'One of the most compelling contemporary writers of crime fiction and psychological suspense. I firmly believe Eva Björg Ægisdóttir's novels are not written simply to scare or thrill her readers, although they can very often do both, rather they are crafted to absorb you through their tantalising prose'
Duncan Beattie

'The author writes so beautifully you get immediately immersed into the chilly surrounds and in *Night Shadows* there's a cleverly obfuscated mystery intertwined with personal developments for our series protagonists. A genuinely excellent novel again from Eva. Can't wait for the next'
Liz Loves Books

PRAISE FOR THE FORBIDDEN ICELAND SERIES

WINNER of the CWA John Creasey (New Blood) Dagger

WINNER of the Storytel Award for Best Crime Novel

WINNER of the Blackbird Award for Best Icelandic Crime Novel

SHORTLISTED for the Amazon Publishing Readers Award for Best Debut Novel

SHORTLISTED for the Amazon Publishing Readers Award for Best Independent Voice

'Fans of Nordic Noir will love this' Ann Cleeves

'An exciting and harrowing tale' Ragnar Jónasson

'Beautifully written, spine-tingling and disturbing ... a thrilling new voice in Icelandic crime fiction' Yrsa Sigurðardóttir

NIGHT SHADOWS

ABOUT THE AUTHOR

Born in Akranes in 1988, Eva Björg Ægisdóttir studied for an MSc in globalisation in Norway before returning to Iceland and deciding to write a novel – something she had wanted to do since she won a short-story competition at the age of fifteen. After nine months combining her writing with work as a stewardess and caring for her children, Eva finished *The Creak on the Stairs*. It was published in 2018 and became a bestseller in Iceland, going on to win the Blackbird Award, a prize set up by Yrsa Sigurðardóttir and Ragnar Jónasson to encourage new Icelandic crime writers. *The Creak on the Stairs* was published in English by Orenda Books in 2020, became a number-one bestseller in ebook in three countries, was shortlisted for the Capital Crime/Amazon Publishing Awards in two categories and won the CWA John Creasy (New Blood) Dagger in 2021. *Girls Who Lie*, the second book in the Forbidden Iceland series, was published in 2021. Dubbed the 'Icelandic Ruth Rendell' by the British press, Eva lives in Reykjavík with her husband and three children. Follow Eva on Twitter @evaaegisdottir.

ABOUT THE TRANSLATOR

Victoria Cribb studied and worked in Reykjavík for a number of years and has translated more than forty books by Icelandic authors, including Arnaldur Indriðason and Yrsa Sigurðardóttir. A number of these works have been nominated for prizes. In 2021 her translation of Eva Björg Ægisdóttir's *The Creak on the Stairs* became the first translated book to win the UK Crime Writer's Association John Creasey (New Blood) Dagger. In 2017 she received the Orðstír honorary translation award for services to Icelandic literature.

The Forbidden Iceland Series
The Creak on the Stairs
Girls Who Lie
Night Shadows

NIGHT SHADOWS

Eva Björg Ægisdóttir

Translated by Victoria Cribb

**ORENDA
BOOKS**

Orenda Books
16 Carson Road
West Dulwich
London SE21 8HU
www.orendabooks.co.uk

First published in the United Kingdom by Orenda Books, 2022
First published in Iceland as *Næturskuggar* by Veröld Publishing, 2020
Copyright © Eva Björg Ægisdóttir, 2020
English translation copyright © Victoria Cribb, 2022

A catalogue record for this book is available from the British Library.

Paperback ISBN 978-1-914585-20-3
Hardback ISBN 978-1-914585-37-1
eISBN 978-1-914585-21-0

The publication of this translation has been made possible through the
financial support of

ICELANDIC LITERATURE CENTER

Typeset in Minion by typesetter.org.uk
Printed and bound by CPI Group (UK) Ltd, Croydon CR0 4YY

For sales and distribution, please contact info@orendabooks.co.uk or visit
www.orendabooks.co.uk.

NIGHT SHADOWS

Pronunciation Guide

Icelandic has a couple of letters that don't exist in other European languages and that are not always easy to replicate. The letter ð is generally replaced with a d in English, but we have decided to use the Icelandic letter to remain closer to the original names. Its sound is closest to the voiced *th* in English, as found in *th*en and ba*th*e.

The Icelandic letter þ is reproduced as *th*, as in *Th*orgeir, and is equivalent to an unvoiced *th* in English, as in *th*ing or *th*ump.

The letter *r* is generally rolled hard with the tongue against the roof of the mouth.

In pronouncing Icelandic personal and place names, the emphasis is always placed on the first syllable.

Names like Alexander, Begga and Elma, which are pronounced more or less as they would be in English, are not included on the list.

Aðalheiður – AATH-al-HAYTH-oor
Ævar – EYE-var
Akrafjall – AAK-ra-fyatl
Akranes – AA-kra-ness
Akureyri – AA-koor-ay-ree
Andri – AND-ree
Barónsstígur – BAA-rohns-STEE-goor
Birta – BIRR-ta
Borgarfjörður – BORK-ar-FYUR-thoor
Breiðholt – BRAYTH-holt
Brynhildur – BRIN-hild-oor

Dagný – DAAK-nee
Esja – ESS-ya
Finnur – FIN-noor
Fríða – FREE-tha
Fúsi – FOOS-see
Gerða – GYAIR-tha
Gígja – GYEE-ya
Grímur – GREE-moor
Guðlaug – GVOOTH-loig
Hannes Hreiðar Þorsteinsson – HAN-nes HRAY-thar THOR-stayns-son
Harpa – HAARR-pa
Hrafnkell – HRAPN-ketl
Hörður Höskuldsson – HUR-thoor HUSK-oolds-son
Húsafell – HOOSS-a-fetl
Hvalfjörður – KVAAL-fyurth-oor
Ína – EENA
Ísak – EES-sak
Jaðarsbakkar – JAA-thars-BAKK-ar
Jens – YENS
Jóel – YOH-ell
Jökull – YUR-kootl
Jón – YOEN
Júlía – YOO-lee-a
Kári – COW-rree
Katrín – KAA-treen
Laufey – LOIV-ay
Lise – LEESS-uh
Marinó – MAA-rin-oh
Mosfellsbær – MORS-fells-bye-r
Örnólfur – URD-nohl-voor
Óskar – OHSS-gar
Ragnar Snær Hafsteinsson – RAK-nar SNYE-r HAAF-stayns-son

Rúna – ROON-a
Sævar – SYE-vaar
Seyðisfjörður – SAY-this-FYUR-thoor
Skógahverfi – SKOH-a-KVAIR-vee
Snorri – SNORR-ee
Sonja – SON-ya
Stormur – STORM-oor
Tómas – TOH-mas
Unnar – OON-nar
Vilborg – VILL-borg
Villi – VIL-lee

PART ONE

The Night Before

Once the rain stopped, there was a risk someone would notice the smell. He made a phone call and said again that he wanted to move the body. It was making him increasingly anxious to think of it lying there, the decomposition advancing by the hour. The idea filled him with such anguish that he could barely sit still.

It was turning out to be incredibly difficult to dispose of a corpse. He couldn't think of any way to carry it out to the car without being seen. The nights weren't dark enough yet to provide sufficient cover. And even when he'd got it into the back, where could he go? Where was he supposed to bury it? He had never travelled much outside town and had no idea where to find a suitably out-of-the-way spot or even what the ground would be like. Was the soil deep enough, or would he hit rock? The last thing he wanted was for some farmer to dig up the body. Throwing it in the sea was one possibility, but there was always a risk it would wash up on a beach somewhere. He wasn't familiar with the currents; had no idea whether the tide would be in or out right now.

Last night he had gone to check on it. In his drunken state he had been curious to observe the changes in the colour and texture of the skin. He had pulled back the covers, unwrapped the plastic and run a finger along the bare arm. There was an undeniable thrill in seeing a dead person. The sense of unreality was so overwhelming that it made him dizzy and sent the blood rushing to his fingers and toes. For a moment, thinking he was going to faint, he put his head between his knees. Then, when the spell had passed, he poured the rest of the vodka down his throat and turned his attention to the face. He prised open the mouth, inspecting the tongue and teeth, then carefully pushed up the eyelids. Underneath them, the eyes were dull and fixed, covered in a white film. It was then that the fact of death became too real for him and he stumbled away.

When he got back outside, he thought he was going to throw up, but instead he fell to his knees, overcome by a fit of weeping. He couldn't stop picturing them, those unseeing eyes, staring back at him so emptily.

Saturday

Akranes's wooden church was so tightly packed with mourners that the windows had started to steam up. Elma surreptitiously fanned her face with the hymn sheet. Yet although the building was full, the only sounds were the creaking of the narrow wooden pews and the occasional sniff or cough.

Hörður was sitting at the front with his family. Elma could see the back of his head, the grey-streaked hair and smooth shirt collar. He sat bolt upright, staring straight ahead, and didn't look round when the doors opened and the people who'd entered walked down the aisle. Not even when his daughter laid her head on his shoulder. He sat so still it was as if nothing could stir him, or, perhaps, as if the slightest movement would shatter his hard-won composure.

Elma's gaze moved from Hörður to the photo of Gígja on the service sheet. It was a recent picture but taken before the cancer had left its mark on her. She had gone downhill rapidly after her diagnosis. In a few short months they had watched this energetic woman growing ever weaker, the weight falling off her, until in the end she was bedbound, dependent on strong painkillers. Elma had last seen Gígja a month before she died. A few of them from the police station had gone to visit her, bearing pastries and a bunch of flowers.

Hörður too had lost so much weight that his trousers hung in loose folds around his thighs and his shirts were far too big for him. In the week since Gígja died, he hadn't come near the police station.

Elma blinked back her tears and swallowed the lump in her

throat. Sævar smiled sadly as the organist began to play, filling the little church with music, and the choir joined in, raising their voices in unearthly song. Only then did Elma notice Hörður's head droop and his shoulders begin to shake.

◆

The glass cabinet in the sitting room was a legacy from Laufey's parents. She had never been able to get rid of the musty, old-cupboard odour that clung to everything they stored in it: the coffee set that had belonged to her parents, the Royal Copenhagen dish or the beautiful crystal glasses that had been a wedding present. Every time they wanted to use any of these items she had to wash them first to remove the smell.

It was the only job she had left to do. Everything else was ready. The potatoes were sitting on the kitchen counter, covered with aluminium foil; the meat had been browned and wouldn't need much longer in the oven, and the dessert was waiting in the fridge – a large meringue cake filled with strawberries and chocolate-coated liquorice balls.

Unnar came into the kitchen, freshly shaven and wearing a fitted shirt. Unlike her, he'd had ample time to shower, shave and choose his clothes. She'd pulled on the same old dress when she found a minute, less than half an hour before the guests were due to arrive.

'Champagne?' Unnar asked, holding up the bottle.

'No, thanks.' Laufey untied her apron, trying not to be irritated by him. She didn't want a quarrel when they were expecting their friends any minute.

'Tired?'

'Seriously, Unnar?' Laufey asked. 'Just so there are no arguments, you're clearing up after dinner. I'm not lifting a finger.'

'Sure, no problem.' Unnar took the wineglasses into the sitting room and changed the music. While Laufey was toiling away in the kitchen, he'd had so much time on his hands, he'd been able to prepare a playlist for the evening ahead.

Laufey took a cloth and wiped away a smear that his damp fingers had left on one of the glasses. After a moment's pause, she poured herself some champagne and took a sip, then another.

'They must be here soon,' she said, sitting down in an armchair.

Unnar shrugged. 'You know what it's like; no one turns up on the dot.'

'No, I suppose not.' She started and put down her glass.

'Is everything OK?'

'Yes, but I almost forgot to light the scented candle.' Laufey got up and opened a drawer. She had bought an outrageously expensive candle at some luxury shop in Reykjavík, and if they didn't use it now, when would they?

'We can't have that,' she heard Unnar murmur sarcastically as she rummaged for a lighter.

Laufey took a deep breath and told herself that there was no point reacting. It wouldn't do any good. She placed the candle on the hall table, lit all three wicks, and almost immediately the fragrance began to spread through the house. 'Champagne Toast' it said on the label. How appropriate, Laufey thought, and knocked back the rest of her glass.

As the evening wore on, people began to show signs of fading. Laufey sank lower in the sofa, losing the thread of the conversation. Villi started yawning, and shortly before midnight he and his wife Brynhildur got up and said goodbye. Óskar and Harpa, on the other hand, were nowhere near ready to throw in the towel. Harpa had downed eight glasses of champagne and was talking nineteen to the dozen. Óskar was no better; he'd taken over the playlist and was putting on songs that had been hits in their youth.

Laufey, feeling rather the worse for wear herself, went into the kitchen for a drink of water. The dining table was covered with dirty dishes and leftovers. She longed to tidy up, but that wouldn't be fair: she had cooked and the clearing up was Unnar's job. He wouldn't get away with dodging it this time.

She folded a dishcloth, her gaze on the window.

It was raining outside, big, heavy drops falling vertically in the windless weather. She closed her eyes, breathing out slowly through her nose, and felt everything moving up and down inside her.

It was a long time since she had drunk this much, and she revelled in the sensation of being so relaxed and carefree. Her drowsiness had dissipated the instant she stood up, and she felt a sudden crazy urge to hit the town. But Akranes had no fun night clubs where you could dance until the early hours. They would have to make do with the sitting room.

Laufey got out another bottle of red wine and poured herself a glass. To hell with the dishes – she'd definitely make Unnar do them in the morning. She took a big mouthful and only then did she register the silence. The music had stopped, and she couldn't even hear a word from Harpa.

Laufey went into the sitting room and saw the glasses on the table beside the cheeseboard.

'Unnar?' she said, but there was no answer.

It was as if they had all vanished into thin air.

Sunday

Ævar became aware of the fire when he looked out of the bathroom window and noticed a strange glow above the expensive property adjoining their back garden. At first he thought, sleepily, that the sun must have gone down behind the house in the middle of the night, but then he heard a piercing wail shattering the tranquillity and realised what was happening. He yanked up his briefs and made for the door, without stopping to wake Rósa or put on his coat.

The wet branches tore at his skin as he forced his way through the hedge dividing the two properties. The fire was at the front of the house, so Ævar made straight for the back door and tried the handle. When it wouldn't open, he banged on the glass.

'Hello!' he called, pressing his forehead to the pane. 'Is there anyone home?'

He expected to hear screams or see figures come running, but nothing happened. The house was home to a couple with two kids. In fact, they weren't kids anymore; both must be around twenty, though they still lived with their parents.

Ævar was aware of his heart pounding under his thin vest but didn't even register the cold. He wondered if he should break down the door. It looked easy enough in the movies, but he knew it was different in real life.

Instead, he ran round the corner of the house and saw to his dismay that there was a car parked in the drive. Somebody might well be home.

'What's going on?'

Ævar turned to see the man from the neighbouring house

running over. What was his name again? Jón. Jens. Something like that.

'Fire,' Ævar gasped between panting breaths. 'I can't get in. I don't know if anyone's home. I…'

'I'll call the emergency number,' said Jón or Jens, who'd had the presence of mind to pull on a coat and bring his phone with him. Ævar was barefoot and in his underwear, but this was no time to worry about such trivial things.

'You ring, I'll try the front door,' he said and set off at a half-run. He winced with pain as the gravel cut into the soles of his feet.

The front door turned out to be locked as well and wouldn't budge, despite all his efforts to force it.

A moment later there was a loud explosion. He saw that the glass in one of the windows had blown.

Ævar tried shouting again. 'Is there anyone in there?' he yelled into the blaze, but there was still no answer.

The heat and smoke were so bad that he couldn't get any closer. He held his arm over his face, coughing, then heard the sirens and knew there was nothing more he could do.

❦

Unnar woke up to find himself in bed, fully dressed. His white shirt was sticking to his body, and his suit trousers were unbuttoned to reveal his briefs. His mouth felt so parched that he worked his lips to try and summon up some saliva, then put his hands over his eyes to shield them from the dazzling sunlight that was streaming in through the window.

When he tried to sit up, pain knifed through his head, so he lay straight back down again and closed his eyes. After a while, he crawled out of bed and, with difficulty, made it to the bathroom, where the residue of the previous night's excesses ended up in the toilet bowl.

Unnar was too old for this. Although he drank regularly, he didn't normally get as wrecked as he had last night.

As he stood under the shower, he tried to remember what had happened. He recalled the dinner party and the first part of the evening. The bottles of Bollinger they'd drunk with the starter, the roast that had melted in the mouth after its long *sous-vide* cooking, the Hasselback potatoes. Everyone had praised the food, and afterwards they had polished off a bottle of ten-year-old malt that Villi had brought with him.

After that, though, the events of the evening grew hazy, and by the end of his shower Unnar was still no closer to remembering how he had come to be in bed with all his clothes on. The ominous feeling wouldn't leave him as he was dressing, but the harder he tried to piece the evening together, the more it seemed to slip from his grasp.

His seven-year-old daughter, Anna, was practising gymnastics in the sitting room when he emerged.

She raised both arms, extended her leg, then bent over backwards and executed a full turn. Anyone would think she was double-jointed.

'Wow,' Unnar said, impressed. 'What a clever girl I've got.'

Anna glowed with pride, then wrinkled her nose. 'Daddy, your breath stinks.'

In the study he found Laufey seated at the computer, her glasses perched on her nose. The instant she became aware of him, she closed the window that had been open on the screen.

'What, are you booking a flight?' He thought he'd seen the logo of an airline.

Laufey turned. 'Yes, actually,' she said. 'I still need to buy the tickets to Sweden.'

'Still? But that's only two weeks away.'

'Yes, I know, I'm terribly behind.' Laufey took off her glasses and rubbed her eyes, studying him as if she were seeing him properly for the first time in a very long while. 'How are you feeling?'

'Fine,' Unnar lied.

'You put away a hell of a lot last night.'

'So did you.'

Laufey didn't reply to that.

Unnar couldn't actually remember whether Laufey had drunk a lot. He could hardly recall anything about her behaviour last night, except that she had chatted to the other wives while he and his friends were reminiscing about their schooldays. And she had given him the evil eye when he didn't immediately clear away the dishes after supper.

He tried to read from her expression whether anything else had happened, but her face was inscrutable. She asked him if he wanted a coffee.

'No,' Unnar replied. 'No, thanks.'

He watched as she went into the kitchen and poured some beans into the automatic coffee machine they had bought last Christmas.

His wife had once been beautiful, but these days she gave little thought to her appearance. A few years ago she'd had her hair cut short and started wearing glasses – God, how he hated those glasses. They made her look at least ten years older.

When they'd met she had been a fifteen-year-old with dreams of becoming a hairdresser. They had always been a bit wild, having sex wherever they wanted to: in an alleyway behind a club, in his parents' bed, on a hotel balcony in Spain. Today she was forty-two, sat on Akranes town council, taught yoga and was studying for a degree of some sort. Whenever she spoke in public, her grating voice made him cringe. They rarely had sex and when they did it was over quickly.

Many of his colleagues' wives looked much better and seemed to care far more about their appearance. But none of them could compare to Tommi's new girlfriend, Helena. Tommi, who worked with him in the export department, had divorced his wife last year and his two kids were teenagers, so he rarely saw them. Helena had dark hair, a slim waist and big breasts. She'd just completed a degree in tourism studies and loved hiking. She was always dragging Tommi off into the mountains, and Unnar thought he seemed a changed man. But when he mentioned this, Tommi said it wasn't the mountain hikes but all the sex that did it. Tommi had shown him a picture of Helena, bare-breasted, fast asleep in bed, then laughed uproariously.

Unnar was perfectly aware that his thoughts were superficial. After a long marriage, things like this shouldn't matter to him, and yet they did. And it wasn't just Laufey's appearance that got on his nerves. She'd changed: she was no longer the fun, carefree, adventurous person she had once been.

Sometimes it felt as if they had nothing in common anymore apart from the children, but the day would come when the kids moved out. Then it would just be him and Laufey alone together, and he had no idea what they would say to each other.

'What?' Laufey asked, noticing him staring at her. She dunked half a biscuit into her mug, then stuffed it in her mouth.

'Nothing,' Unnar said.

'Hangover that bad, is it?'

'Are you sure you want to eat that biscuit?' he retorted. 'I thought you were on a diet.'

Laufey gave him a weary look and turned away.

A shrill, persistent sound penetrated her dreamless sleep. Elma buried her face in the pillow, not yet ready to wake up. There was a pause, then the sound started up again, and Elma realised it was the doorbell. She got out of bed, wrapped herself in her flannel dressing gown and went to the door. On the way, she caught sight of herself in the mirror and grimaced. Her hair, flattened by the pillow, clung to her face, her eyelids were swollen and the dark circles reached halfway down her cheeks.

Judging from Dagný's expression, she hadn't failed to notice the state her younger sister was in.

'What happened?' Dagný asked in concern, as she and her two little sons, Alexander and Jökull, came in. 'Are you ill? Or … don't tell me … were you out on the town last night?'

'Have you only just woken up?' Alexander asked, before Elma could answer. 'But it's like *seriously* late, man.' He gaped at her in disbelief, stressing the 'seriously'.

'Yes, I know, but I was awake all night,' Elma told him, ruffling his blond head. After the unusually fine Icelandic summer, his hair was bleached white and his skin was tanned golden brown. Elma raised her eyes to her sister. 'Don't worry, I wasn't having fun – I just couldn't sleep.'

'I see. By the way, did you hear about the fire—?' Dagný's gaze suddenly darted past Elma, and she groaned. 'Jökull, don't open that drawer.'

Jökull, soon to be three, had made a beeline for the most interesting place in his aunt's flat. The biscuit drawer was well within his reach, and he invariably opened it and helped himself when he came round.

'Oh, Elma, can't you move the biscuits somewhere else?' Dagný said, sounding resigned as she watched Jökull dropping crumbs all over the kitchen floor.

'I don't want a biscuit,' Alexander announced. 'My coach says that if you want to be good at football, you should eat healthily.'

Elma raised her eyebrows. 'Is that really something for a seven-year-old to worry about?'

'Yes, of course, man,' Alexander said. Recently his vocabulary had become peppered with new phrases and slang terms. The latest fad was to end all his sentences with 'man'. 'Aren't you going to get dressed, Elma? The show's about to begin, man.'

Elma glanced at the clock and saw that they'd be late if she didn't get a move on. She'd promised to take her nephews to a play that was being performed at the local cinema.

'Give me five minutes and I'll be ready.'

'It'll take you more than five minutes,' Dagný said, and now it was her turn to raise her eyebrows.

'Here, Jökull, have another choccy biccy.' Elma stroked the little boy's head, then went into her bedroom and started dragging on her clothes. 'What's that you were saying about a fire?' she called to her sister, but just then her mobile rang.

It was her boss, Hörður, head of West Iceland CID, on the other end, and it soon became clear that she wouldn't be going to any plays that day.

◆

The house was of an ultra-modern design, with large windows and a double garage. It had walls of varying heights and a steeply pitched roof, suggesting unusually high ceilings inside. A statement wall of cut stone added to the striking impression, reminding Elma of the places featured in the architecture and design magazines a friend of hers subscribed to. Surrounding the building was a large garden and a veranda that was evidently little used. There was no patio furniture, no barbecue nor any of the other clutter that was found in the gardens of the neighbouring houses. The fire damage was confined to the front of the building; the glass in one window had blown, and black streaks radiated out from the gaping hole.

They were in Akranes's new Skógahverfi Estate. It was a quiet residential area, dominated by large villas, which were mainly occupied by families, including Elma's friend who read the design magazines and had three kids. That summer they had sat out on her deck, drinking coffee. The surrounding gardens had been full of life in the good weather, with the sounds of children bouncing on trampolines or splashing in hot tubs.

On the way to the scene, Hörður had filled Elma in on what had happened. During the night a fire had broken out in one of the bedrooms, where a young man was sleeping. A neighbour had called the emergency number when he saw the blaze, but although the fire brigade had arrived promptly, they had been too late to save the boy.

'His name was Marinó Finnsson, and he was twenty years old,' Hörður said, as they got out of the car. 'His parents were at a hotel in Borgarfjörður, and his twin sister was staying with her boyfriend, so he was alone at home. The fire seems to have started in his room.'

'Is that it?' Elma asked, pointing to the broken window.

'Yes, that's his room,' Hörður said. 'The forensic team's in there now. I spoke to them earlier this morning and they're fairly sure it's arson. When the fire brigade turned up, Marinó was still in bed.'

Perhaps it was her imagination, but the area seemed unusually quiet to Elma. Looking around, she saw a few curious eyes watching them. On one of the houses, the Icelandic flag was flying at half-mast.

'Was there no smoke alarm in the house?' she asked.

'Yes, there was. It woke the neighbours.'

'But Marinó didn't wake up?'

'No,' Hörður said, 'apparently not. There was an alarm in his room that must have gone off almost immediately. In normal circumstances he would have had time to get out, or at least you'd think so. Mind you, when I spoke to the lead firefighter, he told me that it was only a matter of seconds sometimes.'

'Could they tell straight away that it was arson?'

'They suspected it pretty quickly,' Hörður said, opening the front door of the house. 'But, like I said, the fire originated in Marinó's room, which is strange if we're talking about arson. The front door was locked, so I find it unlikely that anyone could have entered uninvited. Unless the person in question locked the door on their way out.' Hörður bent a little closer to Elma and added in an undertone: 'But of course it's possible that the victim started the fire himself.'

'I suppose so,' Elma said, after a pause. 'Or that the person who started the fire had access to the house.'

◆

Finnur couldn't stand his mother's flat. He couldn't stand the red velvet sofa in the sitting room, the painting of the little girl by the stream, the blue-checked cover on the double bed. A faint smell of cigarette smoke clung to all the furnishings, even though his mother had quit smoking around the time his father succumbed to lung cancer.

An oppressive silence had hung over the house when he was growing up, in spite of the constant blare of the television. His parents used to spend their days slumped in front of it. Both had been registered disabled, subsisting on a low income, yet somehow there had always been enough money for booze and fags. Finnur had learnt early on that the only rules were: don't touch Mum's drink. And don't touch Dad's drink. Apart from that he could stay out to all hours, as long as he didn't disturb his parents in the morning, when they would invariably be hungover. They were never mean to him, not directly, but if anything their indifference was worse.

While still young, Finnur had promised himself that he would escape this miserable existence as soon as he could and would never turn into his parents. He had kept his word. He was now fifty-five, he'd been sober since he was nineteen and he was very comfortably off financially.

As he watched his bank balance growing over the years, he'd felt as if he was simultaneously growing in stature. He'd felt both proud and powerful; like one of life's winners.

But what had he actually won? he asked himself now, studying the photograph in his hands. Where was the victory?

The photo was of a five-year-old Marinó holding a kitten the twins had been given one Christmas. Although Marinó had been pestering them for months to have a cat, he had grown nervous the moment the animal was put into his arms, and his fear showed in his expression. His eyes were stretched wide, his body tense, as if he were expecting the cat to shoot out its claws and scratch him. Finnur ran a finger over the picture, aching to touch his son one last time.

Since hearing of Marinó's death, he'd felt as if he were sinking into a bottomless abyss. It couldn't be true that his son no longer existed. How could the world go on without Marinó?

There was a stabbing pain in his chest. For a moment he felt crushed by his grief, but an instant later rage flared up inside him.

It wasn't an accident. Someone had deliberately done this to his son, and Finnur thought he knew who. He opened his laptop, found the old emails and reread the angry messages. They hadn't really got to him at the time; other people's problems had seemed irrelevant. As far as he was concerned, it had just been some pathetic, sick individual, who would never dare to put their threats into action. But he saw things differently now.

He typed the sender's name into the search engine and saved the address. Then he closed his laptop and picked up the photo again, losing himself in memories of a past he would never get back.

❧

'I don't understand it,' Marinó's mother, Gerða, said, her hands trembling as she put down the glass of water. 'I don't understand what happened. It must have been the wiring. The light in Marinó's room was always flickering and I told—'

'No,' Hörður intervened hurriedly. 'There's nothing to suggest the fire was caused by the wiring.'

Gerða closed her eyes and drew a long, shaky breath. Elma saw how much it was costing her not to break down.

They were sitting in a flat belonging to Finnur's elderly mother, Agnes. When Agnes opened the door to Elma and Hörður, her movements had been slow and her face frozen. Of course, the circumstances were nothing to smile about, but Elma had got the impression that Agnes wouldn't have smiled regardless of the occasion. Without saying a word, the old woman had pointed to the sitting room, then disappeared into another room herself, closing the door behind her.

'The forensics team is still examining the scene,' Hörður said, 'but I'm afraid it's fairly clear that it was arson.'

'But that's impossible,' Gerða said, stunned. 'Who...?'

'I'm afraid we don't yet know who was responsible,' Hörður said. 'But we've found traces of a flammable substance, and the behaviour of the fire also points to arson. That's to say, it spread far more quickly than it would have done naturally.'

Silence descended on the room, then the clock struck the hour, and they all looked up. All except Finnur. The short, delicately made man, sitting so rigidly on the sofa, appeared to be miles away. His thick, bushy eyebrows gave him a rather dour expression.

'Where were you staying on Saturday night?' Elma asked, breaking the silence.

'We were at a hotel in Borgarfjörður,' Gerða replied, referring to the countryside around the large fjord some thirty kilometres north of Akranes.

'What's the name of the hotel?'

'Hótel Húsafell. We got there at five on Friday afternoon and stayed for two nights. We went to the, er ... to the Krauma nature baths and had our meals at the hotel restaurant.'

'Do you remember when you last heard from Marinó?' Elma asked.

'He rang me just after midday on Saturday, saying he couldn't find his swimming trunks. He was going to the gym and wanted to use the hot tub afterwards.'

'Did he seem at all different from usual?'

'No,' Gerða said. 'No, he didn't.'

'What about in the last few days or weeks?'

'No,' Finnur said suddenly. 'No different.'

'Actually, he was a bit distracted, Finnur,' Gerða said quietly. 'Now I come to think of it, he wasn't home much last week. He went out in the evenings and got back late.'

'Was that unusual?'

'Well, it happened sometimes, but not that often.'

'Did you get the feeling something was bothering him?'

'To be honest, I didn't even think about it,' Gerða said. 'But now that you mention it…'

'It was nothing.' Finnur sounded almost angry. 'There was nothing bothering him; nothing wrong with him. He was exactly like his usual self. Exactly…' His voice cracked and he turned his face away.

'Can you think of anyone who might have wanted to harm Marinó?' Elma asked. 'Had he fallen out with someone recently?'

'No,' Gerða answered quickly. She sniffed, fighting back her tears. 'Marinó wasn't like that; no one had it in for him. He was a good student, he had a nice group of friends and lived a very normal life. He … he was ambitious, he had opinions about politics, he played the saxophone and wanted to work in IT. And he was interested in history and Greek philosophy too – he read all those books by Plato and Aristotle right the way through. He wasn't in any kind of trouble.'

'Marinó had just started a degree in computer studies at the University of Iceland,' Finnur said, having regained control of his voice. 'As my wife says, he was never in any kind of trouble, if that's what you're trying to imply. He wasn't mixed up in bad company; he didn't take drugs or anything like that.'

'Who were his friends?'

'Marinó's had the same group of friends since he was at school,' Gerða said, wiping a tear from her cheek with a quick movement.

'Ísak, Andri and Fríða – Marinó's twin sister. Oh, and her friend, Sonja.'

Elma asked for their full names and noted them down.

'Who has access to your house?' she asked next.

'Only us.' Gerða glanced at her husband.

'Yes, only our family,' Finnur confirmed. 'Why do you ask?'

'The door was locked when the fire brigade reached the scene,' Elma said, 'but the fire was started inside the house.'

'I don't understand,' Gerða said. 'What does that mean?'

'We're wondering if Marinó could have forgotten to lock the door and the person who started the fire locked it behind them on their way out,' Elma said. The idea didn't sound very convincing to her, but it was all she could come up with. If someone from outside the family had started the fire, then logically they must have got in somehow. She doubted that Marinó had let them in voluntarily, if he had been in bed.

'No, that can't be right,' Finnur said.

'That he'd have left it unlocked?'

'No, not that. The door doesn't lock automatically – you have to use a key.'

'I see.' Elma shifted in her seat. 'So, someone must have locked it from outside, using a key.'

'But...' Gerða moved forwards to perch on the edge of the sofa. 'But we're the only ones with keys.'

'Are you absolutely sure about that?' Elma asked.

'Yes, only us and the twins,' Gerða said. 'Oh, and Agnes, Finnur's mother.'

Hörður cleared his throat, and Elma could tell he was uncomfortable about asking the next question. 'Was Marinó on any drugs?'

'Drugs?' Finnur repeated indignantly. 'No, he wasn't.'

'Were there any drugs in the house?'

'What ... why are you asking that?' Gerða sounded bewildered.

'I was just wondering if Marinó could have unwittingly taken some medication,' Hörður said. 'Accidentally taken some pills, for example, under the impression that they were painkillers.'

'I don't know what you're insinuating,' Finnur said angrily, 'but, I told you, Marinó didn't do drugs. He didn't have any problems of that kind.'

'Do you think there's any chance he could have started the fire himself?' Hörður asked warily.

'That's it. I'm not putting up with any more of this.' Finnur sprang to his feet, tight-lipped.

Hörður added hastily: 'I ask, because your son doesn't seem to have woken up when the smoke alarm went off, although it was loud enough to disturb the neighbours. As I said, Marinó was still lying in bed when the fire brigade arrived and didn't seem to have made any attempt to get up.'

❧

The conversation with Marinó's parents had taken its toll. Elma always dreaded having to ask next of kin probing personal questions, but it couldn't be avoided. The most uncomfortable questions were often the most important, but people reacted very differently to them. Finnur had been seething with rage by the end. He had stalked off into another room without a word, leaving it to his wife, Gerða, to escort them to the door.

It was understandable that Marinó's parents had a hard time believing someone could have entered his room in the middle of the night, started a fire then left again, locking the door behind them – all without waking Marinó. Yet Elma wasn't about to rule out the possibility; it was vital to keep an open mind.

Gerða told them that the only spare keys to the house were hidden under a stone by the wall. So there was a chance, however slim, that someone could have found the key and let themselves in. A neighbour, perhaps, who knew where it was kept. Elma was also considering the possibility that Marinó had a girlfriend his parents weren't aware of. It was the only thing she could think of to explain why he would have let someone in, then been found lying in bed.

'Which stone do you think it is?' Sævar asked.

'Gerða said it was quite a big one, under the window,' Elma told him.

Following the visit to Marinó's parents, she had picked up her colleague, Sævar, from the police station. Hörður had stayed behind in his office, saying he would go over the press release before heading home. She couldn't understand why he was at work at all, given that it was only a week since Gígja had died. When she had spoken to him the previous week, he had talked about taking several months off, but this morning, the day after the funeral, he had turned up at the station. Elma longed to tell him to go easy on himself but didn't know how to put it tactfully.

'They're all pretty big,' Sævar pointed out.

He was right. A number of large stones had been lined up, decoratively, along the house wall.

'It's not a bad hiding place,' Elma remarked. 'Most people put their keys in a flower pot or in the light fitting over the door.'

When she was growing up, she would retrieve the spare key from the flower pot by the front door – on the rare occasions it had been necessary. Usually the house had been left unlocked, regardless of whether anyone was home.

Elma pulled on a pair of latex gloves and turned over the largest stone below the window. Seeing nothing underneath, she moved on to the next.

'There are no keys here,' she said at last. Straightening up, she surveyed their surroundings.

There was an unusual amount of traffic in the street: vehicles were slowing down as they passed, presumably to get an eyeful of the damage caused by the fire. News of last night's incident had spread fast, and it was all over the national media today.

When Elma drove through the town earlier, she had noticed a number of flags flying at half-mast. Although she could think of plenty of disadvantages to growing up in a small community like Akranes, there were advantages too, and the feeling of solidarity was probably one of the biggest. Whenever anything bad happened, it brought the locals together.

Elma tried not to dwell on thoughts of Marinó's family and friends. She and Sævar had to focus on solving the case, and their first step must be to talk to the neighbours. With any luck, one of them might have witnessed something that could explain the terrible tragedy.

After they rang the bell, there was a short interval before the door opened. The man who came out was around their age – thirty-something – with thinning hair and glasses. They followed him into the kitchen, where a woman was sitting with her hair pulled back in a loose bun.

'I gather it was you who called the emergency number last night?' Elma said.

'Yes,' the woman replied, looking at the man. 'Jens rang.'

'That's right,' Jens said. 'I couldn't sleep and I was here in the kitchen when I heard the alarm go off. I went over to the window and saw smoke coming from Gerða and Finnur's house, so I ran outside and saw another neighbour, Ævar, banging on their door. That's when I called the emergency number. If I'd known the son was in the house, I'd have tried to do more to…'

'But we heard the fire brigade coming almost straight away,' the woman said, as if to comfort him. 'Jens had hardly hung up before we heard the siren.'

'Did either of you notice anyone near the house when you looked outside?'

'Near the house? No, I … Jens?'

Jens frowned. 'No, I didn't see anyone. But then I wouldn't have been able to see even if someone had come out of their front door.'

Elma glanced out of the window where Jens was pointing and saw that he was right. The garage jutted out further towards the street, blocking the view of the entrance to Gerða and Finnur's house.

Jens had cottoned on immediately. 'You think it was arson – I saw on the news.'

'We're looking into all the possibilities,' Sævar replied, though Jens's comment hadn't been a question. 'The origin of the fire's not entirely clear yet.'

Apparently unconvinced that Sævar was telling them the truth, the couple waited, presumably hoping their silence might elicit more information. But then a voice called 'finished' from another part of the house, and the woman excused herself and left the room.

'Do you know Gerða and Finnur well?' Elma asked.

'Not exactly well but, you know, we're neighbours, so we have to talk to each other occasionally.' Jens's lips twitched ironically. 'I noticed that they were off somewhere for the weekend. Finnur put a suitcase in the boot of their car on Friday afternoon. There's been quite a lot going on there over the last couple of days.'

'Really?'

'Yes, or mainly on Friday.'

'Could you be more specific?'

'Oh, you know: the kids obviously took advantage of their parents' absence to throw a party. I'm not really complaining but there was quite a lot of noise on Friday night. It wasn't us who called the police, though.'

'Did someone call the police?'

'Yes, apparently there was a spot of bother, but the police came round and put a stop to it. I didn't see anything myself, but I heard about it from Rósa and Ævar, who live opposite. They were the ones who called the police.'

'I'm so sorry, I don't know what to say. Poor Finnur, poor Gerða.' Rósa looked out of her kitchen window with a heavy sigh. 'I can hardly believe Marinó's dead. He was such a nice boy.'

Rósa and Ævar lived in the property backing onto Finnur and Gerða's place, their gardens separated by a thick hedge.

'I hear you were the first person to notice the fire,' Elma said, turning to address Ævar.

'Yes.' Ævar stared across the table at them, his brows heavy. 'But it's not like I was any use.'

'Could you tell us what happened?'

Ævar cleared his throat then briefly related how he had seen a strange glow when he woke up in the middle of the night. He hadn't realised what was happening at first, then he had heard the smoke alarm and run outside.

'I tried to get in but…' Ævar lowered his eyes, and Rósa put a hand on his arm. Her fingers were puffy, her wedding ring far too tight.

'It wouldn't have made any difference,' Elma assured him. 'The fire spread so fast that you would only have been putting your own life in danger if you'd gone inside.'

'They said on the news that it might have been arson,' Rósa remarked, after a little silence.

'There are various indications that it might,' Elma said. 'That's why we wanted to check if you'd been aware of any unusual activity around the house.'

'No, I didn't see anything,' Ævar said. 'But then all my attention was focused on the fire.'

'Ævar ran out in his underwear,' Rósa said. 'I doubt he was thinking about anything except getting into the house.'

'What about you?' Elma asked Rósa.

'No, but…' Rósa paused to think. 'But I did hear a car earlier last night, and I also heard people talking outside.'

Ævar snorted. 'You're imagining things. The other day you were sure you heard a baby crying in the middle of the night.'

'But I did. I'm sure I did.'

Ævar shook his head and addressed Sævar and Elma. 'There are no babies in any of the neighbouring houses; not a single one.'

'What nonsense,' Rósa said. 'Of course there's a baby in the street.'

'That little boy lives three doors down,' Ævar said. 'Do you really think you can hear him through three houses? You can't even hear when I call you from the other room.'

'Selective deafness can come in handy sometimes.' Rósa smiled at Sævar and Elma. 'But I'm absolutely sure I heard a car.'

'Did you see the car or the people who were talking?'

'No, it was around one in the morning. I was lying in bed and only woke up because Ævar was tossing and turning.'

'We heard there was quite a party there on Friday night?' Elma said.

'Oh. Yes,' Rósa said. 'But it wasn't me who rang the police. I don't mind kids having a bit of fun. You're only young once.'

'The music was far too loud,' Ævar protested. 'It was impossible to sleep for the racket. There are young children…'

'Aha!' Rósa exclaimed. 'So now you're admitting there are babies in the street?'

'Young children, not babies,' Ævar corrected her.

'We hear things got a bit rowdy,' Elma said. She'd already been in touch with her uniformed colleagues who had attended the callout and put a stop to the party. According to them, the kids had been drunk and playing loud music but there had been no sign of a fight.

'Well … I heard smashing sounds and people having a row,' Ævar said.

'Again?' Rósa asked. 'I heard them quarrelling the other day.'

'Who did you hear quarrelling?' Elma asked, since Rósa didn't seem to be talking about the party.

'Oh, the twins,' Rósa said. 'Fríða and Marinó.'

The roast lamb had been taken out of the oven by the time Elma made it to her parents' house. Her father was laying the table, her mother standing at the stove.

'How's Sævar?' Aðalheiður asked, the moment Elma walked in. Then she picked up a carton of milk and poured a thin stream into the butter and flour in the saucepan, deftly stirring all the while.

'Fine, I think. Why don't you ask him yourself?' Elma said, pinching a slice of cucumber from the salad bowl.

'I would if he was here.'

Ever since Elma and Sævar had gone to Tenerife together last Christmas, her mother had been regularly asking after him. To her mind, going abroad together must mean they were more than just friends.

Elma and Sævar had decided at the last minute to jump on a plane to the Canary Islands for the holidays. They were both at a similar stage in their lives – single and childless – and somehow neither had felt in the Christmas spirit; their yearning for sun, sand and sea had been much stronger.

Sævar had lost his parents many years before, and his brother, Maggi, who used to live in a group home for the disabled in Akranes, now had his own flat. Maggi had wanted to spend Christmas with his new girlfriend and her family, which meant Sævar had been faced with the prospect of a lonely festive season. His only other option – an invitation to stay with an aunt up north in Akureyri – hadn't tempted him, so he'd been more than up for it when Elma had suggested, half joking, that they go on a beach holiday together.

After supper, Elma and her father cleared up while her mother settled in front of the television with her knitting needles.

'Mum,' Elma said, when she finally sat down beside her. 'What do you know about Finnur and Gerða?'

Her mother worked for Akranes council and had done ever since Elma was a little girl, and she could be relied on to know everything about everyone. This case turned out to be no exception as Aðalheiður immediately launched into a detailed account of the family, without slowing the pace of her knitting.

'You mean the parents of Marinó, who died in the fire last night? God, that was terrible. Marinó was such a promising boy. A talented saxophone player, I'm told.' Aðalheiður paused to glance at her knitting pattern, then carried on. 'Let's see. Marinó had a twin sister called Fríða. They've had a bit of bother with her since she got involved with a much older boyfriend. I hear they recently pranged their car...' The knitting needles clicked rhythmically as Aðalheiður talked. By the time she'd finished, Elma had a pretty good picture of the family, certainly far more complete than anything she could have gleaned from the internet. Her mother's nosiness came in extremely useful at times.

When Elma got home later that evening, she ran herself a bath, thinking over what her mother had said. Propping her toes on the edge of the tub, she reclined her head and wallowed in the soothing warmth.

Finnur was a local, born in Akranes, while Gerða came from the mountainous Dalir district, further up the west coast, but the couple had lived in the capital, Reykjavík, for most of their married life. In typical Icelandic fashion, Aðalheiður had digressed onto the subject of Finnur's family tree, mentioning the names of his parents and even his grandparents. Since Elma hadn't heard of any of them, most of what her mother said on the subject had gone in one ear and out the other. But she had sat up when Aðalheiður explained that Finnur had made a killing out of buying up properties from the Housing Financing Fund after the 2008 financial crisis; in other words, properties that had been repossessed after their owners failed to keep up with their mortgage payments. Finnur had bought them cheap and later sold them on for a steep profit. Many people had looked askance at the couple as a result and muttered about unethical behaviour, while others had simply regretted their failure to spot this chance of making a quick buck themselves. Not that it would have been possible for just anyone to buy up the flats; for that, you would have needed Finnur's connections.

At the time the banks went under, he had been working for an investment fund in Reykjavík. Later, when many people found themselves saddled with loans they couldn't pay back, he had purchased a plot of land in Akranes and built a large de-tached villa. The house was so swanky that it wasn't uncommon to see cars slowing down as they drove past, their owners gawping out of the windows. Some didn't even try to hide their curiosity and stopped outside for a closer look.

While the house was under construction, there had been a lot of gossip among the townspeople about the family who were planning to move there. They had pictured a bunch of snobs, as Elma's mother put it, but, in the event, it turned out Finnur and Gerða were not into showing off their wealth. The couple were in their fifties – they'd had the twins fairly late – and with the ex-ception of their ostentatious house, they kept a low profile in Akranes society. Both were short and slight. They rarely used the car that was parked in the double garage, preferring instead to get about by bike or on foot. Their friendly, unaffected manners soon put a stop to the gossip, and the town gradually lost interest in them.

The twins were also very ordinary kids, who didn't make much of an impression at school. Fríða and Marinó had both gone to Grundi School, Elma's alma mater, but had been in dif-ferent classes.

Elma still hadn't met Fríða, who had been staying with her boyfriend the night her brother died. Finnur and Gerða had begged the police to give their daughter a little time, as she was so distressed, but sooner or later Elma would have to talk to her. If anyone had known Marinó well, it was surely his twin sister.

Elma washed her face in the hot bathwater, rubbing the mascara from her eyelashes.

Marinó's parents' grief had really got to her. She couldn't imagine what it was like to lose a child. It was bad enough thinking what it would be like if anything ever happened to her nephews, Alexander and Jökull. Of course she shouldn't let her imagination run away with her like this, but it was hard not to. She found it difficult to avoid empathising with other people's pain and entering into their grief.

Elma had sometimes met parents who had lost children many years previously, through accidents or other causes, and it always seemed as if something had been taken away from them. As if their faces had been permanently marked by their loss.

She slid down until her head was submerged, then sat up again and wrung out her hair before heaving herself to her feet.

Today was one month since she had realised that all was not as it should be, and three weeks and five days since she had received confirmation of the fact. She had about seven months left until her whole world would be changed beyond recognition.

◆

By Sunday evening Unnar couldn't stand it any longer and rang Villi.

'What the hell happened last night?' he asked. 'I can't remember a bloody thing.'

Villi laughed so hard that he choked on his energy drink.

'Were you that drunk?' he asked, when he had finally caught his breath.

Unnar wanted to scream. He wasn't used to losing his cool like this; as a rule, he liked to be in control. 'Come on. Did anything happen?'

'We finished my whisky.'

'And?'

'And?' Villi coughed into the phone, and Unnar pictured his beer gut wobbling up and down. The keto diet he'd been following for the last year didn't seem to have done any good. If anything, Villi had put on weight from all the bacon and cheese he had been putting away. 'You started playing U2 and Prince and then I knew it was time to leave.'

Unnar bent forwards over his desk and rubbed his temple. 'Was Laufey … How was Laufey?'

'What do you mean?'

'Was she drunk too?'

'Well…' There was a pause at the other end. 'She was probably the most sober of all of us. Brynhildur and I were wrecked next day. Brynhildur had invited her parents to lunch and we had to cancel, claiming I had a stomach bug. And obviously I don't know what happened after we left you.'

'Did you leave that early?'

'Not *that* early … We went home at midnight, leaving you two with Óskar and Harpa. The last thing I remember was you and Harpa involved in some big discussion, and Óskar taking over the music. I have to say, he has better taste than you.'

Unnar hung up, racking his brains to remember the discussion, the music, anything. But all he could recall was the smell of damp grass and the feel of his wet shirt clinging to his back.

Monday

'Good news.'

Elma started as Begga burst into the kitchen with her usual noisy bustle. Begga wasn't a detective like Elma but a uniformed officer who worked shifts. The two women had been friends ever since Elma joined the Akranes police, and she was always glad when Begga had a day shift during the week. As a member of CID, Elma worked conventional hours, and they didn't always coincide with Begga's.

That summer they had spent many an evening sitting in the hot tub on Begga's veranda. She lived alone, apart from her big ginger cat, but often had guests over, and that spring she had extended the invitation to the entire police station. The result had been a colourful affair, with several individuals revealing terrible singing voices and others, uninhibited by their lack of a swimming costume, getting into the hot tub in their underwear.

'Oh?' Elma said now. She felt more than ready for some good news. There had been precious little recently.

'I've gone round all the houses, talking to the neighbours,' Begga continued, dropping heavily into the seat opposite Elma. 'No one's seen anything of interest. Most people were asleep at the time, and the ones who were awake didn't hear a thing because they were busy shoving a dummy in their kid's mouth or something. But there's one guy about three doors down, on the other side of the road, who's a real technology freak. He's got a house full of computer screens, a sort of photography studio in the living room and a giant dish on his roof that must pick up at least a trillion stations – is anyone seriously still putting up satellite dishes these days? I thought they were totally out—'

'Yes, and?' Elma prompted, impatient for Begga to get to the point.

'Anyway, he's got cameras all over the house too. In almost every nook and cranny indoors – though hopefully not in the toilet.' Begga grinned. 'And outside too, of course. One on every corner of the house so he can see all round it, and, luckily for us, they cover the street too. He sent me last night's recordings.'

'Cover the street? That's against the law – but you're right, it's extremely lucky for us.' Elma rose and put her mug in the sink. 'Shall we have a look at the recordings, then?'

❧

The neighbour's camera footage was of such high quality that they had a remarkably clear view of the entrance to Finnur and Gerða's house, the pavement and the street outside. On Saturday, the weather had chopped and changed between sunshine and showers, causing the screen to dim periodically. When the sun set, the quality deteriorated a little, but the camera appeared to have a night setting, so it was still possible to make out everything that happened.

It was fortunate that the house with the cameras was set a little further forwards, closer to the pavement than the other buildings on the street, and that it had no trees in front of it, as this meant they had a good view of the cars driving by.

Suddenly two figures appeared, walking past the house, and Elma started.

'There,' she said.

But Begga drew her attention to the time setting. It still wasn't that late and the figures were walking away from Marinó's house rather than towards it. They continued watching.

For a long time there was no activity, apart from a couple of cats padding along the pavement. Since it was a quiet neighbour-hood, some distance from the town centre, that was to be expected. But just as the clock on the screen was approaching 03.00, Elma started again.

She paused the tape and bent closer.

The figure in the frozen image was wearing a bulky down jacket with the hood up, obscuring their face, which seemed odd for September. Although Iceland was often chilly, even in summer, the weather had been unusually mild recently and few people were sporting winter coats yet. It was mainly foreign tour-ists who wore thick anoraks in the Icelandic summer, which made them stand out like sore thumbs among the lightly dressed locals. Then again, it had been raining on Saturday evening: perhaps the person in question didn't own a waterproof and had put on a down jacket instead.

'Keep going,' Begga said, and Elma pressed play.

The figure walked rapidly along the pavement towards Marinó's house, head lowered, hands in pockets. Several minutes followed in which nothing happened. Elma held her breath.

Then the figure reappeared, this time walking quickly away from Marinó's house, so quickly they were almost running.

Elma's father, Jón, was wandering around the shop with his hands in his pockets as if going for a Sunday stroll rather than looking for clothes. Elma, who had long ago given up trying to steer him towards the smart shirts, took matters into her own hands and started lining up garments along her arm.

'Right, Dad, you go in there,' she said, pointing to the fitting room.

'In there? What for?'

'To try them on, of course.'

'Do I have to? Can't we just buy them?'

'You have to try them on.' Elma put a hand on his shoulder and gave him a push. 'Otherwise we won't know if they fit.'

'I buy all my clothes without trying them on,' he muttered, but obeyed and went into the cubicle.

'Pull the curtain, Dad,' Elma said, then did it herself before the whole shop got an eyeful of her father's gut.

She sighed and the shop assistant smiled at her sympathetically.

Elma realised her mother must be hugging herself with glee at having got out of this trip to the shops. According to Aðalheiður, all Jón's shirts, T-shirts and shorts were too small for him since he'd put on weight, and they needed to replenish their hot-weather wardrobe as they were off on a beach holiday in a month's time. Elma's father didn't take it to heart when his wife criticised his flab. 'You should be pleased, shouldn't you?' he'd said, and Aðalheiður had regarded him in surprise. Why should she be pleased about his extra kilos? 'Well, because now the whole town has living proof of what a good cook you are,' Jón had replied, and Aðalheiður had no answer to that. Particularly since, at that moment, she had been standing in the kitchen, kneading dough.

'It's too big,' Jón said now, pulling back the curtain.

'What are you talking about?' Elma inspected him. 'It's a very smart shirt and just the right size.'

Jón stared at her for a moment, visibly engaging in a mental struggle about whether to argue or abandon the fight. In the end he opted for the latter approach, almost certainly because he couldn't be bothered to try on any more clothes.

'Right, great. Now we know my size,' he said, grabbing several more shirts of the same size. 'So we can go. Can I buy you an ice-cream?'

'But Dad...'

'What?'

'All right.' She gave up. 'Let's pay and get out of here.'

On the way home, her father talked about the plots of land the local council was planning to sell off by drawing names out of a hat. Dagný and her husband, Viðar, were going to put theirs forward but they would have to be incredibly lucky to be selected.

Elma ate her ice-cream while her father talked, her thoughts on Marinó rather than the Akranes property market.

They had viewed the camera footage repeatedly at the police station and kicked around various theories. The timing and the odd behaviour of the figure in the down jacket were a strong indication that he or she was connected to the fire, but however much they enlarged the image they couldn't see the face. With the help of forensics, though, they had at least established that the individual's height was around 175 centimetres, suggesting either a tall woman or a short man. Furthermore, they could tell that the coat was dark, probably black, and came from the 66° North Icelandic clothing store. The shoes were Nike trainers, but it was impossible to work out the size.

Since the evidence suggested that the fire had been started by someone other than Marinó, the next step would be to search for anything in his life that might explain who would want to do him harm. His parents were adamant that their son hadn't fallen out with anyone or had any issues with drink or drugs, but it would be interesting to hear what his friends had to say on the subject.

The post-mortem should have started by now. Elma was relieved not to be present, as the body was in a bad state, almost entirely covered in third-degree burns. Meanwhile, the examination of the scene had been completed, and CID were now waiting for the preliminary report. After that, they could start interviewing Marinó's friends and associates.

Elma had been wondering whether the incident could have been aimed at someone other than Marinó. On the face of it, Finnur seemed more likely to have made enemies than his son. He worked in finance and had been mixed up in some controversial business deals from which he had made a fat profit. But arson struck Elma as an unusually dramatic way of getting even. To her, the choice of a destructive weapon like fire suggested violent hatred; a desire to inflict the maximum amount of damage in a short time.

Once she had finished her ice-cream, Elma said goodbye to her father, took out her phone and entered a number that she hadn't forgotten, although it was a long time since she had last called it.

Rúna was a brilliant and ambitious psychologist who had been working with the Icelandic State Prison Administration ever since completing a post-graduate course in criminology at a university in the Netherlands. She and Elma had been on the same psychology degree course at the University of Iceland until Elma quit two years in and decided to join the police instead. In spite of this, their friendship had endured, though they hadn't seen much of each other in recent years.

Rúna lived in the small town of Mosfellsbær, twelve kilometres east of Reykjavík and an easy half-hour drive from Akranes via the Hvalfjörður tunnel. Elma enjoyed this chance to get out of town and go for a spin, following the Ring Road as it wound round the lower slopes of Mount Esja, hugging the shoreline. It was one of those astonishingly clear autumn days, with every rock and gully standing out, sharp-etched, against the mountainside, and the grass glowing yellow and russet in the September sun.

Mosfellsbær had been transformed almost overnight from a rural farming district to a town with a population of twelve thousand, which made it considerably larger than Akranes these days. Elma drove past the modern estates of white low-rise houses with colourful roofs, eventually finding the address she wanted. The house turned out to be old and a bit shabby, which was Rúna all over. She had never been one to pursue the latest fads or find fulfilment in material possessions.

The two women took a seat in the lino-floored kitchen at a small table with steel legs. While Rúna was boiling the kettle and taking out the cups, she asked Elma about her life and work in Akranes.

'You swore you'd never move back there,' Rúna remarked, studying Elma. 'But naturally you'll have wanted to go home after Davíð died. For the sense of security.'

Elma didn't know how to respond to this. It was correct that when her long-term boyfriend had taken his own life two years ago, she had gone home. She hadn't even stopped to think about it, just got in the car and didn't stop driving until she reached her parents' house.

Rúna had always been blunt; she didn't have the patience to pussyfoot around sensitive subjects, and seemed to regard it as a personal challenge to analyse people – qualities that no doubt came in useful in her job as a prison psychologist.

She put the kettle and a box of teabags on the table, along with a Christmas cake she'd taken out of the freezer.

'Are you seeing anyone new?' Rúna asked before Elma could respond to her previous comment.

'No, not exactly…'

'But there's someone special.' Rúna smiled and nodded slowly. 'I can see it's done you good to go home. You know, you actually seem happy.'

'Do I?'

'Yes, there's a glint in your eye.'

'I see,' Elma said, a little embarrassed. 'But…'

'But that's not what you came here to talk to me about,' Rúna finished for her. She pushed the kitchen door to and sat down.

'No, not right now,' Elma said. 'What do you know about arsonists?'

'It depends what you mean,' Rúna said in the didactic tone that Elma remembered so well. At university, Rúna had generally taken on the role of teacher and Elma that of student, which made it natural for Rúna to slip into their old mode now. 'Are you talking about someone who starts fires to cause damage to property or harm to people?'

'I mean...' Elma thought for a moment, then decided to tell the truth. 'I mean an individual who would choose arson as a murder weapon. Or start a fire after killing someone.'

'Those are two different things,' Rúna pointed out pedantically, sipping her tea. 'Arsonists often have psychiatric conditions. They're subject to an uncontrollable compulsion to light and watch fires. It's not so different from an addiction to gambling or drugs. Individuals with pyromania, as it's called, are fascinated by anything fire-related and often have an encyclopaedic knowledge of fire-prevention systems, fire services and so on. They derive pleasure – a release of tension – from the act of watching a blaze. Once the fire goes out, they experience the compulsion again. They need to repeat the action. And fire-setting becomes an addiction.'

'Er, that's not what I...' Elma fell silent when one of Rúna's young sons wandered in and asked for an apple.

'You mean murder by arson,' Rúna said, once the boy had left with his apple. 'Or, as you said, setting fire to the crime scene after the act.'

'Exactly.'

'Is this connected to...?' Rúna coughed and tactfully abandoned her question. 'Setting fire to a crime scene would be a pragmatic act, since it would destroy incriminating evidence, preventing any fingerprints or biological traces from being found. But killing someone by setting fire to them would be an entirely different matter. It would imply hatred, maybe even a desire for revenge, but not necessarily a psychiatric condition. The desire to kill someone and dishonour their body in that way – that's hatred pure and simple.'

Elma considered this. Was it possible that someone could have hated Marinó that much?

'Of course, starting fires is also a well-known insurance scam,' Rúna added. 'Does the person you're dealing with by any chance have money problems? Would they stand to gain financially from the fire?'

Elma explained that they were still waiting for the bank to provide information about the victim's parents' finances. 'Though I find it impossible to believe they would set fire to their own house, knowing their son was at home.'

'Are you sure they knew?'

'They must have. Why wouldn't he have been at home?'

Rúna shrugged. 'I once read about a man who hired someone to burn down his house for him. Apparently he'd run up big gambling debts from betting on horse racing and hadn't told his family, so he had the bright idea of trying to recoup the money from his insurance company. He instructed the guy to do it in the middle of the day when his wife and child would be out. Only, unbeknownst to him, an hour earlier his wife had got a phone call from the kindergarten to say their three-year-old son was running a temperature. She didn't call her husband, just picked up the boy, took him home, put him in their bed and got under the covers with him. Their bodies were found when the fire brigade arrived.' Rúna took a sip of tea, before finishing: 'Or what was left of them.'

✦

Hannes Hreiðar Þorsteinsson probably devoted more time to thinking about death than most people. It wasn't that he was pre-occupied with his own mortality or the fate of his soul, as he didn't believe in such things; rather it was the biology of death that fascinated him: the changes a body underwent post mortem, and the influence of local conditions and other environmental factors on the process.

The subject hadn't always gripped him. Hannes didn't read

crime novels or watch the sort of TV shows in which a detective works out the murderer's identity by stooping to pick up a hair and sniff at it. Unlike the police, Hannes had limited interest in the *who* or *why*; what concerned him was the question of *how* death had occurred.

In Iceland, deaths were rarely suspicious. The majority of the cases that came Hannes's way were exactly what they appeared to be: the result of a heart attack, a blood clot or some other natural cause. Along with the occasional suicide that generally appeared straightforward.

He wasn't only concerned with the dead; he also assisted the police with the living, in cases of grievous bodily harm or domestic violence: children with injuries that they couldn't or wouldn't explain, for example. For some reason he found these cases far more troubling than the cadavers he usually dealt with. He rarely had intrusive thoughts about the dead once he got home in the evenings, whereas the faces of the living children haunted him long after he had left the anonymous building at the corner of Reykjavík's National Hospital campus on Barónsstígur.

After reviewing his day's schedule, Hannes was ready to start work. He put on his green overall and tied the plastic apron behind his back. Then he snapped on his gloves and lined up his instruments in a neat row on the steel table. While he was doing this, his assistants were preparing the body on a table in the middle of the room.

The flames had made a mess of the young man, and there was a lingering odour of charred flesh in the air. The clothes were stuck to his arms and legs, and his hair had been singed off.

Hannes began by taking photos of the body from every conceivable angle, focusing single-mindedly on this task.

The remnants of clothing proved tricky to remove: the T-shirt had completely fused with the skin in several places. Hannes worked slowly and methodically. It wasn't the first post-mortem he had done on the victim of a fire, nor the worst. One of his earliest jobs when he worked abroad had been an autopsy on an elderly couple who had died when their caravan went up in flames while they were asleep. There were grounds to suspect that they had been dead before the fire broke out.

They hadn't, but Hannes didn't know whether that made it better or worse.

The same task awaited him now. He would have to discover whether the young man had been alive or dead when the fire started. If he had been alive, Hannes would expect to find traces of soot or smoke in his lungs. He would look for heat damage, like bleeding in the airways or inflammation in the windpipe or lungs. Occasionally there was no detectable evidence of this type, even when there was nothing suspicious about the case. For example, some materials released cyanide fumes that could result in a swift death from poisoning before the victim had a chance to inhale any smoke or soot.

Hannes talked as he worked, describing everything he found, or didn't find, for the recording. It was crucial to be meticulous, since the tiniest detail could turn out to be of vital importance. In his discipline, the details were what mattered.

He picked up a small torch and shone it up the victim's nostrils, then pressed his thumb on the chin to open the mouth. It required a bit of effort as rigor mortis had set in, making the body more unwieldy. The young man's oral cavity turned out to be intact and there were no obvious signs of swelling or bleeding in the windpipe or respiratory system. Frowning, Hannes continued with his examination.

After a while, he stretched, arching his back until the vertebrae cracked. While he was peeling off his gloves, he reflected that it was the first time in ages that the results of a post-mortem had taken him by surprise. For he was fairly satisfied in his own mind that Marinó Finnsson had not been killed by the fire.

◆

Unnar was exhausted by the time he eventually got home. His day had been spent arguing with an overseas client who was claiming that part of their consignment was missing. Unnar had long ago become fed up with his job in the export department of a freight-forwarding company, but hadn't yet done anything about moving on.

Once the girls were asleep, he opened a bottle of Coke and filled his glass to the brim. Laufey was in the bath, and the perfume of her soap infiltrated the TV room. She always made such a performance of having a bath: lighting candles, pouring all kinds of oils and other potions in the water and listening to music. Unnar couldn't understand how she could bear to lie there and parboil like that. She always emerged scarlet in the cheeks and smelling like a bunch of flowers.

There was nothing particularly exciting on TV; he had limited interest in a programme about volcanoes, so he opted for something on their streaming service.

When his glass was empty, he went into the kitchen again for a refill. To his surprise, he saw Laufey standing there in the dark. She was staring out of the window, hugging herself, apparently miles away.

'What are you thinking about?' he asked, and noticed the way she jerked at his voice.

'Nothing,' she said, unwinding the towel from her head.

He saw that she hesitated for a moment before fetching a glass and helping herself to some Coke.

'I don't believe that,' Unnar said.

'What don't you believe?'

'That you weren't thinking about anything special.' The corner of his mouth twitched and he leant on the table. 'All your thoughts are special.'

'You're in a good mood all of a sudden,' Laufey remarked.

It was true: he was in a good mood, in spite of his tiredness and boredom with work. He didn't know quite what had come over him, but all of a sudden he was flooded with optimism. After months of being on edge and avoiding the house as much as possible, he felt he could finally relax.

'Do you remember when we first met?' he asked. 'You were always coming out with philosophical stuff that no one but you was interested in. Like, if a tree falls in a forest and no one hears it—'

'Oh, Unnar,' Laufey protested, though she couldn't help smiling. 'That was such a long time ago. I don't think about philosophy anymore.'

'So now you believe that the tree falls, even if nobody hears it?'

'God, I don't even remember the point of that nonsense.'

'Who says it's nonsense?'

'You. You always said it was nonsense.'

'Did I?' Unnar frowned and went over to her.

Laufey looked rather cute without her glasses and with her wet hair sleeked back like that.

'All I can remember is thinking how hot you were when you talked that way,' he said. 'Even if it was a load of nonsense.'

'What made you think of that now, after all these years?' Laufey was eyeing him a little doubtfully, as if suspicious of this sudden happy mood.

'Klara,' Unnar said. 'Our daughter's just like you. She asked me earlier where people go when they die.'

'And what did you say?'

'Well, to heaven,' Unnar said. 'But she just sighed and said she didn't believe in God and that she'd meant people's bodies. Like whether they turned into dust and if that dust was just like any other dust.'

'Could she have heard about the fire?' Laufey asked. 'It's so terrible. Poor Marinó.'

'You've never particularly liked his mother.'

'So what?' Laufey said. 'That's irrelevant in the circumstances.'

Unnar shrugged. He had no real desire to talk about Finnur and Gerða. 'I know it's irrelevant. I was just stating a fact.'

'I'd never wish it on her to ... to lose her son. It doesn't matter that Gerða and I have never...'

'That's not what I meant.'

'You've never had any time for Finnur either.'

'I know.'

Laufey looked out into the garden again and exhaled slowly through her nose.

Unnar put down his glass. 'You smell nice.'

'Do you think so?'

'Mmm.' Unnar was standing close to her now. He bent down to breathe in the perfume of her hair, then kissed her on the neck. She stood perfectly still for a moment before surrendering. She tilted her head to one side and didn't object as his hands untied the knot in her dressing-gown cord.

Tuesday

Hörður summoned Elma and Sævar to see him first thing. They arrived simultaneously at the door of the meeting room, Sævar's dog Birta following at his heels. Birta greeted Elma joyfully, wagging her entire backside. Sævar, meanwhile, hung back, allowing Elma to enter ahead of him.

'Ladies first,' he said formally, and Elma made a face. There was nothing ladylike about her, as Sævar well knew. She preferred trainers to heels, had never sported a pair of fake nails in her life and, on the rare occasions she wore nail varnish, she would be picking it off in no time. And since she couldn't be bothered to remove it properly, she usually left it to flake off on its own.

'I got the provisional results of the post-mortem yesterday evening,' Hörður announced once they were seated. He stroked the pale stubble on his chin, a deep crease forming between his brows.

Elma tried to hide the fact she was still chewing her sandwich. Outside in the corridor, she heard two of the regular officers discussing their summer holidays. Kári was going into loving detail about the food in Italy.

Hörður stood up and closed the door before continuing. 'There were no signs of smoke inhalation or soot in Marinó's lungs. You can read the proper medical terminology in the report, but what it boils down to is that he may have died before the fire broke out.'

'Couldn't the pathologist confirm it one way or the other?' Sævar asked, reaching down to Birta, who was lying under his chair, and scratching her behind the ears.

'I rang Hannes this morning for a more in-depth explanation, and he's fairly confident that Marinó was already dead. Though he did hedge his bets by saying there were other factors that could explain why there was no soot in his lungs – something about cyanide poisoning.'

'Where's the cyanide supposed to have come from?' Elma asked, looking over at Birta. The dog immediately lifted her nose as if Elma had called her, then got up and walked unhurriedly over to lie under her chair instead. Sævar pretended not to notice.

'Apparently, some soft furnishings like mattresses can release cyanide gas when burnt, which brings about death so quickly that the victim has no time to inhale any smoke,' Hörður explained. 'Hannes says it's very uncommon nowadays, but you do get the odd incident when the furnishings are dated. I called forensics following our conversation, and they agreed with Hannes that it was unlikely. The furniture in Marinó's room was modern, and I gather there's now a law against manufacturing the kind that emits cyanide. But the blood test should remove all doubt, and we'll have the results of that by tomorrow at the latest.'

'Did Hannes find any injuries on the body?'

'No. Apparently it was too badly burnt,' Hörður said.

'But we're working on the basis that someone other than Marinó started the fire, aren't we?' Elma asked. 'And if he didn't die in the fire, the same person could have murdered him?'

They had all watched the security-camera footage and agreed that the mysterious figure who appeared in it must have been the arsonist. There could be no other explanation for such suspicious behaviour at precisely that hour of the night.

'Yes, it's possible,' Hörður said. 'Assuming he was murdered. In that case, the purpose of the fire would have been to destroy the evidence.'

'We interviewed the neighbours, who told us that Marinó and

his sister had a party on Friday evening and that there were sounds of a loud argument,' Elma said. 'So I had a word with the guys who were on duty. According to them, there was no evidence of any trouble of that kind when they arrived.'

'We still need to find out what the quarrel was about,' Sævar added. 'And if it could have had any repercussions.'

'I suppose so,' Hörður said, stifling a yawn. His eyes were weary and his shirt was uncharacteristically crumpled, with a coffee stain on the sleeve. Elma felt an impulse to tell him to go home and rest; leave the inquiry to them.

But she could understand why he would rather work than sit around doing nothing. The house must seem so empty without Gígja. She'd been such a big personality; always talking, with that loud, infectious laugh. The polar opposite of her quiet, restrained husband, who was sparing with his smiles.

'Sævar and I will take care of that,' Elma said.

'Tread carefully,' Hörður warned them. 'I don't want the news spreading that Marinó might have been dead before the fire. We can't do that to his family until we're absolutely sure. But I'll ask forensics to go over the house again, just to be on the safe side.'

Örnólfur's flat was located fairly centrally in Reykjavík.

Finnur had encountered him one evening several years ago at a restaurant downtown. He had just concluded a meeting about a potential investment opportunity. The two guys pitching their business idea to him had been on fire. They were both young, in their late twenties, clearly ambitious, and had made a favourable impression on him.

After they had left, Finnur stayed behind to finish his drink. He was in no hurry, having taken the precaution of booking a hotel room in the city centre, since he had known in advance that it would be a late meeting involving booze and that he wouldn't be in a fit state to drive back up the coast to Akranes that night.

He hadn't been sitting there long when a man came over and introduced himself as Örnólfur, saying that he recognised him: Finnur never did work out where from.

'I couldn't help overhearing your conversation.' Örnólfur was wearing a tight black shirt that showed off a bodybuilder's physique, and he was holding a large beer. 'It sounded like an interesting opportunity.'

'It is,' Finnur said, without elaborating, a little disconcerted to learn that the man had been eavesdropping. For most of the evening the place had been fairly empty, which meant there had been plenty of room for people to spread out. Since there were deep armchairs in every corner, there had been no need to sit overly close to the other customers.

Örnólfur carried on chatting and asking questions, and before Finnur had emptied his glass, he'd blurted out everything that emerged in the meeting. But Örnólfur kept wanting to know more and asking questions about Finnur's company, although he seemed pretty well informed already and eventually admitted that he'd had his eye on Finnur for a while.

By this stage, the drink had gone to Finnur's head, and he took it as a compliment. After all, he was prominent in the Icelandic financial world, though mainly among insiders. He wasn't well known to the public and was keen to avoid the media spotlight, unlike some other venture capitalists. Finnur had always been careful to keep his name out of things when he was involved in big deals.

'Isn't your wife waiting for you?' Finnur asked, nodding towards a young woman who was sitting at the bar, casting glances their way.

Örnólfur waved dismissively. 'Oh, she can wait.'

The young woman looked away with a sour expression when she saw Örnólfur's gesture, and the next time Finnur glanced at the bar she had gone.

The two men, on the other hand, stayed on until late. Örnólfur ordered them more rounds of drinks, and Finnur ended up considerably drunker than he had intended.

In hindsight, maybe he shouldn't have talked so much and been so open. Örnólfur told him that he had a considerable sum of money at his disposal and was just waiting for the right investment opportunity. Finnur gave him the young men's names before they parted, then made his way, a little unsteadily, to the nearest fast-food joint and bought himself a kebab wrap before returning to his hotel room.

Several weeks passed, and when another business idea came up, similar to the one the young men had pitched but much further developed, Finnur was relieved that he hadn't acted too hastily in committing himself to the first project.

Then, one day, he heard a commotion in the corridor outside his office and hurried out to see what was going on. A man he didn't immediately recognise had just swept a pile of papers off the reception desk, and the receptionist was standing as if pinned to the wall, her face a picture of alarm.

'You,' the man said hoarsely, advancing threateningly towards Finnur and keeping his eyes trained on him even as he stumbled and lurched. Only then did Finnur place him as the man he had met in the bar.

'It's your fault,' Örnólfur slurred, pointing at Finnur. His eyes were red and sunken, and when he spoke, saliva sprayed from his mouth. 'It was everything I owned – do you understand?'

Finnur had just managed to close and lock his office door before Örnólfur reached him. He stood there, frozen, while the other man banged on the door, abusing him and demanding that they sort the matter out there and then.

The police arrived promptly and removed Örnólfur from the premises, but following the incident Finnur began to receive strange emails. They were anonymous, sent from a variety of addresses, but clearly all came from Örnólfur. Most were sent at night and so peppered with spelling mistakes and typos that Finnur suspected the man was drunk when he wrote them. They all contained threats that the sender was going to get even and that he knew where Finnur lived.

In spite of this, Finnur had never seen Örnólfur again. He felt a slight pang of guilt sometimes, thinking back. The man had obviously been a novice when it came to finance and had taken Finnur's words too literally. Perhaps Finnur should have warned him against investing in the young men's venture, but it wasn't his job to nanny grown men and tell them what to do with their money. Personally, he never put his trust in anyone other than himself, so he had little sympathy for the wretched man.

What had Örnólfur been thinking of to sink all his money in a start-up like that? Finnur had a rule that he never invested more than he could afford to lose. He had certainly never intended to commit a large sum to the project, which was something he only ever did with very careful consideration. So he dismissed Örnólfur's emails as the ravings of a sick man – a harmless drunk. After all, Örnólfur had never followed up on his threats, and Finnur didn't think it was necessary to involve the police.

A year had passed since the last email. Admittedly, that message had alarmed Finnur since Örnólfur had sent an attachment containing an old conviction he had received. It was then that Finnur realised the man was not nearly as harmless as he'd imagined.

Finnur parked outside the block of flats and switched off the engine. He opened his window a crack while he was waiting, never taking his eyes off the front door. Sooner or later Örnólfur was bound to emerge, and Finnur had plenty of time.

It was over an hour before the door opened. Örnólfur had changed a lot in the intervening years; the tight black shirt wouldn't fit him now. Yet there was no doubt it was the man Finnur had met in the bar. The tattoo running from his chest up his neck was the same, and he towered over the woman beside him.

Finnur broke out in a sweat when he saw the size of the man. He had remembered that Örnólfur was a big guy, but seeing him now, in the flesh, was daunting. Face to face, Finnur wouldn't stand a chance. He had never been involved in a fight, not even when he was a kid at school.

But Finnur had no intention of getting into a punch-up with the guy; there were other ways to inflict damage.

Instead of heading to a car, Örnólfur and his wife walked off down the street, holding hands and talking. Finnur started the engine and slid off after them.

◆

Once the morning briefing was over, Elma set to work checking out all the calls to and from Marinó's phone in the days before the fire. There weren't that many, and once she had discounted the numbers belonging to his parents, there were only a handful left. Kids his age simply didn't call each other much anymore. Communications had moved on and mainly consisted of messages or pictures sent on social-media platforms, which could take the police far longer to access – if they could access them at all.

Elma looked up a few numbers and noted down the names of the owners. The most frequent callers were Marinó's best friends, Andri and Ísak. His mother had mentioned three names when Elma asked who Marinó used to hang out with. In addition to Andri and Ísak, she had mentioned Sonja, who was the mother of Ísak's child and a friend of Marinó's sister, Fríða. The five of them had formed a tight little social group, and if anyone knew what was going on in Marinó's life, it was bound to be one of them. Elma noted that the last phone call Marinó made had been to Sonja, at suppertime the evening before he died.

Nevertheless, Elma decided to start by talking to Fríða,

Marinó's twin. She would have preferred to do it far earlier but had wanted to respect Fríða's parents' request that they give the girl a bit of space, as she was so distraught about her brother's death. There were, however, limits to how long one could delay an interview this urgent. In the end, the interests of the investigation had to take priority.

She was relieved to hear that Fríða was staying at her boyfriend's place, because she didn't want to have to interview her with Gerða and Finnur present. However old they were, kids were invariably less forthcoming around their parents. Fríða gave her the address, and Elma and Sævar got in the car.

'Is everything OK?' asked Sævar, who was driving. On the way, they had stopped off at his building to leave Birta with his neighbour, an elderly man who regularly dog-sat for him and enjoyed taking Birta for walks when Sævar was too busy with work.

The question took Elma by surprise, and she turned to him, puzzled. 'What? Yes. Why do you ask?'

'Oh, it's just that normally you talk nonstop.'

'I do not.'

'All right, fair enough.' Sævar grinned. 'But you generally talk more than this.'

Elma had been sunk in her own thoughts, preoccupied with more than the case.

'Everything's fine with me,' she said, trying to sound upbeat.

'Right.' Sævar pulled into a parking space and switched off the engine.

He studied her for a moment or two as if waiting for her to go on. Elma smiled, determined to give nothing away. She knew Sævar could sense that something was up but hoped he wouldn't start pestering her for an answer. They had known each other for two years, ever since Elma had joined West Iceland CID. Sævar was one of the main reasons why she was so contented in Akranes, but right now all she wanted was to get out of the car and away from his observant eyes.

When Fríða came to the door, Elma immediately noticed the tell-tale signs of grief. The girl's face looked tired and drawn, and she had dark circles under her eyes, but her grip was firm as she shook their hands.

'This is Hrafnkell,' she said as they entered the sitting room.

A broad-shouldered young man looked up from his laptop and greeted them.

'Would you prefer to talk in private?' he asked.

'Oh no, it's fine,' Sævar replied.

'I'll go into the bedroom then,' Hrafnkell said, as if he hadn't heard. He snapped the laptop shut and left. Elma noticed that his feet were bare.

'We can sit down here,' Fríða said, pointing to a rather grubby velour sofa.

'I'm afraid we need to ask you a few questions about your brother,' Elma said gently, once they were seated.

'OK,' Fríða said, grabbing a strand of hair and twisting it round one finger.

'Your parents said you and your brother were very close?'

'We're twins,' Fríða replied, as if that was answer enough.

'I mean—'

'I know what you mean,' Fríða interrupted. 'Yes, we've always got on well.'

'Did you hang out with the same group of friends?'

'Yes, I suppose so. Since we moved to Akranes, anyway. It wasn't as easy at our old school in Reykjavík.'

'Why not?'

'Oh, just…' Fríða shrugged. 'Kids being nasty.'

'To you?'

'No, mainly to Marinó.'

'In what way?'

'Does it matter? We were only nine or ten at the time, and the boys have all apologised since. They're not to blame.' Fríða hesitated. 'Marinó was never everyone's cup of tea. He could come across like he was pleased with himself. The other kids thought he was a snob, but they were wrong; really he wasn't. He was just a bit out of it sometimes, like he wasn't interested in anyone else, and people can find that kind of annoying. They reacted like he was arrogant, but it wasn't true.'

'What about Marinó's current friends?' Elma asked. 'Can you tell us about them?'

'What do you want to know?'

'Whatever you think matters,' Elma said.

Fríða thought for a while, her eyes becoming unfocused. 'Marinó had two best mates, Ísak and Andri. He met Andri first, and they hit it off straight away, although they were such different types.'

'In what sense?'

'Oh, just … Marinó had, like, zero interest in sport, while Andri's heavily into football. Marinó plays … played … the saxophone, and I think he had dreams of becoming a music teacher, though he'd just started a degree in computer science. He'd always been a computer nerd, so the course suited him fine, but music was his real passion. Andri used to find it funny, but really I think he admired the way Marinó did his own thing and wasn't afraid of being different. Andri's the kind of guy who's obsessed with appearing cool. He thinks a lot about his clothes and his hair and so on. Girls are crazy about him, but when you know him, you realise he's not as tough as he seems. Really, he's just shy.' Judging from the affection in her smile, Fríða had a lot of time for Andri.

'Did they ever fall out?'

'No, never.'

'What about Ísak?'

Fríða picked up a cushion and hugged it before answering. 'Ísak used to go out with my friend, Sonja. They've got a five-month-old son and they'd been together, like, forever. Ísak works for Icelandic Alloys as a mechanic. But the thing is, he's always been a bit...' Fríða was silent for a moment, searching for the right word and fiddling with the frayed corner of the cushion. 'Out of control. A few years ago all the younger kids were scared of him. He used to steal bikes and spray them black, then either sell them or just chuck them in people's gardens. By the time he started hanging out with Marinó and Andri he was already going out with Sonja – in year nine, that is.'

'Did he change after that?' Sævar asked. He was leaning forwards a little, perhaps because Fríða was speaking so quietly. Elma couldn't work out whether it was because her voice was naturally low or she didn't want to disturb her boyfriend.

'Not at all.' Fríða shook her head. 'He still behaved like an idiot sometimes.'

'Had there been any friction between Ísak and Marinó recently? Did they quarrel at the party, by any chance?'

'The party?' Fríða looked puzzled.

'Yes, we spoke to your neighbours,' Elma said. 'They said you had a party on Friday.'

'Oh, right. Mum and Dad were away and...' Fríða paused for breath, then said in a rush: 'Ísak and Marinó had a bit of an argument on Friday. Marinó and Sonja were shut in the bedroom for ages, talking, and when Marinó came out he was annoyed and wanted a word with Ísak. They disappeared for a while, then Ísak stormed out and ... I don't know what it was about, but Marinó was shaking with rage afterwards. Then the police turned up.'

'So the neighbours heard them quarrelling?'

'Did they?' Fríða asked. 'I thought they'd called the police because the music was too loud.'

'No, they heard a row,' Elma said. 'Followed by the sound of something breaking.'

'Oh,' Fríða said. 'I think maybe a glass got broken. It was nothing serious.'

'Didn't Marinó tell you what happened after Ísak had left?'

'No, he didn't want to talk about it.' Fríða shrugged. 'I don't know what was going on but it was all very ... weird. It wasn't even supposed to be a party – we'd just been planning to play board games, but then Marinó suddenly seemed totally wasted, and I had no idea what was going on.'

'Was it unusual for him to drink?'

'Well ... Marinó didn't often drink, at least not as much as he did on Friday.'

'Did you two ever quarrel?' Sævar asked.

'What?' Fríða seemed startled by the question. 'Not very often.'

'Only, the neighbours claim they heard you two having a row several days ago.'

'Oh, that. That was just over something stupid,' Fríða said. 'We both wanted to use the car. Mum and Dad bought one for us to share, but Marinó hogged it most of the time because Hrafnkell's got a car. Then his broke down last week and we wanted to go and see a film in Reykjavík, and the one time I wanted to borrow the car, Marinó got all pissed off because he said he needed it.'

'I see,' Elma said. If anyone understood about quarrels with siblings, it was her. She and her elder sister, Dagný, had fought cat and dog throughout their teens, and it would be interesting to hear what the neighbours would have had to say about their relationship twenty years ago.

'Do you usually keep the front door locked at home?' Sævar asked.

'Yes, always. Why?'

'We couldn't see any signs of a break-in,' he told her. 'No smashed window or anything like that, and the fire brigade had to force the door. Do you think Marinó could have forgotten to lock it?'

'No, he'd never have done that. He was quite paranoid about that kind of thing.'

'Do you know who else has keys to the house?' Elma asked.

'Just us in the family.'

'Is there anyone who can confirm where you were on Saturday night?'

Fríða didn't seem offended as she met Elma's gaze. 'Hrafnkell. We were here together.'

In contrast to its chic exterior, Finnur and Gerða's house turned out to be rather underwhelming inside, let down by the décor and furnishings. Admittedly, it had high ceilings, the floor was tiled with natural slate-coloured stone, and the kitchen, dining and sitting room formed an airy open-plan space, but the dark furniture was dated and clumsy. Mediocre landscape paintings and a brown leather three-piece suite further contributed to the downmarket impression. Although none of it looked as if it had been bought in junk shops, the overall effect was curiously taste-less. The furniture was badly arranged, the shelves were cluttered and the pictures haphazardly placed. The yellow walls were the final straw.

Since forensics were still at work, re-examining Marinó's bedroom, Elma went for a wander around the house.

It was plain that Finnur and Gerða had been away over the weekend: the kitchen sink was full of dirty dishes, and there were two empty Coke bottles and a takeaway pizza box on the table. Someone had obviously been making themselves a smoothie since the blender was on the table too, along with an empty plastic bag that had contained frozen strawberries.

There were no signs of the fire in the open-plan area, apart from a lingering acrid smell.

Elma walked over to a glass cabinet that was as cluttered as the other shelves in the room, with figurines, photos of the twins and a pile of books.

'What do you think?' Sævar asked.

'Not quite my style, though the house looks good from outside.'

'Does it?'

'Yes.' Elma turned and smiled. 'Don't you agree?'

Sævar shrugged and came over. 'I picture myself buying something a bit older. With more personality.'

'Can houses have a personality?'

'Sure they can,' Sævar said. 'Just like people.'

'You're kidding.'

Elma turned back to the cabinet and opened it, releasing a musty smell of old books and varnish. Most of the volumes seemed to belong to the same series as they had identical black bindings with gold lettering on the spines.

'Anything of interest?' asked Sævar, who had gone over to the window and was staring out at the veranda.

'Maybe. If you like Laxness and poetry.' Elma turned her attention to the top shelves, which were lined with picture frames. Most of the photos had been taken in a studio, with everyone dressed up and carefully posed, their smiles neat and controlled.

Elma took down a family portrait and studied the younger versions of Finnur and Gerða: Finnur with much more – and darker – hair; Gerða wearing big earrings and a silk shirt. The twins, who looked as if they were about five years old, were standing between their parents. The resemblance between them was unmistakable then, but time seemed to have erased it. Elma didn't think the brother and sister had been particularly alike as young adults, but she had nothing but their appearance from which to judge. She'd never got a chance to observe Marinó talking or moving, and family resemblance could go deeper than surface impressions.

Hörður appeared in the hall and called them over. 'Forensics are finishing up,' he said, and they followed him into Marinó's room.

The smell of burning was still present, though it was fading a little, mingled now with the reek of the chemicals the crime-scene team had been using. A large part of the room was blackened by the flames and smoke, but the rest was more intact than Elma had expected. The window was broken, and the front wall would probably have to be totally rebuilt, but the rest looked almost untouched. She wondered if Marinó's parents would repair the wall or move out. Would they ever be able to face living in the house again after the tragedy that had occurred there?

Most of the furnishings and Marinó's belongings were badly damaged; the desk that stood against one wall had been engulfed by the flames and so had the bed. The fire had left black scorch marks up the walls and strange dark streaks on the floor. Elma guessed that these were the result of the inflammable liquid that had been poured onto it. She couldn't stop staring at the charred bed and hoped it would be removed before Finnur and Gerða came home.

The room was large, and the floor-to-ceiling wardrobe at the opposite end looked more or less untouched. The firefighters had obviously got there before the flames could reach it.

'If there was any evidence, it's almost certainly been destroyed,' Hörður remarked. 'But Marinó's laptop survived because it had been left in the living room. His phone was damaged, though.'

A member of the technical team came in. 'I'll send you the report later this week,' he told Hörður. 'Otherwise we're nearly done here.'

'Was it definitely arson?' Sævar asked.

'Yes.' The man pointed to the floor. 'You can see that the fire originated there, in the middle of the room. Petrol was splashed over the floor – that's what those irregular marks are. I'm actually surprised the room isn't in a worse state than it is. Did the fire brigade arrive that quickly?'

'Yes,' Hörður said. 'The fire station's close by and they were here in just a few minutes.'

'Sadly, it often only takes a few minutes,' the technician said. 'Still, it's strange the victim wasn't woken by the smoke alarm, as that's still in good working order.'

They all glanced up at the ceiling and saw the little red light flashing regularly on the alarm.

'Anyway,' the man said, holding up a transparent plastic bag. 'We found this in the wardrobe.'

'Marinó's phone?' Elma asked.

'I doubt it,' the man said, turning the bag round.

The back of the phone was studded with purple and silver rhinestones.

❧

'What happened?' Gerða threw up her hands when she saw Finnur. He didn't answer, just marched across the kitchen and opened the fridge. His blood was still boiling and the sweat was pouring off him.

'What are you looking for, Finnur? I haven't been to the shops.' Gerða caught hold of his arm, trying to make eye contact with him. 'For God's sake, what's happened? Where have you been?'

'Water,' was all he managed to gasp.

'Water?' Gerða stared at him for a moment, then fetched a glass, filled it from the tap and handed it to him.

Finnur drained it in one go. After that he went into the sitting room and collapsed onto the sofa.

Every time he closed his eyes, he imagined how satisfying it would have been to feel the car smacking into Örnólfur's body and see him falling lifeless to the ground. For a brief moment he would have felt as if justice had been done. But, when it came to the crunch, he hadn't been capable of it and had just roared past the man at high speed. In his rear-view mirror he had seen Örnólfur gaping in surprise at the departing car.

'Finnur, where have you been?' Gerða repeated. She had followed him into the sitting room and was standing over him with her hands on her hips. 'I've been alone here all day, wondering where the hell you were. I thought … I thought…'

She clasped a hand over her mouth and closed her eyes. Finnur stared at her, then jumped up and put his arms round her.

'There's nothing to worry about,' he said soothingly.

After a while they both sat down on the sofa.

It was as if Finnur was only now registering where he was. He'd rented the flat through a colleague as he hadn't wanted to stay with his mother any longer. The owner lived abroad and the flat was for sale, but in view of what had happened, he had agreed to rent it out temporarily to Finnur and Gerða. They wouldn't move back into the house they had built. Finnur never wanted to set foot in it again.

He rocked Gerða gently back and forth, aware that it wasn't only her he was soothing but himself as well. His nerves were still tightly wound. He had driven home from Reykjavík at such reckless speed that it was pure luck he hadn't been stopped by the police. But that probably wasn't a good thing. Really, he'd deserved to be pulled over. His grief was no excuse for putting other lives at risk.

'I went into town,' he said, after a while.

'What for?' Gerða stared at him.

'I wanted to get my revenge.'

'Revenge on who?' Gerða asked. 'I don't understand, Finnur.'

It wasn't surprising she didn't understand. Finnur had never told her about Örnólfur or the emails he'd received. He hadn't wanted to cause her unnecessary alarm. But it was even harder to do it now that he knew their son's death was his fault. If he'd reported Örnólfur ages ago or requested some kind of protection, Marinó might still be alive.

He moved away from Gerða, unable to meet her eye as he told her the whole story.

The gym on Vesturgata stank of rubber and sweat. The squeaking of shoe soles on the parquet floor reached Unnar's ears as he made his way down the narrow corridor to the changing rooms.

He was looking forward to getting some exercise, having been in a bad mood all day and unable to concentrate at work. That morning he'd made a complete fool of himself during a phone call with their Swedish office. He'd never been particularly good at English, though he could get by, but on the phone his tongue had suddenly seemed too big for his mouth and he had started stammering, couldn't remember the simplest words and was just grateful he'd been alone in the room so no one could see his scarlet face. He'd felt like hurling the phone across the office after the call was over, but it wasn't a good idea to give in to the violent fits of rage that sometimes seized him.

Unnar sat down on the wooden bench in the changing room and caught a pungent whiff of sweat from his jumper as he pulled it over his head. A twinge in his back made him grimace; he was stiff from sitting at his desk all day and could do with a massage. At one time he used to massage Laufey's shoulders in the evenings when she complained after a long day at the hair salon. He could just picture her face if he asked her for a back rub now. She always behaved as if his job was a breeze and she was the one who deserved a rest after looking after the children. As if he spent all day having fun.

Óskar was waiting for him in the gym, having already set up the badminton court, fixed the white posts into the holes in the parquet and hung the net between them.

'Hey, look who finally decided to show up!' he called as Unnar entered, and smashed the shuttlecock in his direction. Unnar only just got his racket up in time to stop it hitting him in the face, but somehow he managed to return it.

'You can talk,' Unnar retorted, because, although he was at fault this time, Óskar owed him. He and Harpa had turned up outrageously late to dinner on Saturday evening, blaming the kids, but Unnar had seen from the twinkle in their eyes that something else must have detained them. It was difficult having three children under five, and they didn't often get a babysitter, so he couldn't really blame them for grabbing the chance for a quickie.

Óskar just laughed and batted the shuttlecock back over the net.

'Have you recovered from the weekend?' Óskar asked an hour later, when they were sitting on the bench in the changing room.

'Yes, more or less.' Unnar paused to put on his shirt. 'But I don't actually remember what happened.'

'How do you mean?' Unlike Unnar, Óskar was already fully dressed and in a hurry to head home.

'I just mean that evening in general.' Unnar laughed, trying to sound amused. 'I rather lost count of how many drinks I put away, and the whole thing's a blur. Quite like old times.'

Óskar smiled but there was a quality to his smile that set Unnar's teeth on edge.

When they were younger, Óskar used to take his lead from Unnar. He'd bought the same kind of clothes as him, repeated the same phrases and even tried to imitate the way he moved. But after Óskar got together with Harpa, he'd gradually changed. He'd stopped going out with the boys in the evenings, stopped laughing properly at their jokes and only turned up to parties with Harpa in tow.

Unnar could understand why Óskar wanted to hang on to her. She was way out of his league, with a bewitching laugh and a wide smile. No one could understand what Harpa saw in Óskar, and Unnar had bet his mates that the relationship would only last a few days. Now, many years later, they were still together, and the light that came into Óskar's eyes when he talked about Harpa had only grown brighter with the passing of time.

Anyone would think Óskar had swapped sides, from the boys' to the girls' team. He always supported the women's point of view in any argument and at dinner parties he stuck to Harpa's side, chatting to the other wives or keeping an eye on the children. Over the last ten years he had changed into Óskar who built dens for his kids, Óskar who travelled around Iceland in a brand-new caravan, Óskar who didn't drink except with his wife, and Óskar who voted for the Left Green Party and wrote Facebook posts about feminism.

To make matters worse, these days Óskar's admiration of Unnar seemed to have turned into pity, as if he looked down on some aspect of Unnar's life. Their friendship had become limited to games of badminton and dinner parties with their wives.

'Yes, right,' Óskar said. 'Just like old times.'

'What, er…?' Unnar coughed. 'After Villi and his wife left—'

'Brynhildur.'

'Brynhildur, right,' Unnar said. 'Did you two stay long or…?'

'No, not very. Harpa and I left just after one. She got so cold in the rain.'

'Rain? What rain?' Unnar asked.

'You and Harpa spent ages chatting in the garden when you went out for a smoke. She was soaking when she finally came in.' Óskar folded his sports kit and put it away in his bag. 'I can't understand why she always has to smoke at parties. Anyway, I thought you'd quit, Unnar.'

'Oh, well,' Unnar said, feeling the sweat grow cold on his back. 'I have one from time to time.'

Óskar slung his bag over his shoulder and stared at Unnar for a few seconds too long, as if he were considering whether or not to say something.

'Best get going,' he said eventually, and, smiling stiffly, he left.

Unnar remained sitting there, gazing unseeingly at the grubby white wall in front of him.

He now remembered smoking that cigarette – and the rain too. As the fragments of memory began to assemble themselves into a more complete picture, Unnar knew exactly what had happened.

Sonja tried the number one more time, watching the phone ring and ring until the voicemail kicked in. She stared, disappointed, at the name on her screen, remembering how she'd felt the first time she'd seen it there; how her heart had leapt with excitement. It was years since Ísak had made her pulse race like that.

The doorbell rang, and only then did Sonja notice that Jóel was awake. Unlike other babies, he never woke up crying, just lay in his cot, making happy gurgling noises.

Sonja picked up the entry phone, sure for a moment that it was *him*, but the voice she heard was her mother's. Panting a little, as if she'd been running, though she hadn't. The slightest effort left her mother out of breath, but then it wasn't easy carting around all those excess kilos.

'You look terrible!' her mother exclaimed, sweeping in through the door.

She always blew in like a whirlwind. She dumped her bag, dropped her jacket on the pram in the hall and barged past Sonja towards the bedroom, still trying to catch her breath.

Before Sonja had a chance to answer, her mother was talking to her grandchild.

'Hey, if it isn't Granny's darling little boy,' Sonja heard her cooing in a sugary-sweet voice. 'Are you lying here? Isn't your mummy taking care of you? Do you want to come to Granny, my poppet?'

As Sonja went back into the kitchen, she caught sight of her own reflection. Her mother was right; she looked ill, with shadows under her eyes and scruffy hair. She'd fallen asleep while it was still damp, and now it was sticking out in all directions. With a shrug, Sonja went and filled two mugs with coffee.

'His baby-grow's dirty,' her mother said accusingly, once she was installed at the kitchen table with Jóel in her arms. 'He's been sick down the front of it.'

Sonja put the coffee mugs on the table and took a seat.

'I'll change him in a minute.'

Her mother's gaze rested on her. No doubt she was taking in every sign of weariness, every expression that suggested something wasn't quite right. Sonja's mother had always been infuriatingly sharp, able to spot instantly if something was wrong or her daughter was lying or had misbehaved. She seemed to have a sixth sense for trouble, the way she was always popping round uninvited just when Sonja was at her lowest.

'What's Ísak done this time?' her mother asked, taking a sip of coffee. 'Give me a drop of milk, would you?'

Sonja got up and fetched the carton. 'Nothing. Ísak hasn't done anything.'

'I told you not to trust that boy. Ever since that first time you brought him home I could tell he was trouble.' She dropped a kiss on Jóel's brow as if to apologise for talking about his father like that. 'When he came home with you in those ... those girl's trousers and tight top and could hardly be bothered to say hello, just marched straight into your room and shut the door. Like it was acceptable to walk into my home and be with my daughter without even saying hello or introducing himself.'

'Mum...' Sonja said quietly.

'I'm just saying it like it is, Sonja,' her mother continued, unperturbed. 'I knew then that he wasn't a proper man and never would be. He would never be the man you needed. Sure, Ísak's good-looking and he's not all bad – your grandfather says he's a hard worker and punctual.'

'Punctual?' Sonja repeated, trying to hold back a smile. 'Is that the only good quality you can see in him? That he's punctual?'

'Oh no – he gave you this wonderful little boy too. Didn't he, Jóel, sweetie? You're a very good thing, aren't you?' Her mother bounced her grandson on her knee, and Jóel's face split in a grin. He always preferred his grandmother to Sonja. Her mother claimed that was why she had no interest in losing her excess kilos: grannies were supposed to be soft and cuddly.

Sonja smiled. Her son's preference didn't bother her; she was just grateful for a break.

'So, go on, what's Ísak done now?' her mother said, turning her inquisitorial gaze back on Sonja.

Sonja tipped her coffee mug until the brown liquid touched the rim. 'Ísak hasn't done anything,' she repeated, her voice suddenly husky.

Her mother waited.

Sonja gulped and raised her eyes. 'There's another boy who—'

'Another boy?' her mother said harshly. She had provided Sonja with a shoulder to cry on once too often during her relationship with Ísak. 'Is he treating you badly?'

'No, Mum, you don't understand,' Sonja said, and carried on tipping her mug. A dribble of coffee spilt over the rim and dripped onto the table.

'What do you mean?'

'It was me who did something bad this time, not him,' Sonja said, her voice breaking on a sob. 'Like really, really bad, Mum.'

Wednesday

The pathologist's full report was on Hörður's desk by Wednesday morning. Hörður summoned Elma and Sævar to a briefing and told them the blood test had confirmed that there was no cyanide in Marinó's bloodstream.

'But what they did find was rather surprising,' Hörður continued. 'Marinó's blood contained a fairly high concentration of the prescription sleeping pill Imovane, in addition to a small amount of alcohol.'

'A fairly high concentration?' Sævar repeated. 'You mean, like he'd taken an overdose?'

'Yes, it appears so,' Hörður replied. 'Finnur came to see me this morning, and I took the opportunity to ask him about the drug. He said they had it in the house but he wasn't aware that Marinó had been taking it. Finnur had been prescribed it himself a while ago when he was having trouble sleeping.'

'So Marinó may have taken an overdose the very same night that someone decided to break into the house and set fire to it.' This struck Elma as a little too convenient.

'It appears so,' Hörður said again. 'Sleeping pills are commonly used in suicides, so we have to ask whether this could have been true in Marinó's case, though I'm not denying it's extremely odd that a fire should have been started in his room the same night.'

'I just don't buy the idea that it was a coincidence,' Sævar said.

'Finnur's convinced the arson attack was directed at him,' Hörður went on. He proceeded to tell them about a man called Örnólfur, who had accused Finnur of conning him into making a bad investment. 'When it didn't work out, Örnólfur blamed

Finnur. For the last few years he's been sending Finnur abusive emails containing all kinds of threats, including the threat to burn down his house.'

Elma took the printouts Hörður was holding out, and skimmed through the emails.

'But the last message is from nearly a year ago,' she pointed out. 'Why would he have waited until now to take action?'

'You don't need me to tell you that men like him can be un-predictable,' Hörður replied. 'Örnólfur has been getting into trouble with the law since he was fifteen. He did a spell in prison in 2006 for cumulative offences, including theft, assault and drugs. He received a further ten-year sentence in 2009 but was released in 2015.'

'Isn't this a bit implausible?' Elma asked, passing the printouts to Sævar. 'It's one thing to make threats, but I find it pretty far-fetched that the guy would go and set fire to Finnur's house, knowing that his son was in bed. And even more unbelievable that he would have murdered Marinó.'

'What was his 2009 conviction for?' Sævar asked.

'I was just coming to that,' Hörður said. 'Örnólfur fell out with one of his associates over a drugs deal. The associate was no novice – he lived in an expensive house in Garðabær with his wife and two sons. One evening, Örnólfur turned up at his place, and you can read for yourselves what happened.'

Elma perused the paragraph Hörður pointed to and felt her heart beat faster. On the evening of Saturday, 20 December 2008, Örnólfur had broken into his associate's house, armed with a can of petrol and a box of matches. Once inside, he had emptied the can over the Christmas tree that was standing fully decorated in the sitting room, and while the family were asleep in their beds, he had lit a match and held it to the tree.

🌲

'What's this? Is it … is that really a pizza? How long's it been there?'

'Oh, Mum.' Ísak turned over in bed. 'Can you just go away?'

'That's disgusting, Ísak. Your room's a pigsty and it stinks like something's rotting in here. Can't you at least open a window?'

'No, I'm resting.'

'Resting?' His mother spat out the words. 'I don't know what the matter is with you, Ísak. You're twenty-one years old, but you call in sick to work, move back home to your mother's and can't even keep your bedroom tidy. And you a father too…'

'Could. You. Just. Go.' Ísak tried to stay calm but could feel his fingers tingling and his muscles tensing. He heard his mother moving around the room as she talked, collecting plates and glasses, emitting frequent bursts of tutting.

'This is absolutely revolting, Ísak. And I want you to pay me rent.'

'Rent?'

'Yes – what, you think you can live here for free, do you?' she asked mockingly. 'With full service on top?' She then continued in a saccharine tone: 'You think your mummy will do your laundry for you and cook for you as if you were a baby? A little baby that—'

'Get the fuck out!' Ísak flung off his duvet and sat up. He was shaking with rage and couldn't care less if his mother was shocked. 'Out, now.'

'How dare you, Ísak? You don't get to talk to me like that. I know your friend's just died but that's no—'

'Out!' he bellowed at the top of his voice.

His mother froze and stood there without moving for a moment, looking at him.

'I don't know who you are anymore, Ísak,' she said quietly, before finally leaving the room.

Ísak fell back against his pillow, putting an arm over his eyes. He was so tired of it all. But his mother was right: he was no father. It was crazy to think that he had a son.

He and Sonja were only kids when they got together and, as far as he was concerned, it hadn't been serious. She was never supposed to be anything more than a one-night stand. But Sonja had other ideas. She wouldn't let him go. It didn't matter what he did, she forgave him everything; always came crawling back to him and overlooked the terrible things he'd said to her or the fact he'd been with other girls.

Part of him was impressed by her determination. Before she came along, no girl had thought he was worth fighting for. When Sonja was in a good mood, there was nobody like her; she was up for anything and spoilt him rotten. When he was a kid of sixteen or seventeen, all that attention had been good for his ego, but at some point their relationship had ceased to be healthy. He couldn't understand how Sonja could do this to herself. Sometimes he could have sworn she actively wanted to be treated badly.

Something had been different from usual at Marinó's house on Friday evening. Sonja had been all over Marinó the whole time, and Ísak had caught them in the bedroom, sitting on the bed together, Marinó's hand on hers. When they looked at him, Ísak had seen that Sonja was crying. Marinó had stood up, glaring at Ísak, and shut the door.

By the time they emerged a while later, Marinó was wasted, and that was when the evening had really got out of hand.

Marinó had behaved like an idiot, but it was Ísak who regretted everything. He regretted the way he had strung Sonja along and how he had treated her, but most of all he regretted the way he and Marinó had parted.

Elma knew she should have taken the wheel. Sævar always got hopelessly lost in Reykjavík but refused to use the satnav. After being given the address, he'd claimed to know more or less where the flat was.

Elma groaned as he missed yet another turning.

'Stop and turn round,' she said. 'This is a cul-de-sac.'

Sævar obeyed and finally agreed to let her navigate.

'Were there no repercussions when Örnólfur set fire to his associate's house?' she asked, once they were back on course.

'Repercussions?' Sævar asked.

'Yes. I mean, I know he was convicted, but surely the other guy can't have taken it lying down and just left it to the police to sort out? Even though the family got out of the house in time, he must have wanted to get his revenge on Örnólfur.'

'I haven't a clue,' Sævar said. 'If he did, the police obviously never got wind of it.'

'I suppose,' Elma said. She couldn't understand what could have caused the two men to fall out badly enough to have led to such a drastic act. What could possibly justify endangering the lives of two young children? But she knew that people who behaved like that weren't thinking rationally and were usually under the influence of alcohol or drugs. Örnólfur had a two-year-old son himself now, and Elma just hoped he'd come to realise how dangerous his behaviour had been.

'I'm more interested in finding out where Örnólfur got the money from,' Sævar said. 'He comes across as a complete idiot, yet, according to Finnur, he sank a big sum in the start-up that turned out to be a dud.'

'I very much doubt he came by it honestly, wherever it was from,' Elma said, pointing to the block of flats where Örnólfur lived. 'Up there.'

The man who opened the door to them was so tall that even Sævar had to crane his neck to look him in the eye. Finnur had described him as powerfully built, but these days Örnólfur's bulk appeared to be made up of flab rather than muscle. A tattoo emerged from under the long sleeved sweatshirt he was wearing and ran up his neck.

'Come in,' he said, holding the door open for them.

Once they'd taken a seat, Sævar asked about the nature of his relationship with Finnur.

'Finnur.' Örnólfur was chewing gum, his jaws working vigorously. 'I know who he is. What about him?'

'His son died at the weekend,' Sævar said.

'Oh, did he?' Örnólfur replied. 'I'm sorry to hear that.'

'Do you want to know how?'

'What? Er … sure.' Örnólfur eyed them doubtfully.

'He died in a house fire,' Sævar told him. 'Someone poured petrol all over the floor of his room and set it alight. Sounds kind of familiar, doesn't it?'

Örnólfur's jaws paused in their chomping, then started up again. He didn't say a word.

'How did you say you and Finnur knew each other?' Sævar asked.

'We hardly know each other at all,' Örnólfur replied.

'Yet you've been busy sending him emails.'

'It's ages since I last sent him a message,' Örnólfur said. 'I wasn't in a good place then. I … I'd lost a shedload of money.'

'And blamed Finnur?'

'I wasn't in a good place,' Örnólfur repeated.

'Are you in a good place now?'

'Five months tomorrow.'

'Five months?'

'Sober.' The pride in the big man's face didn't escape Elma. She noticed that he darted a glance at the photo of a little boy that was hanging on the otherwise bare walls.

'Your son?' she asked.

'Yes.' Örnólfur smiled for the first time. 'That's Stormur.'

'There's a name that packs a punch,' Elma remarked. 'He looks like you.'

'He's a good-looking kid.'

'Your business associate had a son as well. Two, in fact,' Elma went on. 'They almost died when you took it into your head to set fire to his house. And from what I hear, you reckoned you had reason to get even with Finnur too.'

Örnólfur's gaze was still resting on the picture of his son. His mouth twitched down at the corners.

'I wasn't myself then. There's nothing I regret more. I can hardly bear to think of the fact that, because of me, two little boys almost...' He lowered his head.

Elma caught Sævar's eye and he shrugged.

'We need to know where you were on Saturday night and during the early hours of Sunday morning,' Elma said.

'At an AA meeting.'

'How long for?'

'I went to a midnight meeting. Afterwards I went to a café with some mates. We were there until about half past two, then I went home.'

'Great, then we shouldn't have any problems getting your alibi confirmed.'

Örnólfur escorted them to the door but stopped them on their way out.

'Look, I always meant to ring Finnur and apologise. Could you give me his number? I can't find it anywhere online and...'

'I think it would be best to leave it for now,' Sævar said. 'I think Finnur has enough on his plate as it is.'

◆

Unnar watched his wife all afternoon without being able to make up his mind. She behaved normally for the most part, helping the girls with their homework and getting on with her own studies while he cooked.

'Supper's ready,' he announced at twenty to seven.

Laufey put aside her textbooks, smiling at him, and Unnar felt a rush of relief.

She obviously didn't have the faintest clue what he and Harpa had got up to at their dinner party.

When Óskar said that Unnar had gone out for a smoke with Harpa, it had all come flooding back to him with sudden, harsh clarity. He and Harpa, out in the garden; how he had lit her cigarette and she had leant towards him until he could smell her perfume. How they had stepped, as if by chance, out of the glow from the outside light and Harpa had leant back against the wall. She had raised her chin and taken a drag on her cigarette, staring at him provocatively, then moistened her lips, and he had taken the bait.

Although the kiss hadn't lasted long, it had been eager and he hadn't wanted to stop. It was Harpa who had finally torn herself free and adjusted her blouse. She had given him a hungry look before stubbing out her cigarette and going back inside.

Unnar had stayed behind, smoking another cigarette and wondering what was wrong with him.

Why had he turned into the type who cheated on his wife? He used to despise men like that, regarding them as pathetic shits. Now he was one of them.

But Laufey couldn't know anything about it, Unnar thought, as he forked the creamy pasta into his mouth. He swallowed, studying her. She was still in her yoga gear, a tight sports top, half unzipped at the front, her short hair scraped back in a stubby pony-tail, no make-up. The wedding ring looked too small for her finger: her hands had filled out over the years and now she could hardly get it off.

All of a sudden he was hit by a feeling of such pity for Laufey that he could hardly bear to look at her. She was caught up in an endless competition with herself; a desperate compulsion to educate herself, keep the house clean, eat healthily and lose weight, all while being the world's best mother. At some point in the last twenty years her true self had got lost in this obsessive pursuit of perfection. Standing for Akranes town council had been one of the challenges she had been so excited about. She had managed to get herself elected, contrary to all his predictions, and now she was buckling under the strain.

It got on Unnar's nerves that Laufey, who went to such great lengths to have everything perfect, should neglect her marriage. For years she hadn't made the slightest effort to improve their relationship, and that was precisely why he was forced to look elsewhere.

Everyone needs validation and love, and he was no exception. He was, when it came down to it, only human.

Thursday

The staff at the café confirmed that they had seen Örnólfur there the night Marinó died. Besides, at a good 190 centimetres, Örnólfur was considerably taller than the figure caught leaving the crime scene in the neighbour's security-camera footage.

It continued to bother Elma that there were no signs of a break-in at Finnur and Gerða's house and that the front door had been locked – a door that required a key. She reflected that she really ought to get one of those put in herself; then she'd never lock herself out again and would save a fortune in annual locksmith's fees.

This was what convinced her that the person who started the fire couldn't have been a stranger. Either someone had known where the spare keys were kept or they had access to the house, maybe even their own key.

Elma pushed down the plunger in the cafetière and poured herself a mug. Recently, she'd noticed that she wasn't experiencing her normal craving for caffeine; she could drink her morning cup but then didn't feel like any more for the rest of the day. Of course, she had often heard about women's appetites changing during pregnancy; she just hadn't expected it to happen this fast.

Tomorrow she had an appointment with a midwife who would be able to tell her whether she was imagining things and all her pregnancy testing kits were faulty, or whether she really was expecting a baby. In that case, she would have to spend the next few weeks breaking the news to people until, in the end, everyone knew: her parents, her sister, her colleagues ... and the child's father.

Elma inhaled deeply, trying to get her stress levels under control. It wasn't as if she had a choice and could just ignore the problem until it went away.

Hearing sounds of movement from the bedroom, she took another mug from the cupboard. There was plenty of coffee left as she had made enough for two.

'Örnólfur has an alibi for the night Marinó died.' As Elma told Finnur and Gerða this, she felt almost like the bearer of bad news. She had been hoping for a speedy and convincing solve, which made it all the harder to have to admit that the police were still completely in the dark.

'How's that possible?' Finnur looked anything but pleased.

'Örnólfur has been sober for five months and was at a midnight AA meeting,' Sævar said, taking over. 'After that he was with a couple of other AA members until half past two in the morning, and they were both able to confirm his alibi. The barman remembered them as well. We're just waiting for a CCTV recording that will remove all doubt about the time he left.'

Finnur sat in silence, his gaze fixed on something behind them. There was a hopelessness in his expression that Elma understood only too well. Getting closure was vital. The worst part was to be left hanging, never knowing what had happened.

She experienced such a flood of relief on leaving the flat that she felt guilty. Unlike Marinó's parents, she could walk out of there and dismiss the case from her mind, temporarily, at least.

'What now?' asked Sævar, who seemed equally glad to get out of there.

Elma answered with a sigh.

Forensics had taken various samples from the house, but so far none of these had provided any leads. The police were still waiting to get their hands on any data that could be retrieved from Marinó's computer, and Elma was putting her hopes on this. Computers were almost like an extension of their owner nowadays, as so much of a person's life was conducted on that small, illuminated screen. It was where people met, socialised, worked, wrote down their most intimate thoughts and planned their future.

While they were waiting for forensics to send over the files, they would just have to find out as much as they could by traditional means, and Elma knew who to ask.

'Something happened at the party he held the day before, on the Friday,' Elma said. 'It's time we got to the bottom of what Ísak and Marinó were quarrelling about.'

'So you want to go and see Ísak?'

'No,' Elma said. 'Let's start with Andri.'

◆

Andri's converted garage flat gave him a bit of space from his family – without it he'd probably have moved out long ago. It didn't matter that the pipes running along the wall emitted regular, loud hissing noises or that the branches of the trees tapped against the window when the wind picked up. He could live there rent free, which gave him a chance to save his money. He'd already put aside enough for the deposit on a small flat in Akranes, but that had never been the plan. Ever since he was a child he had dreamt of playing football abroad, but now he just wanted to get out of Iceland, by any means.

'What are you thinking about?' Júlía asked, propping herself up on her elbow. Her long, blonde hair lay like silk on the black pillowcase.

Andri liked her fine. She was pretty, with long eyelashes and pale-pink lips, and clever too, much cleverer than him. She had won countless prizes when she graduated from the commercial college, and was now starting a law degree at Reykjavík University.

'Nothing special,' Andri said. He had never been good at expressing himself in words; couldn't begin to describe how he was feeling or why, but this had never bothered the girls who had chased him over the years. If anything, it seemed to have the opposite effect, making them redouble their efforts to elicit something from him, though he didn't know what. They inevitably tried to read him, and grew ever more disappointed and despairing when they failed. They didn't seem to realise that he wasn't sending them any coded messages or experiencing emotions that he was trying to hide. Not consciously, anyway.

Júlía pursed her lips and studied him. Her penetrating gaze made him uneasy, and he closed his eyes, faking a yawn.

'If you want to talk about … you know.' Júlía laid her chin on his shoulder.

Andri felt his heart beginning to race, his palms growing sweaty, and experienced a sudden, overpowering desire to be alone. He couldn't stop imagining the flames fastening their burning claws into his friend's body. He'd been having nightmares about Marinó rising, ablaze, from his bed and trying to call for help. But he didn't want to talk about it, especially not to Júlía.

'Júlía.' He swallowed, but knew he would have to talk to her sooner rather than later. 'I, er...'

The phone rang and Andri broke off.

Several minutes later Júlía had gone, taking all her stuff: the clothes, cosmetics and shoes, leaving only a sweet scent lingering in the air and a smear of foundation on his pillow.

Andri turned the pillow over, spread the cover on his bed and opened the window. As he did so, there was a knocking on his door – three firm raps.

His visitors introduced themselves as Sævar and Elma, explaining that they were from the police. They both looked older than him but younger than his parents. Sævar was tall, dressed in the kind of jeans and T-shirt that could easily have belonged to a boy of twenty, like Andri. Elma wasn't exactly pretty but she was attractive in a way that Andri couldn't quite put his finger on.

'This place isn't bad, is it?' Sævar said, sitting down heavily on the bed.

'It's OK.' Andri didn't know what to do with his hands, so he put them in his pockets.

'No being disturbed by your parents,' Sævar continued. 'Free to come and go as you please, without them knowing.'

'Yes, I suppose so,' Andri said.

Elma smiled as if to excuse her colleague. Instead of taking a seat, she remained on her feet, surveying her surroundings.

Andri wondered what it was she saw. Probably a typical young man's room: black furniture, greyish parquet and grey walls. He and Marinó had painted them that summer. They'd chucked the furniture in the garden while they were decorating, going outside at regular intervals to flop, bare-chested, in the sun and quench their thirst with ginger ale.

'I'm sorry about your friend,' Elma said.

'Thanks,' Andri muttered, dropping his eyes to the floor.

'As you know,' Elma went on, 'it seems likely that the fire in Marinó's bedroom was started deliberately.'

'Yeah, I heard.' Andri tried to put his whirling thoughts into some kind of order.

'When did you last speak to Marinó?' Sævar asked.

'On Friday evening, at the party,' Andri said. 'Actually, no, it was on Saturday. He rang me around lunchtime, wanting us to hang out that evening.'

'Why didn't you go?'

'I had other plans. With my girlfriend.'

'How did Marinó sound on the phone?' Elma asked.

'I don't know. Just normal.'

'Are you aware of anything that might have been on his mind recently?'

'No, nothing.' He didn't mean to sound curt but he couldn't help it: he just wanted to get the conversation over with as soon as possible.

'Andri,' Elma said, trying to fix and hold his gaze. Andri looked into her greenish-brown eyes. 'When we spoke to Marinó's parents, his mother thought differently. She said he'd been unlike himself for the last week. But you're saying you didn't pick up on that?'

'I, er … I didn't see much of him last week.'

'Are you quite sure about that? You have no idea what could have been bothering him?'

Andri took a deep breath and shook his head. 'No. No, I don't know.'

'All right,' Elma said. 'Then, do you have any idea what Marinó and Ísak were fighting about on Friday evening?'

He and Marinó had been friends for nine years. Andri had counted back in his head as he lay there last night, unable to sleep. It was nine years since his mum had pointed to the short kid with the glasses and the big shock of hair. 'Go and talk to him,' she had ordered. Andri hadn't realised then, but knew now, that his mother had felt sorry for Marinó. She'd heard what had gone on at his old school. Come to think of it, that was typical of his mother, who couldn't bear to see anyone suffer. All through Andri's time at school she had insisted on inviting the whole class to his birthday parties, despite his dad moaning about the horde of kids charging around the house.

'I…' Andri began. 'It's not for me to say.'

'Not for you to say?' Sævar repeated. 'What do you mean by that?'

'It's just…' Andri hesitated. 'Marinó used to take stuff to heart, you know? He hated it when people did bad things.'

'What people?'

Andri hesitated. 'Just people.'

'Like your mate Ísak?' Elma asked.

Andri nodded.

'Did Ísak treat someone badly?' Elma persisted, her eyes fixed on his face.

'Well … yeah, but, like, I don't think that's any secret.'

◆

A missed call was waiting for Elma when she got back to the car and checked her phone.

'Hörður's been trying to reach me,' she told Sævar, and returned the call.

Hörður answered after the first ring. 'Hello, Elma. Where are you two now?'

'We were at Marinó's friend Andri's place and now we're on our way to see Sonja,' Elma said. 'Is there any news?'

'Yes.' There was the sound of a door closing, then the creaking of an office chair as Hörður sat down. 'I've just had a call from forensics. They found traces of sleeping pills in the blender that was on the kitchen table at Marinó's house.'

'In the blender?' Elma repeated. Sævar was staring at her. The volume on her phone was turned up so high that he must be able to hear everything Hörður said.

'Yes, it appears that the sleeping pills were mixed with … with fruit and alcohol, which Marinó then drank.'

'Do you think he could have made the drink himself?'

'I went back to the house,' Hörður continued, without answering her question, 'and looked through the medicine cabinet. There were still some pills left from his father Finnur's prescription; there certainly weren't enough missing to match the levels in Marinó's bloodstream.'

'So he didn't get the drug from there?'

'No. Either he got hold of the pills by other means or somebody else brought them round.'

'And offered to mix him a drink?'

Elma hung up and looked at Sævar.

'Well, at least one thing's clear,' he said. 'If Marinó didn't do it himself, you can bet it was someone he knew.'

❦

The first time Unnar cheated on his wife, he was so drunk that he could remember only snatches of the night. The girl, a single mother, had been won over by his expensive suit and the fat wad of notes he had brought out to pay for their drinks. She'd probably let herself fantasise that he was some rich guy who would take care of her and her son; move them out of their tower block in Breiðholt. Unnar had allowed her to hold on to her dream for that night.

The girl – he couldn't remember her name – had thin, brown hair and lips that disappeared when she smiled. Although the details of the night were hazy, he had a clear memory of waking up the morning after in a bed with rose-patterned sheets, and seeing his underwear on the floor. On the way out he encountered her son, sitting, eating cereal in the kitchen. It hadn't occurred to Unnar that the son she kept talking about would turn out to be at least twelve and seriously overweight. Unnar had made himself scarce after slipping the boy a thousand-krónur note, feeling as if he was paying him for sex with his mother.

That was eleven years ago, shortly before Klara was born and a few years before Anna came along. Anna was totally unaware of all the stupid things her father did: in her eyes he was perfect.

Unnar knew it was wrong to have a favourite child, but he loved Anna more than anything else in the world. Perhaps because she had been premature and he had never seen anything so tiny and fragile. Her curled fist could hardly encircle one of his fingers, yet she had clung to him in search of security and warmth.

It was Anna who wrapped her skinny arms round his neck and whispered that he was the best. Her face lit up every time she saw him, and, even though she was seven now, she would still clamber onto his lap and lay her head on his chest. He had promised himself that whatever the state of his marriage, he would hang in there until she reached her teens.

There were three years between the sisters, but Klara had always seemed older than her true age. She was wary and suspicious by nature, and there were times when Unnar felt he must have earned her distrust somehow. He would catch Klara watching him now and then with an expression he didn't like.

After that first one-night stand, others just seemed to fall into his lap. Girls he met in bars or worked with. Some he did no more than kiss, others he slept with. Despite the twinges of guilt afterwards, he didn't have the strength to resist.

Laufey was too busy to notice. They shared a house and had a family, but sometimes it felt as if they lived in two separate worlds. On the rare occasions they quarrelled, she would never defend herself properly. As a result, their problems were never thrashed out, they simply became part of the background to their life. At times he said things simply to provoke a reaction from her, but the only sign that his words had hit home would be a tiny twitch of her jaw muscles or a momentary pause. She wouldn't show anything else.

❧

A small wet patch had formed on the girl's white strappy top, on the breast that wasn't hidden by the child. Sonja didn't seem to have noticed. She opened the door a little hesitantly when they knocked.

'Cute kid,' Sævar said, grinning at the baby. 'What's his name?'

'Jóel. Jóel, after my grandfather,' Sonja said, sounding relieved. She stepped aside and let them in.

'Hi, Jóel,' Sævar said, making a face at the child.

Elma couldn't help smiling. Sævar's baby voice needed some work, but then he probably didn't get much practice.

'I'm sorry about your friend,' Elma said, once they were seated.

Sonja nodded and hugged Jóel tighter. The little boy was obviously tired as he cuddled up to his mother's breast, avidly sucking his dummy. His eyelids kept drooping, though he tried to keep them open.

'We won't disturb you long,' Elma said. 'I can see this little fellow's about to drop off. But we do have a few questions we need to ask you.'

'That's fine,' Sonja said, rocking the baby.

'How long had you known Marinó?' Elma began.

'Ever since he started at my school.'

'So you were in the same class?'

'No, the same year,' Sonja said. 'I got to know Fríða first, then Marinó through her.'

'Marinó rang you at suppertime on Saturday,' Elma said. 'Could you tell us what he wanted?'

'He wanted to apologise,' Sonja said. 'To check if everything was OK.'

'To apologise for the fight he had with Ísak, you mean?' Elma asked.

Sonja nodded.

'What were Marinó and Ísak fighting about? Ísak's the father of your baby – of Jóel, isn't he?'

'Yes. Oh, God.' Sonja could no longer hold back the tears that started trickling down her cheeks. 'It's all my fault.'

Elma and Sævar waited for her to say more, but she didn't.

'Sonja,' Elma prompted.

'Hang on,' Sonja said, sniffing. 'I'm going to put Jóel down in his cot. Then I'll tell you everything.'

When she came back, she had pulled on a baggy knitted jumper. She fetched a glass of water and sat down again.

'Me and Ísak started going out in year nine, though we'd known each other for ages. I'd had a crush on him since the first year.' Sonja smiled shyly. 'So when he finally showed an interest, I was so happy that I was prepared to put up with anything. He was never that kind to me. You know, like, he used not to bother answering my calls or texts when he didn't feel like it, though he'd send my friends messages at the same time, so I knew he had his phone. Then people started saying they'd seen him with other girls but … I just refused to believe it. We were such kids. Then about two years ago everything suddenly seemed to get better. I finally stopped being scared of losing him. I got pregnant, and we rented this flat, then Jóel was born.'

Sonja took a mouthful of water before carrying on.

'The birth was terribly difficult; I lost a lot of blood and it took me ages to recover. I was in hospital for two weeks. Ísak was working, so he didn't stay with us, apart from the first night. When I finally got home he was great, constantly spoiling me, running out to buy me food and treats and so on. Then one evening I got a call from a girl who felt she just had to share with me the fact that while I was in the maternity ward, she'd slept with Ísak. Not once but five times. That's what she said: five times. She sent me pictures to prove it.'

Sonja picked up her phone, scrolled through her messages, then held it out to them. On the screen was the back view of a boy lying in bed with the duvet rucked up between his legs. He was clearly asleep, unaware that the picture was being taken.

'The sad thing is that I wished she hadn't called me,' Sonja said. 'I wished everything could just have gone on the same.'

'But I don't understand,' Elma said. 'Marinó and Ísak can hardly have been fighting about that? Unless Marinó was angry on your behalf?'

'No, but…' Sonja paused. 'That evening Marinó and I got talking, and I told him about everything that had happened between Ísak and me, though up to now I haven't liked to tell people about it. I mean, Ísak's Jóel's dad, in spite of everything, and I don't want stories like that circulating about him.'

'So that was why Marinó lost it with Ísak?' Elma asked.

'I think so, but … actually things were a bit weird that evening,' Sonja replied. 'I don't understand what happened to Marinó. He suddenly got so angry.'

'For no reason?'

'He was fine while we were talking, but suddenly he went for Ísak and after that he just kept muttering the same thing over and over again.' The baby began to make noises in the other room, as if waking up. Sonja ignored him. 'What have I done?'

'What have I done?' Elma repeated.

'Yes, that was what he kept saying: "What have I done?",' Sonja explained. 'At first I thought he was talking about Ísak but then … then I wasn't so sure.'

Ísak had just got out of the shower. He smelt of newly washed hair and aftershave.

Sævar launched into the questions the moment they were seated. 'We know you and Marinó had a fight last Friday evening and we want to know why.'

Ísak looked at them for a long time in silence, before saying slowly, 'I just don't understand what happened that evening.'

'What do you mean?'

'Marinó suddenly went completely mental. He started yelling at me. Something about Sonja and … It was like she'd been feeding him some…'

'Feeding him what?'

'Bullshit.' Ísak shrugged.

'Bullshit?' Sævar raised his eyebrows.

'Yes…' Ísak hesitated. 'Marinó thought I'd hit Sonja. That's not true.'

'Why did he think that?' Elma asked. Sonja hadn't mentioned

anything about domestic violence to them, but perhaps she had confided in Marinó.

Ísak shook his head, dropping his eyes. Elma studied him. He had a thin face, sharp jawbones and slightly protruding ears. There was an air of sensitivity, of fragility even, about him.

'You have a child together,' Sævar remarked.

'So what? That doesn't mean we're a couple.' Ísak ran a hand through his hair. 'Our relationship has never been easy. It's always been kind of on and off. Then Jóel came along, and after that everything got ... more complicated.'

'More complicated in what way?'

'Just...' Ísak sighed. 'I wasn't ready for it. Sonja told me she was on the pill, then next minute she's pregnant. I know accidents can happen but I reckon she did it on purpose. To ... to tie me down or something.'

'To tie you down?' Elma repeated. She hoped Ísak could hear from her tone how ridiculous this sounded to her. It wasn't like many girls got pregnant just to trap a boy.

'I know it sounds crazy,' Ísak said. 'But you don't know Sonja.'

'Marinó knew you both,' Elma pointed out. 'And he chose to believe Sonja.'

'She can be very convincing,' Ísak muttered, shifting in his chair. 'She ... she's good at making stuff up.'

'Making stuff up?'

'Yeah. Making people feel sorry for her,' Ísak said. 'And the thing is, I reckon Marinó always secretly fancied her. She could wrap him round her little finger.'

'Was that why you two had a fight?' Sævar asked. 'Because you were jealous of their relationship?'

'No, I couldn't care less.' Ísak snorted. 'It's not like Marinó would ever have done anything about it and, even if he did, I wouldn't have given a shit.'

Somehow this answer didn't come as a surprise. From all Elma had heard, it seemed Ísak didn't believe he'd committed to a relationship with Sonja.

'Where were you on Saturday night?' she asked.

'At home.'

'Can anyone confirm that?'

'My mum,' Ísak said.

'And would your mother necessarily notice if you went out in the night?'

'No, but I didn't,' Ísak said, his manner reminding Elma of a sulky child.

'One more thing,' Elma said, as they were preparing to leave. 'Were you mixing yourselves drinks on Friday? Using the blender, I mean?'

'Yeah,' Ísak said. 'The girls were making cocktails.'

'Who was in charge of mixing the drinks?'

'Fríða,' Ísak said. 'Why do you want to know?'

Elma had printed off a photo from Gerða's Facebook page, showing Marinó and his friends standing in the garden, all dressed up. The twins, Fríða and Marinó; Marinó's best friends, Andri and Ísak, and of course Fríða's best friend, Sonja, the mother of Ísak's child.

Elma found it surprising that they had all stuck together in spite of what had happened between Ísak and Sonja. Friends often take sides when a couple splits up. But perhaps the bonds they had formed during their schooldays had been strong enough to hold the group together.

Fríða was standing at the edge of the picture, and Elma had to check the date again to be sure that the photo really had been taken last summer. The girl must have been ten if not twenty kilos heavier then, and the contrast with her current appearance was startling. Today, Fríða was so thin that her trousers hung off her.

Beside Fríða stood Sonja, leaning against Ísak, who was resting an arm on her shoulder. She was tall and slender, with long, smooth, chocolate-brown hair, small features and a wide smile, which hadn't been in evidence when Elma and Sævar went to see her. She and Ísak made a strikingly good-looking couple. In the photo he was much smarter than he had been when they visited him earlier, in a shirt and waistcoat, and a pair of distressed, light-washed jeans. Not exactly conventional smart wear, but then he didn't come across as the kind of boy who would wear a classic suit.

Ísak's other arm was slung around Marinó's shoulders. Marinó was much shorter, with reddish-brown hair and tanned skin. With his straight trousers that barely reached his ankles and shirt buttoned up to the neck, Marinó looked as if he had been cut out of an old photo and stuck onto this one.

Next to him was Andri. Elma got the sense from his expression that he was ill at ease in his suit trousers and shirt. No doubt sports gear was more his style. She examined his face. Andri was undeniably good-looking. He had tucked his longish, dirty-blond hair behind his ears and wore a half-smile, as if feeling a bit foolish but also amused at having to pose like this. When Elma met him this morning, she'd had a niggling feeling that she recognised him, but she couldn't work out where from. Perhaps it was from the football match she'd been to last summer. Andri played for Akranes and was supposed to be pretty good. Apparently he was moving abroad in the autumn to play for a foreign club.

'You're always so organised.'

'You say that like it's a bad thing.' Elma didn't have to look up to recognise Sævar's voice.

He sat down by her desk, and Elma tried to interpret his expression. They had known each other almost two years, spent practically every day together, and yet there were still times when she couldn't read him at all.

'Got any theories yet?' Sævar asked, clasping his hands behind his head. 'Did any of them fall out with Marinó?'

'I don't know,' Elma said with a heavy sigh. 'I mean, we know that something happened between Marinó and Ísak, but it would have had to be pretty major to end like that.'

'It's very subjective, of course.'

'What is?'

'What seems major to one person may seem trivial to anyone else,' Sævar said. 'You just can't tell.'

'You're very philosophical all of a sudden.' Elma grinned. 'But of course you're right. Maybe the whole thing revolves around Sonja. I mean, she must have been important to Ísak, though he won't admit it.'

'So your money's on Ísak?'

'I think it's a possibility,' Elma said, returning her attention to the group photo. 'It would have been a bit of an over-reaction, but what do I know? People are forever surprising me.'

Her gaze paused on Ísak. Unlike his friends he wasn't smiling, just turning up one corner of his mouth slightly. Elma's attention was drawn to the arm that was draped over Sonja's shoulders. She picked up the picture and squinted at it. Sonja was wearing a strapless dress and Ísak had his arm around her, but there was something strange about the way he was gripping her. On closer inspection, it looked as if he was digging his nails into Sonja's bare flesh.

❦

Laufey sat on the bed, changing her trousers. Her broad thighs were pure white, despite the fine summer they'd had, and the purple varicose veins seemed to spread with every year that passed. She sometimes talked about having an operation to remove them but never got round to it.

'What?' Laufey asked, when she noticed Unnar standing in the doorway, watching her. She stood up, sucking in her stomach as she buttoned up her jeans.

'I just wanted to let you know that I'm going out this evening,' he said. 'It's Villi's birthday.'

'Oh, right.' Laufey opened the wardrobe and scanned her shirts, most of which had some kind of flower pattern. 'Are partners not invited?'

'Sure. Actually, he said you'd be welcome,' Unnar replied. 'But I don't think it's really worth getting a babysitter again. I won't be long.'

Laufey took out a blue blouse and held it up.

'Do you mind?' Unnar asked, when he got no response.

'No, not at all.' Laufey looked round and smiled. Her vest had lace at the front and there was a glimpse of bra through the thin material.

'Are you going out somewhere?'

'Yes,' Laufey said and went into the en-suite bathroom. She opened the cabinet and started putting on face cream with firm, circular strokes.

'Where?'

'Just a little "meeting" with the other councillors,' she said, making air quotes with her fingers.

'A meeting?' Unnar echoed, looking at the clock. 'On a Thursday? What time does it start?'

'In half an hour. At eight.'

'Who's going to babysit?'

'I've sorted that,' Laufey said, plugging in the hair dryer.

'And when were you planning to tell me?' he asked, but Laufey didn't hear him over the noise of the dryer.

Unnar took off his shirt and fetched a new one while Laufey was getting ready. He put on his best trousers and a dark-blue shirt. Then he examined his cheeks in the mirror, wondering if he needed a shave.

At that moment Laufey appeared behind him in the mirror, her hair smoothed back, wearing lipstick and foundation. She reminded him suddenly of when they were young, before they had kids. In those days they were always travelling, heading to places that few other people would think of visiting. They'd jet off to Spain, hire a car and leave the tourist spots behind, making for the mountain villages. Or travel through the English country-side or the Scottish Highlands. The old Laufey couldn't keep her hands off him; she'd been happy to sleep on thin mattresses on the floor, drink beer before lunch and stay up late.

'What?' Laufey asked, fluffing up her hair.

'Nothing,' Unnar said, buttoning his shirt.

'Were you thinking about anything in particular?'

'Me?' Unnar coughed. 'No. You just...'

'What?'

Unnar heard the plea in her voice and knew what she wanted to hear.

'Try not to be back too late. I don't know when I'll be home, but we can't pay the babysitter to stay up half the night.'

Laufey was silent for a moment, then turned away.

'Yes, of course. I won't be long,' she said and left the room.

❧

Langisandur beach stretched out on either side, its fine, light-brown sand streaked with vein-like marks by the retreating waves. There were crowds of people out walking and swimming in the sea, and the new geothermal pools were almost full. Last year, Guðlaug, an innovative concrete structure containing two pools overlooked by a viewing platform, had been built into the rocks above the beach. The lower pool was generally lukewarm but could be icy cold at high tide when the waves broke over it. At the moment, the tide was out and it was packed with sea-bathing enthusiasts trying to get the heat back into their bodies. Elma, meanwhile, was wallowing in the hot water of the upper pool, gazing out over the bay, where sea merged into sky at the horizon.

Elma's mind was not on the view. Instead, she was preoccupied with her psychologist friend Rúna's suggestion that the fire could have been intended to hide incriminating evidence. Since Marinó had already been dead, it appeared that the act of arson had indeed been an afterthought, rather than the killer's initial aim; an attempt to hide his or her tracks and the fact that Marinó had been murdered – assuming he had. The police still couldn't rule out the possibility that he had taken the overdose voluntarily and started the fire himself as soon as the drug began to take effect. But in that case who was the person acting suspiciously in the security-camera footage?

'I thought we were going to clear our heads,' Sævar murmured.

'I am,' Elma said. It had been a long day and she needed to distract herself from the case. All that awaited her at home was a sleepless night of spiralling thoughts, so Sævar's suggestion of relaxing in the hot pool had sounded tempting. In practice, though, she was finding it impossible to switch off.

'I can almost hear your mind whirring.' Sævar gave a wry smile. 'What is it?'

'I just … I was wondering why Marinó kept muttering those words to himself.'

'"What have I done?"'

'Exactly. What do you think he was referring to?'

'Well, he'd just had a fight with his mate,' Sævar pointed out.

'Yes, but Sonja didn't think he was talking about that.'

'Isn't it possible he was mixed up in something that we haven't discovered – yet?' Sævar turned over to rest his head on the edge of the pool.

'I suppose so.'

'I did a background check on the guy Fríða's living with – Hrafnkell. He's thirty – ten years older than her – and already has two bankruptcies behind him.'

'What kind of business was he involved in?'

'His first venture was importing energy drinks, but then it

turned out that some of the ingredients were banned,' Sævar said. 'The second was some kind of online shop selling goods from AliExpress for a huge mark-up. When the news got out, the shop, unsurprisingly, went bust. So it's pretty convenient for him to have hooked himself a girlfriend with rich parents. I bet the fact didn't exactly scare him off Fríða.'

'No, I bet,' Elma said. 'But Marinó's unlikely to have been involved in his business, surely?'

Before Sævar could answer, some people he knew got into the pool and started chatting to him, so Elma went back to contemplating the view.

One of the things she had learnt during her police training was to approach every case as objectively as possible, which meant taking nothing for granted and casting a critical eye over everyone and everything involved. What looked initially like an open-and-shut case could turn out to be a complicated criminal investigation. You couldn't assume that a fall from a ladder was an accident; instead, you had to adopt a certain mindset and follow set procedure. As straightforward as this sounded, it was something she was constantly having to remind herself about. She had to keep an open mind: the case might have nothing to do with Marinó's friends or father but with something that had yet to emerge. In spite of this, the image of Ísak kept rising before her mind's eye, with his sly smile and his fingers digging deep into Sonja's shoulder.

❧

Eventually, Hörður had ordered Sævar and Elma to go home. They had stayed late, discussing their next steps and reviewing the evidence, but so far they had virtually nothing to go on. The video footage had provided few leads, and there was nothing to suggest that Örnólfur was linked to the fire. What's more, it seemed no one had anything bad to say about Marinó.

Hörður knew he should head home to bed as well, but instead he lingered in the office. He made himself some toast, had a cup of tea, then dialled his daughter's number. There was a little interval before she answered, audibly out of breath.

'Any contractions yet?' Hörður asked.

'No, none.' There was a sound of hammering in the background. His daughter and son-in-law were doing up the flat they had just moved into.

'It can happen fast,' Hörður said, taking the phone over to the window.

'Dad.' Katrín's voice was tired. 'It's not even due yet. There's still another three weeks to go.'

'I know, I know. But when you were born...'

'I know I arrived early, but that doesn't mean my baby will be the same.'

'No.' Hörður sat down in his chair again and turned on his monitor. 'No, I suppose not.'

'I just hope he hangs on a bit longer,' Katrín continued. 'We're in the middle of moving and absolutely nothing's ready yet.'

'Snorri'll take care of the move.'

'Is that a question?' Katrín laughed. 'No, actually: Snorri's not going to do it all on his own. He's putting up shelves, and I'm unpacking boxes, and, yes, Dad, I'm being careful.'

Katrín was always doing that – answering questions before he'd even asked them and finishing his sentences for him. He hated to think he was that predictable, but Gígja used to do exactly the same. Sometimes he felt as if his family knew his mind better than he did.

'Right, well. You'll let me know.'

'Yeah, yeah.'

There was a short pause, and Hörður had the impression that Katrín wanted to get rid of him. She had more than enough to do and little time to spare for her old dad.

'Just don't choose the colour of the nursery yet,' he said, then immediately regretted it. He hadn't meant to say anything, but he still couldn't believe that his daughter had chosen to find out the sex of her baby in advance. It was like stealing a peek inside a Christmas present. In their family it had always been the tradition to wait and see. Honestly, he couldn't understand people's impatience nowadays: all those baby showers and gender-reveal parties, or whatever they were called. What if something went wrong? Wouldn't the parents have to come home, empty-handed, to be faced with a pink- or blue-themed nursery, full of toys and clothes? That would be devastating, but then he supposed it would be difficult in any circumstances.

'*Dad*.' He couldn't fail to hear the note of warning.

'What if *he* turns out to be a *she*?' he persisted, against his better judgement.

'I'm hanging up now.'

'I'm done.'

'Good.' Katrín cleared her throat. 'Dad?'

'Yes?'

'Is, er … is everything all right? Would you like to come round for supper? I wasn't planning to cook but we could get a takeaway.'

'No, thanks, love, there's no need. I'll drop by tomorrow.'

Hörður put the phone down on his desk. Ever since Katrín had told him about her pregnancy he'd had a knot in his stomach. His daughter had always been over-sensitive and touchy, ever since she was a child, and it didn't take much to upset her. But now, although it was only two weeks since Gígja had died, Katrín seemed suddenly to have decided to be the strong one in the family. Hardly a day passed when she didn't call him or invite him round for a meal. It was as if their roles had been reversed and she meant to take care of him now. Apparently she was more like her mother than he had realised.

The phone rang, interrupting his thoughts. It was the technician from forensics, who had been tasked with going through Marinó's computer.

'There was activity on the computer until 23.12,' the technician said. 'Just the usual web surfing. Nothing interesting or unusual to see there. Then there's a pause for...' There was a brief silence at the other end. 'Here it is: he wasn't on the computer again until 00.23 hours, and that's when it gets strange.'

'In what way?'

'I'm coming to that.' The eagerness in the man's voice suggested that he had found something significant. 'At 00.23 hours he types the following search entry in English: "How to hide a body".'

'And did he get any results?' Hörður picked up a pen and made a note of the time.

'Oh, yes. There's no shortage of suggestions floating around online. He looked at a number of different sites; I'll send you a list.'

'Great. How long did he spend looking at this stuff?'

'At 00.52 hours he switched off his computer,' the man said.

After hanging up, Hörður took a piece of paper and wrote down the times he had been given – 23.12, 00.23, 00.52 – trying to make sense of Marinó Finnsson's last night alive.

Then he examined the list of websites Marinó had visited, which the technician had sent over. For most of the evening, the young man had been clicking between various sites of no particular interest, but shortly after midnight he had asked the search engine how to hide a body, then spent half an hour visiting sites that had come up in the results.

Hörður tried to think of an innocent reason for the search. Perhaps it had been prompted by no more than natural curiosity, but he couldn't remember giving any thought to that kind of question when he was young.

Nevertheless, he doubted that Marinó's research had been serious. The only suspicious death in Iceland at the moment was his own; the one they were currently investigating. Admittedly, there were old, unsolved cases – not murders but missing-persons cases – which could conceivably turn out to be crimes. Hörður made a note to check on recent disappearances to see if any of them could have a connection to Marinó.

Just before one in the morning, Marinó had switched off the computer, and Hörður didn't know what he'd done after that; whether he'd gone to bed or watched TV.

Hörður leant back in his chair, his eyes still on the sheet of paper. All those times and question marks. The fire hadn't started until around three, but Marinó had probably died a while before that. At some point between his turning the computer off just before one and the fire starting at three, Marinó had consumed an alcoholic drink containing sleeping pills and died as a result. The question was, who had mixed the drink?

◆

The babysitter had sent them to bed far too early, but Klara didn't care. The girl, a fifteen-year-old called Vilborg, had barely looked up from her phone all evening, though she'd had the TV on far too loud. She could never be bothered to talk to them or play with them. Klara was fairly sure Vilborg didn't even remember her name.

The good thing about the babysitter's indifference was that Klara could read as late as she liked. She didn't even have to use her torch, she could just switch on the wall light, because she knew no one would come in and order her to turn it off.

She must have fallen asleep, though, because all of a sudden she started up and saw that her book had fallen on the floor. According to the clock on her bedside table it was nearly three in the morning. Klara retrieved her book, put it on the bedside table and switched off the light. She was just dropping off again when she heard a noise, a quiet pattering like footsteps, carrying in through the open window. She strained her ears, lying perfectly still, but nothing happened.

It was quiet in the house. The TV had finally fallen silent, so

Vilborg had obviously gone home, and either her mother or her father must be back. They had both been very dressed up when they went out earlier, especially her mum. Klara loved the smell of her perfume and the colour of her lipstick. When her mother made an effort, it was like she became a new person, and Klara couldn't take her eyes off her.

Feeling wide awake now, she sat up, then got out of bed and padded over to the window. Where had the noise come from? It was probably just next door's cat, which was always coming into their garden and lounging on their deck. Klara longed for a pet, though preferably a dog, and was always asking her parents, but in vain.

She lifted the blinds a little and peered out, hastily scanning the garden: there were the goalposts, the trampoline and the washing line that flapped around when the wind got up.

Then she jumped and her heart began to pound when she saw that there was a figure standing in their shadowy garden: a girl with long dark hair, wearing a bulky coat.

Klara shrank back from the window, not wanting the girl to see her. What on earth was she doing in their garden in the middle of the night? The girl glanced around quickly, apparently looking for something, but what? Could she be a burglar who was planning to break into their house? Klara hoped her parents had remembered to lock the door; they usually did, but sometimes her mum was cross in the morning and would tell off her dad for forgetting.

The girl turned away, so Klara could see only her back view. She thought she recognised her but knew that was impossible. The girl went over to one of the windows, laid her palms flat on the glass and peered inside. Klara wanted to shout at her to go away. She wondered if she should run to her parents' room and tell her mother, but didn't dare move.

Without warning, the girl whipped round and stared straight at Klara's window.

Klara froze, scarcely daring to breathe. Could the girl see her standing there?

The girl stood still for a moment, then came rapidly towards her, with long, purposeful strides, never taking her eyes off the window.

Klara reacted by dropping the blind and leaping back into bed where she pulled the duvet over her head and squeezed her eyes shut, as tight as she could.

Friday

There was silence in the meeting room after Hörður had filled them in on his conversation with the forensic technician. Their heads all turned to the whiteboard where he had written down the relevant times and the activity on Marinó's computer the night he died.

'Could he have been planning something?' Elma ventured after a while. 'Or was he just fantasising about it?'

'Fantasising about murdering someone?' Sævar queried.

'I don't know. Maybe. People look at all kinds of stuff online.'

'The fact he died shortly afterwards puts it in a rather different light.' Hörður stood up and went over to the board.

'Did they examine his browsing history over a longer period?' Sævar asked.

'Yes, but this is what stood out,' Hörður said. 'The rest was the kind of thing you'd expect.'

'It's amazing how often people get caught out that way,' Elma reflected. 'It doesn't seem to occur to them that if they're under suspicion, the police are bound to look into their search history.'

'Except that Marinó hadn't murdered anyone,' Sævar objected.

'But...' Elma paused. 'Are we quite sure about that?'

'What do you mean?' Sævar asked. 'We've only got one body, unless I'm missing something?'

Although she knew Sævar was right, Elma couldn't help wondering if Marinó had been involved in something bigger. Something that would explain his sudden fit of rage the evening before he died and why he hadn't been himself all week.

'And there's another thing,' Hörður said. 'Forensics have traced the owner of the phone to the Netherlands.'

'Hang on, what phone?' Sævar asked.

'The phone they found in Marinó's wardrobe.'

Elma had almost forgotten the new-looking smartphone, studded with purple and silver rhinestones, that forensics had discovered in Marinó's room.

'The Netherlands?' she repeated in surprise. 'Are any of Marinó's friends Dutch?'

'I've got the name of the owner here,' Hörður said. He picked up a piece of paper from the table and read out: 'Lise Ragnarsdóttir Visser.'

'Lísa?' Sævar repeated. 'That's an Icelandic name, isn't it?'

'Lísa's common in lots of countries,' Elma said. She held out a hand for the paper. 'Anyway, the name's spelt with an "e" at the end: Lise.'

'Yes, but the patronymic Ragnarsdóttir is obviously Icelandic.'

'Perhaps she had a Dutch mother?' Elma suggested. 'Or was married to a Dutchman and adopted his surname.'

'But no one's mentioned any Lise in connection with the investigation,' Sævar said. 'Is it possible the phone just ended up in the wrong hands? Maybe Marinó came across it lying around somewhere and took it home with him.'

'I haven't had time to look the woman up yet,' Hörður said, starting to collect his papers. 'Maybe you could do that, Elma?'

Who was this Lise and how on earth had her phone found its way into Marinó's wardrobe? The phone looked new and was in good working order. Elma was aware that models like that cost a bomb. She herself made do with a cheap older phone that cost a fraction of the price. But, as if the phone company wanted to punish her, she was constantly being bombarded with notifications that her device didn't support this or that upgrade.

Elma thought Lise's phone looked exactly like her sister's, and she knew Dagný always had the latest model because her husband Viðar worked for a telecom company. It seemed highly unlikely that this Lise Ragnarsdóttir would have deliberately discarded something so expensive. She might have mislaid it but, if so, surely she would have searched for it as soon as she noticed it was missing.

Of course, it was always possible that Marinó had stolen it, but today's advances in security had made phone theft much trickier. It required technological know-how, as phones were generally locked and equipped with tracking software, which meant that a casual thief was unlikely to be able to turn off all the protections so as to use the device.

No sooner had Elma sat down at her desk than her own phone rang.

'Elma Jónsdóttir?' a clear female voice said formally.

'Speaking.' Elma typed her password into the computer.

'You had an appointment with us at ten.'

'I know, I called earlier.' She had rung in a hurry that morning to cancel her appointment with the midwife when she realised she wouldn't have time to drive down the coast to Mosfellsbær. She had deliberately booked one there rather than in Akranes, where the news was bound to leak out.

'Yes, no problem,' the woman replied. 'But you asked if we could ring you to arrange a new appointment?'

'Oh, right,' Elma said, glancing up. Sævar was standing in the doorway. 'I, er...'

'Can you come in on Monday at ten?'

Sævar sat down in the chair facing her and waited.

'Mm,' Elma replied, unobtrusively turning down the volume.

'How far along are you? I can't see the information here but—'

'OK, thanks,' Elma said briskly and hung up.

'Who was that?' Sævar asked, looking at her.

Elma could feel her cheeks starting to burn.

'No one,' she said airily. 'Nothing important.' She was a terrible liar. Why hadn't she just said it was her mother? Or a friend – anyone?

Sævar eyed her suspiciously for a moment, then obviously decided to let it drop.

'Are you hungry? I was thinking of popping out to Galitó and fetching a takeaway, if you're interested.'

'Oh, yes.' Elma smiled. 'Please.'

She gave a sigh of relief once he had gone. She couldn't face telling him about her situation quite yet. She still thought of it as a situation, though really she knew that although it was temporary, the consequences would last a lifetime.

Elma drained her glass of water in one go, pushing away visions of a huge, distended belly, then typed 'Lise Visser' into the search engine. Judging by the countless results on all the main social-media platforms, Lise Visser was a common name. She tried adding Ragnarsdóttir and soon narrowed it down to the right person. On the screen before her appeared a young girl with olive skin and dark hair. Elma bent closer and began to read.

'Lise Ragnarsdóttir Visser was born and brought up in Amsterdam but she had an Icelandic father, Ragnar Snær Hafsteinsson, who died earlier this year.'

'What about her mother?' Sævar asked.

'She died a long time ago. I couldn't find out much about her, apart from the fact she was Dutch.'

'OK, and have you found any clue as to how Lise's phone ended up in Iceland?'

'Well, I learnt that she flew to Iceland in February.'

'February? But that's months ago.'

'I know,' Elma said. 'I couldn't find out what she was doing here, and her last posts on social media date from January, a week or so before her father died.' Elma had the impression that the father's death might have been sudden. Perhaps the shock had been so devastating that the girl had quit social media.

'So, her father dies in January and she comes to Iceland in February?' Sævar said. 'Could she have been visiting family?'

'Possibly. Though I can't find many living relatives. Her grandparents are dead and Ragnar was their only child. The only family members I can trace are second cousins.'

'Any of them live in Akranes?'

Elma shook her head. 'No, most are in Reykjavík.'

'But it's not impossible that she was planning to visit them?'

'No, exactly. I made a short list of her relatives and was going to ask if you could maybe ring them?'

'No problem. Perhaps Lise will turn out to be staying with one of them.'

'In the meantime, I was thinking of paying Fríða a quick visit,' Elma said. 'She should know if Marinó was acquainted with Lise.'

'What if he was?' Sævar asked. 'That doesn't necessarily mean anything.'

'No.' Elma nodded calmly, then added: 'Not if we find her alive and well.'

Sævar closed his office door, something he rarely did. He preferred to have his colleagues around him. Since being promoted to detective, he had been given his own office but he found himself missing his old desk in the open-plan area. When he was younger he could only revise for exams while listening to music on headphones and sitting in cafés or other places where he was surrounded by life.

He filled Birta's bowl with food before sitting down at his computer. Elma had given him the names of several people related to Lise's father, Ragnar. The first person he decided to call was a cousin of Ragnar's; the set of grandparents they shared had died before the millennium. Sævar was hoping this man might be able to enlighten him about Lise's movements.

Lise had been orphaned at only nineteen years old. Sævar knew what that felt like from personal experience. But rather than losing his parents to illness many years apart, he had been robbed of them both on the same night, in the same instant. From one moment to the next, he and his brother Maggi had been left alone in the world, he at twenty, Maggi at sixteen. Sævar hadn't been remotely ready to care for his brother on his own, especially as Maggi had special needs. Up to that point, Sævar's only responsibility in life had been to ensure that he woke up early enough to get to college on time.

The man who answered the phone had a cheery, sing-song voice. But when Sævar explained why he was calling, there was a lengthy silence. He had begun to think he'd lost the connection when he heard the sound of a throat clearing.

'The only time I remember meeting Ragnar's daughter was about ten years ago when he and his wife were over for a visit,' the man said. 'To be honest, Ragnar and I didn't have much contact, except when we were very young and used to stay with our grandparents.'

'I assume you're aware that Ragnar passed away earlier this year?'

'Yes, sure. I heard about it, but I didn't go over for the funeral, and as far as I'm aware none of the rest of the family did either. Ragnar's parents died years ago, and after that we gradually lost touch. He lived over in Amsterdam with his wife and daughter, and I don't think he visited Iceland much. I wondered if that would change when his wife died and he was left alone with his daughter, but they never came over.'

'So, as far as you're aware, none of your family were in contact with them?'

'No, and now I'm curious to know why you're asking?'

'We're trying to get hold of Lise in connection with a case we're investigating,' Sævar said. 'But she's not in trouble.'

'And you think she's in Iceland?'

'According to our information, she came over in February of this year.'

'Really?' The man sounded astonished. 'Well, I'll ask around and get back to you. She may have been in touch with another member of the family without my knowledge.'

'That would be great,' Sævar said and ended the call. He contemplated the other names on the list. Perhaps it would be better to wait for the man to ring back.

◆

Usually football practice was what kept him going, but today Andri couldn't wait for it to be over. He kept catching himself checking the time.

'Eyes on the ball, Andri,' Ingi barked from the sidelines. The coach never missed a trick. He was a stern man who rarely smiled, even when things were going well. The only sign of pleasure he ever betrayed was a slight nod of the head.

When the training session finally ended, Andri's teammate Grímur came over.

'Everything OK?' he asked in a low voice.

'Yes, sure. Everything's fine,' Andri replied breezily.

He and Grímur got on well, though they weren't close friends. In spite of being a few years older, Grímur had always had a soft spot for Andri. He was a decent enough player in his own right but would never rise any further. Not that he had any ambitions in that direction.

'Heading for the hot tub?'

'No, not now. Júlía's waiting,' Andri lied. He wasn't actually planning to meet Júlía until this evening, but he didn't want any company just now; he'd rather be alone.

Andri had always been rather a weird kid, with few friends, so he was used to solitude. During his early years at school he hadn't been exactly unpopular, but neither had he found any common ground with the other boys in his class. Football was his only interest, and it wasn't until he was in his early teens that his classmates finally seemed to notice him. Shortly after he was picked for the national youth team, the girls began to look at him with new eyes, and the boys suddenly wanted to invite him along to places. Being popular didn't even require any effort on his part. All he had to do was turn up, and somehow everyone just accepted that he was silent. The only boy he had formed any kind of connection with was Marinó, and that was mainly because Marinó had taken care of the talking and didn't seem to mind if Andri had little to contribute.

Marinó had a talent for seeing qualities in people that others couldn't. It was why he had also befriended Ísak, who could be a bit of an idiot. Andri and Ísak had known each other for years but only became friends when Marinó appeared on the scene.

Ísak used to be good at football when he was younger, better even than Andri when it came to technique. They used to compete for attention during training, but, when the chips were down, Ísak simply didn't have what it takes. Because, in football, talent was far from being the only quality that counted.

Andri walked home quickly, looking neither left nor right. To his astonishment, he could feel a lump in his throat. All his life he had been good at football and nothing else. He'd had one dream, and only one, ever since he was a little kid, and that was to become a professional. But now that his goal was within reach, it was like he'd suddenly had enough. He felt no excitement or anticipation, and hadn't for a long time now.

Football had long ago ceased to be a game; it had become a job. Before matches he got so sick with nerves he couldn't sleep. Everyone expected so much of him; sometimes it felt as if they all wanted a piece of him: his team, his town – even his country. Contrary to what his parents believed, he read all the news about himself and it filled him with depression rather than pride. Such a profound, crushing sense of depression that he felt as if he were being suffocated and couldn't breathe.

For the second time in two days Elma parked in front of the new block of flats. Though, now she stopped to think, it wasn't really that new. It had been built ten or even fifteen years ago, yet somehow she thought of everything that had been built since her childhood as new. Akranes had undergone profound changes since Elma was young. The population had doubled in size, from four thousand to eight thousand, and the urban area had spread out over the flat Skagi Peninsula, spilling over into the surrounding farmland and creeping ever closer to the foot of Mount Akrafjall. Among the orange blocks of flats where Fríða's boyfriend, Hrafnkell, lived, there was one building that stood out from the rest. It had once been a small, traditional farmhouse with horses grazing in the paddock, but now it looked lost and out of place, swallowed up by the modern developments.

Elma had taken a closer look at Hrafnkell following her conversation with Sævar, not because she thought he was mixed up in the case, so much as out of pure curiosity. He seemed to be a big fan of off-roaders and motorbikes, judging by all the pictures of them he posted on social media, alongside photos of himself on mountain hikes, sometimes accompanied by tour groups. Where Fríða fitted into his life, Elma couldn't guess, because she didn't turn up in a single photo, though she seemed to spend a good deal of time over at his place.

'Oh,' Fríða said, when she saw Elma standing at the door. She didn't seem particularly pleased to see her. 'Come in.'

'Thanks, it won't take a moment,' Elma said, slipping off her shoes and following Fríða inside.

Hrafnkell, who was sitting at the coffee table, holding a toasted sandwich, said hello. He had both elbows on the table and there was a mountain of cocktail sauce on his plate.

Elma took a seat at the dining table facing Fríða. She was feeling queasy, having narrowly avoided throwing up as she climbed the stairs to the flat, and just hoped her face wasn't green.

'Is there any news?' Fríða asked, chewing gum with her mouth shut.

'Not much as yet,' Elma said. 'But I wanted to ask if you knew this girl?' She took out her phone, found the photo of Lise, and laid it on the table.

Fríða bent over it. The sun shone in through the window behind her, illuminating her reddish-brown hair.

'That's Lise.' Fríða smothered a yawn with the back of her hand. 'She is – or was – an au pair.'

'Was?'

'Yes, she went home last weekend. Or … no, it would be the weekend before last, now.'

'Who was she au pairing for?'

'Andri's parents. His mum and dad are so "busy" that they don't have time for their kids.' Fríða put air quotes around the word busy.

'Were she and Marinó—?'

'Going out?' Fríða finished. 'No, they weren't in a relationship – no way. Andri introduced her to us. She's a year younger than us and seemed really nice. She spoke fluent Icelandic because her dad was from here or something. Anyway, Andri used to bring her along sometimes when we met up.'

'Do you know where she is now?'

'Gone home,' Fríða said. 'We saw her the weekend before … before the fire. She told us then that she was leaving.'

'And…' Elma hesitated. 'Are you sure she left?'

'Haven't a clue,' Fríða said. 'Why don't you ask Andri or his parents?' Giving a sudden, exasperated sigh, she added: 'What's this got to do with Marinó? I don't understand why you're wasting time on Lise instead of trying to find the person who killed my brother.'

Elma nodded and changed the subject. 'Was Marinó…?' She

paused again. 'Did he often mix himself drinks in the, er … the blender?'

'What? You mean like a smoothie or…?'

'Yes,' Elma said. 'Or a cocktail.'

'Er … no. I sometimes make cocktails for us girls, but Marinó only used to drink beer. Why are you asking about that? What does it matter if he made drinks in … in our blender?' Fríða's manner was in marked contrast to the last time they had spoken. Then she had been composed and perfectly willing to talk. In fact, she'd seemed oddly calm, considering that her brother had just died. This time her calm had broken and she seemed angry.

'I can't understand why you haven't found the person who did it yet,' she burst out, her voice rising. 'We haven't heard anything. Don't you need back-up, like from Reykjavík or something? From people who are more experienced at dealing with cases like this?'

'I'm sorry if you feel we haven't been keeping you well enough informed about the progress of the investigation,' Elma said steadily, 'but you can rest assured that we're working as fast as we can.'

'Oh, really?' Fríða said, pursing her lips.

'Yes, really,' Elma said. She wasn't offended by Fríða's anger; the girl had a right to feel frustrated. The police had no motive, no leads, no witnesses in her brother's case. That's why Elma was clinging to the hope that this girl Lise might be able to tell them something, though she had to admit it was a long shot.

Once Elma was sitting outside in the car again, she gripped the steering wheel with both hands and hunched over, resting her forehead on the black vinyl. Closing her eyes, she waited for the nausea, which had assailed her again halfway down the stairs, to pass. She concentrated on breathing slowly and steadily through her nose, and after a while she was able to sit up and start the car.

According to Fríða, Lise had been on her way home to the

Netherlands, which wasn't unnatural. Au pairs were only placed with families for limited periods. Perhaps Lise had come to Iceland at a difficult time, shortly after losing her father, and got homesick before her placement was over. The problem was that Elma had already been in touch with all the airlines that served Iceland, and none of them could find Lise's name on their passenger lists. Elma had even contacted the operator of the Norröna ferry, which sailed between Denmark and Seyðisfjörður in the east of Iceland, to check if the girl had left by sea, but they had no record of her.

Assuming Lise hadn't left the country undetected, as a stow-away, logically she must still be in Iceland. So either the girl had lied about leaving or something had occurred to prevent her from returning home.

※

Some days the wind seemed to take a brief holiday and everything would fall perfectly still, the faded leaves hanging unmoving on the branches.

Anna had suggested going to the beach at Langisandur and, after a bit of persuasion, Klara had agreed to come too. As Anna ran ahead, Unnar thought it was no surprise that the advertising agency had been in touch again. Last summer, Anna had been invited to act in an advertisement for a new kind of ice lolly. Unnar had rarely been prouder than when he saw the ad for the first time, with Anna racing around on screen among a group of wildly excited kids. Although there had been lots of other children taking part, Anna had naturally played a starring role, and the camera had lingered lovingly on her. As a result, her fame had lasted rather longer than the ice lolly being advertised, which hadn't been on sale again this summer. The attention the little girl got, not just at school but in the town, had given her a foretaste of celebrity. Now she dreamt of becoming an actor, and a champion gymnast on the side.

This time the agency needed a girl to star in a music video for a foreign band that was to be filmed in Iceland. The concept sounded cool. It would feature the traditional autumn sheep round-up against the backdrop of the Icelandic landscape. Anna was to play a young girl who became absorbed in chasing a tiny field mouse. The idea was that the girl would forget the time and get lost. Then an elf woman would emerge from the rocks, take her by the hand and lead her home. Unnar liked the concept and was sure Anna would be beside herself with excitement at the idea.

'Daddy,' called Klara, who was lagging a little way behind.

'Yes?' Unnar glanced back at his elder daughter. She was trailing along as if her limbs were heavy and sluggish.

'Can't I just go home?' Klara screwed up her eyes against the sun like a vampire seeing daylight for the first time.

'Aw, don't you want to spend a bit of time with your dad?'

Klara didn't answer.

Unnar was feeling pretty rough after last night; he'd got home late – much later than intended. He and Villi had stayed on long after everyone else had left, and his memory of the walk home was hazy. Though he did remember seeing a light on in the bedroom window when he got home and wondering why Laufey was still awake. When he got in, though, she was fast asleep and didn't stir even when he prodded her.

He had lain awake for a long time, thinking things over. He wasn't particularly proud of his past exploits and, just before dropping off, he had resolved to do his best to patch up his marriage. He loved his children and Laufey too. If only she could relax sometimes and be more like her old self; not so uptight all the time. Maybe he should invite her away on a weekend break, to Paris or New York: that might put some life back into their relationship.

Anna had taken off her trousers and was paddling at the water's edge, while Klara had halted and was scratching at the sand with a stick. Calling to the girls that he was going to get into his swimming trunks, Unnar headed over to the changing huts, not having had Anna's foresight to put on his costume under his clothes. On his way back out to the hot pools, he spotted his son walked unhurriedly along the coast path.

'Andri?' Unnar shouted. 'What are you doing here?'

'Just on my way home from training. What about you? Are you ... Is Mum here too?' Andri seemed equally surprised to encounter his father at the beach.

'No, just your sisters.'

Andri nodded, hesitated a moment, then carried on walking. Unnar watched him go.

'Andri,' he called after him. 'You wouldn't like to, er ... join us in the pool?'

Andri turned and looked at his father. 'No,' he said. 'I've got to go.'

'All right. No problem.'

Unnar watched his son walking away and was taken aback by the wave of sadness that suddenly descended on him. Andri was so grown up these days; it was too late to change his opinion of him: Unnar would never be the father Andri wanted him to be.

Unnar sighed and climbed up the steps to the hot pool. The sound of Anna's laughter, echoing around the beach, brought the smile back to his lips. At least he still had his little girls.

The street Andri lived on was not far from Elma's parents' house. She had often walked along the paths that crossed the neighbourhood, behind the houses, and knew which gardens had the biggest redcurrant bushes and which playgrounds were good sources of rhubarb and sorrel in summer.

Elma had often been to the house too, as it had once been home to a classmate of hers, and she had attended birthday parties there every year. In those days, the floors had been carpeted, the furnishings dark and the garden full of trees, bushes and other plants. The lush greenery had been banished now, leaving only the garden hedge, a few neat flowerbeds and shrubs, and a patch of lawn with goalposts, while most of the plot was taken up by an impressively large wooden deck.

When the door was opened to them by Andri's mother, Elma noticed that the carpet had gone too and the floor was now covered in blond parquet.

'Andri's at training but should be home' – the woman looked at her watch – 'in about a quarter of an hour.'

'Do you have a few minutes to spare?' Sævar asked.

'Yes, of course, come in,' the woman said, and introduced herself as Laufey.

As they followed her inside, Elma could see little to remind her of the house she used to visit as a child. The dark furnishings had been replaced by white fittings and the furniture looked as if it was made of walnut. There was evidence of Andri's younger sisters wherever you looked: a gym mat on the floor, two pairs of sandals by the garden door and brightly coloured school books spread out over the dining table. Laufey reached up into a cupboard and took down two cups decorated with black ravens.

'Please, don't go to any trouble for us,' Elma said quickly.

'It's no trouble; it's as simple as pressing a button,' Laufey said, gesturing to a large automatic coffee machine. 'Wouldn't you like a cup?'

'No, thanks.' Elma smiled. 'This will only take a moment.'

'Oh, OK.' Laufey put the cups down and took a seat.

She was in her forties, a little plump but fine-boned, with delicate features. She was an attractive-looking woman today but Elma guessed that twenty years ago men wouldn't have been able to take their eyes off her.

'Marinó Finnsson was a friend of your son, Andri,' Elma

began. It wasn't a question so much as a statement, but Laufey nodded anyway.

'Yes, that's right. Ever since year five, when Marinó and his sister Fríða moved here from Reykjavík. Marinó and Andri hit it off straight away.' Laufey talked fast and Elma noticed her ribcage moving up and down under her top.

'So they spent a lot of time together?'

'Yes, they did,' Laufey said and swallowed. 'The news hasn't properly sunk in yet. The whole thing seems so shocking and unreal. Are you any closer to finding out what happened? We've been following the news, but they haven't reported any developments.'

'Things should hopefully become clearer soon,' Elma said noncommittally, and decided to get straight to the point. Taking out her phone, she laid it on the table in front of Laufey. 'This is Lise Ragnarsdóttir Visser. I gather she au paired for you.'

Laufey looked down at the phone, then back at them, wearing a puzzled frown. 'Yes, that's Lise, but I don't understand...'

'We found something that belongs to her at Marinó's house and need to get hold of her.'

'Then you'll have to look a lot further,' Laufey said. 'Lise went home to Amsterdam nearly two weeks ago.'

'Had she reached the end of her placement?'

'No, actually.' Laufey sighed. 'Something came up unexpectedly, or so she said. I have to admit that it was terribly inconvenient. I teach yoga in the mornings and after that I often work in the salon until six, and on top of that I have council meetings every other Tuesday. I've had to cancel quite a few appointments thanks to her leaving at such short notice.'

'Did she say what it was that came up?'

'No,' Laufey replied. 'I don't know what happened. But she ... she'd seemed so down for the last few days.'

'Why was that?' Sævar asked.

'I'm not sure,' Laufey said, thinking. 'At first she was so open and cheerful, and always out here in the kitchen or sitting room, even when we were all home. But towards the end she became more withdrawn and spent a lot of time shut in her room.'

'And you have no idea what could have been wrong?'

'No, but I expect it was connected to her father,' Laufey said. 'He died at the beginning of this year.'

'We're aware of that,' Elma said. 'Do you remember when you first noticed the change in her? Did it happen slowly or overnight?'

'She changed quite suddenly,' Laufey said reflectively, as if only just realising the fact. 'I was away the weekend before she left and when I got back something had changed. I asked my husband Unnar if anything had happened, but he said no.'

'So your husband was here with her the weekend you were away?'

'Yes, though I doubt he would have been home much. I went to a summer house with friends, and Unnar had to work that weekend, so Lise was looking after the girls. We paid her extra.'

'Where was Andri?'

'That weekend, you mean?' Laufey asked. 'He was at home, but he's always got a lot on.'

'Lise and Andri got on well, didn't they?' Elma asked. 'I hear he took her along to parties and introduced her to his friends.'

'Yes, that's right.' Laufey thought for a moment. 'But I don't know if I'd go as far as to call them friends. Andri felt sorry for Lise because she was a bit lonely but didn't make any effort to get to know people. She didn't want to go to the strength-training classes I suggested or to meet the other kids who were au pairing here. I think her father's death must have hit her harder than she wanted to admit, and of course I completely understand that.'

Elma found herself wondering if Lise might have applied for the position of au pair in a desperate attempt to acquire a new family. Perhaps, in the end, she had realised that the world didn't work like that, and this was what had precipitated her decision to leave.

'What kind of phone did Lise have?' Sævar asked.

'It wasn't an iPhone,' Laufey replied. 'Some other model. She had little stickers on it – sparkly ones.'

'Did she always have her phone on her?'

'When she went out, yes.' Laufey wrinkled her brow. 'Why, have you found her phone somewhere?'

'It turned up at Marinó's house,' Sævar said. 'Do you have any idea why that might be?'

Laufey glanced out of the window as a car drove past with a loud roar.

'Well … I suppose she must have forgotten it there.'

'Two weeks ago?' Sævar said sceptically. 'Kids her age are usually so dependent on their phones that they can't go without them for two minutes.'

'Tell me about it.' Laufey smiled. 'But Lise wasn't like that. Unlike my son, she hardly ever carried her phone around, except when she went out. She could well have left it lying about somewhere and not noticed immediately.'

'Not until she'd left the country?' Sævar asked.

'It's possible,' Laufey said.

'When was Lise supposed to fly out?'

'She left us on Sunday, nearly two weeks ago.' Laufey paused to think. 'On the Saturday she went round to Marinó's with Andri. Yes, that's right, so she must have forgotten her phone there. She'd left by the time I got home from yoga at Sunday lunchtime. I don't actually know if she was due to fly out that day, but that's when she packed up and left our place.'

'And this was two weeks ago?' Elma asked. 'A week before Marinó died?'

'Yes,' Laufey said. 'I expect Lise had an early flight and didn't have time to say goodbye. It all happened rather fast. I offered to pay for her ticket and give her a lift to the airport, but she refused. If I'd known she was leaving so early, I'd have said goodbye to her that morning before I went out. She didn't even say goodbye to the girls, and they were rather hurt.'

'So you didn't see her at all on the Sunday?'

'No.'

'Then how do you know she came home on Saturday night?'

'Because her luggage had disappeared next morning and I remember seeing it in her room the day before.'

'The trouble is,' Sævar said, leaning forwards slightly, 'Lise never flew home. We've searched for her name with all the airlines offering flights out of the country in the last few weeks, and they have no record of her. She's not staying with her relatives here in Iceland either; we've been in touch with them and none of them have seen her.'

'Are you serious?' Laufey looked shocked. 'How can that be?'

'We were hoping you'd be able to tell us.'

'I wish I could help,' Laufey said. 'But I haven't a clue where she could have gone.'

'Where was Andri last Saturday night – I mean the weekend of the seventh to the eighth?' Elma asked.

'He came home between one and two, so I can confirm that he had nothing to do with the fire,' Laufey said, adding hurriedly: 'Not that you think that, of course. Anyway, we were having a dinner party and some of our guests were still here when Andri came home, so there are witnesses who can confirm that.'

'Doesn't he sleep in the garage?'

'Yes, he does.'

'So you wouldn't necessarily have noticed if he went out again, would you?'

Laufey opened her mouth to protest, then paused a moment before saying: 'No. No, I wouldn't have noticed.'

Elma was deep in thought as they returned to the car. She was extremely keen to find Lise but was beginning to suspect that the girl might have engineered her own disappearance. After the conversation with Laufey, it seemed obvious to Elma that far from getting over the loss of her father, Lise had run away to

Iceland and cut herself off from her friends at home. The recent change in her behaviour wasn't necessarily significant, since grief was a bumpy ride: people could be on a high one minute and deeply depressed the next.

But when Elma shared these thoughts with Sævar, he shook his head.

'No,' he said, starting the car. 'I reckon something else is going on. Think about it: Lise and Andri go round to Marinó's house, and no one has seen her since. The following weekend Marinó googles how to hide a body, and shortly afterwards he's dead and someone's started a fire in his bedroom. Does that sound like a coincidence to you?'

'But we can't be sure no one's seen Lise since then,' Elma objected. 'It's not like we've asked all the possible witnesses yet.'

'No, that's true,' Sævar conceded.

'But you still think something happened the evening she and Andri went round to Marinó's?'

'Yes, I do.' Without warning, Sævar took the turning to Akranes Folk Museum and the cemetery, and pulled into the car park. Then he looked at Elma. 'Say Marinó did something to Lise and the search question means he was looking for a suitable place to dispose of her body.'

'Do you really think that's possible?'

'Why not?' Sævar asked. 'If Marinó killed Lise, it wouldn't be implausible for him to kill himself as a result. Maybe even start a fire to hide the evidence.'

'Yes, I suppose.' Elma rubbed her eyes. 'This whole thing's getting so confusing and far-fetched. Do you genuinely believe it's possible?'

Sævar shrugged. 'I can't think of any other reason for him to have been googling that question. I mean, Marinó wasn't writing a novel or anything that would have given him an excuse to be researching the subject.'

'Can we sure about that?' Elma smiled wryly. 'Couldn't it have been an essay question? "How would you hide a body?" Life Skills 103.'

'Very funny.'

'No, but seriously,' Elma said. 'I think it's much more likely that Lise took her own life. She obviously hadn't got over her father's death.'

'And there's another thing,' Sævar went on, clearly not listening. 'Marinó typed in that search question the evening he died, which must mean he hadn't got rid of the body yet. If I'm right, logically there should be a body somewhere.'

'Sævar, you're not going to start searching for a body?'

'It can't have been at Marinó's house, because forensics have carried out a thorough examination.'

'What about in the car?' Elma suggested.

'Fríða and Marinó shared a car,' Sævar countered.

'Yes, but Marinó wouldn't let Fríða borrow it,' Elma reminded him. 'That's why they quarrelled.'

'Good point.' Sævar started the car again and set off in the direction of the Skógahverfi estate. Elma realised that he was taking them to Marinó's house.

'But if Marinó was hiding a body somewhere, we would surely know by now. The smell…' Elma protested, reliving the times she had visited the pathologist's lab. The sweet stench of decomposing flesh was something she would never forget.

Sævar swung into the modern estate with its roads lined with single-storey detached houses.

'If I remember right,' he said, 'Marinó's car was still parked in the drive. It occurred to me that we ought to take a look inside.' He parked by the kerb in front of the house.

'But Lise was at Marinó's more than a week ago.'

'Right, which isn't actually that long a time. Maybe Marinó managed to keep an eye on the car somehow while he was plotting where to dispose of the body.'

Sævar took out his phone.

'Who are you calling?' Elma asked.

'Hörður,' Sævar replied. 'I'm going to ask for permission to search the car.'

❧

When Unnar and the girls got home they all had wrinkled fingers and red cheeks from sitting in the hot pool too long. There was no sign of Laufey in the sitting room or kitchen.

'Laufey,' Unnar called, but there was no answer.

'Daddy, can we watch TV?' Klara asked, and he nodded distractedly. When he'd entered the house, he'd had an uneasy sensation that he couldn't explain, as if something wasn't where it should be, as if it had been displaced or disappeared.

Once the girls were installed in front of the television, he went into the room that had been used by Lise, the au pair who had come into the family's life back in February and lived with them for more than six months.

The room was painted light blue and contained a wardrobe, a desk and a single bed. Lise had left nothing behind. The wardrobe was empty, the desk bare apart from a wilting pot plant. The air was stale, but he was reluctant to open the window as he didn't want Laufey to know he had been in there.

Unnar went over and sat on the bed. Then he carefully turned back the duvet, as if he were uncovering a sleeping person – as if Lise were still in the bed. Laufey hadn't changed the sheets since Lise left and they still smelt of the exotic scent he had been so aware of every time the girl came near him.

Unnar inhaled deeply and closed his eyes.

'Unnar.'

He jumped and flicked his eyes open again. Laufey was standing in the doorway, watching him.

'What are you doing?' she asked slowly, keeping her voice low.

'I…' Unnar shot to his feet. 'I've got a headache. I just needed to be alone for a while.'

Laufey was silent.

'Where were you?' he asked, with as much composure as he could muster.

'In the utility room,' Laufey replied. 'Anna's going to a birthday party later, so I was looking for the outfit she wants to wear. How was Langisandur? I tried to ring you.'

'Oh, right, I left my phone in my coat pocket,' Unnar said. 'But Langisandur was fine. The pools were very busy.'

'Mm, I can believe it.' To Unnar's considerable surprise, Laufey smiled.

'The girls had a good time,' he said, following her into the kitchen.

'Thanks for taking them.' Laufey got out two cups and asked if he wanted a coffee, which he did. 'I need to visit these famous pools myself.'

'Haven't you been yet?'

'No.' Laufey laughed. 'I'm probably the only person in Akranes who hasn't tried them.'

'Maybe we should go together one evening?' Unnar suggested.

'Sure,' Laufey said, handing him a cup. 'Maybe.'

Unnar smiled and sipped his coffee.

The weather was uncharacteristically calm that Friday afternoon, allowing sound to carry with unusual clarity: cars driving past, doors slamming, children playing. The street was lively at this time of day. The family who lived opposite had just got home. The woman was half inside the back of the car and when she emerged, she was holding a little girl. The man opened the boot and took out a couple of shopping bags, one from a supermarket, the other containing alcohol from the Ríki. Beside him stood a boy of about five, who was clamouring to be allowed to carry something inside. The man handed him a packet of cereal, which looked huge in the child's arms. Soon the neighbourhood would be permeated by the savoury smell of grilling meat; wineglasses would be filled and cans of beer ripped open by the barbecue.

After securing permission to search Marinó's car, Elma and Sævar had stopped by the office to fetch the keys from Hörður. The big bunch they had been given contained a number of other keys as well. Although Hörður was sceptical about Sævar's theory, he'd agreed to contact Finnur and Gerða. Elma didn't know how Marinó's parents had reacted or what explanation Hörður had given, but the upshot was that she and Sævar now had the keys and had returned to Marinó's house.

They walked over to the car, a new-looking Nissan Leaf, which was still parked in the drive.

Elma held her breath as Sævar opened the boot, half expecting a foul stench to be released, but nothing happened. The boot was empty.

'I think we're making too big a deal out of Marinó's Google search,' Elma remarked, re-locking the car. 'I doubt he laid a finger on Lise.'

'Maybe,' Sævar said. He surveyed the garden. 'Can you think of any other places?'

'To hide a body?' Elma asked. 'No, I can't, actually.'

Sævar set off along the shady side of the house, and Elma followed.

The sun was still shining in the garden. At the back of the property there was a thick belt of trees and a hedge, which gave way to a fence, made partly of concrete, partly of dark cherry wood. In the right-hand corner there was a shed, made from the same kind of wood as the fence. It didn't have a window, just a door which was so unobtrusive it looked as if it had been cut out after the unit had been built.

'What about the shed?' Sævar asked.

'We can check,' Elma said. 'But if we don't find anything, I think we should call it a day.'

Sævar didn't answer: he was too busy trying the different keys on the ring. Finally, one of them slid into the lock but wouldn't turn. Sævar put his shoulder to the wooden planking as if he was planning to force it, then turned the key, shaking the door as he did so.

'Are you sure it's the right one?' Elma asked dubiously, but just then there was a click and the door flew open.

'It was only sticking,' Sævar said with a smile. 'You know, I don't quite see the point of this shed. They've got a double garage: why do they need to keep their gardening stuff in here?'

Elma was about to reply when she was hit by the smell. Peering into the dark space, which couldn't have been more than six to eight metres square, she made out a lawnmower on the floor, a green petrol can beside it, then some garden tools fixed to the wall.

Sævar's attention had been caught by something in the corner. At first glance it looked as if the cover from the barbecue had been chucked on the floor. Underneath it, there was a glimpse of matt plastic. Sævar bent down and reached out to take hold of the cover, then seemed to realise what he was doing and paused to extract a pair of rubber gloves from his pocket.

'Shine a light over here for me,' he said, while he was snapping on the gloves.

Elma took out her phone and turned on the torch, illuminating the motes of dust floating in the air. In the next-door garden they could hear someone bouncing on a trampoline, the creaking of the springs penetrating the thin walls of the shed.

Cautiously, Sævar pulled off the cover. Underneath it was a dark wool blanket with a traditional *lopapeysa* pattern. Neither of them said a word as he folded back the blanket, then pushed the plastic aside.

Elma pressed the sleeve of her jumper to her nose as the throat-catching stench intensified.

Lise Ragnarsdóttir Visser was lying on the floor, her eyes open. She was wearing gold earrings and a black vest with narrow straps. Her slim arms were crossed over her chest and her black nail varnish was chipped.

Elma backed out of the hut without saying a word and put her phone to her ear. Next door, a voice was calling the children to come in for supper.

PART TWO

February 2019

Lise was perfectly aware that she was running away, so there was no need for the repeated warnings. Yet she kept hearing Anita's voice admonishing her: 'Are you sure you're making the right decision?' 'No, miss,' she told Anita in her imagined conversation, because the truth was that she wasn't sure. Far from it. But she knew that Anita didn't have a clue either about whether the trip would be good for her or not. Lise had long ago learnt that no one else really knew what was best for her.

Over the last few days and weeks, she had been forced to listen to endless advice that was intended to be helpful but might as well have been so much hot air. Words couldn't make her father come back, couldn't undo the past or influence the future. So, yes, she was running away from her home and the city that filled her with such unbearable feelings of loss. She was running away to Iceland in the hope that this would prove better than staying at home.

Raindrops slid vertically down the window as the bus drove past endless bare fields that were hardly visible in the gloom. It turned out that February evenings were pitch-black in Iceland, and Lise felt silly to have expected any different. She had imagined herself being treated to magnificent views of mountains and lava; all the things her father had described for her so often but she herself hadn't seen since she was small. Back then, the whole family travelled to Iceland together, she, her mother and her father. They had stayed with her grandparents, played card games like Olsen Olsen late into the evening, gone swimming in geothermally heated pools, and visited waterfalls, hot springs and wide lava fields. She could still remember what it had been like to stand in the middle

*of the petrified lava flow, feeling as if she were on another planet.
In her memory, the trip had been perfect. It was incredible to think
that less than a year later her mother had been dead.*

The bus came to an abrupt halt, and Lise stretched in her seat.
She hadn't even noticed that they had arrived. Akranes – such an
odd name for a town. Although her Icelandic was fluent, the three
syllables still seemed hard and clumsy in her mouth, as if the letters
didn't belong together.

'This is the stop,' the driver called, twisting round in his seat.

When she first climbed aboard, Lise had held out a note to him
with the name of the street where she was supposed to get off, afraid
she wouldn't know when to ring the bell. Now, rising hastily to her
feet, she took her case from the luggage rack and struggled down
the steps with it and out onto the pavement.

The air smelt different from how it did at home. She could
almost taste the sea and glaciers on her tongue. She smacked her
lips and filled her lungs with its cold freshness.

When the bus pulled away, Lise spotted the couple waiting on
the other side of the road, Laufey in lace-up boots and a raincoat,
Unnar in a thick down jacket with a fur trim on the hood. Lise
waved, then looked both ways before hurrying across the road.

'Welcome,' Unnar said, holding out a hand that felt warm and
soft when she took it.

'It's so nice to meet you,' Laufey greeted her, smiling.

'We made the girls wait at home because we weren't sure how
much luggage you'd have.' Unnar opened the boot and picked up
her case. 'But you obviously travel pretty light.'

'Yes.' Lise tucked a lock of hair behind her ear, but the wind blew
it straight back over her eyes. 'I only brought the essentials.'

'Oh, well, do let us know if there's anything you need.'

He opened the rear door and Lise got in. There were two sports
bags on the seat, one pink, the other green, marked with the names
'Anna' and 'Klara'.

'Just push that mess out of the way,' Laufey said. She had put

back her hood, revealing quite short, fair hair. 'The girls always
forget to take their games kits inside with them. They're probably
going mouldy by now.'

'No problem,' Lise said.

'They insisted on staying up to see you,' Laufey added, once the
car was moving. 'They're so excited about meeting you.'

'I'm excited about meeting them too,' Lise said, and it was true.

She had found the couple through an online matching agency
for au pairs. Now, just over a week later, here she was in Iceland,
where she was supposed to live for the next year. Anita had been
right; the decision had been an impetuous one. But for the first
time since her father died, it had given Lise something new and
exciting to focus on and look forward to.

She heaved a sigh of relief, feeling as if she were exhaling all her
grief and loneliness, able to breathe freely for the first time in weeks.
As she did so, she caught Unnar's kindly, reassuring gaze in the
rear-view mirror.

Friday

The shrieking of girls' voices carried into the street. Laufey braced herself before knocking on the door.

'We've been having a great time here,' Nína said as she let her in. Laufey could just imagine how great it must be to have fifteen seven-year-old girls tearing around the house for two hours.

'Just be glad you don't have boys,' Laufey replied, remembering what children's parties used to be like when Andri invited his class round. Cake crumbs all over the floor, kids screaming and crying, balls hurtling through the air and puddles of wee in front of the toilet. God, it had been a relief when Andri turned twelve and decided he didn't want any more children's parties.

'Oh, I don't think boys are any worse.' Nína laughed. 'Anyway, come in, have some coffee. The girls are just finishing watching the film.'

Laufey had been hoping she could be straight in and out, but clearly that was wishful thinking. She was forever being required to stop for coffee; it went with the territory. Sometimes she felt as if all she did was put on a mask for the world: smile, be polite, show an interest. What would happen if she dropped the act? If one day she simply said and did exactly what she liked?

'Anna told me you don't have an au pair anymore. What happened? I thought everything was going so well?'

'Oh, she went home.'

'Really? I thought … She'd only been with you a short time, hadn't she?'

'Well, not that short. She'd been with us since February – that's more than seven months. But something came up unexpectedly

and she had to leave.' Laufey took the cup with a forced smile.
She wondered if she should tell Nína that the police had been
round to say they couldn't find any evidence that Lise had left
the country, but decided against it. She didn't want to have to
fend off a barrage of questions and, besides, she was in no mood
to discuss Lise right now.

'There's nothing to stop you getting another one, is there?'

'No, I suppose not.' Laufey turned the cup in her hands.
'Though ... to be honest, it's a bit of a nuisance having someone
else living in the house. More difficult than I'd expected. I'm not
sure I'd do it again.'

'Hm.' Nína smiled as if she knew something Laufey didn't. 'I
expect you and Unnar will be happy to have your evenings to
yourselves again?'

'Yes.' Laufey could feel herself blushing. 'Yes, that'll be nice.'

Nína laughed, putting down her cup and abruptly standing
up. 'I don't know how you do it. Could you teach me a few
tricks?'

'What do you mean? How I do what?'

'You and Unnar are still mad about each other; anyone can
see that.' Nína laughed again and put her cup in the sink. She
leant her back against the kitchen counter, watching Laufey.
'Seriously, though. Palli and I don't do it anymore. Ever. And I
don't even miss it, at least not with him. Though sometimes I
wouldn't mind—'

'Mummy.' The birthday girl came running into the kitchen,
interrupting the conversation.

Laufey took a sip of coffee. This was yet another reminder of
how great things could appear on the surface. To be fair, Unnar
wasn't entirely devoid of good qualities: he could be affectionate
and considerate, especially in public. Sometimes she allowed
herself to give in, forgetting all the bad stuff and welcoming him
with open arms. On other days she could barely look at him
without seeing all the betrayals and broken promises.

What good were fair words when Unnar spent so many nights away from home? What about all the mornings he wasn't there when Anna was weeping from tiredness, Klara refused to go to school and Andri was too sick with nerves to eat any breakfast?

Laufey got up, leaving half her coffee, and went in search of Anna. The little girl was sitting in the middle of the group, her hands full of snacks. She emitted a loud groan when she saw her mother but got to her feet anyway and said goodbye to the other girls in a voice so affected that Laufey barely recognised it as hers.

Once they were in the car, the smile vanished from Anna's face.

'Why didn't Daddy pick me up?'

'He's got a headache.'

'Ohh-h,' Anna whined, drawing the word out into two syllables. 'He promised to buy me a top with flip sequins – the ones where the picture changes when you run your hand over it. All the other girls have got tops like that. Even Ína, and her mummy and daddy haven't got any money, and…'

Anna chattered on as Laufey turned out of the cul-de-sac, the comfortably familiar drone of her voice filling the car and leaving no room for Laufey's own troubled thoughts.

'I can't see any obvious injuries that could have led to her death,' the pathologist, Hannes, announced, emerging from the shed. He put a hand to the small of his back and arched his spine as if it was aching, which wouldn't be surprising given the amount of time he had spent stooping over the body in the cramped space.

Forensics had already completed their examination of the shed. Not many technicians had been required this time, as the space was so restricted that only a couple of people could fit inside simultaneously. By shortly after ten that evening they had packed up and headed back to Reykjavík.

The consensus was that Lise had not died in situ but had been moved there post mortem. There were no signs of a struggle inside, nothing had been broken or knocked out of place. The crime-scene team had found no blood, no bodily fluids – nothing, though it was possible that biological traces would turn up on the blanket, the plastic sheeting or the barbecue cover that had been taken away for analysis.

'So there's no way of establishing the cause of death?' Hörður asked.

'No, I'm afraid not,' Hannes said. 'Not until I've got her on the table in my lab.'

'And there are no visible injuries?'

'I didn't say that, just that I couldn't see any that would have been fatal. There's a bruise on her upper arm, where someone may have gripped it. But the bruise had begun to turn purple, which means it must have been inflicted at least twenty-four hours before she died.'

'Can you give us an idea of the time of death?'

'That's hard to say with any certainty; I'll need to do a more thorough examination. But I'd say at least a week – two at the outside. It all depends on the weather conditions.'

'One to two weeks?' Hörður repeated. 'Are you sure?'

'Fairly sure, judging by the state of the body. It's been lying there at least a week, but I think we're probably looking at a slightly longer period.'

Hörður looked at Elma and Sævar. The crease between his eyebrows had deepened. If Lise had been dead for about two weeks, she had in all probability died the weekend before the fire, which meant there was every chance she had lost her life shortly after visiting Marinó's house with Andri.

Hannes adjusted his glasses. 'Two bodies in one week – unbelievable. What's going on with you lot in Akranes?'

'Us lot in Akranes?' Hörður exclaimed. 'You can hardly blame the whole town.'

The pathologist smiled faintly. 'Anyway, you'll have my report early next week.'

After the ambulance had removed the body, Elma and Hörður were the only ones left. Sævar had headed off at the same time as the pathologist, since he needed to drop by his flat to tend to Birta.

Silence had descended on the housing estate, apart from the occasional sound of voices carrying from open windows. The police had succeeded for the most part in keeping the operation discreet, thanks to the unusually tall, thick belt of trees around Finnur and Gerða's garden. The autumn gales hadn't arrived yet, and the leaves still hung on the branches. Elma had only been aware of one neighbour watching them through a gap in the foliage, and that was Ævar, the owner of the property backing onto Marinó's; the man who had discovered the fire. He had a good view of the garden and made no secret of the fact he was watching, standing there defiantly on the other side of the hedge, hands on his hips.

'Could it have been an accident?' Elma mused. 'Seeing as there are no visible injuries.'

'Well, I think we can be fairly confident that she didn't die of natural causes,' Hörður said slowly. 'If she had, or if it had been an accident, her body wouldn't have been lying in the shed, would it?'

The phone rang in Hörður's pocket. He pulled it out, checked the screen then stepped aside. When he came back he beckoned Elma to follow him.

'I'll give you a lift home.'

Elma got into the four-by-four after moving Hörður's fur hat from the passenger seat and placing it beside a pair of leather gloves on the centre console. She couldn't help smiling as she did so. The sight of Hörður wearing this hat in winter always struck her as a bit incongruous. He looked like an extra from *Game of Thrones*; all he lacked was the fur coat. Not that he resembled the characters from the TV series in any other respect; he was far too gentle and amiable.

'This is an ugly business,' Hörður said once he had started the car. 'What can have made those kids do it?'

'Are you sure they were involved?'

'I'm not sure of anything,' he replied. 'But the fact remains that Lise was last seen in their company, and now her body's turned up in Marinó's garden – or rather his parents' garden.'

'I don't get that feeling about them,' Elma remarked.

'How do you mean?'

'These kids aren't mixed up in drugs or anything dodgy,' Elma said. 'They all seem pretty straight to me.' No sooner had she said this than her thoughts flew to Ísak. He seemed different from the others – what was it Fríða had said? That he used to be a bit wild, stealing bicycles and that sort of thing, and that the younger kids had been scared of him.

'They aren't kids anymore,' Hörður reminded her.

'Not in the legal sense, anyway,' Elma agreed. They had all reached the age of twenty, which counted as adult, but, when she thought back on her own life, she reflected that she'd scarcely been more than a child at that age.

Hörður drove sedately, both hands on the wheel, the radio burbling away. A presenter asked a psychologist whether face-to-face contact was becoming less common among young people nowadays, and the psychologist answered that it was being supplanted by other methods of communication. The second presenter laughed and asked if it wasn't far-fetched to suggest that all communication would take place online in future, since humans would surely always need real-life social contact. Elma was just waiting to hear the expert's reply when Hörður turned down the volume.

'So, how long have you and Sævar been an item?'

'What?'

'I remember when Gígja and I first got together,' Hörður continued, turning into Elma's street. 'It sometimes feels as if it was yesterday, but then I look in the mirror and realise I've become an old man since then. We were only teenagers when we first caught each other's eye. She was a year older than me, which was considered out of the ordinary in those days. Usually it was the other way round.' Hörður stopped the car, but Elma didn't immediately get out. 'The first time we had a proper date, I invited her to go for a walk. Just imagine: I had to pluck up the nerve to go and ask her. No emails or ... or text messages, just me and her, looking each other in the eye, talking face to face. I'm often grateful I wasn't born later, though I have to say I find sixty-three quite old enough to be getting on with.'

'Did you get together straight away?' Elma wanted Hörður to keep talking. She had seldom discussed anything personal with him before and could tell that he was enjoying reminiscing.

'Well, to be honest, Gígja wanted nothing more to do with me after that first walk. I barely said a word, just stammered and sweated like an idiot. But then we bumped into each other later, when we were both on our way home from the shop. Our paths crossed, quite literally, and that time I found my tongue. I finally managed to win her over.' Hörður smiled. 'After that there was no going back. We've been together ever since.'

Until now, Elma thought, but didn't say it.

All at once she was filled with rage at the unfairness of life, but when she glanced at Hörður, she couldn't see any anger in his eyes. His expression was tinged with sadness, but more than anything he looked contented, as if the memory made him happy. Elma suspected that from now on all Hörður's memories of Gígja would be a blend of joy and sorrow.

'What I'm trying to say to you,' Hörður resumed, 'is that if I've learnt anything in the past few weeks it's that time is all we have. Make sure you and Sævar don't waste it.'

'But ... how did you know?'

'Everyone knows, Elma.'

'Seriously?'

Hörður inclined his head slightly and smiled. 'Good night. See you in the morning.'

February 2019

The girls woke Lise early the next morning. She heard them giggling and coughing outside her room, and it was obvious what they wanted. In the end she relented and called out to them to come in. At first they stood in the doorway, gazing around curiously, at the open suitcase on the floor, the backpack on the desk and the clothes she had laid on the office chair.

Klara, the older girl, was wearing a light-green top with an elephant on the front. Anna, who was three years younger, was in a flowery white nightie and had purple toes. Klara's nails were free of all varnish. Her glasses had dark-red frames, and her curly mop was unruly, with small stray hairs sticking up all over her head. Anna's hair, in contrast, fell in fetching waves, framing a delicate face.

The sisters were so different in appearance that Lise found herself wondering how well they got on. Although she had always dreamt of having a brother or sister of her own, she knew that siblings weren't always that close.

'Girls, you're not bothering Lise, are you?' Laufey called, then appeared in the doorway herself, shooting a stern look at her daughters. 'Sorry, Lise, I told these monkeys not to disturb you.'

'That's all right, I've had a good night's sleep,' Lise lied.

'Oh, well, in that case I'm making some bacon and eggs. Would you like to have breakfast with us?'

'That sounds nice.'

'Good. Just join us when you're ready.' Laufey laid her hands on her daughters' shoulders. 'You two come with me. At least give Lise a chance to wake up and get dressed in peace.'

The girls left, reluctantly tearing their inquisitive gazes away from her.

Once they had gone, Lise lay back on her pillow for a moment. It was an odd feeling. For nineteen years she had lived in the same flat, which she knew like the back of her hand. If she were at home now, she would wander out in her pyjamas and drink a cup of coffee in the comfy armchair overlooking the Amstel, watching the citizens of Amsterdam waking up and the first rays of sunlight gleaming on the water. Her father would sit at the table with her, reading the newspaper while she was eating breakfast, and commenting on what he had read: 'Honestly, Lise, I can't believe Rutte would decide to do that after what happened last week. What do you think?'

Lise's father used to encourage her to engage with current affairs, expecting her to be well informed enough to take part in conversations with adults, so she'd always made sure she had an answer ready. If she came out with something ignorant, her father would shake his head and tap her on the crown with his paper. 'Read, Lise,' he'd say. 'That way you'll get a head-start on the other kids your age. It'll help you go far in life.' When she gave an intelligent reply, on the other hand, his face would light up with pride and satisfaction. These discussions had come to form an increasingly important part of their relationship, because Lise's interest had been roused. They might not always have agreed on everything, but in their heart of hearts they were in sympathy. But now her father wasn't there anymore and everything seemed so alien: the smell of the duvet, the voices in the house, the sounds outside the window.

Lise closed her eyes and took a deep breath. Then she got up, pulled on yesterday's clothes, ran her fingers through her hair to tidy it and opened the door.

Mother and daughters were in the kitchen, seated at a round table that was laid with a plate of pancakes and a tray bearing bacon and fried eggs, as well as strawberry jam, maple syrup and melon slices.

'Do sit down,' Laufey said with a smile. She was holding a mug but there was no plate in front of her.

Lise took a seat beside Klara. Across the table, Anna was greedily shovelling bacon onto her plate. Lise didn't need to look under the table to be sure that she was simultaneously swinging her legs.

Klara picked at a fried egg with her fork. 'Mummy,' she said, 'can I have another slice of bacon?'

'You've already had one,' Laufey said. Although she smiled at her daughter, her voice was firm.

'But Anna's got three.'

'Klara.'

Klara sighed and reached for a slice of melon instead.

'Morning.' Unnar walked into the kitchen, a shopping bag in either hand. He dumped them on the table and started unpacking the contents. The paper bags he took out were full of pastries that had stuck to the sides.

'But I've just cooked,' Laufey protested. 'I made pancakes.'

'Well, I'm absolutely starving,' Unnar said, winking at the girls.

He pushed aside the dishes of bacon and pancakes that Laufey had made. He had such an infectious smile. His face may have been that of a middle-aged man, with stubble and deep wrinkles around the eyes – he was forty-five, Lise knew – but there was something boyish about that grin.

'How did my two rascals sleep?' he asked, reaching for the jam.

'Badly,' Anna announced. 'My bed's far too small. Whenever I move I bump into the wall or—'

'Anna,' Laufey said. 'You're only seven and not that tall. You do not need a larger bed yet.'

'But Ína's bed is this wide and she's much shorter than me.'

'Anna.'

Anna sighed theatrically and directed a beseeching gaze at her father in the hope that he would take her side. But Unnar just grimaced and in the end Anna had to smile.

'How big is the town?' Lise asked. 'How many people live here?'

'In Akranes, you mean? I suppose there must be about ... what? Eight thousand.' Laufey looked at Unnar.

'Yes, that's right. Something like that.' Unnar's mouth was full. He took a sip of orange juice. 'Why don't we go for a drive when we've finished breakfast? I can show you around.'

'Good idea,' Laufey said. She looked at Lise. 'You'll need to know the way to the school and the sports club the girls go to. Anna does gymnastics and Klara plays football.'

'You promised I could give up this summer.'

'Oh, Klara.' Laufey caught Lise's eye and explained: 'Klara doesn't particularly enjoy sport.'

'I hate football.'

'Now, now, don't start on that nonsense again.' Unnar ruffled Klara's hair. 'You can't hate football when your brother's one of the best players in the country.'

'I do,' Klara said, licking her finger, then using it to pick up the crumbs on her plate.

'Andri trains at the sports club too, of course,' Laufey said, ignoring Klara.

'Andri?'

'Yes, you know.' Laufey wrinkled her brow. 'Our son – Anna and Klara's big brother. Andri's your age.'

'Oh,' was all Lise could say. They hadn't mentioned anything about an older brother when they interviewed her over the phone. He wasn't in any of the pictures they had posted on the au pair website either, but Lise supposed that wasn't surprising. After all, they could hardly expect her to babysit him.

'Right,' Laufey said, standing up. 'I'm supposed to be at my yoga class in a few minutes. Do you want to wait until I get back?'

'Oh, no, we'll manage,' Unnar said. 'It shouldn't be a problem, should it, Lise?'

'No.' Lise smiled. 'No problem at all.'

The town wasn't what Lise had been expecting, perhaps because all the photos she had seen online had been taken either in summer when the grass was green or in winter when everything was buried under a blanket of snow. That February day there was neither sun or snow and the tarmac was still damp from yesterday's rain. Dark clouds hung unmoving in the sky, casting a twilit gloom over the scene, though it was only midday. The cars they met were filthy, the grass on the verges was brown and shrivelled, and the trees in the gardens were bare of leaves. As a result, the whole place seemed rather bleak.

The houses were mostly single-storey and the ones they were passing appeared rather rundown. The majority were plain, white boxes with A-line roofs, lacking any decoration or aesthetic appeal. The flat Lise had shared with her father in Amsterdam had been in a tall, thin house with a stepped gable and sash windows. There was nothing to compare to that here. Yet the more she looked, the more she realised that the simplicity of the buildings had a charm of its own. She stared out of the car window, her mouth a little open, taking in the wintry gardens around the houses, the people they passed. She tried to imagine what their lives were like, what they did for kicks around here. There were a few pedestrians, the odd car out and about, but apart from that the place seemed so empty it might have been asleep. She couldn't think of a greater contrast to the teeming streets of Amsterdam.

'So, what do you think?' Unnar asked.

Lise was beside him in the passenger seat. Anna, who had demanded to come with them, was sitting behind Lise, humming a tune as she played a game on her iPad. Klara had opted to stay at home. She had shut herself in her room straight after breakfast and hadn't emerged since. Anna, in contrast, had followed Lise into her bedroom and watched while she brushed her hair and put on moisturiser. The little girl had fiddled with Lise's belongings, even the things that were still in the suitcase.

'Yeah, all right,' Lise replied to Unnar now.

'The town looks better in summer.' Unnar laughed. 'Hopefully you'll still be with us then.'

'Oh, but I...' Lise was a little disconcerted. She had been under the impression that her placement was for twelve months. 'I was planning to stay for a year,' she ventured.

'I know that's what we discussed,' Unnar said, 'but it doesn't always work out that way. As we've learnt from experience.'

Lise looked at him in surprise. 'Have you had au pairs before?'

'Yes, one. Didn't we mention that?'

Lise shook her head. She had assumed the experience was equally new for them. There had been nothing in their profile about them having an au pair before.

'When was that?'

'Oh, about ... a year ago. Her name was Lena. She was Polish.'

'What happened?' Lise asked. 'Did she leave early?'

'Yes. I can't remember exactly why. I expect she was homesick.' Unnar took a left-hand turn, down towards the sea. 'Look, you get a better view from here. In fact, this place is the pride of Akranes.'

'How long did she stay?' Lise persisted, ignoring Unnar's attempt to change the subject.

'Who? Lena?' Unnar coughed. 'Only about a month. Maybe two.' He stopped in a parking space facing the sea. 'This is the best view in town. You can see the whole place: the beach itself is called Langisandur, then there's Mount Akrafjall, Faxaflói Bay, and over there in the distance is Reykjavík. And if you look to your right, you'll spot the town's two lighthouses. We'll head over there next.'

Lise was itching to ask more about Lena but didn't like to as Unnar seemed reluctant to discuss her. Obediently, she followed his pointing finger, taking in the long, sandy beach below them, the grey sea, the mountain with its twin white summits and the dip in between, and the two lighthouses in the distance, apparently rising out of the sea beyond the town. For a while Lise's worries were forgotten as she drank in the panorama.

'Beautiful, isn't it?' Unnar smiled at her, almost proudly, as if he had created the scenery himself.

Lise nodded, feeling suddenly terribly self-conscious as she met his gaze. Her dark hair was dragged back in a childish pony-tail and her hoodie had a stupid picture on the front.

'Yes,' she replied. 'Yes, it's very beautiful.'

Saturday

Andri was sick to death of people breathing down his neck all the time. Of the constant pressure for him to be on top form and put in a perfect performance whatever the circumstances. Maybe that was why he'd done it. Or maybe it was just that he couldn't stand the little prick, who had joined the team a year ago and was so full of himself. He was forever showing off, copying what the others said and doing his best to be one of the lads. Well, now he was lying on the ground, clutching his nose, the blood oozing out between his fingers.

'What the fuck do you think you're doing?'

Ingi, the coach, sprinted over before the other boys in the team could reach them.

'Shit.' Someone seized Andri by the shoulder and shoved him roughly aside. Andri wiped his face with his sleeve and finally looked around him. Most of the other players had stopped in their tracks and were standing about the pitch, unsure what to do. Ingi was bending down, trying to make contact with the young man on the ground.

Fúsi, the guy who had grabbed Andri, was one of the oldest players on the team and had a lot of time for the new kid. Fúsi had taken him under his wing when he joined the team that spring, clearly revelling in having a young lad following him around and laughing at all his jokes.

'What were you thinking, man? Why the fuck did you do that?' Fúsi was right in Andri's face. He gave him another shove. 'Answer me. I'm talking to you.'

Andri didn't budge, just stared back at Fúsi as if he had nothing to do with him.

'Why are you smirking like that? Think it's funny, do you?' Fúsi wouldn't drop it. He seized Andri by the scruff of the neck, and Andri couldn't hold back a grin: there was something so ridiculous about Fúsi's outraged expression, his popping eyes and gaping mouth.

Andri's grin only provoked Fúsi into giving him another hard push, but Andri didn't fall, just stumbled a few steps backwards and spat off to the side. Fúsi was trembling with rage now. The other players watched, frozen into immobility, not daring to interfere.

Fúsi was a defender, much bigger and stronger than him, yet Andri wasn't in the least intimidated. He knew Ingi could be relied on to stop Fúsi before he went too far. The coach was looking from one of them to the other, but his gaze lingered longest on Andri. His face wore an expression that Andri hadn't seen before. Ingi was a serious guy who didn't hesitate to give the boys a piece of his mind when he felt it was called for, but there was no anger in his eyes now, just an emotion that Andri found difficult to read. It looked almost like pity.

'What are you playing at, Andri?' Ingi asked in an undertone, taking him aside now. 'What's the matter with you?'

'I don't know,' Andri mumbled, avoiding his eye.

'Look.' The coach laid a firm hand on Andri's shoulder and forced him to meet his gaze. 'I know the lad who died in the fire was a mate of yours. If you need a bit more time to get over it, just let me know.'

Andri was silent.

'You reckon you'll be OK?'

'Yeah, yeah. I'm fine.'

'Are you sure?'

Andri nodded, but Ingi gave him a long, searching look before finally letting him go.

Sunday

Two young lives lost in two weeks. Two people who'd had their whole lives ahead of them. Elma was having a hard time getting to grips with the fact. She couldn't imagine what could have led to such a catastrophe.

The lack of background on Lise made matters more complicated. Both her parents were dead, and it transpired that none of her relatives in Iceland had been in contact with her. In Amsterdam she was registered at the address where she had lived with her father. The police had no details about next of kin or any friends they could talk to in order to learn more about her.

Naturally, Elma's first thought had been to approach Unnar and Laufey. Laufey had appeared concerned when they told her that Lise hadn't boarded any plane. Elma's immediate suspicion was that Andri might have had something to do with the deaths. He was the only clear link between Lise and Marinó, though of course they could have been meeting up without his knowledge.

When Elma came back in, Sævar was sitting up in bed, talking on the phone. Birta was lying beside him, sound asleep. She was getting old and tired, and seemed to do little else but sleep these days. Sævar smiled at Elma, said yes into the phone, then rang off.

Elma had got dressed in the other room, putting on a pair of tracksuit bottoms that had never been used for sport and an old knitted jumper.

'Are you going to have a shower too?'

'Yeah, sure.' Sævar settled back in bed, patting the duvet beside him. 'In a minute.'

'We need to go soon,' Elma reminded him, but sat down anyway.

'I know.' Sævar pulled her towards him but didn't kiss her, just wrapped his arms round her.

She laid her head against his chest, feeling his ribcage rise and fall, enjoying the warmth that radiated from him. She thought about all the blood his heart was pumping around his body, about the biological processes involved, all those complicated systems that made it possible for him to breathe and be alive.

Sævar pressed his lips to the top of her head and it occurred to Elma that this would be the perfect moment to break the news to him. It was peaceful in the bedroom, the pale morning light filtering through the slats in the venetian blinds. *Say something,* a small voice said inside her, and her heart beat faster at the thought.

'Right, I'm going to jump in the shower.' Sævar let her go.

'Sævar.'

'What?' He was sitting up.

'I…' She cast about in vain for the right words.

'You…?' Sævar raised his eyebrows, that small smile playing over his lips – the one that never seemed entirely absent.

'I, er…'

'Don't you want me to go?'

'Yes, sure. Of course you should go and shower.'

'Because I can stay longer if you like.' Sævar lay down again, putting an arm around her.

'Sævar.' Elma gave him a push. 'We'll be late.'

'I don't really care,' he said and loomed over her.

'You don't mean that.'

'Don't I?' He rested his chin on her chest. Close to, his face seemed so big, with its thick eyebrows and stubble, and dark hair.

'We've got to go,' she murmured but could feel herself sinking ever deeper into the mattress.

It was unbearably hot in the meeting room and Elma had to try hard to distract herself. The photo in front of her showed Lise Ragnarsdóttir in a red jumper with her hair in a pony-tail. She looked very young, less than her nineteen years, with that straight fringe and wide smile. Her hair was brown, so dark it was almost black, and her skin was olive. Elma had scrolled through Lise's Facebook page and seen that she took after her mother in appearance. Her father, in contrast, had been a typical Icelander, with pale-pink skin and light-brown hair.

'Her father, Ragnar, died in January of this year,' Elma said, recalling the information she had gathered about Lise. The case appeared in a totally different light now that they had found the girl's body. 'Lise came to Iceland not long afterwards. According to Laufey, her placement with them was arranged at short notice.'

'How short?' Hörður asked.

'A week or so.' Elma got up to open the window. 'I thought maybe she'd wanted to visit her Icelandic relatives, but apparently she made no effort to contact them – did she, Sævar?'

'No, the ones I talked to hadn't heard from her,' Sævar confirmed. 'So her visit must have had some other purpose.'

'Did she speak Icelandic?' Hörður asked.

'Fluently. I gather father and daughter used to speak it at home,' Elma replied.

'And her mother died ten years ago?' Hörður rubbed his chin, contemplating the photo of Lise.

'Yes, after a short illness,' Sævar said. 'None of the relatives here seem to know exactly what of. One said cancer, another pneumonia.'

'And the father, what happened to him?'

'Heart attack,' Elma said, thinking what a sad fate the little family had suffered.

'We'll have to inform the authorities in the Netherlands,' Hörður said. 'Someone must have started to worry about her. In fact, it's strange no one's reported her missing to the Dutch police yet.'

'Have you confirmed that?'

'Yes – no one's been in touch,' Hörður said. 'But I assume she had less contact with her family and friends at home after she came to Iceland.'

'I suppose so,' Elma said. 'I doubt she would have been in daily contact with them. But surely her friends will soon start wondering what's happened to her? And what about the data from her phone? Did anything of interest turn up there?'

'She didn't use it much,' Hörður said. 'I imagine she mainly communicated with people through social media.'

'Right,' Elma said, recalling what Laufey had said about Lise rarely carrying her phone around. Elma had looked up Lise's relatives in the Netherlands and found a few names but didn't know how close Lise was to them. Certainly, none of them seemed to have noticed that she wasn't answering her phone.

Lise had been only nineteen when she was left to fend for herself after her father's death. Adult in the eyes of the law, but in reality still so young that she would presumably have been preoccupied with what she was going to study or with her future career options. Elma didn't know if the girl had been at college or working before she came to Iceland, let alone how she'd envisaged her future. It seemed she'd inherited something from her father, though, as the flat in Amsterdam was now registered in her name.

'Why didn't Unnar and Laufey report her missing?' Hörður asked.

'Lise was going home.' Elma repeated what Laufey had told them: that Lise had announced out of the blue on Saturday, 7 September that she was leaving. Laufey didn't know the specific reason for her decision, and Lise had already packed her belongings and gone by the time Laufey got back from yoga on the Sunday morning.

'I see.' Hörður took off his glasses and rubbed his eyes. 'Tell me, how do these … these au-pair arrangements work? Do the young people come and go as they like, or do both parties agree on a fixed length of stay?'

'Usually they agree a fixed duration,' Elma said. 'Lise still had nearly six months left of the year she had agreed to spend with them, so it was news to Laufey that she wanted to go home all of a sudden.'

Hörður put his glasses back on, picked up the photo from the table and stared at it, as if hoping to find the answers hidden behind Lise's dark eyes.

'Where's her luggage, then?'

'What?'

'You said she'd packed her belongings and gone. We've found Lise, but where are her things? Did she come back and fetch them or could someone else have removed them?'

'You've got me there.'

To Elma's embarrassment, the question hadn't even occurred to her. She had been working on the assumption that Lise had gone to Marinó's party on the evening of Saturday, 7 September and never left. According to Laufey, Lise's luggage had been in her room on the Saturday evening but by the Sunday morning it had vanished. So it stood to reason that either Lise had come back for it or someone else must have taken it.

'The person who took her things obviously had access to Laufey and Unnar's house,' Hörður remarked, giving voice to Elma's thoughts.

She nodded. Only one name came to mind. 'Andri,' she said. 'Andri Unnarsson, their son.'

'Ah, yes, the footballer,' Hörður said, as if to himself.

'Yes, he's moving abroad. Transferring to some Swedish club...'

'Örebro,' Sævar supplied.

'That's the one.' Elma could never remember the name.

'We questioned him a couple of days ago in connection with the fire,' Sævar said. 'He was Marinó's best friend and had invited Lise along with him a few times to meet his mates. They went round to Marinó's together the weekend before he died.'

'Did the subject of Lise not come up at all when you spoke to him?' Hörður asked.

'No, he didn't mention her,' Elma replied. 'But then we weren't asking about her or what he did the weekend of the seventh to the eighth. We just asked him questions relating to the fire, which was the weekend after that.'

'So, we're saying that Andri turned up at Marinó's house with Lise the weekend before the fire and also happened to be with Marinó the day before he died?' Hörður put down the pen he'd been holding. 'In that case, I think we should definitely have another word with him.'

February 2019

'You'll need to make the girls' packed lunches and take them to school.'

Laufey moved around the room while she was talking, showing Lise the girls' school bags and lunch boxes.

'Klara likes pâté,' she continued, 'but Anna can't stand it. She's a terribly fussy eater and would rather just have bread with chocolate spread, but she's only allowed that on Fridays. I want the girls to eat healthily, especially Klara. There's no question of them having biscuits after school. We tend not to keep them in the house, anyway.'

Lise stifled a yawn as she followed Laufey around.

'Did Unnar show you the school?'

'Yes, we drove past.'

'Good, so you'll know how to find it.'

'I'm not sure—'

'The girls know the way,' Laufey interrupted. Then, as if realising this sounded a bit brusque, she gave a quick on-off smile. 'Are you hungry?'

'Maybe a little.'

'I'm going to get some sushi for supper. Do you eat sushi?'

'Yes, I love it,' Lise said. She used to go with her father to a place in Amsterdam where the dishes came past on a conveyor belt. He had forbidden her to waste any time worrying about how much they cost. 'It ruins the whole pleasure of eating out and, besides, what are we here for? To worry about money? In that case, we can just eat pot noodles at home,' he had said, covering the prices with his hand.

'Good. Then I'll pop out now if that's OK with you.' Laufey put a black purse on the table and started rooting around in it.

'Shall we play a game?' Anna asked, the moment her mother had closed the front door behind her. Without waiting for an answer, the little girl ran into her room and came back with a box that she laid on the kitchen table.

'What sort of game is it?' Lise asked.

'Spooky Stairs. I got it for my birthday.' Anna opened the box, took out the board and put it in the middle of the table. Every movement she made exuded confidence; she showed no hint of diffidence or shyness. When she spoke, she expressed herself with her whole face, stretching her eyes and mouth wide open.

'Shouldn't we ask Klara to play too?' Lise suggested.

'OK. But she's probably busy.' Anna rolled her eyes at Lise, adding in a world-weary tone: 'Klara's always busy.'

'What's she doing?' Lise looked over at Klara's bedroom door. She hadn't seen her since that morning.

'I don't know. Drawing or something.'

'Drawing?'

'Yes, she draws, like, amazingly well,' Anna said. 'But she's terrible at sport. I'm very good at sport, actually, especially gymnastics. Mummy says we've got different talents.' Her voice was free of all conceit, as if she were simply stating a fact.

'I look forward to seeing you practise,' Lise said.

Anna's face lit up. 'Klara,' she bellowed, making Lise jump. She shouted her sister's name again, even louder, and Klara emerged from her room.

'What?'

'We're going to play a game. Lise says you've got to play too.'

'I didn't say you've got to,' Lise corrected, 'just that it would be fun if you did.'

Klara hesitated, then came over. She drew up a chair beside Anna and sat down.

The game was straightforward. The object was to remember the *colour of the pawn hidden under each ghost piece. When Lise finally took the ghost off her pawn and realised that it was Anna's piece, she threw up her hands in defeat and Klara laughed.*

'Girls,' Lise said after a while. 'Your dad said you had another au pair before me?'

'Oh, yes,' Anna said. 'Lena.' She moved her piece back to the beginning, having clearly taken the decision for them that they were going to play another game.

'Did she stay long?'

'No,' Klara said, forestalling her sister.

Lise threw the dice and moved her piece. 'Why not?'

'Because she said that—'

'Anna,' Klara hissed, shooting her sister a look.

'What? I wasn't going to say anything, you know...' Anna broke off mid-sentence when Klara nudged her.

'What?' Lise looked at them both in turn. The sisters' embarrassment had roused her curiosity. 'What did she say?'

Anna looked uncertainly at Klara, who scratched at a brown stain on the table with her fingernail.

'She didn't tell the truth,' Klara muttered down at the table.

'Didn't tell the truth? You mean she told fibs?' Lise said.

Klara raised her eyes, but before she could answer the front door opened.

Laufey was back.

'Daddy.' Anna took a brief pause from doing cartwheels around the sitting room and stood poised, her arms held straight up in the air, one foot extended. 'Why are some people fat?'

'*Anna*,' Laufey said in a warning tone.

'She's allowed to ask,' Unnar said. He took off his glasses and folded the newspaper. 'Some people find it harder than others to control what they eat.'

'That's not the only—' Laufey began, but Unnar cut her off.

'Look at your mother, for example. She loves eating biscuits.' Unnar grinned at Laufey, and Anna giggled. 'She's never been able to control what she eats, and that's why ... well, you see what I mean.'

'But why's Klara fat?'

'Really, Anna!' Laufey glared at her daughter.

'It's just a fact, Laufey,' Unnar said. 'Klara takes after you in that respect.'

Laufey ignored Unnar and tried to keep her voice calm as she replied: 'There's nothing wrong with being fat, Anna. Lots of things are worse, like being mean, for example, or saying spiteful things.'

Anna shrugged. 'I don't want to be fat like you and Klara. I want to be like Daddy.'

'That's my girl.' Unnar laughed and stroked her hair.

'I think there are more important goals in life than looking a certain way,' Laufey said, trying to force herself to smile. Her gaze went to Klara, who was sitting at the kitchen table, drawing. She didn't appear to be listening to them, but rather concentrating hard on the paper in front of her, the deft movements of her hand seeming not to belong to a ten-year-old.

'Yeah, right,' Unnar said, pinching Laufey's shoulder. He winked at Anna. 'But it doesn't exactly hurt to think about your appearance, does it?'

Laufey chose not to answer, knowing full well that anything she said would only lead to an argument that she couldn't win. It was a conversation they'd had so often. Unnar was well aware of what Laufey had gone through as a girl when her mentally ill mother had projected her own food fixations onto her daughter. Growing up, Laufey had been subjected to daily sessions on the scales, after which her weight had been recorded in a little book and her supper rationed accordingly. She'd had to put up with constant needling from her mother about her clothes not fitting her, her bed not being strong enough to support her weight and comments along the lines of how could she dream of going out in those shoes with feet like that?

Even now, long after her mother's death, Laufey was still coping with the fallout. It had taken her years to rid her head of her mother's voice and even longer to come to terms with her own body.

Yet Unnar continued to justify his comments about her weight by claiming it was all in fun and that she had no sense of humour; she couldn't laugh at herself. Laufey had long ago given up trying to make him see how painful his comments were, but now she could feel her face burning with rage.

She had made such an effort to bring up her daughters with healthy priorities. Conscious of this, she had begun early to praise them for the right things. She never told them they were 'pretty', but that they were 'hard-working' or 'clever'. Appearance was something people were born with, not a quality they earned or worked hard to achieve, so it shouldn't be the focus of praise. Once the girls started going to school, though, Laufey's influence had waned. Klara got to hear that she was fat and Anna that she was pretty. And however often Laufey told them that neither of these things was important, it had no effect. Klara lost confidence and retreated into her shell, while Anna spent hours in front of the mirror, pouting and smiling, and was always asking for new clothes and nail varnish.

Children were shallow, and Laufey couldn't change that. All she wanted was for her girls not to be overly influenced by what other people thought of them but to be proud and happy, however they looked. But then Unnar came along and mocked all her efforts. Although he pretended he was only joking, he made no attempt to hide his scorn for people who put on weight, especially in the case of women in the media or on the news. Laufey was forever calling him out on this, but Unnar ignored her and remained unrepentant.

Klara collected up her drawing things and went into her room. Laufey wiped the table, her thoughts on her older daughter. Then she looked at Unnar, who had sat down again with the paper and was humming to himself. He had been in an unusually good mood all day, apparently untroubled by the news that Lise was missing. When Laufey told him the police had been round to ask about her, he had just said 'hmm', then started talking about his colleague who had apparently split up from his much younger girlfriend.

Laufey, on the other hand, hadn't been able to think about anything else. She had to admit to herself that she had never really taken to Lise, not that this was in any way relevant. The girl simply hadn't been what Laufey was expecting. Too careless, untidy and absent-minded, and her personal hygiene had left a lot to be desired. Laufey almost had to force her to take a shower at least once a week, and the girl never seemed to have the slightest interest in going out and meeting people. Instead, she had hung around the house every evening, getting underfoot, when Laufey would have preferred some time to herself. She had also slipped Klara and Anna sweets when Laufey was out, and rummaged through her cosmetics in the bathroom.

Laufey was still thinking about Lise several minutes later when there was a knock at the door.

+

Unnar and Laufey were both there to receive Elma and Sævar this time. Their daughters could be heard talking loudly in one of the bedrooms, but there was no sign of Andri. Elma suspected he spent most of his time in his garage flat.

'Have you found Lise?' Laufey asked, as soon as they were seated. 'I saw on the news that a body had turned up. Was it … was it by any chance her?'

'I'm afraid so,' Elma replied. 'Lise's body was found on Friday evening.'

Laufey gasped, and Unnar turned white. They were sitting in the living room, where a carved wooden clock ticked on the wall and the aroma of coffee wafted in from the kitchen.

'She was found at Marinó's house,' Elma continued. 'But it's not yet clear how she died.'

'At Marinó's house?' Laufey exclaimed. 'But … how's that possible? Christ, what can have happened?'

'We don't know,' Elma said. 'When did you two last see Lise?'

Laufey was staring rigidly into space, as if the news was still sinking in. Her lips were slightly parted, and she had wrapped her arms around her ribs, hugging herself.

'It must have been on Saturday evening two weeks ago,' Unnar replied. 'Isn't that right, Laufey?'

'What? Yes, I…' Laufey sat up straighter. 'Like I told you on Friday, I last saw her two weeks ago. Remember, Unnar? It was the evening Andri took Lise with him to Marinó's.'

'Yes, I remember,' Unnar said.

'I had yoga early next morning, so I went to bed before you. You stayed up late, didn't you?' Laufey said to Unnar. 'Do you remember seeing Andri and Lise come home?'

'No, I don't.' Unnar tugged at the neck of his jumper as if to let in some air. 'I may have seen Andri come home but I didn't see Lise. I'm fairly sure of that.'

'Was Andri alone when you saw him?' Elma asked.

'Yes. He went straight into the garage, as usual.'

'Just so we've got this straight,' Elma said, taking out a pen to make notes. 'Lise and Andri went to Marinó's house on the evening of Saturday the seventh of September?'

'That's right,' Laufey said.

'And Unnar, you saw Andri come home that night,' Elma went on. 'Do you remember what time it was?'

'No, I...' Unnar clicked his tongue. 'Around four or five in the morning, maybe.'

'Four or five.' Elma raised her eyebrows. 'And he was alone?'

'Yes.'

'Are you absolutely sure you didn't hear Lise come in?'

'Yes. Absolutely positive.'

'Laufey, you said Lise's luggage was in her room on Saturday evening but that it had vanished in the morning,' Elma said. 'So someone must have come and taken it, mustn't they?'

'Yes,' Laufey whispered. 'They must have.'

'So all that time, from Saturday evening to Sunday morning, one of you was home – the house was never empty.' Elma put her notebook back in her pocket without taking her eyes off them. 'What I don't understand is how Lise's luggage could have disappeared during that time. You yourselves must see that it just doesn't add up.'

'We'd like to ask you a few questions about the weekend before Marinó died, specifically about Saturday the seventh of September,' Elma said. They had called Andri into the police station to take his statement. 'Do you remember what you were doing then?'

'I was playing in a match,' Andri answered promptly. 'In Akureyri.'

'How did it go?' Elma asked with a smile.

'We lost,' Andri said, without apparent regret.

'Sorry about that,' Elma said. 'I don't follow football much but I've heard you're pretty good. Aren't you going to play for some club abroad?'

'I'm moving to Sweden. Flying out next week.'

'That's exciting.' Elma sensed that Andri was more relaxed now than when he had first come in.

Andri took a sip of water and glanced around him. There wasn't much to see: the interview room was very plain and non-descript: cream walls, a birch-wood table and chairs. The curtains were drawn and the window was shut, which made it quite hot in there when the sun was shining.

Elma noticed how still Andri was sitting. She was used to interviewees constantly shifting and fidgeting: shuffling their feet, picking at their nails or rhythmically tapping a hand on their thigh. Since the situation was inherently nerve-racking, such reactions were normal. But Andri sat perfectly still, breathing easily, and didn't seem remotely concerned.

'You knew Lise, didn't you?' Elma asked. 'What can you tell me about her?'

'Not much,' Andri said. 'Lise was our au pair. She looked after my sisters.'

'Weren't you two friends?'

'Friends? Mum sometimes made me take her along when I was going out, in the hope that she'd get to know some other people. She'd been with us for months but she hardly left the house.'

'So, when you got home from the match in Akureyri,' Elma said, 'you invited Lise along to your friends' house because your mother asked you to?'

'Yes. Well, no.' Andri took another sip of water. 'I'd introduced her to my friends before. The girls invited her round to Marinó's that evening, and she got a lift with me.'

'I see,' Elma said. 'How did you get home that night?'

'I don't really remember,' Andri said, seeming awkward for the first time. 'I, er … I don't usually drink, but I did then. I got home quite late.'

'Why were you drinking?'

'I…' Andri shrugged. 'I don't know.'

'Did Lise come home with you?'

'No, she stayed behind at Marinó's.'

Elma looked at him searchingly. 'Why? Why didn't she come back with you?'

'She fell asleep,' Andri said, looking down at the table. 'She got very drunk, you know, so we thought we'd better leave her to sleep it off.'

Elma said nothing for a while, her eyes meeting Sævar's. It was possible that Andri was telling the truth. They had already questioned him about the evening Marinó died in the fire, but Elma decided to ask him again; get him to repeat his story and see if it was consistent with the first version.

Andri answered all her questions succinctly. On Saturday, 14 September he had not seen Marinó at all; Andri had been with his girlfriend, but they hadn't spent the night together, and he had got home between one and two. His parents had been having a dinner party, and their guests had seen Andri.

'When did you last see Lise?' Sævar asked, returning to the earlier theme when they had run out of questions about the night Marinó died.

'At Marinó's party on the Saturday evening,' Andri said. 'I don't think she was that used to alcohol because by the end she was throwing up. Then she lay down on Fríða's bed, and I left her there. I thought it would be better for her to sleep it off there than at home.'

'Weren't you surprised when you didn't see her again?'

'Not really,' Andri said. 'Lise had told us it was her last evening in Akranes. Then on Sunday evening Mum told me she'd left.'

'Without saying goodbye?'

'Yeah. Maybe that was kind of strange.'

'Did Lise tell you why she wanted to leave Iceland?'

'She just said she was feeling homesick,' Andri said. 'She'd been here for six months, which was a pretty long time. Much longer than Lena.'

'Who's Lena?'

'The Polish au pair who was with us last year.'

'Did she go home early as well?' Elma asked.

'Yeah, she only lasted a month or so.'

'What happened?' Sævar asked.

'Don't ask me,' Andri said. 'I'm not home much. I mean, I live there, but the garage is separate from the house, so it's almost like I live alone.'

'We know that,' Sævar said, and smiled. 'Did you have any contact with Marinó after the evening Lise stayed over at his place? Didn't he say anything about her – like whether anything had happened between them?'

Andri stared at Sævar for a moment or two, as if he didn't quite follow. Then, apparently cottoning on, he shook his head.

'There was nothing going on between them. They hardly knew each other. I told you, Lise went to lie down in Fríða's bed.'

'So Marinó told you she'd gone home the next day?'

'No, he...' Andri hesitated. 'He didn't actually say that, but then I didn't ask.'

'So you didn't care?' Elma said. 'You two arrive together, she gets pissed out of her skull and ends up spending the night with your friend, and you don't even ask about her?'

'Er ... no,' Andri said. 'Why should I?'

March 2019

The moment Lise woke up she checked the alarm clock and got a shock. Then she leapt out of bed so fast that she almost fainted but didn't have time to bend over and wait until the blood had returned to her head.

How could she have overslept? The girls started school at half past eight, and she had conscientiously set her alarm for seven to give her plenty of time to make their lunches and get breakfast ready before they woke up.

'Girls.' Lise opened the doors to their rooms. 'Girls, we overslept.'

Anna sat up and rubbed her eyes. 'You overslept,' she said accusingly. 'You were supposed to wake us.'

'I know but the alarm didn't go off and...' Lise tried to breathe calmly. There was no point making excuses. She was supposed to keep an eye on the time, and if the alarm hadn't gone off, she must have done something wrong. 'We'll have to hurry. I'll make your lunches but you need to be dressed by the time I'm done.'

'Can't we have breakfast?' Klara asked plaintively.

'No, but you can take a banana with you.'

Anna lay back in bed, groaning loudly. 'But we always have breakfast at home. Mummy says—'

'Girls!' Lise snapped, and Anna shut up. 'Get dressed now, or you'll be late.'

Twenty minutes later they were all outside in the damp air. It was still dark. Luckily the school was only a short walk away, and they reached the gate just before the bell rang. Lise watched the girls run inside. The moment they vanished from sight, her control broke and the tears started rolling down her cold cheeks. She wiped *them hastily away. Then she walked back to the house, head down, hoping no one would see her face. Thank God it was dark.*

Once she had closed the front door behind her, she broke down completely. Leaning back, she slid down to the floor and sat there sobbing.

'Hello?'

Lise gasped. She got hurriedly to her feet, drying her cheeks. Could that be Unnar home at this time of day? The voice was male, but it didn't sound like Unnar; it was too light and ... Before she had time to wonder any further, a young man appeared in the doorway. She recognised Andri from the photos in the sitting room. The eldest son – Anna and Klara's big brother, Andri – who had been away on a two-week training trip and had presumably just got back.

'I...' Lise stammered. 'I didn't know there was anyone home.'

'Oh, right.' Andri coughed. 'I, er ... I've just got back from a training trip. Are you, er ... the babysitter?'

'Yes,' Lise said, trying to smile. 'I'm Lise.'

'Andri.' He smiled ruefully. 'How's it going?'

'Great.' As she said it, Lise pictured herself: wild hair, red cheeks streaked and swollen from crying. Suddenly she couldn't hold back her laughter. The situation was so ridiculous: the way she had left the kitchen looking like a bomb site, with clothes strewn all over the place, the breakfast spreads still on the table, and the contents pulled out of all the drawers because she hadn't been able to find the girls' lunch boxes. Andri would think she was crazy, but the thought only made her laugh harder.

'Sorry,' she gasped. 'I just ... God. It's not like this every day. It just ... I overslept and that's why...'

Andri raised his eyebrows and smiled. 'That's why the kitchen's been turned upside down?'

'Mm.'

'I thought there'd been a break-in,' he said. 'Though it seemed kind of odd that the burglar had only been interested in the contents of the fridge and my mum's Tupperware.'

'That would be odd,' Lise agreed. 'Unless the burglar was a deranged mother in search of ingredients for her kids' packed lunches.'

Andri laughed, and Lise noticed that he had unusually small teeth. Although he took after his mother in looks, he'd unquestionably inherited his smile from his father.

Lise had barely seen Unnar all week. Since their drive around town the previous Sunday he had been more or less absent, though Lise sometimes heard him coming home late in the evening, warily opening and shutting the front door and turning on the television in the den. One night she had been woken by the sound of someone moving about at two in the morning and had peered out of her bedroom door to see Unnar standing at the kitchen island with a glass of water, his hair tousled, his white shirt creased and unbuttoned. After tipping the water down his throat, he'd wiped his mouth on his sleeve, staring absently into space. The overhead light cast his weary eyes in shadow and his features were set in harsh lines; very different from the warm, charming demeanour Lise was familiar with.

'Anyway,' Andri said, gesturing in the direction of the garage. 'I'm going to my room, so I'll let you get on.'

Lise nodded and stepped aside to let him pass. After he had gone, she caught sight of herself in the hall mirror. Her cheeks were still flushed and her eyes a little red. She smoothed her hair back behind her ears and inhaled deeply, then began to tackle the mess she had left behind that morning.

By the end of the day Elma was exhausted. Following their in-terview with Andri, she had called his girlfriend, Júlía, who confirmed that he had been with her until midnight last Saturday. Afterwards he had gone home to his parents' house. Elma wondered if Laufey and Unnar would be prepared to lie for their son. The evening Marinó died they'd held a dinner party, which meant there were other witnesses to Andri's home-coming. But, of course, he could have gone out again later. Marinó had probably been murdered and the fire started at some point between two and three in the morning. The police were now waiting for data from Andri's phone, which would provide confirmation of his movements.

'So, basically, your theory is that Marinó killed Lise and hid her in his garden shed until he could find a better place to dispose of her body,' Sævar said, dunking a piece of sushi in soy sauce with his fingers, then popping it in his mouth.

'It's by far the likeliest explanation,' Elma replied. 'We know Lise hasn't been seen since she spent the night at Marinó's, and, after all, her body did turn up in his shed.'

Sævar swallowed and opened his mouth to speak, but Elma got in first.

'I know there are some loose ends. Like, for example, who took away Lise's luggage and where is it now?'

'But Marinó's search history is a pretty strong indication that he knew about the body, isn't it?' Sævar said.

'Yes,' Elma replied. 'So we can assume that at least two people knew Lise's body was in the shed.'

'Really? Can we necessarily assume that?' Sævar sounded sceptical. 'We know Marinó was aware of the body, but it doesn't follow that anyone else was. Marinó's murder doesn't have to be connected to Lise.'

'No, maybe not.' Elma stabbed a piece of pickled ginger, which she knew Sævar couldn't stand, and put it in her mouth. 'But I still don't believe he was acting alone. I reckon two people hid Lise's body, and Marinó's death is connected somehow to that.'

'In other words, you think the second person was responsible for the fire?'

'Yes.' Elma took a swig of Coke. 'But I can't work out why. Whether it was to stop Marinó talking or because the second person discovered what he had done to Lise.'

Sævar held out the sushi tray to Elma, but she shook her head. 'Aren't you hungry?'

'No, and it's Mum's birthday, so I'm invited to dinner.'

'Oh, right. Wish her a happy birthday from me.' Sævar took back the tray and ate another piece of sushi.

'Will do,' Elma said, a little awkwardly. 'But there were no obviously fatal injuries on Lise's body. Her death could have been an accident. Perhaps she had a bad reaction to some drug. But, in that case, why hide her body? Why not call the police?'

'There may be injuries we haven't discovered yet,' Sævar said through a mouthful of raw fish.

'When's Hannes planning to do the post-mortem?'

Sævar shrugged. 'As soon as possible.'

The smell of sushi suddenly got to Elma. She stood up, went over to the window and stared out for a moment. After another swig of Coke, the queasy feeling passed. She leant her back against the kitchen countertop.

'I was going to be an au pair once. In Spain. I'd found a family and everything. We'd talked on the phone, and the only thing left was to book my flight.'

'What happened?'

'They changed their minds.'

'Why?'

'They split up.'

The family had lived in a small village in northern Spain, and the plan was for Elma to look after their three-year-old son and five-year-old daughter. She could still remember the photos: the good-looking couple with their arms around their two children. The father holding the camera as far away as possible to get the whole family and himself in the picture; the wooded mountains in the background. The little girl had been dark, with a gap between her front teeth, while the boy's pure-white hair had formed a striking contrast to his brown eyes.

Elma couldn't wait to meet them, but a month before her departure she'd received an oddly personal email from the husband. In it, he had explained how his wife had walked out on them because she had met another man and moved in with him. If Elma still wanted to come, that would be OK, but she would have to pay for the flight herself as he wasn't sure what was going to happen to the family's finances. Elma had wanted to go, but her parents had put their foot down, and now she understood why.

She finished the rest of her Coke and said goodbye to Sævar.

'Don't forget to give my regards to your mother,' he called after her.

❧

On the TV screen, a thin, bony woman with shoulder-length hair was announcing: 'Our information suggests that the discovery of the body in Akranes may be connected to the house fire that—'

Laufey pressed the top button on the remote control, and the screen went black. The girls were asleep and Unnar was playing badminton with Óskar, so there was complete silence in the house. She heard a car pull into the drive, and a few moments later the garage door slammed.

Laufey put on a cardigan and shoes and went outside.

Andri answered her light tap, and she stepped into the garage flat, closing the door behind her.

'Andri, what on earth happened at training yesterday? Ingi rang; he's worried about you.'

'*He's* worried?' Andri said derisively.

'I'm worried too. Are you sure everything's OK?'

'Yeah.'

'How did you get on at the police station?'

'Fine.'

'What did they want to know?'

'Just where I was and that kind of thing.'

Laufey stared searchingly at her son. He was lying on his unmade bed, still in his training gear. His room smelt of sweat and trainers, mingled with a faint hint of aftershave. Andri had always been a bit of a slob, but right now she had more important things on her mind.

'I know it's not...' Laufey stopped herself and said instead: 'What do you want to do?'

'You know what I want to do.'

Laufey nodded and went out again, leaving him in peace.

Back in the house, she couldn't resist the temptation to take out the old photo albums. She missed simpler times. Andri had become an adult. She had been trying to work out when it was that she had finally lost him. When was the last time they'd hugged without him waiting impatiently for her to let him go? When was the last time she had touched him without feeling self-conscious?

Andri had always been withdrawn, even as a kid. He used to have problems concentrating and seemed incapable of remembering anything. They'd had to give him constant reminders: don't forget your school bag, close the front door, come home at the right time, turn off the lights and close the fridge – obvious things, you would think. But they weren't obvious; not to Andri.

He hadn't been disobedient, just forgetful and absent-minded, something Unnar had been unable to understand. He had believed that tough love was the answer, insisting that the boy would learn in the end if his forgetfulness resulted in reprimands or punishments. Laufey had noticed how Andri began to avoid his father, becoming silent and tense in his presence.

The only good thing Unnar had done for Andri was to take him to football practice when he was four. Laufey remembered how stressed she had been beforehand, imagining the other kids barging into him and Andri starting to cry in front of the parents. Unnar couldn't stand public displays of tears, and Andri was an awful cry-baby. Laufey had sat on the benches, watching him clamber over the obstacles, so unsteady and fragile, as tender as a blade of grass. But then he had gone over to join the other kids who were being split up into two teams and made to kick a ball around. Andri had simply stood there at first, watching and getting in the way. Then he had started to run.

Later, Laufey remembered the moment that had decided the future direction of his life. Andri had run, taken the ball, run with it and scored. Laufey had gripped her seat, laughing with emotion. She had nudged Unnar, who was busy talking to one of the other fathers. Andri had taken the ball again, run with it and scored a second time. And so it had continued. At four years old, he may have been smaller and skinnier than all the rest, but he was faster and nippier too. It was as if the ball had been glued to his feet. After that there was no turning back; Andri's life had come to revolve entirely around football.

As he grew older, though, football had ceased to be a game and became a job. Laufey had been around the club long enough to know that the culture within the football world left a lot to be desired. The better Andri performed, the more expectations were placed on his shoulders, and when he didn't meet those expectations, people were quick to denigrate him. They said such ugly things that Laufey was shocked. Andri didn't handle pressure well; it made him anxious and stressed. And now Laufey was afraid that his anxiety was getting the better of him.

✦

'Just sit down.' Aðalheiður took the cutlery from her daughter. 'Honestly, you're not helping.'

'Mum, I'm perfectly capable of laying the table,' Elma protested, the yawn she stifled immediately afterwards belying her words.

'Is that right? Elma, dear, you've got knives and spoons there. Are you intending to eat your roast with a spoon?'

Elma looked down and saw that her mother was right. She was holding a bunch of soup spoons and knives. Was she really that shattered? She put the spoons back in the drawer and sat down with the mug of coffee she had helped herself to the moment she came in. Clearly, she needed it.

'I'll lay the table,' volunteered Dagný, who had been standing in the kitchen with their mother when Elma arrived. 'Mum, why don't you sit down too? After all, you're the birthday girl.'

'Yes, but—'

'The joint's ready, I've made the salad, and the only thing left is the table. That and waiting for the potatoes to cook. Go on, sit down.'

'Right.' Aðalheiður dithered for a moment, looking at Dagný, then wiped her hands on her apron and took it off. 'Right,' she said again and sat down across from Elma. 'How's work?'

'You mean how's the inquiry going?'

'Yes.'

'Urgh,' Elma sighed. 'I can't face talking about it.'

'That badly?'

Elma answered with another heavy sigh.

'You know you used to babysit for him, don't you?'

'Him?'

'That boy Andri. You and Silja looked after him one summer. You used to take him to the playground and so on. How old were you, fourteen, fifteen?'

'We were probably fifteen or sixteen,' Elma said, realising that this was why Andri's face had seemed so familiar. 'But we weren't both paid to look after him. Silja used to babysit for him sometimes in the evenings and at weekends; I just went along with her a few times.'

'Yes, well. You were never that keen on babysitting. Not exactly the world's most maternal type.'

Elma quickly changed the subject. 'Have you done anything special today? Apart from cooking for us, I mean?'

'Yes, your father and I went for a walk down to the harbour and stopped off at the bakery. Then your aunt Lóa came round for coffee.'

'You're quite a respectable age now.'

'I am, aren't I? Can't complain.'

'But you still seem as young as ever,' Elma said, and she meant it. Her mother didn't appear to have changed a bit since Elma was a little girl.

'Ooh, I don't know.'

'It's no age these days,' Dagný said, joining them. The potatoes had a bit of time left and they were in no hurry. For once, Alexander and Jökull were sitting quietly in front of the TV with the toy box. Viðar, Dagný's husband, had gone into another room to take a work call, and the sisters' father, Jón, was in the shower.

Dagný picked up the open bottle of wine from the table and poured them all a glass.

'Oh, really,' Aðalheiður protested, but Elma could see that she was smiling.

Dagný raised her glass, and the others followed suit. 'Cheers.'

There was a clinking of crystal.

Elma took a big mouthful, the wine tasting pleasantly acidic on her tongue, and was about to let it trickle down her throat when she realised what she was doing. Abruptly, she bent over and dribbled the lot back into the glass.

Dagný and Aðalheiður stared at her in astonishment. Then a small smile appeared on Dagný's lips. A smile that grew wider by the second.

'I knew it!' She took another sip of wine herself. 'I knew it.'

'What?' Aðalheiður's head swung back and forth between them. 'What did you know?' When neither of her daughters answered, she put down her glass and demanded, almost crossly: 'Girls! Come on, tell me: why the strange looks?'

April 2019

Andri knew a lot of girls. At least that's how it looked on social media. They wrote comments under his photos and liked every-thing he posted. In fact, he posted very little and most of the pictures of him had been taken by other people. If they weren't linked to football, they were selfies taken with girls, in which he was smiling awkwardly – as if he was embarrassed, Lise thought.

She had only seen him bring one girl home, though. Her name was Júlía; she was blonde and leggy, and always dressed as if she was on her way to a party. Lise sometimes watched them go into Andri's garage flat. Then she would lie in bed, imagining what must be happening a few metres away from her. She knew they weren't just sitting there chatting, not when Júlía didn't go home until late at night or early the following morning.

'Lise.' There was a knock on her door, and she sat up in bed. 'Supper's ready.'

She went out and joined Laufey and the girls at the kitchen table. The burgers they were having for supper looked like beef but were probably made of beans or some other kind of vegetable. Laufey cooked a lot of veggie dishes, especially when Unnar was out, and Lise had soon discovered that on weekdays Unnar mostly didn't come home for supper.

Lise took a seat beside Klara. As she was helping herself to sweet corn, the front door slammed.

'Andri,' Laufey said, rising instantly to her feet. 'I didn't know you'd be here for supper.'

'No.' Andri sat down beside Lise and took a plate from his mother.

He smelt of fresh air and sweat; just come back from football training, no doubt.

Laufey talked and talked throughout the meal. Lise ate slowly, unwilling to leave the table while Andri was there. As he was clearing away his plate, Laufey eyed Lise thoughtfully.

'Andri,' she said. 'You should introduce Lise to some people. How would you like that, Lise? You haven't got to know anyone yet, have you?'

'No,' Lise said, toying with a kernel of corn on her plate.

'Andri, why don't you take her to meet some of your friends?'

Andri just shrugged. Lise didn't know how to interpret this, but later that evening he knocked on her door.

They went round to see his friend Ísak and Ísak's girlfriend Sonja, who was heavily pregnant. The twins, Marinó and Fríða, were there too, and they sat around all evening, playing board games and eating snacks. Lise enjoyed herself. It brought home to her just how much she had been missing Anita and her other friends back in Amsterdam.

Next day, the two of them went out together again and drove around town. Lise assumed they were going to see Sonja and Ísak, but Andri kept driving.

At first neither of them said a word.

Andri seemed preoccupied and ignored his phone, which kept vibrating in his pocket. He didn't even glance at it.

'Your girlfriend's incredibly pretty,' Lise remarked, guessing that she was the one calling, because who else would try him again and again like that?

'Who? Júlía?'

'Have you got others?'

'No.' Andri laughed.

'Anyway, she's incredibly pretty. Like an actress or something.'

'Yeah, I know,' Andri said, as if it wasn't important. Lise sometimes fantasised about what it would be like to be that stunning. Compared to girls like Júlía, she felt like an overgrown child, with

her trainers, hoodie and pony-tail. But she didn't know how to be any different.

'Have you been together long?'

'About a year.'

'What will happen if you go abroad?'

'I haven't actually thought about it.'

They drove down to the harbour, and Lise looked up at the four tall blue tanks that stood by the quay. Only a month ago the area had been dominated by a big white chimney, part of the defunct cement factory, but it had now been demolished. The townspeople had gathered to watch the controlled explosion, either from a safe distance or via live stream. Lise had marvelled that it should have been such a big deal to them, until Laufey explained that, although it had been derelict for many years, the chimney had been an important landmark in the town. Lise had been living in Akranes long enough now to understand that the community was a bit like a small neighbourhood in Amsterdam; a neighbourhood where everyone knew each other and took an interest in local affairs.

She turned back to Andri. 'Really? I bet she has, though.'

'I guess so,' Andri said.

'Do you think you'll miss her?'

Andri slowed down by the harbour. The sun was setting, casting pink and orange rays over the surface of the sea.

'No.'

'And your parents?'

There was a pause before Andri answered: 'Yeah, I suppose.'

'You're lucky,' Lise said, gazing out to sea. Andri had stopped the car by the jetty. 'Sometimes I miss my dad so much I can hardly breathe. At least you'll get to see your parents again.'

'I've never lost anyone. Well, except my granddad, and he was very old.'

'That's different.'

'I know.'

Lise scratched at the fabric of her seat. 'Are your parents … Have

they always been happy together?'
  'My parents?' Andri shook his head. 'No.'
  'What? Seriously?'
  'Yes, they … they're not like they seem.'
  'In what way?'
  'Just, you know…'
  Lise waited.
  'Mum can be a bit difficult,' Andri said, 'but that's only because she wants everything to be perfect. Sometimes it's like she tries too hard. But, er … you know, Dad's worse. We've never been particularly close or anything. Not like you and your dad.'
  Lise looked at him, chewing her lower lip. Now that she thought about it, she had never seen Unnar and Andri talking to each other. Unnar didn't even turn up to his games, unlike Laufey, who attended every match, kitted out in yellow and black. She also talked constantly about Andri when her friends came round.
  'Dad's kind of just…' Andri fiddled with the steering wheel.
  Lise raised her eyebrows enquiringly, but Andri left it at that.

Monday

It was only half past six when Elma gave up trying to sleep and got out of bed, unable to face lying there any longer, plagued by her thoughts. She'd been very taken aback by her mother's reaction. She hadn't expected Aðalheiður to get all weepy like that, almost too choked up to speak. The hug she'd given Elma had been long and heartfelt, and there had been fewer questions than she'd expected. Her normally nosy mother hadn't said a single word about the child's father, just looked at Elma archly, as if she already knew more than she was letting on.

Elma had extracted a promise from her mother and sister that they wouldn't breathe a word to anyone, as she hadn't meant to break the news until she'd spoken to Sævar. It wouldn't be fair on him.

She knew she'd have to do it as soon as possible but felt she needed to be a hundred per cent sure first. She had booked another appointment with the midwife in Mosfellsbær, but Dagný had insisted that she come to her instead, ordering her to turn up at nine o'clock sharp on Monday morning. Elma wasn't in a position to object, though she found the idea of having her sister as midwife a little uncomfortable. Still, Dagný had seen it all, and of course a pregnancy was the most natural process in the world.

It wasn't the pregnancy or the birth that scared Elma. She was sure that when the time came her body would take over and all she would have to do was endure the labour pains. It was what came afterwards that frightened her: becoming the mother of a child, having to be responsible for another human being. How would anyone be able to look at her and feel secure? How would she stand comparison with her own mother, who was supremely resourceful and knew everything. Literally everything. Elma had to ring her to ask her advice about the most trivial problems, like how to get red-wine stains out of clothes or how long to roast a chicken. Was someone like her, who wasn't even clued up enough to cook a chicken, suddenly supposed to be in charge of a newborn baby and know what to do?

Whenever her worries about the future became too pressing, Elma tried to distract herself by thinking about the case instead. She'd had an idea.

After her own abortive au pair experience, if you could call it that, she knew a little about how such things were arranged. The girls or boys usually went abroad through specialist matching agencies or services, and Elma knew exactly where to call.

The man who answered the phone at the au pair agency clearly wasn't a native English speaker. He had a hard accent that Elma couldn't begin to identify.

'I've got her profile up in front of me now,' the man said. 'Lise Visser, nineteen, from Amsterdam. Where did you say she was au pairing?'

'In Iceland.'

'OK. No, she didn't go through our agency.'

'But she created a profile with you, didn't she?' Elma had been hoping the agency would be able to tell her more about the circumstances surrounding Lise's sudden decision to leave Laufey and Unnar.

'Yes, but anyone can set up a profile. Prospective au pairs can register for free, while host families seeking au pairs have to pay to use our platform. It's not uncommon for people to make private arrangements, though, without going through us.'

'What services do you offer, then? I mean, why should the girls – or boys – use your matching agency rather than simply arranging their own placements?'

'We strongly recommend that people use an agency rather than going independently. It's a safety issue,' the man said, rather mechanically, as if he had given the same speech countless times before. 'We take care of all the preparations and arrange an initial meeting between the host family and the prospective au pair; we do background checks on all the applicants; organise events for au pairs based in the same country; send out all the forms, visa applications and so on, as well as offering advice and solutions if problems arise. We work closely with both the au pair and the host family during the placement.'

'What are the most common types of problems that can come up?' Elma asked. 'For example, why might an au pair want to leave their host family?'

'Naturally, I can't discuss individual cases.' There was a slight pause on the line, then the sound of a door closing, cutting off the ambient noises. 'But, for example, although we have a system for matching host families with au pairs, we still get regular cases where individuals simply don't get along. They often have unreal expectations: the families make too many demands on the au pairs, or the au pairs don't do what's required of them. In other words, misunderstandings can arise about the nature of the arrangement, especially when the young people go privately. Our agency requires both parties to sign an agreement specifying their roles and duties. The experience can be hard to beat when everything goes according to plan, but that can't be guaranteed.'

'I see.' Elma closed the window as a chilly breeze was beginning to blow the papers around on her table. 'What about if something came up unexpectedly? Do you have any examples of … how shall I put it? Of a situation arising that would mean the au pair wanted to leave the host family immediately?'

'Well, naturally incidents like that do occur, but they're not very common. It's more usual for problems to develop over time and for both sides to do their best to rescue the situation before they give up on it.' The man hesitated before adding in a low voice: 'But very occasionally we've had cases of au pairs suffering abuse from a member of the host family. Once a mother slapped a male au pair in the face, and there have also been a few cases of fathers sexually harassing female au pairs. This applies especially to Filipino girls placed with wealthy European families. It goes without saying that we do our best to prevent that kind of incident by doing background checks on all our applicants, but of course it's impossible to be a hundred per cent sure. Some men have brilliant careers and look excellent on paper but turn out to be complete sleazebags in practice.'

❦

When Hörður arrived at the office he found a message waiting for him from the Reykjavík police. Unable to make head or tail of it, he put in a call to DCI Borghildur.

'We had a phone call today from a young woman trying to track down a friend of hers, who she hasn't been able to contact for some time,' Borghildur explained. 'A girl by the name of Lise Ragnarsdóttir Visser. I'm assuming this will mean something to you?'

Hörður got up and closed his office door.

'It certainly does. Lise's the girl whose body we found on Friday evening.'

'I thought she might be.' Borghildur was silent for a moment, and Hörður heard the rattle of a drawer being closed, followed by the rustling of paper. 'I've got the woman's number here. I think it would be best for someone from your office to speak to her.'

She reeled off the number, and Hörður wrote it down. He was about to say goodbye when Borghildur's tone suddenly changed and became less formal.

'I, er…' she began. 'I'd like to offer you my deepest condolences about Gígja.'

'Thank you for that.'

'How are you coping?'

'Oh, fine,' Hörður answered. As a rule he tried to make the best of things and give the impression that everything was all right. But now, suddenly, he couldn't bring himself to keep up the pretence and, after a brief pause, he added: 'Up and down – you know how it is.'

'It's so awful. Gígja was a lovely woman,' Borghildur said, and Hörður remembered that she and Gígja had got on like a house on fire at one of the annual police parties. They had discovered that they were distantly related and had spent ages tracing their family tree. They both had memories of a farm in the West Fjords that they had visited as children, and had a good giggle about the old farmer who used to spit his chewing tobacco into the sink, to the disgust of his wife.

'Yes, she was,' Hörður said slowly.

After ending the call, he reflected that it would probably be sensible to let Elma take care of talking to Lise's friend. He wasn't in the kind of shape emotionally to cope with a difficult conversation like that. At the time of the fire, he had been desperate to return to work, but now his reserves of energy were running low and he could feel himself growing wearier with every day that passed.

Elma had told Hörður that she would be in late because of a dental appointment. Strange how it was always the dentist that sprang to mind when she needed to lie. She was sitting in the car in front of Akranes Hospital, trying to psych herself up to switch off the engine, open the door and go into reception.

Her phone rang and Dagný's name flashed up on screen.

'I'm outside,' Elma answered.

'I'm waiting,' Dagný replied, sounding eager.

Dagný was standing talking to the receptionist and smiled from ear to ear when she saw Elma.

'Right, come on in,' she said.

Elma followed her into a small office containing a couch.

'Ooh, this is so exciting,' Dagný exclaimed, lightly clapping her hands. She paused and inspected Elma more closely. 'Though you look as if you're about to go on trial. Relax, there's no need to be so stressed.'

'I'm not stressed,' Elma lied.

'Sure, you're not.' Dagný smiled wryly and switched on the computer.

The white coat suited her sister, Elma thought. Her blonde hair was loosely tied back, she wore no jewellery and her face was bare. As a rule, Dagný liked to dress up and put on a lot of bling and make-up, but evidently not at work.

'OK,' Dagný said, her fingers dancing on the keyboard. 'I can fill in most of this myself.'

'Great.' Elma surreptitiously wiped her clammy palms on her jumper.

'Except perhaps the father's name.' Dagný didn't take her eyes off the computer screen as she spoke. 'But maybe you'd like to leave that blank for now?'

'Yes.'

Elma had been expecting more pressure, but Dagný didn't say another word, just turned her chair to face her.

'Have you done a test?'

'A test?'

'Yes, you know. Have you peed on a stick?'

'Yes.' Elma cleared her throat. 'Three of them.'

'All positive?'

Elma nodded, and Dagný smiled.

'Sorry, but I'm dying of excitement. This is so fantastic, Elma. I can't wait to meet my little niece.'

'Niece?'

'Yes, oh, I've always had the feeling your first would be a girl.'

'OK.' Elma hadn't got as far as thinking about the baby's sex. Up to now she had just thought of it as a baby. Pictured a tiny, hairless creature rather than a girl or a boy. She wondered which she would prefer.

'And to think I'll get to deliver her,' Dagný added, her eyes sparkling.

'But the tests might have been wrong. Maybe—'

'They're fairly reliable, the tests – especially if you did three,' Dagný interrupted. She put on her professional face again, although she was obviously having trouble wiping off her smile. 'What date did your last period start?'

As Elma told her, she found her gaze straying to the model of a female body with a child in the womb that was on the desk. A poster on the wall showed the various stages of foetal development, from embryo to nine months.

Dagný picked up a round dial made of cardboard and turned it.

'Given the date, you should be eleven weeks gone, which means there's a good chance we'll be able to hear a heartbeat.'

'A heartbeat?' Elma repeated, feeling her own heart jump. She didn't know what she had been expecting; perhaps another test, a pat on the back and an appointment for an ultrasound.

'Lie down on the bed and pull your jumper up a bit,' Dagný ordered, opening a drawer in the desk.

Elma obeyed, getting onto the bed and lifting her jumper to reveal the pale skin of her midriff. If anything, her stomach looked flatter than it had a few weeks ago. She had little appetite these days, had given up eating breakfast altogether and only really craved cucumber, as strange as it sounded.

'This is going to feel a little cold,' Dagný said, smearing gel on her stomach, which gave Elma goose pimples. Then Dagný picked up what looked like an old-fashioned telephone receiver and started running it over her belly.

Elma heard the low hum of the machine and over it the sound of her phone vibrating in her coat pocket. Dagný's face took on a concentrated look as she turned up the machine until the hum filled the small office. She ran the ultrasound back and forth over Elma's stomach, pressing down and frowning.

Elma watched her, afraid that something was wrong. Was she not pregnant after all? Had the tests been faulty? Or could she have miscarried without realising? That would make everything simpler, she thought, but at the same time she was caught out by an unexpected stab of regret.

It wasn't until Dagný's facial muscles relaxed into a smile that Elma could give way to relief. Immediately followed by another emotion, as a rhythmic thudding suddenly made itself heard over the hum of the machine. Loud and clear.

'Ah, there it is,' Dagný said. She met Elma's eye and smiled again. 'A strong heartbeat, as you can hear. My little niece is obviously fighting fit.'

Elma nodded, suddenly finding herself having to sniff and blink.

April 2019

Spring was delayed by an unexpected snowfall late in April. It had fallen so heavily during the night that the shrubs in the garden were bowed down by the weight. Lise opened the window and felt the icy air flooding in. It was unusually quiet outside. The snow muffled all sounds, even the traffic. The only thing she could hear was the cheeping of the sparrows as they hopped from branch to branch, and the drips that landed on the window sill as the sun began to melt the snow.

After breakfast, she went to see Laufey.

'I was wondering if I could take the girls sledging?'

Laufey looked up from the brochure she was reading, which had a picture of a beautiful home on the cover. 'Yes, of course. I'm sure they'd love to go.'

She closed the brochure, and Lise got a shock when she saw the back of Laufey's hand. It was greenish purple and so swollen that it hardly seemed to belong to her wrist. Laufey noticed Lise's gaze and put her good hand over the swollen one.

'I sprained it during yoga this morning,' she explained, rising to her feet. 'I'll get out the girls' snow gear. They'll be ready in a few minutes.'

Lise's thin anorak wasn't designed for wet snow or a biting wind, though it had been perfectly adequate against the dry, still cold of the Dutch winter. Laufey took one look at it, then rooted around in the hall cupboard and handed her a down jacket, a pair of padded trousers, a scarf and some gloves.

Lise and the girls were standing in the hall, all bundled up, when Unnar came in.

'Hello, where are you three off to?' he asked, hanging his wool coat in the cupboard.

'We're going sledging,' Anna told him. She tugged at his hand. 'Come with us, Daddy. Then we can go to the mountain.'

'The mountain?' Lise asked.

'Mount Akrafjall,' Unnar explained. 'We don't climb all the way up, of course, but there's a pretty good run on the lower slopes.' Unnar hesitated, then gave in to Anna's pestering. 'All right, then, I'll come.'

So the girls got in the car instead of walking to the nearby slope they called the 'big hill'. Unnar drove them out of town, turning off soon afterwards towards the local landmark of Mount Akrafjall, which always looked to Lise as if it had collapsed in the middle. Unnar parked at the foot of the slope, and the girls jumped out. Lise followed more slowly and stood there for a moment, taking in the white fields near at hand, the blue waters of the fjord beyond and the distant ranks of snowy peaks stretching away as far as the eye could see.

'Not bad, eh?' Unnar was holding a sledge under each arm. 'We've been coming here since the girls were small. We usually have the slope to ourselves.'

Lise watched him striding up the mountainside, carrying the sledges, the girls scampering after him. Anna squealed with joy as she whizzed down the smooth white run and even Klara was beaming.

'Lise, you have a go,' Anna called eventually, out of breath after several more descents. 'It's amazing. You must try.'

Unnar had hardly been able to keep up with their demands to carry the sledges to the top, and his face was shiny with sweat.

'All right,' Lise said. 'I'll have a go.' Up to now she had been standing, watching enviously as the girls hurtled down the run. But as she reached out to take the sledge from Anna, Unnar beat her to it.

'You get the same service as the girls,' he said in a jokey tone, and walked ahead of her up the slope.

'It's so beautiful here,' Lise said, once they were both standing at the top of the run. The girls waited at the bottom, red-cheeked, their breath forming clouds in the cold air.

'It is, isn't it?' Unnar gazed out over the fjord as if only just noticing his surroundings. 'You couldn't do this in Holland, could you?'

'No,' Lise replied. 'And anyway my dad hated the cold and snow. He used to say he'd had more than enough of that when he was a kid. So we always went somewhere hot on holiday.'

'Like Spain?'

'No, Dad couldn't stand touristy places. We always went to small towns that didn't have many visitors.' Lise smiled at the memory. 'It was getting harder to find them, though, as there seem to be tourists everywhere these days.'

'Sounds like paradise. I wouldn't mind being abroad right now.'

'Really?' Lise smiled. 'I can't think of anything better than this. The snow and the mountains and...'

Unnar laughed and was about to say something when they heard a shout.

'Are you two coming down or what?'

Lise got on the sledge and pushed herself off. She felt a thrill in the pit of her stomach and couldn't have stopped smiling if she'd been paid to. The icy air whooshed against her face and the snow crystals swirled around her like white powder.

She didn't notice the rock until it was too late. The sledge ricocheted off it, hurling Lise onto her side. After a moment's shock, she became aware that her arm was hurting and there was freezing snow on her face and neck.

'Are you OK?' Unnar asked, his voice full of concern, when he reached her. He squatted down beside her. Lise sat up.

She began to laugh in spite of the pain in her cheek and arm. 'I don't know what happened. I...'

She broke off in confusion as Unnar stroked her cheek, his warm fingers melting the snow.

'You've got a small graze,' he said and smiled. 'It's not too bad.'

Lise nodded and put out a hand to push herself up, then winced as a stab of pain shot up her arm.

'Did you land on your arm?' Unnar asked, quickly catching hold of her.

Puffing and panting, the girls arrived.

'What happened?' Anna demanded. 'Did you hurt yourself?'

'Are you all right?' Klara asked.

'Yes.' Lise laughed again. 'Yes, I'm just so clumsy.'

'Terribly clumsy,' Anna agreed.

'Girls, you carry on by yourselves,' Unnar ordered. 'I'm going to take Lise back to the car. I want to check she's OK.'

'Do we have to go home already?' Anna asked, her voice petulant with disappointment.

'No,' Lise said quickly. 'Of course not. There's nothing wrong with me.'

They trudged back to the car where Unnar made Lise get into the passenger seat while he went round to open the boot, then returned with a first-aid kit.

'Seriously, I'm fine,' Lise said, feeling like an idiot. Couldn't she even have a go on a sledge without managing to hurt herself?

'I'll be the judge of that.' Unnar got down on one knee. He didn't seem to care that his trousers were getting wet from the snow. Taking hold of her hand, he pushed up the sleeve of her coat.

'Just relax and make yourself floppy,' he said, moving her wrist back and forth.

Lise felt like a doll. Her hands looked so small in Unnar's big ones. She could smell the fragrance of his shampoo and a faint whiff of sweat from inside the jacket he had unzipped. A scarf hung loose from his neck, black with brown and dark-blue stripes. He had short stubble on his throat and cheeks, his hair had been recently cut and there was a small, dark-brown mole on his left cheekbone.

'Does that hurt?'

'Hm?' Lise blushed when he glanced up, and wondered if he'd sensed her studying his face.

'Does it hurt when I move your wrist?'

'Not really,' Lise said.

'Good.' Unnar released her hand and inspected her cheek. 'Would you like a plaster for that graze? It's stopped bleeding.'

'No, it's fine.'

'I'll clean the grit away, all the same.' Unnar took out a small bundle, tore it open and pulled out a wet wipe. Then he hesitated. 'Or would you rather do it yourself?'

'No, that's fine,' Lise said breathlessly.

Unnar dabbed gently at the graze. He was so close now that she could see every tiny detail of his face. A small crease had formed between his brows. He paused briefly and his eyes met hers. For an instant the world stood still, and Lise sensed that he didn't want to draw away. Then he dropped his gaze and cleared his throat, embarrassed.

Lise remained sitting in the car while Unnar went back to join the girls. His scarf was lying on the driver's seat, still a little damp from the snow and his sweaty neck. Lise picked it up carefully and stroked the soft wool, then darted a glance at the slope where Unnar and the girls were safely occupied.

Quick as a flash, she raised the scarf to her nose and inhaled its scent.

'Hello?'

There was a rustling and crackling, then complete silence.

'Hello,' Elma tried again. She stood up and took the phone over to the window in case the reception was better there.

'Hello, can you hear me?' a voice said suddenly at the other end.

Elma answered in her best English. 'Yes, I can. Hi, Anita.'

Anita turned out to be a close friend of Lise's, who was worried sick. Apparently Lise had asked Anita to pick her up from Schiphol Airport on the afternoon of Sunday, 8 September, but she hadn't been on the flight. Since then, Anita had been trying and failing to get hold of her. They used to be in regular contact, but this had changed when Lise went to Iceland.

'I wanted to give her a bit of space to think,' Anita explained. 'She left in such a hurry after her father died that I don't think she gave herself a proper chance to grieve. She felt she had to get away, but I was against the idea. I thought she should stay at home with the people who care about her. She wouldn't listen to me, though.'

Elma could tell that Anita was pacing around. Her voice trembled a little as she spoke, and she was breathing fast.

'Can I talk to her?' Anita asked. 'I just need to hear her voice so I can be sure she's OK. She *is* OK, isn't she?'

Elma braced herself. 'I'm sorry to have to tell you, but your friend was found dead at the weekend.'

The silence at the other end was different in quality now, accompanied, after the first shock, by a faint, muffled sobbing.

'I don't understand,' Anita said after a moment, in a broken voice. 'That's not possible.'

'I'm extremely sorry.' As usual in this situation, Elma found herself floundering, lost for words. What could she do but tell the blunt truth? Part of her longed to soften it and say that everything would be all right, but that would be a lie. There was no way of softening death. It was what it was – as inescapable a fact as life itself.

'What happened?' Anita whispered.

'We don't know how she died yet,' Elma said. 'It may have been an accident.'

'*May* have been an accident,' Anita repeated slowly. 'What do you mean? Is there another possibility? Did she kill herself?'

'We still don't know,' Elma said again, wishing she could give a clearer answer. 'When did you last hear from Lise?'

'About three weeks ago. She rang me for the first time in ages. Apart from that we've mainly chatted online. I felt she'd been quite short with me recently and I was wondering if everything was all right.'

'And how did your conversation go?'

'I don't really know. Lise was…' Anita stopped to think. 'Lise seemed strange. She didn't sound happy and she actually said she was planning to book a flight home. It sounded out of character for her. She was always so stubborn and never quit anything. Like I said, we'd argued about whether she should go to Iceland in the first place; I wanted her to wait a bit, but she wouldn't hear of it. I was expecting her to stay the full year, just to prove she'd been right, however she might be feeling.'

'Did you get the impression she was unhappy here?' Elma picked up a pen and began to scribble notes on the pad in front of her.

'For the first few weeks she was on top of the world, raving about how everything was so great and the people were so friendly. Then suddenly she went a bit quiet – not unhappy exactly but like there was something she didn't want to tell me. I kept asking her what was wrong, and in the end she told me she'd fallen for a boy.'

'Oh?' Elma put down her pen. 'Do you know who he was?'

'No, she didn't tell me his name, but of course it wouldn't have meant anything to me if she had. I asked her to send me a picture of him, but she never did.'

'And she didn't tell you anything else about this boy?'

'No, but when I last talked to her she said something a bit strange. She told me she wouldn't be coming home alone.'

'You mean that the boy would be coming with her?'

'I think so,' Anita said. 'She seemed excited at the thought.'

'I don't understand how we're going to make it work. Long-distance relationships are always a hassle.'

'Yeah,' Andri said. 'I know.'

Júlía turned towards him, tipping her head on one side. 'Why don't I just come with you?' She asked as if she was joking, but Andri knew she meant it. He could hear the plea in her voice. It was so pathetic it almost made him want to cry.

Next minute she was leaning forwards and giving him a long, affectionate kiss, as if trying to force some kind of emotional response from him. When she finally pulled away, she was smiling.

'What?' she asked, all unsuspecting, completely unaware of what was going through his mind.

'I was just thinking about what it would be like if you came with me.'

'And?'

'Oh, just how sad it would be. Do you seriously want to sit around in the flat, waiting for me to finish training? What would you do with yourself all day?'

He could see that Júlía was thrown.

'I could take a distance-learning course or...'

'Or what?' Andri sat up and looked at his phone as he was talking. 'You'd be just like one of those stupid WAGS who go after footballers simply so they can go abroad with them and spend their money. Mainly to hide the sad fact that they're not capable of achieving anything on their own apart from looking like sluts on Instagram.'

'Are you joking, Andri?'

Andri looked at her, raising one eyebrow. 'No. Are you saying it's not true?'

'Yes.' Júlía pushed the duvet aside and began to pull on her jumper. 'If you think I'm like that, you've got me all wrong.'

'Oh, yeah? Because you never post slutty pics of yourself online?' Andri opened her profile and laid his phone on the bed between them. 'It's just so ... so tragic. You're so self-obsessed. I mean, look at you.'

Júlía didn't so much as glance at the phone. She slipped her shoes on and opened the door, turning to look back at him.

'Andri, I ... I don't understand what's got into you. You can call me when you're ready to apologise.'

'Oh, I can, can I?' Andri said sarcastically. 'Thank you so much. Really ... thanks a bunch.'

The door slammed so hard that the contents of the room rattled.

Andri yawned, picked up his phone again and sent a terse message:

It's over.

❧

So Lise had met a boy, but the family she was living with hadn't been aware of the fact. According to them, Lise rarely went out in the evenings and didn't have any social life to speak of. Elma knew that these days people didn't need to meet in person; they could easily get to know someone who lived in another part of the country or even abroad, for that matter. Perhaps Lise hadn't wanted to go out in Akranes because she already had a social life online, chatting to some boy who could live just about anywhere.

Or locally, Elma reminded herself. Lise could have been chatting to someone who lived nearby but was posing as a different person. There was no shortage of online creeps using fake identities. If that was the case, it would considerably expand the list of possible suspects. To make things even trickier, the police didn't have Lise's computer. They had her phone, but forensics hadn't found anything of interest there.

Elma had called Anita and asked if she remembered the exact date of the phone call during which Lise had told her she would be coming home to Amsterdam and bringing someone with her. Anita had rung back several minutes later to say that their conversation had taken place on 4 September. That meant that Lise must have been in a relationship with someone recently – with a boy who was planning to go abroad with her.

Elma was inclined to believe that this mysterious young man was someone Lise knew or had met in the flesh, rather than some shadowy figure online, because the fact remained that Lise had been found in Marinó's garden shed. It seemed implausible that a stranger would have gone round to the house, murdered her, then left her body there.

No, Elma was sure that wasn't what had happened. She was also sure that they had already met the boy Lise had been involved with, and that somebody wasn't telling the truth.

Sævar was sitting in his office, staring at his computer. In front of him was a bag of liquorice toffees and a bottle of Coke. Elma sat down by his desk and reached into the bag for a toffee, only to discover that it was empty.

'Lise was intending to take some boy home to Amsterdam with her,' she announced.

'You what?' Sævar finally tore his gaze away from the screen, rubbing his chin.

'Lise said she wasn't going home alone.' Elma loosened the

elastic band from her pony-tail and ran her fingers over the back of her head where it had been tugging at the roots of her hair.

'Where did you pick up that information?'

Elma told him about her conversation with Anita.

'I've been going over it in my head,' she said, 'and to me the most likely scenario is that Lise was involved with Andri or one of his mates. Laufey said she hardly ever went out in the evenings, so I doubt she had a chance to meet any other boys, unless it was online. Still, my money's on Andri.'

'They were both at home a lot during the day,' Sævar remarked.

'Exactly,' Elma replied. 'And could have been having a relationship without his parents knowing.'

'Yes,' Sævar agreed. 'But the question is, did that necessarily have anything to do with the deaths? I can't see why it would.'

'No,' Elma sighed. 'I can come up with all kinds of motives and scenarios, but I don't have any evidence for them. I don't even know where to look. Who can we talk to? We've already spoken to most of the people associated with Lise.'

'Yes, but someone obviously knows more than they're letting on,' Sævar said. 'We just have to find out who.'

It took less time than Hörður had been expecting to secure a warrant to examine Andri's phone and trace his movements over the last two weekends. It took longer to puzzle over what the numbers meant and work out the chronology, but Hörður eventually managed to piece together a fairly complete picture. He leant back in his chair, squinting through his glasses and reminding himself that he needed a new prescription.

Hannes still hadn't sent through the results of the post-mortem. However, he had said that he believed Lise had died the weekend of 7 to 8 September, though he couldn't be certain. His conclusion was based on the assumption that she had been in the shed the entire time and on the known temperature fluctuations during the period in question, which would affect the decomposition process.

The police were also going by when Lise had last been seen. Laufey had talked to her on the Saturday, and Andri had taken her to Marinó's that evening. There had been four other people there who could all confirm that Lise had been alive on the Saturday evening, but she hadn't been seen since. There was still a possibility, of course, that she had still been alive on the Sunday morning, since someone had removed her luggage, but, on the other hand, her body had been found in Marinó's garden, which made it unlikely she had gone back to Unnar and Laufey's house in between.

Hörður sighed aloud as he tried to collect his thoughts. If Lise hadn't fetched her luggage herself, someone with access to the house must have done it, which meant it could only have been a member of the family.

'Andri,' Hörður muttered under his breath, collecting up his papers. 'Andri Unnarsson.' A variety of clues seemed to point to him, and yet, when his phone records were examined, there turned out to be precious little evidence to support that theory.

May 2019

Lise and Klara were sitting in the kitchen with school books spread out on the table in front of them. Klara needed help with her maths homework, and Lise had volunteered. Laufey was standing at the stove, browning mince. Water was boiling in another pan, sending steam rising into the extractor fan. It was Friday, and Anna, who had been allowed to choose what they had for supper, had opted for her favourite: spaghetti bolognese. Beside the hob was a glass of red wine that Laufey was taking occasional sips from.

'Mummy,' Anna's voice came from the hall.

'Yes?' Laufey called back.

'Do you know? At gymnastics I did such a good jump that the coach said I was sure to win the tournament.' Anna came into the kitchen, her hair smoothed back in a bun.

'Great,' Laufey said, and took another sip of wine. But Anna had already gone back into the hall to practise cartwheels.

'Hi, girls.' Unnar came in and smiled at Lise and Klara. He was wearing a tailored dark-blue suit with a blue-checked shirt, his greying hair swept back. He went over to Laufey and took hold of her hips. 'Hello, love.'

'Hello you.' Laufey turned her head and they kissed.

Lise looked away and tried to concentrate on the problem in Klara's maths book. She wondered if her mother used to stand at the stove like that, and if her father went over to taste the cooking. Raising her eyes again, she watched Unnar's hands stroking Laufey's broad hips. Watched the way he leant against her and rested his chin on her shoulder.

'Where's Andri?' Laufey asked, glancing around once they were all sitting down.

'Here,' a voice called from the TV room. Andri shuffled into the room in his slippers, still typing something on his phone.

After their last outing, Lise had expected another invitation to come for a drive, but Andri had barely even looked at her. Since then, Júlía had been round to see him three times. Lise had caught herself monitoring Andri's comings and goings, as she could see the garage door from her bedroom window and often peeked out between the curtains. Sometimes she fantasised about entire conversations she might have with him. Andri wasn't someone who smiled much, which made it feel somehow special when he did. She wanted to make him smile more.

'Mummy,' Anna said, after wolfing down her food in record time. 'Is there any pudding?'

'I bought some popcorn for you in case you wanted a cosy evening with your dad,' Laufey said.

'With me?' Unnar raised his eyebrows. He had taken off his jacket and stuffed a napkin into the neck of his shirt.

'I'm going to meet Brynhildur and Peta.' Laufey put down her fork. 'I told you earlier this week.'

Unnar met his wife's eyes across the table. She lowered hers and toyed with her spaghetti.

'I though Peta was getting a divorce. Weren't you saying you were fed up with her whingeing?'

'Unnar.' Laufey laughed. 'I never said that. It was you who—'

'It doesn't matter,' Unnar interrupted. 'I've promised to go out this evening. It's work related.'

'Oh.' Laufey put down her knife and fork, and raised her glass to her lips without realising it was empty. 'What time are you planning to leave? I could be back—'

'I need to head out soon. Sorry, love. I'd completely forgotten.'

Laufey looked pleadingly at Andri. 'Could you babysit this evening, Andri? I did so want to meet up with the girls.'

'I'm going out,' Andri said, the phone vibrating in his lap.

'Who with?'

'I'll babysit,' Lise said. 'It's no problem.'

'But it's your evening off,' Laufey said.

'It's no problem,' Lise repeated. 'Really.'

'Great. That's sorted then.' Unnar smiled at Laufey, and she nodded.

'Fine. Lise will babysit.'

'You can see here that Andri's phone connected to a mast in Akureyri at 19.38 on the evening of Saturday the seventh of September. That fits, as he caught a plane back to Reykjavík just after eight p.m. Then, here, you can follow the progress of his phone all the way to Akranes. He stops moving for about half an hour, presumably at home, then goes here.' Spread out on the table was a map of Akranes, on which Hörður had marked the locations of the transmitters and the times the phone had connected to them.

'Andri was at Marinó's house until five the next morning.'

'Which means he was there with Lise,' Sævar said.

'Then this is the following weekend – the fourteenth to the fifteenth,' Hörður went on, paying no attention to Sævar. 'Andri's clearly moving around the town during the day. Here, between one and four, he's at the Jaðarsbakkar sports centre, playing a home match. At eight o'clock he's picked up by the mast near the flat of his girlfriend, Júlía, and just before two in the morning he's back home.'

'Exactly as he said.'

'The problem is,' Hörður continued, 'that Júlía lives close to Marinó's place. When I checked, forensics told me that he was connected to the same mast at both houses.'

'In other words, his phone information doesn't provide much help.'

'I'm afraid not,' Hörður said. 'Though it does confirm Andri's story and shows that he probably didn't go out again after he got home.'

'Unless he left his phone behind,' Sævar pointed out.

'So, the phone locations can't help us prove or disprove anything in this case,' Elma said.

'Right,' Hörður agreed, gathering up the papers. 'We have

nothing to locate Andri at Marinó's house around the time the fire broke out.'

'Lise and Andri weren't going out, if that's what you think,' Fríða said flatly.

Elma had gone to the café on the square where Fríða worked, ordered a cup of cocoa and a *kleina*, and asked the girl if she could have a quick word. They sat down at a table outside and, much to Elma's surprise, Fríða took out a packet of cigarettes and lit up. She'd thought young people smoked nothing but e-cigarettes these days.

'Are you sure they weren't going out?' Elma asked, trying not to breathe in the smoke.

'Of course I'm sure.'

'But friends don't always tell you everything,' Elma said. 'For example, you weren't aware that Marinó and Ísak had been fighting about Sonja. You know, I still don't quite understand why Marinó was so eager to protect her all of a sudden.'

'Oh, Sonja's good at making people feel sorry for her. She and Marinó locked themselves in his room and had this big heart-to-heart, and no doubt she told him what Ísak did to her. Marinó couldn't stand it when people behaved like bastards.'

'But she didn't confide in you? I thought you two were great friends.'

Fríða grimaced as if she found the comment irritating. She blew a stream of smoke sideways before answering. 'We…' She paused and stubbed out the cigarette. 'We are. But she's just the way she is.'

'What do you mean by that?'

'She just does what she likes and always has.'

Elma sipped her cocoa and felt the hot liquid warming her all the way down to her stomach, then took a bite of her cardamom doughnut.

'Don't you think he deserved it, though?' Privately, Elma was quite impressed at the way Marinó had sided with Sonja against his friend.

'Who? Ísak?'

'Yes. I gather he treated Sonja quite badly.'

'Look…' Fríða sighed. 'I don't want to interfere. All I'm saying is that Sonja can be a bit melodramatic sometimes, and I learnt a long time ago not to believe everything she says.'

'So she tells lies?'

'Not exactly lies. It's more like … she exaggerates things. When we were in year eight, Sonja had a crush on this boy. I mean, like, she was totally obsessed with him. She could hardly talk about anything else.' Fríða took another drink of water. 'She wasn't exactly subtle about it either. She liked all his photos and bombarded him with messages. The boy was interested at first but then he started ghosting her.'

'Ghosting?'

'Yes – oh, you know: when someone sees your messages but doesn't answer them.'

'Ignoring her,' Elma corrected.

'Whatever. Anyway, Sonja did *not* react well. She kept crying and writing poems about it. I didn't know what to do, because it wasn't like she really knew him. They weren't going out or anything. They'd only met up, like, about three times and hadn't even gone all the way. Then the boy got together with another girl, and that's when Sonja really lost it. Not with him but with the girl.' Fríða shifted in her seat, glancing around. 'She created a fake profile and started messaging the girl, pretending to be this guy who was really hot. And the girl, who was unbelievably stupid, agreed to send him photos – nudes.'

Elma frowned. 'How old was she?'

'Fourteen,' Fríða said. 'Sonja forwarded the pictures to everyone and it worked: they split up. But unfortunately, after all that, the boy still didn't want anything to do with Sonja.'

Elma felt a pang at the thought of the other girl. The poor thing had only been a child. Kids could be so cruel.

'It was the same with Ísak,' Fríða went on. 'Except he lasted a bit longer. I think Ísak liked the fact she was so crazy. Or maybe he was just interested in getting a shag. When you're fifteen, it's not that easy, but Sonja was up for it.'

'But that was when they were fifteen. They were a couple for a long time after that, weren't they?'

'A couple?' Fríða snorted. 'It was a pretty toxic relationship. Ísak was always trying to break it off, but Sonja wouldn't let him go. And for some reason Ísak always went back to her in the end. It must have been good for his ego to have Sonja so obsessed with him. But one day he just said it was over. Sonja waited, thinking he'd come crawling back, but he didn't.'

'When was this?'

'About a year ago.' A couple walked past and went into the café. Fríða paused until they had gone inside. 'But then Sonja told him she was pregnant, and Ísak, idiot that he is, got back together with her, wanting to do the right thing. Maybe it's because he was brought up by a single mother himself.'

'I see,' Elma said. 'But the relationship still didn't work?'

'No.' Fríða shifted uncomfortably in her chair again. 'Not for long. It worked at first; they stayed together until Jóel was born, but then you know how it ended.'

Elma nodded.

'Look, Sonja's my friend and all that, but she doesn't always tell the truth. The thing is, I know she wasn't pregnant when she told Ísak she was. She'd asked me for a tampon, like, the day before, and then the baby arrived ten months later. I mean, I know babies can be overdue, but ten months is pushing it.'

'Didn't Ísak notice?'

'Ísak?' Fríða snorted again. 'No.'

Elma finished her cocoa and put down her cup. Fríða made as if to stand up.

'About Lise,' Elma said hastily, before the girl could leave. 'When did you first meet her?'

'Lise came along with Andri when we met up to play games back in the spring.'

'Did she say anything about a boy she was seeing?'

'No, nothing like that. She didn't say much at all.'

'And you're absolutely sure there was nothing going on between her and Andri?'

'Positive.' Fríða shivered and hugged herself as a chilly gust of wind swept over them.

'You were at the party two weeks ago when Lise arrived with Andri. How did she seem?'

'She was quite drunk. I went home early that evening but, when I left, Sonja, Marinó, Andri and Lise were still there, and they were all quite pissed. Even Andri.'

'Is it unusual for him to drink?'

'Yes; technically he's not supposed to.' Seeing Elma's expression, Fríða explained: 'Because of the football.'

'Oh, I see.'

'I've never really seen him drunk before, but that evening...' Fríða wrinkled her brow, thinking back. 'That evening he was totally wasted. I've never known him like that.'

Elma could tell that something was troubling Fríða and waited for her to say more. But, as if she'd picked up on this, Fríða just smiled.

'I expect I made the cocktails too strong. Marinó and I mixed them before the others arrived.'

Elma smiled too, then was taken aback to see a tear trickling down Fríða's cheek. The girl wiped it angrily away, breathing hard through her nose.

'Sorry, I...' Fríða's voice broke and tears started pouring down her cheeks. 'I just can't stop thinking about those last few days. Marinó and I kept fighting because ... because he wouldn't let me have the car. Like that even mattered.'

Elma remembered the words of the woman next door who had heard the twins quarrelling. 'Most siblings fight,' she said. 'Believe me, I know what I'm talking about.'

Fríða smiled sadly through her tears. 'I just miss Marinó so much.'

The bed was unmade and the curtains were still closed when Elma got home that evening. She opened the garden door to air the place, then switched on the TV, not because she wanted to watch it but because she didn't like the silence. Noise made the flat feel more homely, and that was what she wanted right now. The phone rang and she flopped onto the sofa before answering.

'Have you eaten?' Aðalheiður asked, without so much as saying hello.

'Yes, Mum.' Sometimes she wondered if her mother realised how old she was. Aðalheiður didn't treat Dagný like that, although she was only three years older. Perhaps it was because Dagný had a husband and two children. Their mother had dispensed with the maternal duties towards her but felt she still owed them to Elma.

'What did you have?'

'Do you want the menu for the whole day or just supper?' Phone tucked under her chin, Elma opened her laptop.

'You need to look after yourself, Elma. Especially now.'

Elma had a sudden vision of what the next few months would be like. Now that her mother knew she was pregnant, she would have no peace at all.

'Actually, I was just about to make supper,' she admitted. 'But I had a banana earlier. And an energy bar.'

'It's nearly nine o'clock,' Aðalheiður pointed out. 'You know you're always welcome to have dinner here. I cooked an Indian meal for me and your dad, and made one of those cucumber and yoghurt sauces to go with it. It was absolutely delicious – your dad had three helpings. And he claims he's not keen on curry.

There are still some leftovers. If you come over now, I'll heat them up for you.'

'To be honest, I'm completely knackered,' Elma said. 'But I'll come over tomorrow.'

'All right, whatever you like, dear.'

There was a brief silence. Elma sensed that her mother wanted to say something.

'I can understand that you're tired. Maybe you should talk to Hörður and—'

'No, that won't be necessary,' Elma interrupted. 'Everything's fine. Honestly, Mum.'

'All right. Have you made an appointment with the midwife? Oh, what am I talking about? Naturally you'll go to your sister. If you like, I can come with you, if there's no father in the picture.'

'*Mum.*'

'I'm only asking. So there is a father?'

'Right, I'm going to heat something up for supper.'

After Elma had finally managed to end the conversation, she let out a groan of exasperation. Her mother meant well but she always went too far. Elma got up and looked in the freezer compartment of the fridge. Rejecting the frozen pizza, she settled for a bowl of muesli and buttermilk instead.

While she was devouring this, she had another look at Andri's social-media profiles. His pages were all open to the public, allowing her to see his friend lists and any number of pictures. Most were football related and had been posted by other people. Andri didn't seem to be very active himself, though he had a large number of friends and followers.

Elma opened his friend list and typed in the name 'Lena'. The search returned a single result, but the Lena in question was Icelandic and therefore not the one she wanted. Of course, the simplest thing would be to get the previous au pair's name from Laufey and Unnar, but how was Elma supposed to explain her request? She could hardly say that she suspected something dodgy had happened in their house and that their son was involved.

Without warning, a memory popped up on her Facebook page. It was a photograph of her that Davíð had posted when she graduated from police training college. He had added a nice message, as they always used to in those days. Elma remembered that evening so well. They had gone out to dinner together to celebrate her achievement. Later, in the summer, Davíð had surprised her with flight tickets to Berlin. In the period leading up to the trip, their relationship had been unusually close, reminiscent of when they had first got together. They hadn't been able to keep their hands off each other.

During the Berlin holiday, however, Elma got to see a darker side of Davíð, which she had only caught glimpses of before. One evening they went out for a posh dinner at the kind of restaurant where the waiters put one arm behind their backs when they pour the wine. Elma and Davíð felt like kids who had accidentally wandered into the world of the grown-up smart set. They drank far too much and giggled like idiots, and afterwards they went to a sleazy bar. There they spent a long time kissing on the dance floor in between dancing. At some point, Elma went to the bar, and a young man offered to buy her a drink. She didn't accept – not that this made any difference. Without warning, Davíð materialised at her side and punched the young man in the face, while Elma stood there frozen with shock. She watched helplessly as people came running over, men lost their tempers and drinks got spilt on the floor. After that, she lost sight of Davíð and couldn't find him anywhere. Not at the bar or in their hotel room or in the hotel bar. She rang his number repeatedly all night, but there was no answer. He didn't reappear until towards lunchtime the next day, refusing to say where he had been. They had spent the rest of the holiday in suffocating silence.

Elma closed her eyes, pushing away a tide of self-recrimination. She had been so angry. So furious with him for doing that to her. She'd punished him for days, and after they got home, their relationship had undergone a change. From then on, it had seesawed between good times and bad. Elma had blamed Davíð and his mood-swings. But now she blamed herself for not spotting what was wrong and urging him to seek help.

It was too late now. He had gone and would never come back. He would never have a chance to be the father he had so often talked about becoming one day. This made it feel unfair somehow that she should get to be a mother.

The phone distracted her again, this time with a message from Sævar:

Home?

Elma wrote a message, then deleted it and composed a new one. She had been planning to tell him about the baby this evening but if she received him like this, her face puffy from weeping, she'd probably frighten him away. Instead she wrote:

Yes but falling asleep. See you tomorrow?

Sævar's answer came back instantly.

Sure, good night ☺

Elma switched her phone to silent and put it down. She forced her mind away from Davíð and concentrated instead on a spot of online research. First she checked Unnar and Laufey's friend lists, then she visited various au-pair agency websites and tried searching for 'Lena'. She realised what a foolish undertaking this was when she was inundated with results. It turned out Lena was a common name in Poland, and Elma had no idea of the girl's surname or what she looked like. Come to think of it, if she'd had a bad experience with Laufey and Unnar, chances were she wouldn't be on the au-pair site any longer.

Elma went back to Laufey's Facebook page and scrolled through the family pictures. There were no photos of Lise or Lena but countless ones of her two daughters and Andri. Beside one picture it was possible to click on the name Klara Unnarsdóttir, and this led Elma to the little girl's Facebook page.

She was surprised that such a young child should have her own page, but Klara only had thirty-two friends and there were no photos of her. Elma scrolled down her friend list and her heart skipped a beat when she saw the name she was looking for.

Lena Maja Kaminski.

Elma clicked on it but was disappointed to discover that Lena's page was locked. She opened Messenger and put down the bowl of muesli without finishing it.

Having composed a brief message to Lena, she sent it, then waited a few minutes to see if the girl would answer. There was no response. In the end, Elma closed the computer, turned off the TV and crawled into bed.

May 2019

Lise knocked on the door of Klara's room, then opened it. The girl was sitting in bed, reading. The dim wall lamp cast a warm glow on her unruly mop of hair.

'What are you reading?'

Klara held up the book.

'Girls in Love,' Lise read.

'It's not really that kind of story,' Klara muttered, putting it down. 'It's a book about girls who are friends.'

Lise laughed. 'I know, I've read it.'

'Have you?'

'Yes. When I was your age, I read everything I could lay my hands on. I wanted to be a writer when I grew up.'

'Did you?'

'But then I realised it's incredibly difficult and you don't make any money. Or at least very few people do. But my dad always encouraged me to keep going. He even gave me a book to write in.'

'What kind of book?'

'Like a sort of diary. Only with blank pages. But I think he actually wanted me to write stories.'

'Did you write any stories in it?'

'No,' Lise said, picturing the green book that was now hidden between the mattress and the wall in her bedroom. 'No, not stories. Just … silly stuff.'

'What kind of stuff?' Klara asked.

'Just silly stuff.' Lise smiled. 'Anyway, you need to go to sleep now. Night, night, Klara.'

Klara took off her red glasses and put them on the bedside table.

She yawned, wriggled down in the bed and pulled the duvet up to her chin. 'Night, Lise.'

Lise closed the door gently, smiling to herself.

The TV was on in the other room, but she decided to switch it off and spend the evening reading instead. The conversation with Klara had made her long suddenly to immerse herself in a book. Unnar and Laufey wouldn't be home until late.

She stopped dead in the doorway when she saw Unnar stretched out on the chaise-end sofa. He was wearing his suit trousers and a dark-blue shirt, and had loosened the knot of his tie. In one hand he was holding the remote control and, in the other, a glass containing something that definitely wasn't water.

'Oh, hi,' he said. 'Are the girls asleep?'

'Yes,' Lise replied. 'You're home early.'

'Am I?' Unnar glanced at his watch. 'Isn't Laufey back yet?'

'No.'

Lise thought she saw Unnar's jaw muscles tense.

'Have you seen this film?' He put down the remote control, sat up a little and gestured at the TV with his glass. He was far more relaxed than Lise was accustomed to seeing him, and this made him seem much younger.

Lise looked briefly at the TV screen but didn't recognise the actors. 'No. I was planning to read this evening.'

'It's Tarantino. A classic.'

Lise hovered in the doorway.

'Sit down.' Unnar patted the sofa beside him. 'Come and watch it with me.'

'I...'

'I insist.' Unnar smiled but his voice was firm.

Lise sat down hesitantly at the far end of the sofa, tucking her legs under her.

'Don't move.' Unnar swayed slightly when he stood up and had to take an extra step to recover his balance. When he came back, he was carrying a glass containing clear liquid and a slice of lemon.

'Gin and tonic for the lady,' he said, handing it to her.

'But I…' Lise looked down into the glass, where tiny air bubbles were popping with a soft, fizzing sound. She rarely touched alcohol and hadn't for a moment expected to drink with her host family.

'Drink up,' Unnar ordered, sitting down on the sofa again, closer to her than before. 'Cheers.'

There was a clink of glasses, and Lise took a sip.

'You have had alcohol before, haven't you? I'm not corrupting you?'

'No, don't worry,' Lise said. 'I've had alcohol before but I don't actually drink much. The first time I tried, I massively overdid it and ended up being sick on my friend Anita's parents' sofa. She took the blame and said she'd been ill, but they could smell the alcohol and grounded her for a month.' Lise bit her tongue, telling herself to stop chattering.

'You're a dark horse.' Unnar laughed. 'Tell me more. How old were you?'

'Sixteen.' Lise traced the pattern on the glass with one finger. 'Dad was mad. He said if Mum was still alive I wouldn't have behaved like that. I told him it didn't make any difference. It wasn't his fault; teenagers were just like that. I ended up having to comfort him. I suppose that's why that phase ended almost before it began.'

'How old were you when your mother died?'

'Nine. But I can hardly remember her.'

'You must remember something?' Unnar said gently.

'I remember some of the things we did and said, but when I close my eyes and try to picture her face, all I can see is photos of her. Sometimes it's like the photos have blotted out the actual memories, because I can't remember her talking or laughing or moving at all. She's always just … still.' Lise took a large gulp of her drink and made a face at the bitter taste. Unnar put a hand on her back and stroked it warily.

'I feel like…' Unnar broke off, then smiled at her. 'I hope this won't come out sounding wrong, because I don't want to make you uncomfortable or anything, but ever since you arrived I've had the feeling you're older than your years. Has anyone ever told you you're an old soul?'

'Yes.' Lise smiled but felt a lump forming in her throat. 'My dad always used to say that.'

Unnar watched her, his silence saying more than words. Lise felt safe. She felt happy. She took another mouthful of gin, and Unnar turned up the volume again. His hand was still there, and Lise leant back until his arm was half around her. She had a sudden flashback to watching films with her father when she was young. His big body had felt like a sea of warmth and softness that she used to let herself sink into.

Her glass was empty before Lise finally dared to ask: 'Are … are you and Laufey happy together?'

Unnar withdrew his arm and bent forwards, his elbows on his knees, and Lise immediately regretted having asked.

'All I mean is that you seem so good together,' she added hurriedly. 'Just like I imagine my parents would have been if…'

'That's a hard one to answer.' Unnar rubbed his chin. 'Laufey's changed since we were young. I expect we both have, but … but I suppose the truth is that sometimes we're happy and other times we're not.'

'I understand,' Lise said, nodding.

'Do you?' Unnar looked round at her, apparently amused. 'Anyway, you'll understand when you're older and have a husband of your own. Marriages are far from straightforward. Sometimes it's like Laufey pounces on tiny things that don't matter and blows them up out of all proportion until they seem so huge that they get in the way of everything else. And of course I've got my faults too – I work too hard.' Unnar sighed. 'Sorry, am I being boring?'

'No,' Lise said. 'I understand what you mean.'

Unnar's eyes gazed into hers. Their colour reminded her of a forest, wild and primitive.

'You know,' Unnar said, 'you're going to make some man very happy one day.'

Lise laughed, but Unnar didn't stop smiling. There was something sad about his smile. Something she didn't quite understand. She stopped laughing and for a long moment they gazed at each other. The world seemed to stand still. Lise felt her heart beating faster. She didn't know what was happening but she was aware of him leaning closer, as if something was drawing him towards her. But then he seemed to come to his senses.

'Wow.' He laughed and shook his head. 'Sorry, I'm not quite myself. I've probably had a few drinks too many. I should go to bed.'

'Me too.' Lise tried to slow her shallow breathing. Her heart was beating so fast it felt as if it was trying to break its way out of her chest.

Unnar gave her a parting look.

'Lise, Lise,' he said, with a crooked smile. 'You're really special, you know that?'

Tuesday

Elma had scoffed down five cinnamon biscuits while waiting for Hörður to finish reading through the provisional report from the pathologist.

'That took a while,' Hörður said eventually. 'It seems quite complicated.'

He licked his index finger and separated two pages, then adjusted his glasses before beginning. 'I have to admit that Hannes's report is rather unexpected. He's not entirely confident about the conclusions himself, as it's a rare case – if he turns out to be right. It, er...' Hörður broke off mid-sentence and leafed through the pages.

Sævar and Elma exchanged impatient glances. What was he on about?

'You see, um...' Hörður resumed, 'Lise died from the impact of a blow to the back of her head. During the post-mortem, a bruise was found on her frontal lobe and there was evidence of a subdural haematoma.'

'But surely the frontal lobe is at the front of the head?' Sævar asked, puzzled.

'Yes, but the blow caused concussion and this produced a bruise on the frontal lobe,' Hörður replied. 'I don't quite understand how, but that's what Hannes says here. In layman's terms, a subdural haematoma is bleeding in the brain. But that doesn't necessarily mean that the blow was particularly hard. In other words, most people wouldn't have died from it.' Hörður took off his glasses and rested both elbows on the table. 'Hannes explained that the haematoma is made up of a lot of smaller bleeds that should, in normal circumstances, simply heal, causing little or no lasting damage. In Lise's case, however, the haemorrhage spread and grew on the outer part of the brain, forming a pool of blood, which then burst, with fatal consequences.'

Neither Elma nor Sævar said anything.

Hörður waved his hands. 'I know, I know, it's hard to get your head round. I had to read it several times myself. But the significant part is that the process could have taken several hours. Possibly even several days.'

'Let me get this straight,' Elma said frowning. 'You're saying that Lise could have received the blow several days before she died. But how…?'

'Yes, according to Hannes. Lise received a blow and would probably have felt a bit dizzy afterwards and suffered from the typical symptoms of concussion, but she would have remained conscious. She may have felt unwell, had a headache and been tired or nauseous. Then the pool of blood burst and she just…'

'She dropped down dead,' Sævar finished.

Hörður nodded.

'But you said that normally that kind of injury would just heal by itself. Why not in Lise's case?'

'Apparently she had a bleeding disorder that meant her blood didn't clot properly. She couldn't take blood thinners, for example. Hannes called her family doctor in the Netherlands for confirmation.'

'So it's possible no one laid a finger on her at the party? She could have received the blow some time earlier, and there's no way of telling exactly when?'

'Right,' Hörður said. 'But she died that evening at the party, and it was presumably Marinó or one of the others who put her in the shed to hide her body.'

'But why?' Elma asked. 'Why not call an ambulance?'

'I have no idea,' Hörður replied.

'Were there any other injuries on her body?' Sævar asked.

'No signs of sexual violence; only that bruise on her arm: a bruise that could have been acquired at the same time as the blow to her head.'

'Could the blow have happened by accident?' Sævar asked. 'I mean, are we sure someone hit her? Couldn't she just have bumped her head?'

'The bruise on her arm suggests otherwise. Hannes reckoned the injuries were consistent with someone having slammed her against a wall, for instance.'

'Could he work out when it happened?'

'One to two days earlier.'

'So it could have been anyone?' Elma let out a defeated sigh. 'Then what are we going to do?'

'There's one other thing you should know, which raises some interesting questions,' Hörður said. 'It seems our guess was right and that Lise was sleeping with someone – that's what you thought, wasn't it, Elma?'

'Yes. Her friend, Anita, said she wasn't planning to come back to Amsterdam alone.'

'Ah,' Hörður said. 'Well, she was probably right, because, according to Hannes, Lise had suffered a miscarriage shortly before she died.'

❧

'Now, turning to the first item on the agenda, item number…'

Laufey switched off the minute the chair started talking, though the subject itself was interesting and one of her pet causes: how to encourage businesses in Akranes to become more sustainable and environmentally friendly. During the election campaign she had devoted most of her time to this policy area, making speeches about companies' social responsibility. She had pored over academic articles evening after evening until she had it all off pat and could field any questions she might be asked.

She took a mouthful of soda water and tried, unsuccessfully, to concentrate on what the first speaker was saying. Just then, her phone started vibrating in her pocket, and she pressed the side button to stop it. No one seemed to notice.

'Some businesses have a much bigger carbon footprint than others, and these are the ones we should be focusing on. We need to implement policies and—'

Laufey's phone started vibrating again and this time several heads turned to look at her. Laufey smiled apologetically, hastily killed the call, then checked to see who had been trying to reach her: Unnar.

Since Lise left, he'd had to come home early to look after the girls on the days when Laufey had council meetings.

During the coffee break, Einar came over to talk to her.

'I heard that the girl they found was your au pair. Is that true?'

'Yes,' Laufey said. 'Yes, Lise. It's absolutely terrible.'

'What exactly happened to her?' asked Vigdís, who had turned round to listen.

Vigdís had been on the council for ten years and had a peculiar knack of making Laufey feel inadequate. Sometimes, when Laufey was making speeches, she caught Vigdís smirking contemptuously. Once, Vigdís had asked who wanted coffee, then made a cup for everyone except Laufey. Although Laufey tried not to read too much into it, she couldn't help being a little intimidated by Vigdís. This was the first time the woman had looked genuinely interested in hearing what she had to say.

'I haven't a clue,' Laufey replied. 'It must have been an accident. I can't believe—'

'It was your son who took her to the party, wasn't it?' Vigdís said.

Laufey could feel her face reddening. 'Yes, but—'

'Doesn't he know what happened?'

'No, of course not,' Laufey said, hearing how angry she sounded.

'Yes, I'm sure it was an accident,' Einar said, coming to her rescue. 'Still, it's pretty strange that they found her in the shed. She can hardly have crawled in there herself.'

'I heard she'd been wrapped in some kind of plastic sheeting,' Tryggvi remarked. He was the most conservative member of the council, and Laufey often wanted to tear her hair out when she was forced to listen to him droning on. 'A colleague of mine lives nearby and saw them carrying her out.'

'You can't help thinking it must be connected to the fire,' Vigdís said, and several other people agreed. 'It looks like that boy Marinó had something on his conscience.'

'What rubbish,' Laufey blurted out, and all heads turned to look at her again.

Vigdís raised her eyebrows, and her supercilious expression was the final straw.

Laufey snapped. 'Honestly, the way you lot gossip. If your constituents could hear some of the rubbish you come out with at council meetings.' She took her jacket from the back of her chair and tucked it under her arm. 'I've had to listen to you talking about all kinds of stuff since I joined the council, but this really is the limit. Spreading rumours like that about a young man who's just lost his life in tragic circumstances.'

She was still shaking when she got in the car and took hold of the steering wheel, her face burning, her armpits sweating. But at the same time a frisson of pleasure was running through her body. At last, she'd had the guts to speak her mind. At last.

When she got home, Anna was nowhere to be seen, but Klara was sitting at the kitchen table, eating ice-cream. It was just after seven, the house was silent, and the soup she had asked Unnar to warm up was still sitting on the countertop.

'Where's Daddy?' Laufey asked, removing the tub of ice-cream from the table and putting it back in the freezer.

'He had to go out,' Klara said, licking her spoon.

'Go out? Where to?' Laufey had tried to ring Unnar after the meeting, but his phone had been switched off. She got out a saucepan, poured the soup into it and turned on the oven. She could feel the elation from the meeting fading fast, to be replaced by a heavy burden of anxiety.

'I don't know.'

'Didn't he say?'

'No. But he tried to call you.'

'Yes, I saw.'

'He said he'd be quick.' Klara stood up, sniffing the air. 'What's that?' she asked.

'Chicken soup. It's very good.' Laufey put some frozen baguettes in the oven and checked her phone. 'What time did he go out?'

'I don't know. Just after you.'

Laufey tried calling again, but his phone was still off. She decided to see what Anna was up to and found her in her room, lying in bed. Laufey saw at once from her red eyes that she had been crying.

'What's happened?' she asked, sitting down on the bed.

Although you could fault Anna for many things, she was no cry-baby. She was the one you could always count on to be brave.

'Is something wrong?'

'Mummy?'

'Yes?'

'What happened to Lise?'

'I don't know, darling.'

'Is she dead?'

'Yes. Yes, she's dead.' Laufey wanted to add that Lise had gone to a better place, but it sounded so hollow. The truth was that she hadn't a clue where Lise was now.

'I'm scared,' Anna whispered.

'Scared? What of?'

'I didn't want to be alone here. I begged Daddy not to go out, because…'

'Because of what?' Laufey stroked her forehead. 'You girls have often been alone at home for a short while. Why are you frightened now?'

But Anna refused to say, and in the end Laufey gave up and told both girls to go and watch TV.

Afterwards, she stood in the hall for a while, wondering what could have set this off. Why was Anna so frightened, and what had caused Unnar to rush out like that? He knew she hated the girls being left alone. Even though they weren't little children anymore, there was no guarantee that they would know how to react if there was a problem. Especially when Klara was drawing in her room, oblivious to everything, and Anna was running around, getting up to God knows what mischief.

Laufey's gaze fell on Unnar's laptop case, which was leaning against the wall in the hall. It was unusual for him to leave it lying around. As a rule, he kept it in the car, though Laufey told him it wasn't safe and that the damp could damage it. Now she came to think about it, she had never actually opened the bag. She'd never had any reason to, as all it contained was Unnar's laptop and other work-related stuff. Or so she'd assumed.

Laufey glanced towards the TV room. The girls had been allowed to choose a film and could be relied on not to emerge until they were summoned to eat. Laufey turned down the soup and went over to the bag. Unnar had bought it himself; a plain black design with a broad shoulder strap. Moving quickly, she picked it up, went into the bedroom and locked the door. Her heart was pounding, silly though it was. After all, there was no reason why she shouldn't touch his laptop bag.

Laufey took out his computer and laid it on the bed. It was password protected but that wasn't a problem. Unnar had been using the same password ever since computers first arrived on the scene and he was unlikely to change now. Laufey smiled when she was proved right, then jumped nervously as the loud start-up chime echoed around the room. She strained her ears for sounds indicating that Unnar had come home, then, hearing only the noise of the television, she returned her attention to the laptop. She clicked on a small envelope in the corner of the screen and his email program opened.

There were countless messages, most of them clearly work related. It would take her forever to go through them all. She wasn't even sure what she was looking for or expecting to find, since she had limited interest in Unnar's exchanges with his colleagues. But then she noticed an open window from a chat Unnar had been having with Tómas. Laufey knew Tómas quite well, as he and Unnar had been working together for years. Unfortunately, he had split up from his wife, who used to be the life and soul of the party. Since her departure, Laufey had found Unnar's work events much more of a drag, though it was a while since she had been to any. It must be a year since his last annual work do, when Tómas had brought along his new girlfriend, Helena. Such a nice girl, though closer in age to Andri than them. Laufey couldn't understand what such a pretty girl was doing with Tómas.

She saw that Tómas and Unnar had last chatted earlier that day, when they had agreed that lunch in the canteen wasn't up to much and they should go out to eat instead. Laufey skimmed through their chats, scrolling up and up until she came across a photo Tómas had sent. She was so shocked that her first reaction was to avert her eyes. The picture was of Helena, asleep in bed, one leg covered by the duvet but the rest of her stark naked. Laufey was horrified. She couldn't believe Tómas was capable of sending a picture like that. Didn't he have a daughter who was almost the same age? Laufey closed the photo, but then it occurred to her that there might be more. She opened the window again and used the arrow keys to jump to the previous photo they had shared. This time it showed not Helena but another girl, a girl Laufey knew only too well.

July 2019

The midnight sun shouldn't have taken her by surprise. She knew quite a lot about Iceland, and her dad had often talked to her about the bright summer nights, but Lise hadn't expected them to mess up her sleep patterns like this. All summer long she'd had trouble dropping off in the evenings, then found herself wide awake in the early hours when everyone else was still fast asleep. During the day she felt slow and sluggish, her thoughts seeming to slip away from her before they were fully formed. On the one hand, she couldn't sleep; on the other, she never felt properly awake. More than anything, though, she felt foolish.

That had nothing to do with the midnight sun but with Unnar. Ever since the evening he'd come home drunk and they'd sat side by side in front of the television, she hadn't been able to stop thinking about him. For a while she had let herself believe that there was something between them. Now, as she lay sleepless in bed, she blushed at the thought of how stupid she'd been. How childish and downright wicked. Her thoughts flew to Laufey, to the girls and Andri. She was so ashamed that she, Lise, a silly girl of nineteen, should for one minute imagine that she could move into their home and do something that terrible.

Unnar had been avoiding her since that evening, rarely showing his face at home. Lise noticed that Laufey behaved as if nothing was wrong, but she suspected their marriage was pretty rocky.

Lise turned over on her side and hugged the pillow. It was getting on for two in the morning, and what she longed for more than anything else was to go home. She wanted to pick up the phone and call Anita. Tell her that she had been right. At that moment Lise tensed, hearing a car stop outside. The music in the car was switched off, then the door closed and there was the faint click of the lock. Lise listened for footsteps, waiting to hear them go past her window, followed by the sound of the garage door opening. She pictured Andri slouching along, hands in his pockets, a little bandy-legged.

His transfer to the team in Sweden had been confirmed, and the media had announced the news, accompanied by a photo of Andri with his coach. Laufey could hardly contain her joy, and that evening they had gone out to dinner, all except Unnar, who was working late. Lise could tell that this got on Laufey's nerves, because after she finished talking to him, she had stared at the phone for a long moment, her face blank, before taking a deep breath and putting on a smile again with a visible effort.

Just then, the bedroom door moved slightly, and Lise jumped. There was a draught.

That meant someone had opened the front door. More, it meant that the person who had just come home was not Andri but Unnar.

Lise closed her eyes and listened. She heard soft footsteps in the hall, followed by the sound of the fridge opening. There was a quiet hiss from a can of fizzy drink. An interval of silence followed. Lise lay perfectly still, hardly daring to breathe. Though she had done her best to distract her waking mind from thinking about Unnar, her unconscious seemed to have other plans, because whenever she fell asleep she dreamt about him, and in all her dreams she thought she was Laufey. That Unnar was hers. That they were a family.

She started up when the parquet creaked outside her room. There was a tap. Two soft taps. For a moment she wasn't sure if there really was someone at the door. Perhaps she had just dozed off, or it was the wind outside. But she got up anyway and opened it warily, and there he was. Lise's heart gave a lurch. She couldn't speak.

'Can I come in?' Unnar smiled his crooked smile, and Lise took a step backwards. He looked around him then sat down on her bed.

'Shut the door,' he said quietly, and she obeyed.

'I think we need to talk,' he said.

Lise could smell the alcohol on his breath. His eyes were red; his shirt was crumpled and stained where something wet had dripped on it. She stood there awkwardly until Unnar patted the bed beside him.

'I don't bite.' He grinned.

Lise sat down, putting as much distance between them as she could.

A little while passed before Unnar said anything. He stared at her, rubbing his fingers together, seeming nervous. Then he smiled boyishly, and Lise felt the age difference between them melt away. It was like sitting in her room with a boy she fancied, not knowing what to say or do. Her heart pounding, she returned his smile.

'Lise, I ... I don't know how...' Unnar heaved a sigh and shook his head. 'I shouldn't tell you this but I can't stop thinking about you. Sorry. I'll go if you like. I'll go now, OK?'

But he didn't go, and Lise didn't want him to.

'What ... why?'

'Why do I think about you?' Unnar smiled again. 'Because you're clever and fun and so, so beautiful. Lise, you're ... you're incredible. I know I shouldn't be saying this. You must see me as some old man but...'

'No,' Lise whispered. 'No, I don't.'

Unnar hesitated, then reached out a hand and she took it. They sat like that for a while, their fingers entwined. So little contact, yet it felt so intimate. Then Unnar pulled her towards him, and all her doubts were drowned in the warmth of his body.

The phone had been silent all evening, and Sonja was tired of waiting. It felt as if she'd spent her whole life waiting for men. Not just Ísak but her father too. For years she had waited every other weekend for a phone call from him, a phone call that didn't always happen. The times her father did ring, she would wait for him to come and collect her, and while they were together, she would wait for him to talk to her, but he didn't. Their conversations were limited to questions about whether she wanted an ice-cream or would be staying for supper.

When her father told her she was going to be a big sister, she was so excited. His new wife was pregnant, and for months Sonja had waited impatiently for her little brother to be born. But when the baby finally arrived, it was her mother who broke the news to her, and Sonja had to wait a year before she actually got to meet him. By then he was one and started bawling when she tried to hold him because he didn't know who she was. And to think she had imagined that her little brother would bring her and her father together. She'd pictured herself kissing and cuddling and playing with him. But she'd been wrong. After the baby was born, her daddy weekends became even fewer and further between, until in the end she grew to despise her little show-off of a brother.

She never spoke about it to her father and hated herself for that. There was so much she wanted to say, but instead she had just nodded when he asked one day if she wasn't too big now for daddy weekends. It was two years since she had last seen him, and even then it had only been by chance. She had bumped into him in Reykjavík, in the Kringlan shopping centre, with his wife and the three children who were supposed to be her brothers and sisters, though she could hardly remember their names.

Well, Sonja was done with waiting. She took out her phone and was about to tap in a number, when the entry phone rang with a loud, peremptory buzz. At first she thought it was kids mucking about, but then she heard Fríða's voice and let her in.

Sonja saw at once that something was wrong. Fríða's eyes were red, and she refused to come any further inside than the hall.

'What did you say to Marinó the evening before ... before he died?' Fríða asked, not even bothering to say hello.

'What did I say?' Sonja stared at her friend. 'I told him what happened with Ísak.'

'What about Ísak?'

'You know, about what he did to me.'

'Sonja,' Fríða said. 'What did he actually do to you?'

'You know what he did. He...'

'Yes, yes, all right.' Fríða hesitated. 'I reckon you know more than you're letting on, Sonja. I haven't been able to stop thinking about it for a minute since Marinó died. I know there was something going on between you. I don't know exactly what, but there was definitely something. And I'm going to find out what happened, both for Lise and my brother's sake.'

'Isn't it obvious?' Sonja whispered.

'No. No, I don't think it is obvious.' Fríða's eyes narrowed. 'What do you think is so obvious?'

'Fríða, I know it's difficult for you to believe that your brother could have done something so terrible, but he said it himself. Surely you remember what he kept repeating all evening? He kept asking what he'd done. Like he was full of regret about something. And I'm pretty sure he wasn't referring to Ísak.'

'So you think Marinó hid ... hid Lise in the shed? That he killed her?' Fríða's eyes blazed. 'Seriously, Sonja? Didn't you know him better than that? Marinó would never have done anything like that.'

'I just ... I don't know.' Sonja lowered her eyes. 'Sorry, Fríða. I didn't mean...'

'Oh, shut up, Sonja.' Fríða had raised her voice, and Sonja could hear that Jóel had woken up in the bedroom.

'Fríða, I really don't know what you're implying,' Sonja said. 'I'm so sorry about what happened and of course I don't think Marinó did anything to Lise.'

Fríða burst out laughing.

'What?' Sonja asked, bewildered. She had never seen Fríða like this before. It was almost as if she was finding it hard to control herself, as if she wanted to attack Sonja.

'I know you're lying. Remember, I know you, Sonja.'

'But—'

'Forget it.' Fríða opened the door of the flat. 'I know you well enough to tell when you're lying, and I'm warning you, the truth's going to come out sooner or later. Don't think you've got away with it.'

'Fríða…' Sonja began, but before she could say any more, Fríða had slammed the door in her face.

Anna couldn't sleep. She hadn't been able to sleep for nights and nights. Every time she got into bed and turned off the light, the shadows would start moving around her room, and she could feel her body growing weak and helpless. She couldn't move. She didn't dare get out of bed for fear that a hand would grab her legs; didn't dare peer out of the window again because *she* might be standing outside, looking in.

When Anna had plucked up enough courage, she jumped out of bed, and ran as fast and quietly as she could to the room next door.

'Klara,' she whispered, sitting on her sister's bed, hurriedly pulling up her feet so no unseen hand could grab them.

'Mm,' Klara mumbled.

'Can I sleep with you?'

Klara didn't answer, just budged up a little so Anna could lie down beside her. Klara's bed was softer and more comfortable than Anna's, perhaps because Anna never took any notice of her mother and was always jumping around on the bed with her friends, leaving sand and crumbs on the sheets.

'Klara,' she whispered again, after a brief silence.

'Go to sleep, Anna.'

'I...' Anna hesitated, then made herself say it: 'I saw Lise.'

For a moment, Anna thought Klara hadn't heard her, then her sister turned over, suddenly wide awake.

'I'm not messing,' Anna said hurriedly. 'I've seen her before. She ... she was in our garden and ... she wanted to come in.'

Her words hung in the air, and Anna shuddered when she thought about that night. She had woken up needing a pee and gone into the bathroom where there was a door you could open out into the garden. She'd been sitting on the loo, half asleep, when suddenly she spotted a movement. Stiffening, not daring to blink, she had stared through the glass panel in the door at the girl standing in their garden.

'Are ghosts real, Klara?'

'No.' Klara's voice sounded unconvincing.

'But it was Lise,' Anna whimpered. She wiped away a tear and felt herself shivering. She wanted to pull the duvet over her head and cuddle up as close to Klara as she could. It wasn't that she didn't want to see Lise; it wasn't her she was frightened of. Lise had been kind and played with her. She'd been her friend.

But Lise was dead, and Anna knew that when people died they didn't come back. Dead people didn't creep around in gardens, peering through the windows. Yet she had seen Lise's long dark hair blowing in the wind when she leant against the window and looked in.

'I know, Anna.'

Anna looked at Klara and saw in the dim light that her sister was staring at her with her eyes wide open.

'I know because...' Klara gulped, then whispered so quietly that Anna could barely hear her. 'I saw Lise too.'

September 2019

It was a mistake, Unnar had said. The moment he sat up in bed, he'd turned to her and said it was a mistake. He just hadn't been able to stop himself after struggling to control his feelings for so long.

Lise was well aware that it was a mistake. As if it wasn't bad enough that Unnar was forty-five and she was only nineteen, he was married too, with children. She felt so bad about Laufey that she could hardly meet her eye. She felt as if her betrayal was stamped on her forehead in bold, black letters.

Stupid, stupid girl, she told herself over and over again. How could she have been such a fool?

It was the beginning of September and she was sitting in the bathroom, staring at two small lines. She was only a week late, but the test was positive: Lise was pregnant.

She kept repeating the fact in her head but couldn't take it in. She tried saying aloud that she was expecting a baby, but that didn't make it seem any more real.

How could this happen?

Of course she knew how it had happened; she wasn't a complete idiot. She'd paid enough attention in biology classes to know that one plus one could sometimes equal three. She'd just never believed it would happen to her; not like this.

It had taken her several hours to get used to the idea, but then she had seen everything clearly. Perhaps having a child wouldn't be the worst thing in the world. After all, her own mother had only been eighteen when she gave birth to her, and Lise hadn't missed out on anything growing up. Age was nothing but a number, she

told herself. There was no reason why she couldn't have the child.
Her father had left her a decent inheritance and the flat as well, so
at least she and the baby wouldn't be homeless.

Everything would work out, and she need never be alone again.
But she knew she couldn't carry on as an au pair much longer, not
when she started to show, and besides she didn't want to. All she
wanted now was to go home.

The day after she had taken the test, she rang Anita and said
she would be heading home on 8 September and that she wouldn't
be coming alone. Anita had done her best to prise more informa-
tion out of her, but Lise had merely laughed and said: 'You'll find
out soon, I promise.'

'I'm starting to believe that this whole case is the result of one big misunderstanding,' Elma said, as they were sitting on the sofa in her flat that evening, with Birta curled up beside them. 'Lise dropped down dead at Marinó's house, and for some reason he felt he had to hide the body. He must have thought it was his fault, though I can't imagine why.'

Sævar had Elma's feet on his lap and was massaging her soles. 'You could be right, but somebody murdered Marinó, and that has to be linked to Lise.'

Although they were both staring at the TV screen, Elma suspected that Sævar, like her, wasn't taking in the programme. She withdrew her feet, feeling suddenly nervous. She wasn't sure she could tell him about the pregnancy after all. But what choice did she have? She couldn't just let her belly go on growing until he noticed it himself.

'Elma.'

She turned to him. 'What?'

Sævar studied her for a moment, his eyes moving slowly and searchingly over her face. 'You're a bit ... I get the feeling something's wrong. Have I done something?'

Had he done something? Good question. Since they started sleeping together, he had given little thought to the possibility that Elma could get pregnant, though it was simple biology – something kids learnt at school. Why should she always have to take responsibility for that side of things? Why was it her role to ensure that there would be no consequences? Elma dropped her gaze from Sævar's face, concentrating instead on Birta's yellow fur. She felt guilty for thinking about the baby as 'consequences'. It was a child. Her child. Their child.

The words emerged before she could form a proper sentence in her head.

'Yes, you certainly have. You've gone and got me pregnant.' She'd meant it to sound like a joke, but instead it came across as accusatory.

'Ha ha.'

'No, seriously. I'm going to have a baby.' Elma raised her eyes to his face again, taking in his dopey expression and open mouth.

'Are you … are you pregnant?' His gaze was flickering back and forth between her eyes, searching for signs that she was serious.

'Yes.' Elma ran a hand over her collarbone, feeling herself growing hot, though she didn't know why. 'Yes, I think so. Or, rather, I don't think so: I went to the doctor – to my sister who's a midwife, I mean – and there was a heartbeat. From the foetus – the baby. So, yes, I'm pregnant.'

Elma swallowed, and the silence hung heavy between them.

'I, er…' Sævar coughed and sat up straighter on the sofa. 'Was that the plan or…? I mean, did you want it to happen?'

'Did I want it? I … No. I mean, it wasn't the plan. But I want it now. Or at least I think I do.'

'Yes, but…' Sævar looked away and bent forwards over his knees. 'Why didn't you say anything before?'

'I didn't plan this. It just happened.'

'Yes, but—'

'I took precautions,' Elma interrupted, her resentment flaring up. 'You've never bothered, Sævar – it's always been my job to take care of that side of things.'

'Yes, I just thought…' Sævar said weakly.

'I told you it wasn't planned.' Elma pursed her lips and forced herself to breathe slowly through her nose. Her sense of injustice was suddenly overwhelming. He was behaving as if it was her fault, as if she should take the blame. But it wasn't as though he would have to carry the child. She was the one who was pregnant; who would have to watch her body growing and changing; who would have to go through the pain of labour.

She got abruptly to her feet.

'Where are you going?' Sævar asked.

'I'm … I'm going to the loo,' Elma said, without looking at him. In the bathroom she locked the door and sat down on the side of the bath. The touch of the cold enamel was a relief. She closed her eyes, doing her best to breathe calmly. Perhaps she had reacted too harshly. It wasn't like her to be short-tempered, and her anger had already given way to a different emotion. She squeezed her eyes shut and forced herself to get a grip. They needed to talk about the future without tempers being lost.

After a minute or two, Elma sent herself a reassuring smile in the mirror, then went back out there.

'Sævar, I…' She stopped mid-sentence when she realised that there was no one sitting on the sofa. Both Sævar and Birta had gone.

❦

Unnar was drunk when he finally got home. Laufey watched him tiptoe inside, drop his phone on the floor and almost lose his balance when he bent down to pick it up. He flung out a hand to steady himself against the wall, then staggered into the sitting room, where he collapsed on the sofa. She watched as his breathing slowed and his body twitched as if he was dreaming. Moving softly, she went into the room, sat down in the armchair and studied him.

This man was her husband, the father of her children. He was forty-five, three years older than her, and they had met when Laufey was fifteen. That meant she had known him for twenty-seven years. Twenty-seven years was a long time.

At fifteen she had moved to Akranes with her father. They had stopped off at a shop to buy milk and other essentials before moving into their new flat. Laufey had walked past the cooler, wondering which flavour yoghurt to choose, when she saw a group of boys standing nearby. They were holding bottles of fizzy drink and bars of chocolate, and all wearing the same kind of trousers with turn-ups. One boy immediately caught her eye. He was in a short-sleeved shirt with the collar up, and when he caught Laufey checking him out he had given her a crooked smile. The smile had made her weak at the knees, and afterwards all she could think about was seeing him again.

Unnar stirred, and for a moment Laufey thought he was going to wake up, but then he took a deep breath and started snoring quietly again.

Laufey's next encounter with Unnar had been many months later at a party given by a new friend of hers. He had pulled her aside and kissed her with a self-assurance that few boys his age possessed. The kiss had taken Laufey so much by surprise that she hardly realised what had happened until afterwards. He hadn't asked permission or even talked to her beforehand, just gone straight in and taken what he wanted. At fifteen years old, she hadn't been able to believe her luck.

Their relationship had always been an unequal one. Even after they were married and had children, she was always afraid of losing him.

Angrily, she wiped away her tears.

'Laufey,' Unnar said in a husky voice, making her jump. 'What … what are you doing? What time is it?'

'Where were you?' Laufey asked, realising, as soon as she'd said it, that she didn't want to know. She didn't care.

'I was out.'

Laufey nodded, then stood up and went into the bedroom. She got back under the duvet and pulled it up to her chin. Unnar followed her in and sat down on the bed.

'I've been trying,' he slurred, pulling off his T-shirt. 'I've been trying to make things better.'

'I know.' Laufey turned over.

'You're difficult.' Unnar lay down on his front, staring at her. He was wearing the same crooked smile as when they had first met. It was still there, under everything he had done to her.

'Am I difficult?' she asked.

'Yes.' Unnar gripped her arm and pushed her down in the bed. Laughing quietly, he kissed her on the mouth, speaking between kisses. 'You should try and be a bit more flexible. I'm trying, Laufey. For both of us.'

'I know,' she whispered, and gave up the struggle.

Unnar was the father of her children; she'd known him for twenty-seven years, but this would be their last night together.

❧

By three a.m. Lena was so drunk that people's outlines had become blurry and seemed to sway in time to the music. The air in the flat was as heavy and muggy as dense fog. A man with a cigarette was dancing in front of her, his eyes travelling down her body. She reached for his cigarette and sucked in the smoke. He smiled and grabbed her by the hips.

Lena took another drag, peering around in search of Olga. The floor was sticky underfoot, and all at once she felt as if she couldn't breathe. The man moved closer, rubbing up against her. His hand moved lower.

Lena tore herself free and moved away quickly before he could protest. She was still holding his cigarette, sucking on it avidly. She scanned the surrounding faces for Olga, but it was hopeless trying to see anyone in this throng.

When she finally got outside into the cool air, the cigarette was finished. She bumped into an older woman who was holding a packet and asked for one but received a blunt refusal. A man standing beside the woman took pity on Lena and offered her his packet. Then he held up his lighter for her and told her to go home: she was too drunk.

Lena pulled a face but couldn't be bothered to reply; couldn't reply. She could barely open her mouth to push the cigarette in. She reeled away from the crowd and leant against a cold stone wall. Luckily, her bag was still on her shoulder, with her phone inside it. She switched it on and saw a message from Olga: *FFS where are you? You always do this!* Lena started to reply but saw that she was writing gibberish, so she gave up and put the phone back in her bag.

She didn't usually drink this much, but the foreign woman's message had brought memories to the surface that she would rather forget. That horrible family. Those horrible people.

Fuck 'em, Lena thought and smoked the cigarette down to the tip.

She slid down the wall until she was sitting on the filthy pavement. Judging by the smell, several people must have pissed there earlier.

It would be easy to ignore the message and never think about it again. But the woman had said it was connected to a girl who was now au pairing for the family. So they had got themselves another au pair after what had happened. *He* must have suggested it. She bet he'd picked the girl himself.

Lena took out her phone and found the message. Her head was beginning to clear and the letters weren't moving about as much as before. She concentrated grimly on what she was writing, read the message over again before sending it, then deleted her account.

Wednesday

Elma was in a hurry to get to the police station that morning. It wasn't far from her flat, only a few minutes' brisk walk between blocks of flats with over-large gardens that were never used and did nothing but take up valuable space. The sun was up, and the weather was still but chilly, the distant mountains standing out sharp and clear, and a definite scent of autumn in the air. There were few other people around. Most hadn't left for work yet, and the schools didn't start until eight-thirty. Elma was out of breath by the time she opened the door to her office.

She sat down at her computer and reread Lena's message. The girl's account had disappeared, so Elma couldn't write back. The message had been sent in the middle of the night and Lena's profile deleted immediately afterwards, making it clear that she was unwilling to discuss the matter further.

Someone walked along the corridor past her office, and Elma stiffened when she heard Sævar's voice. He hadn't come back last night or rung her to apologise, and she was too stubborn to call him. She'd been floored by his reaction. While she'd been prepared for a variety of possible responses: surprise, alarm maybe – after all, he was bound to need time to adjust to the idea – she had never expected him to walk out like that, leaving her in the lurch. She didn't know if she could forgive him.

She got up and opened the door, not caring if Sævar saw the shadows under her eyes that repeatedly splashing her face with cold water had failed to remove. In the light of day she could almost laugh at herself. She was constantly welling up at the moment, which she put down to all the hormones raging around her body. Wasn't that another thing pregnant women had to put up with?

Nevertheless, she got a sinking feeling in the pit of her stomach when she saw Sævar sitting at his desk. It was clear *he* hadn't suffered a sleepless night. He was neatly combed, wearing an attractive blue polo shirt.

'Elma,' he said when she came in, instantly taking his hand off his mouse. 'I—'

'I got a message from Lena last night,' Elma interrupted, surprising herself with how normal her voice sounded. She sat down in the chair facing Sævar and held out her phone.

'Lena?'

'Lena was Laufey and Unnar's au pair before Lise.'

Sævar looked at her for a long moment, then took the phone.

Lena's message provided a succinct account of what had happened. She'd only been with the family a few weeks when Unnar came into her room, drunk, and said things to her that made her uncomfortable. Things about his relationship with Laufey, about how lonely he was and what a beautiful girl Lena was. After that, he tried to kiss her, and Lena was so disgusted that she walked out the very next day.

Elma could see from Sævar's face that he was shocked.

He passed the phone back to her. 'Do you think the same thing happened to Lise?'

'It's not unlikely,' Elma said. 'The other day I rang the au-pair matching agency Lise had a profile with. The guy I spoke to said they sometimes had cases of men trying to exploit girls who come from poorer countries.'

'I'm guessing Laufey didn't know, seeing as she agreed to getting another au pair.'

'No, presumably not.'

Sævar nodded. He was still watching her a little uncertainly, as if there was something he wanted to say. But Elma rose to her feet without giving him a chance.

'Anyway, I don't know if it's significant, but if Lise and Unnar were having an affair, it would give him a motive, wouldn't it?'

September 2019

The sun beat down, its rays hotter than Lise would have believed possible in Iceland. She had offered to do some gardening over the summer, and Laufey had insisted on paying her extra. Every week she mowed the lawn and weeded the flowerbeds. Right now she was kneeling, working on one of the beds in a leisurely manner since the girls had gone back to school. She was relishing this chance to be outside and feel the warm sun on her skin.

Lise hadn't dared break it to Unnar that she was pregnant. She wasn't sure if she ever would tell him, though she supposed he had a right to know about the child, whatever he chose to do with the information. It was up to him whether he told Laufey or not.

She found herself growing more homesick with every day that passed. More than anything, she longed to put this uncomfortable situation behind her and embark on a new chapter in her life. A chapter that was bound to be difficult but not insurmountable. She still had people she could turn to; friends who cared about her.

Lise stood up, wiped her arm across her forehead and was about to return to her weeding when a rhythmic noise reached her ears from the other side of the house. She walked round the corner and saw that Andri was in the back garden, keeping a ball in the air. They knew each other quite well by now since they sometimes chatted during the day, before the others got home. He was different when his family weren't around; more talkative and quicker to smile.

He didn't notice her until she said hello.

'How long have you been playing football?' She sat down on the lawn, reclining backwards on her elbows.

'How long?' Andri seemed to find it an odd question. 'Since ...
forever. I don't really remember a time when I didn't play.'

'Do you enjoy it?'

'Well ... sure.' Andri let the ball drop and left it lying on the
grass.

Picking up on the pause, Lise studied his face. 'You hesitated,'
she said, smiling.

'Yes, I mean, I started playing football when I was a little kid
and showed a talent for it straight away. It's, like, the only thing
I've ever been good at.'

'That doesn't answer my question,' Lise said, tilting her head on
one side.

'No.' Andri came and sat down near her. He pulled up a blade
of grass as he was talking. 'It was just so different when I was a
kid. In those days, it was the most fun thing I could think of. Now
... I suppose it's more like a job.'

'It must be hard when you lose.'

Andri grinned. 'It goes with the territory.'

'Everyone shouting at you and blaming you.'

Andri raised his eyebrows.

'Dad used to watch the football,' Lise explained. 'I never could
because I always felt so sorry for the losing team. It was so sad
when they walked off the pitch. I couldn't help thinking about how
much pressure they must be under, not wanting to disappoint their
hundreds of thousands of fans.'

Andri laughed and shrugged. 'It's only football – you can't take
it too seriously.'

'Your parents seem to.'

'Yeah, well, they're just keen for me to go abroad. You know how
it is.'

'And you're going.'

'Yeah,' Andri said. 'I'm going abroad.'

'Are you excited?'

'Yes, but...' Andri glanced at the house, lowering his voice. 'But,

I mean, if it doesn't work out, that's OK. I just want to get out of Iceland. You know, try living somewhere else and all that.'

'You should come to Amsterdam.'

'I've been to Amsterdam,' Andri said.

'Have you?'

'Yes, but I didn't really see anything. It was just a football trip.'

'Oh, OK,' Lise said. 'You should come in summer. You can't beat walking down by—'

'Andri.'

Lise fell silent and looked up. Júlía was standing by the fence, displaying long tanned legs in sandals. Her blonde hair was held back by a pair of enormous sunglasses.

'Oh, hi,' Andri said, shifting away from Lise.

'What are you doing? I've been trying to get hold of you.' Júlía's eyes were on Lise as she spoke.

'Oh, right.'

'We were meant to be going swimming, remember?'

'Yeah, of course.' Andri got up, dusted down his trousers and left with Júlía. But not without throwing Lise a smile.

Although Lena's message had provided a clue as to what might have been going on at Unnar and Laufey's house, this still didn't bring the police any closer to finding out what had led to Marinó's murder.

For one thing, Unnar hadn't been at Marinó's party the evening Lise died.

The manner of Lise's death raised some interesting questions, though. The pathologist believed she had received a blow to her head hours or even days before she succumbed to its effects. It could have happened on the Friday, for instance, though she didn't collapse until the Saturday night. Elma could just imagine how the young people must have panicked when they realised Lise was dead. She wondered who had been there at the time. Andri and Marinó, possibly. Or Marinó alone. Had he thought Lise's death was his fault and hidden her in the shed in his confusion?

Elma got up and grabbed her bag.

On the way out she didn't even glance in the direction of Sævar's office, determined to prove that she could manage on her own. She didn't need help. From Sævar or anyone else.

The football pitch at Jaðarsbakkar was situated down by the sea. On the side nearest the shore was a small stand with seats in the club colours of black and yellow, arranged to spell out the initials of the Akranes Sports Club. Facing it across the pitch was a grassy mound that had been roughly shaped into benches.

Elma parked in one of the spaces by the swimming pool, then walked over to the stadium. Andri was warming up with the other players. When he saw her, he halted in the middle of the pitch, spoke briefly to his coach, then came to meet her.

'What are you doing here?'

'I wanted to ask you a few questions about Lena,' Elma answered.

'Why?'

'Because she had something rather interesting to say about your father.'

Andri regarded her in silence for a moment, then his shoulders relaxed slightly.

'You knew what happened,' Elma said, watching him carefully.

'I knew she'd said some stuff,' Andri replied. 'But Mum told me it was just a misunderstanding.'

'Do you think it was a misunderstanding?'

'I don't know.' Andri hugged himself, as if suddenly feeling the cold. 'But I do know the local gossip about my dad.'

'Is it true?'

Andri shrugged. 'There's usually some truth in stories like that, isn't there?'

'What about Lise? Do you think they could have been…?'

'No,' Andri said unconvincingly, glancing around them. There was no one near enough to overhear, and his teammates had carried on playing without him. 'When I left Marinó's, Lise was still there. I don't know what happened after that but…'

'But what?'

'But when I got home Dad was awake and…' Andri closed his eyes and swallowed. 'And he asked about Lise.'

'Did you tell him where she was?'

'Yes,' Andri said. 'I did.'

❧

'Dad.'

The voice was low, no more than a whisper, but Hörður knew immediately that something was wrong.

'Where are you?' He opened his desk drawer and rummaged

for his car keys among all the pens and other rubbish before re-membering that they were in his coat pocket.

'At the hospital.'

'I'm on my way.'

'No, Snorri's here with me. I just…' His daughter broke off and he heard a sob that turned into a moan of pain.

Hörður waited, feeling as if the world was standing still. Since Gígja died everything seemed so ephemeral. Before, it had been unthinkable that he could lose a loved one, as if such tragedies only happened to other people, but now he was braced to hear bad news every day.

'Katrín?'

'Sorry, but…' His daughter laughed, sounding choked up with emotion. 'He's on his way. We got to the hospital an hour ago, but it's happening quite fast. I just wanted to let you know.'

Hörður nodded.

'Dad?'

'Yes.' He swallowed and tried to sound normal. 'I'm here.'

'I'll let you know when he arrives.'

Hörður put the phone down and stood there in the middle of the room, at a loss. Should he go and wait outside the hospital? Or carry on working?

He sat down again and stared at the stack of papers in front of him. He knew he wouldn't be able to concentrate for a second, so he was glad when there was a knock at his door.

'Hörður?'

Elma was standing there. He beckoned her in, but instead of sitting down, she stared at him, frowning.

'Is everything all right?'

'What? Yes, everything's fine.' Hörður couldn't hold back a smile as he added: 'It's just … Katrín. She's gone into hospi-tal.'

'Oh, that's great.' Elma beamed at him. 'I didn't think they were expecting him until next month.'

'No, but apparently he's in a bit of a hurry. Gígja was the same. All our children arrived early.'

Katrín herself, though born five weeks before the due date, had been a strong, healthy baby. She'd had such a powerful set of lungs that the midwife had been sure she had a future as a singer. And she certainly was a singer, just not a particularly good one. When she was small, she had sung nonstop, hopelessly out of tune but with so much feeling that he and Gígja had hardly been able to contain their laughter.

'Did you want anything in particular?' Hörður asked.

Elma told him about Lena's story and their suspicion that Lise had experienced something similar, only that it had gone much further. She added that Unnar hadn't mentioned speaking to Andri when he got home that night, which seemed fishy.

Hörður immediately agreed to put in a request for Unnar's phone records, which would require a court order. They would need to track his movements both the weekend Lise died and also the following one, when the fire was started.

'Do you think it'll be enough to justify issuing a search warrant?' Elma asked.

'If something comes to light in his phone records, we might get one,' Hörður said. 'It would also be a good idea to check if Lise's luggage is still in their house somewhere. I'll get onto it and let you know.'

Elma nodded, apparently satisfied.

Hörður set the matter in motion but it took all his self-discipline to tear his eyes away from the phone.

The shouting and shrieking in the gym didn't disturb Laufey in the slightest. She enjoyed sitting there watching the kids and drifting off into a reverie. Sometimes she felt herself growing drowsy and remembered what it had been like in college when sleep used to descend on her in the middle of class. How difficult it had been to keep her eyes open and focused on the board.

'How are you?' someone behind Laufey asked, making her start. Next minute, Brynhildur had sat down beside her, radiating concern, which Laufey guessed meant that Brynhildur already knew too much.

'I'm fine.'

Brynhildur didn't say anything, just looked at her searchingly.

'Honestly.' Laufey smiled but was conscious from the stiffness of her face muscles how forced it must appear. 'Why do you ask?'

'Oh, I just heard something about the police wanting to interview Andri.'

'Yes. And me. They're interviewing everyone.' Laufey didn't bother to soften her tone. She was so tired of play-acting; tired of being polite and pretending everything was OK.

She and Brynhildur were friends through their husbands. They had got to know each other years ago, when Anna had just been born and Klara was only three. Andri had been eleven at the time, and life had long since come to revolve around football. Brynhildur and Laufey had hit it off immediately, which was why the families were close. They used to go on holiday together and have each other round for meals.

Laufey knew that Brynhildur had never been honest with her, but she had quietly put up with it. Pretended they were friends. Now she asked herself: who for?

'Yes, I suppose they must be,' Brynhildur said. 'Let's hope they solve the case soon. It's so awful about that girl – where was she from again?'

'Lise was Dutch.' Laufey waved to Anna, who had executed a perfect jump on the trampoline then looked up at the spectator benches to make sure her mother was watching.

'Oh, yes, that was it. She seemed so nice.'

Laufey looked at her, raising her eyebrows enquiringly.

'When I met her at your house,' Brynhildur explained.

'Right.' Laufey had totally forgotten that Brynhildur and her husband Villi had visited them that spring. They had drunk beer, and Unnar had barbecued hot dogs while the girls were bouncing on the trampoline with Brynhildur and Villi's sons.

'The girls seemed to really like her too.'

'They did.'

Brynhildur was looking at her with her round brown eyes full of sympathy. She had always reminded Laufey of a dog; not a cute little puppy but a large hunting dog with loose jowls and floppy ears.

'And Marinó was Andri's friend too,' Brynhildur continued.

'Yes.'

'How's Andri doing?'

'Fine. He's just fine.' It didn't cross Laufey's mind to share her concerns about Andri with Brynhildur. But the fact was, she had concerns. Andri was distant and seemed permanently on edge. She'd started counting down the days until they left the country and could put all this behind them.

'When are you going to Sweden? Or is that no longer the plan?'

'The plan is to go as soon as the season's over, in a week and a bit.'

'Just the two of you?'

'Yes, to begin with.'

'Leaving Unnar alone to look after the girls.' Brynhildur smiled as if the idea was hilarious. 'He's going to miss you all right.'

The gymnastics class ended, and the girls ran into the changing rooms. The parents around them started picking up their bags and pulling on their jackets.

'Brynhildur,' Laufey said, keeping her eyes straight ahead. 'You know perfectly well that he won't.'

Brynhildur seemed badly thrown, although Laufey's manner was perfectly calm and collected.

'Er, what … what do you mean?'

'Oh, just that Unnar will have more than enough to do while I'm away. You know, with all his girlfriends in town. Villi must have told you.'

Brynhildur opened her mouth then closed it again. The mumsy look was wiped off her face, and under the thick layer of foundation her skin turned a blotchy red.

'I'm joking,' Laufey said and laughed.

Brynhildur joined in half-heartedly. But the red blotches grew more pronounced, and she didn't seem able to meet Laufey's eye.

'Anyway, best get going.' Laufey stood up. 'Say hi to Villi from me. Tell him I'll bake that sticky chocolate cake he was so mad about as soon as I get a moment.'

'Will do.'

Laufey smiled wryly then went to find Anna. She must have finished changing by now.

❧

'Are you planning to avoid me much longer?'

Elma zipped up her coat, grabbed her phone and saw that it was late. Dagný had invited her round to supper and she was starving. She was looking forward to having a cuddle with her nephews. Admittedly, these days Alexander behaved as if he was too big to put up with such indignities, but Elma wasn't going to let him get away with that. At least Jökull was always up for a hug. And Elma could do with one right now.

'Elma?'

'I'm not avoiding you, Sævar.' She smiled. 'I'm just in a hurry. Dagný's invited me to supper.'

She made to walk past him.

'Please, Elma. I didn't mean…' He stopped when their colleague Kári strolled past with a mug of coffee, humming a tune.

'Sævar, everything's fine. Honestly.' Elma faked a smile and met his eye. He wore such a look of misery that she felt almost sorry for him, though she was still too angry for that.

'Can we talk this evening?'

'What about?' Elma's voice came out sounding more hollow than she'd intended. She didn't want Sævar to see how hurt she was. She just wanted to get through the day and supper with her sister without ending up an emotional wreck. Closing her eyes, she inhaled slowly. She couldn't let herself break down. If Sævar wanted to run away, then fine.

'I'll talk to you later, Sævar,' she said.

He returned her smile, his eyes still anxious, but before he could answer she was gone. This time it was his turn to be left standing there at a loss.

✦

'Dad.'

'Has he arrived?' Hörður was still at the office. Home didn't feel like a refuge any more. Without Gígja, it was just a house, not a home. Although it contained all the furniture they had bought over the years and the bed they had shared, everything seemed drained of colour. The rooms, which used to seem over-filled by Gígja's larger-than-life presence, by her voice and scent, were now so silent that they seemed alien.

Hörður was determined to sell the house and move as soon as the right flat came on the market. He pictured a small, modern place in an apartment block by the sea.

'He…' Katrín paused and Hörður's heart missed a beat.

'Katrín?'

'Just get over here, Dad. Your newest grandchild can't wait to meet you.'

'Did it go well?'

'Very well,' Katrín said. 'It hurt like hell but it was worth it.'

'That's good to hear.'

'I'm never doing it again, though.' Katrín laughed and in the background there was a loud, piercing wail. Hörður could have sworn the baby sounded exactly like Katrín when she was born.

The moment he'd hung up, he got to his feet, but as he reached out to turn off the computer, an email appeared. It was the data he had requested from Unnar's phone.

Hörður sighed, knowing it would have to be examined but hoping Elma could take care of that. If he were to be completely honest with himself, he ought maybe to have taken a longer time off. He'd been almost incapable of concentrating this week, and with a case this major that just wasn't acceptable. The victims deserved better. After a moment or two's consideration, he forwarded the email to Elma. His grandson was waiting, and everything else could take a back seat for now.

❧

'What's this supposed to be?'

'A house.'

'A house? What kind of house?'

'My house.'

'The house we're in now?'

'Noooh. *My* house, when I'm big. I'm going to have a swimming pool, a hot tub on the roof and a racing track.'

'A racing track?'

'Yes.' Alexander shrugged nonchalantly. 'So I can race the cars I'm going to buy.'

'I see.' Elma hardly dared touch the Lego house that he had dragged her into his room to admire. 'For bumper cars, you mean?'

'Bumper cars?' Alexander looked at her pityingly. 'No, I'm going to buy a Bugatti. They're the fastest cars in the world.'

'A Bugatti?' Elma repeated. 'I don't even know what that is.'

Alexander made no reply to this, but from his expression it

was clear he was disappointed in his aunt. He carried on tinkering with the house while Elma sat on the bed, looking around his room. Not so long ago it had contained countless soft toys, a small teepee, and a cute bunny lamp. Now the shelves were full of Lego models and pictures of footballers. Where the teepee used to stand, there was a desk piled with Alexander's school books.

'No!' Alexander yelled suddenly. 'Get out, Jökull.'

Seeing what was about to happen, Elma scooped up her younger nephew before he could snatch the hot tub off the Lego roof.

'I want to play,' Jökull shouted, struggling. He was nearly three and obviously felt he was too big for Elma to carry him like that.

'Shall we go and help Mummy maybe? Get ourselves some snacks?'

Jökull vacillated a moment, then nodded.

In the kitchen, Viðar was browning mince while Dagný chopped vegetables and arranged them in small bowls. Elma put Jökull down and gave him some tortilla chips, after which he waddled contentedly into the sitting room, where a cartoon was playing. The brothers were very different: Jökull chubby and keen on his food; Alexander always tearing around, rarely pausing to eat.

'I haven't given you a hug yet, Elma,' Viðar said, wrapping his arms around her. 'Congratulations.'

'Oh,' Elma said. 'Thanks.'

'I hope it was all right for me to tell Viðar?' Dagný said. 'I haven't told anyone else, I promise.'

'Yes, of course.' Elma lowered her eyes. 'I probably can't hide it much longer.' When she'd examined herself in the mirror that morning she'd thought her belly looked a little more rounded than before.

'Right, we're nearly there,' Dagný said, putting a bowl of cucumber slices on the table. 'I see you're hungry.'

'Yes, I am,' Elma said, helping to put the vegetables on the table. It was a long-standing joke in her family that hunger turned her into a mere shadow of herself. Whenever she was in a bad mood, the first question they always asked was whether she'd eaten. Elma had to admit that there had been an element of truth in this when she was a teenager but she didn't feel it was fair nowadays.

Dagný just smiled, then called the boys.

After supper, Alexander and Jökull took their ice lollies into the sitting room. Meanwhile, the adults cleared up then sat down again for dessert.

'I'm longing to...' Dagný made circles in the cream with her spoon. 'Have you thought about where you're going to have it?'

'I haven't even begun to think about that sort of thing,' Elma admitted.

'Have you told the father?'

'Yes. But I don't know if he...' Elma put a spoonful of cream and meringue in her mouth. 'It doesn't matter, though. I'm fine.'

'Do you need me to go and knock some sense into him?' Viðar asked, earning a scornful look from his wife.

'You? If anyone did that, it would be me,' Dagný said. 'You're far too nice.'

'What, and you're not nice?'

'I ... don't take any crap.' Dagný smiled. 'If anyone messes with my family, they won't know what hit them.'

'It wasn't like that.' Elma sighed. 'We ... he ... Oh, let's talk about something else.'

'Well, at least you won't be alone,' Dagný said. 'I was hoping that ... that I could be there with you. You know, be your midwife – deliver the child.'

'Deliver my baby?' Elma's eyebrows shot up. 'Wouldn't you find that a bit embarrassing?'

'Embarrassing?' Dagný scoffed. 'Elma, dear, in case you'd forgotten, delivering babies is my job. It's the most normal, natural thing in—'

'Yes, sure.' Elma interrupted. 'And yes, of course I'd like that. I mean, at least it would be better than having a stranger fiddling about down there.'

She popped a strawberry in her mouth, but when she glanced up at Dagný, she was taken aback. Her sister was holding her spoon in the air and blinking rapidly, as if on the verge of tears.

'Sorry, I'm just so excited,' Dagný said. 'It's so...' She heaved a breath and took a sip of water. In the other room there was an outbreak of shouting from Alexander. Dagný and Viðar both shot to their feet simultaneously, but Dagný pushed Viðar down again. 'I'll go. I'm going.'

Viðar and Elma remained behind, grinning at each other. It was nothing new for Dagný to come over all emotional, but this time Elma felt oddly touched. She had been telling herself all day that everything would be fine; trying to convince herself that she could do this on her own.

It was only now that she realised she wouldn't have to go it alone.

❧

When Katrín announced that she was pregnant they had held a family celebration, not for an instant suspecting that Gígja would never get to meet her fourth grandchild. The thought filled Hörður with such unbearable sorrow that he walked into the hospital with a much heavier heart than the occasion warranted. He, who had almost run out to the car in his excitement, now sank down on a chair in reception, reality suddenly kicking in. Normally, they would have come in together to see their daughter's first child. Gígja would have been at his side, chattering away nonstop as usual, overflowing with warmth and compassion for everyone around her.

Hörður gripped the arm of the chair, aware of his heart labouring in his chest. Ever since Gígja died he'd been having episodes during which his grief became so overwhelming that he started to hyperventilate. The other day he had actually fainted.

After a little while his breathing slowed, and he realised that he needed to get up and go to his daughter.

Hörður was familiar with the way, having gone to meet three new grandchildren in recent years. He mentioned Katrín's name to a white-clad woman he encountered, and she directed him to a room at the end of the ward.

Katrín was sitting up in a double bed with white covers. At her side, Snorri was scrolling through photos on a large camera. The baby was lying in her arms, its head resting on her chest.

'Congratulations, love,' Hörður said, kissing her. 'I'm afraid I didn't bring anything. Your mother always took care of that side of things.'

'Don't worry about it,' Katrín said. Smiling a little teasingly, she added: 'How do you like her?'

'She's perfect. Just as I knew…' Hörður was brought up short. 'Did you say … did you say *her*?'

Katrín laughed. 'Yes, I certainly did. I should have listened to you. Now we'll have to repaint the nursery.'

Hörður stroked the baby's head. Even though she was a newborn, he could see now that she was unmistakably a girl. Those long, dark eyelashes, the delicate lips and nose. The tiny hands.

'Dad.'

Hörður looked up and was startled to see that his daughter was weeping. But she laughed anyway, wiping away her tears and sniffing. 'Meet little Gígja. Do you want to hold her?'

When Elma got home, she opened the email from Hörður. She didn't have to puzzle over the numbers for long to work out their significance. Just before three in the early hours of Sunday, 15 September, Unnar's phone had connected to the mast in the vicinity of Marinó's house – at around the same time as the smoke alarm had gone off, waking the neighbours. Shortly after that, the fire brigade had turned up to save what they could.

Elma examined the phone's other movements. All afternoon and on Saturday evening it had been connected to a mast not far from Laufey and Unnar's house. Then, at half past two in the morning, it had connected to another mast, then another, right up until it stopped by the mast near Marinó's house. It appeared to stay there for around fifteen minutes before returning home.

Elma sat down, considering the implications. Could there be any other plausible reason for Unnar's presence in the vicinity when the fire started?

The timing was extremely suspicious, but an innocent explanation couldn't be ruled out. Unnar hadn't told them he'd gone out that night, but then they hadn't asked. Elma remembered that he and Laufey had mentioned holding a dinner party that evening, and she and Sævar had been satisfied with that.

Elma picked up the phone and rang Hörður but got his voicemail.

Just then, she nearly had a heart attack as a loud knock sounded on the glass door onto her deck.

'Are you trying to kill me?' Elma asked, letting Sævar in.

'Not literally.' He stood in the middle of the room, looking ill at ease.

Elma returned to the sofa, leaving him to stand there uncomfortably. She saw no reason why she should make his life any easier. She picked up her laptop and went back to pondering Unnar's movements.

'I—' Sævar began but Elma interrupted.

'Why did you walk out?' She put the laptop down and folded her arms across her chest.

'I … I don't know.' Sævar threw up his hands in despair. 'I didn't know what to do.'

'So you just left?'

'I … Yes, I left.'

Elma felt a crushing sense of disappointment. She'd expected an explanation, an answer, but instead Sævar just stood there, apparently not even aware of what he'd done wrong. She sighed and picked up the laptop again.

'Oh well, it can't be helped,' she said, trying to sound indifferent.

'Elma.' Sævar sat down on the sofa beside her and lifted the laptop out of her hands. Before she could protest, he took hold of her arm. 'I left because I was afraid of what you might say.'

'What I might say?'

'Yes. I left because I thought you didn't want…' Sævar hesitated. 'Didn't want all this.'

'All this?'

'Yes.' Sævar smiled, embarrassed. 'I'm no good at this, am I?'

'No, not particularly.' Elma looked down at his hand, which was still holding her arm. She couldn't quite work out what had happened between them. 'I thought I'd have to go it alone.'

'You didn't seriously think that?'

'I could manage on my own.'

'I know you're perfectly capable of it.'

'It wouldn't be a problem. If you didn't want—'

'Elma.' Sævar leant forwards and silenced her with a kiss. 'There's nothing I want more.'

❧

What could Unnar say? He was a fool who cheated on his wife and occasionally, just occasionally, took photos of the girls he slept with. Not because he had any intention of posting them online; he just wanted to wallow in the memory of the night a little longer. He didn't show anyone the photos, except maybe Tommi, and Tommi didn't pass them on to anyone else. It was all perfectly innocent.

Yesterday evening he had received a phone call from one of his girlfriends in Akranes; she'd wanted to see him, so he had gone round. He'd only meant to stop briefly but ended up staying longer than planned. When he got home he expected Laufey to be angry, but she had been perfectly calm. After all, he thought, there was no need for her to make such a fuss about the kids; Klara and Anna were quite old enough to be left alone at home for an hour or two.

He needed to get out of the house sometimes to distract himself from thinking about Lise. Whenever he let his mind stray to her, he was ashamed, yet another part of him felt proud. The girl had been genuinely crazy about him, and it had been hard to do nothing about it.

So hard that once, and only once, he had given in.

Unnar's thoughts spun round in circles: one minute he wanted to be a better husband and spend more time with his family, the next he felt he was suffocating and had to get out.

It was just too bloody difficult. When Andri was born, he'd been totally unprepared for the sleepless nights and the endless crying that drove him up the wall. He'd soon realised that he wasn't cut out for fatherhood. If he'd had a clue how much having children would change his life, he'd have thought twice about it.

Of course he loved his kids, but family life just wasn't for him, perhaps because he'd never experienced it himself. His father had been a loser who knocked his mother about, and his mother had been a pushover who let him.

Unnar's heart had hardened in childhood. He had learnt at an early age how easy it was to smile and pretend everything was

OK. But all along he had felt so restless and lost; neither Laufey nor the kids could change that.

Unnar was two different men in one body, and sometimes he barely noticed himself when the change occurred. He might be sitting on the sofa after putting the girls to bed, while Laufey chose a film for them to watch together, when suddenly the urge would kick in and he would have to get out.

The only way he could make things work was if he sought an outlet elsewhere, which was why he was sitting in a bar now, drinking and trying not to think about Lise and how everything had gone to hell the moment she entered their lives.

September 2019

Lise ran out of the house. She didn't know where she was going, she just needed to get away. A couple walking down the street stared at her in astonishment as she sprinted past them as fast as she could. Before she knew it, she was standing in the middle of the cemetery on the other side of the road. She dropped into the grass by the pink clock tower and buried her face in her hands.

What had happened?

She could still see Unnar's crazed eyes; feel his fingers crushing her upper arm.

Unnar had hurt her.

No one had ever deliberately hurt her before, not even when she was at school. The very idea that someone might want to was unthinkable. Yet Unnar had done so. He hadn't just gripped her arm, he had shoved her against the wall so roughly that she had banged the back of her head, and now it was aching so badly that she could barely hold back the tears.

She couldn't understand how he could have changed so fast: one minute he had been sitting at the kitchen table, drinking coffee and listening to what she had to say; the next he had leapt to his feet and grabbed hold of her as if possessed. The eyes glaring into hers were completely alien, and she'd sensed the effort it had taken him to stop himself and let her go.

Afterwards he had tried to apologise, calling after her, begging her not to go, saying he was sorry.

Lise had no intention of forgiving him.

She wiped her eyes and took in her surroundings. Graves scattered the wide-open, grassy area around the clock tower. There was no one else to be seen and the atmosphere was peaceful. Only now did Lise have time to notice that she was feeling a little dizzy and, rather than subsiding, the pain in her head was growing worse by the minute.

Catching sight of Unnar's car emerging from the cul-de-sac where they lived, she got to her feet and dashed, head down, round to the other side of the clock tower. When she peered round the corner, she saw Unnar turning into the cemetery and, taking to her heels, she fled away across the grass.

Thursday

There was a smell of cooking from inside the house, mingled with a sweet fragrance that must come from a scented candle. Laufey's face fell when she saw them, but she invited them in anyway. The couple's two small daughters peered curiously out of their rooms as Elma and Sævar came inside, but the girls soon lost interest, disappointed that they weren't wearing police uniforms.

When Elma asked about Unnar, Laufey said he wasn't back from work yet but offered to call him and stepped out of earshot with the phone. When she came back, she invited them to wait for him in the sitting room.

'He's just emerged from the Hvalfjörður tunnel,' she explained, 'so it shouldn't take him long to reach Akranes.'

They followed her into the sitting room, where she switched on a floor lamp and they sat down. Laufey couldn't decide whether she should join them or not.

'What's this about?' she asked after a pause. 'Can I be of any help?'

'You mentioned you'd held a dinner party on the night of the fire,' Elma said.

'Yes, that's right,' Laufey replied. 'We invited some people over – some old friends of Unnar and their wives.'

'Did you stay up late?'

'Yes, quite late,' Laufey said. 'But everyone had left by about one.'

'Did you and Unnar both go to bed then?' Elma asked.

'Yes. Yes, I think so. At least, I fell asleep as soon as my head touched the pillow, but Unnar still hadn't come to bed at that point.' Laufey ran her hands down her thighs, glancing towards the front door. 'Why do you want to know?'

'We—' Before Elma could answer, they heard a key turning in the door.

'Evening,' Unnar said cheerfully, coming into the sitting room.

'Good evening,' Elma replied more formally.

'How can I help you?' Unnar asked, taking a seat.

'Lise's post-mortem revealed that she had recently suffered a miscarriage,' Elma said bluntly. 'So it's obvious she was involved with someone while she was living with you. Have either of you any idea who that could have been?'

'Lise?' Laufey exclaimed. 'You must have made a mistake.'

Elma and Sævar waited. Silence was often the most effective response at times like this.

Unnar rubbed his fingers together. 'It's quite possible that she—'

'Don't talk rubbish, Unnar. She didn't have any friends here. I often tried to encourage her to meet people. That's why I asked Andri to … Hang on a minute.' Laufey's gaze switched back and forth between Elma and Sævar. 'Surely you don't think that one of Andri's friends got her pregnant?'

'We hoped you might be able to help us there,' Elma said. 'Originally we thought maybe Andri and Lise were having a relationship. It could have happened here in the house without you noticing.'

'But that's ridiculous,' Laufey said. 'Andri's got a girlfriend, and anyway we'd have noticed if he'd been creeping in here at night.'

'But then we talked to Lena,' Elma continued. 'And we learnt some rather interesting information.'

'I see.' Unnar coughed and laid a hand on Laufey's arm. 'Surely you don't believe that's in any way relevant? Lise was found dead in Marinó's garden. Isn't it obvious what happened? He must have killed her, then regretted it and started the fire himself. Just how far are you prepared to go in an attempt to shift the blame onto someone else?'

'We can discuss it at the station, if you'd prefer,' Sævar said amiably.

It didn't take Unnar long to consider the offer. He got to his feet.

'What … why?' Laufey stood up as well. 'Unnar, I…'

'I won't be long.'

Laufey shrugged. 'Right. Fine. I just don't understand why it's necessary.'

Elma smiled sadly, guessing that it wouldn't be long before Laufey found out.

Once he was at the police station, Unnar's self-confidence melted away. He seemed unable to get enough oxygen and kept gasping for air, his ribcage heaving.

The situation didn't improve when Sævar read him his rights and asked if he'd like a lawyer to be present since he was being interviewed as a suspect. Unnar flatly refused the offer, saying he was keen to get the questioning over with as quickly as possible.

'Could I have a drink of water?' he asked, and Elma brought him a glass.

'I assure you, you're barking up completely the wrong tree.'

'Maybe,' Sævar said, taking a seat facing him. 'But now your wife's not present, it would be quickest if you told us everything.'

Elma switched on the recording device and recited the formalities.

Then she raised her eyes to meet Unnar's and began: 'What was the nature of your relationship with Lise Ragnarsdóttir?'

'She was the au pair who looked after my children,' Unnar replied.

'Are you sure you didn't have a closer relationship than that?'

'That's crazy,' Unnar snorted. 'I'm married with three children. Do you really believe—?'

'What about Lena? You were also married with three children when she came to live with you.' Elma handed Unnar a printout of Lena's message. 'She claims your behaviour to her was highly inappropriate.'

'That was just a misunderstanding,' Unnar said. 'I ... I was only talking to her. I can't remember exactly what happened. I was drunk and—' Breaking off, he buried his face in his hands. They waited. 'I was fond of Lise, I'd never have hurt her.'

'Did you two ever sleep together?' Elma asked.

'Lise came to me.'

'Lise came to you?' Sævar repeated. 'Are we supposed to believe that?'

'Believe what you like; it's true. We didn't have an affair but ... but it happened once. I didn't mean to...'

Sævar raised his eyebrows. 'So, in other words, you *were* sleeping together?'

'No,' Unnar burst out. 'It wasn't like that.' He picked up the glass of water and emptied it in one go. 'It only happened once. I was drunk, I came home, and she was there and ... It wasn't supposed to happen. I was so ashamed of myself that afterwards I could hardly look her or Laufey in the eye.'

'Did you know she was pregnant?'

Unnar stared down at the table in front of him. His knuckles were white where he was gripping the glass. When he nodded, the movement was barely perceptible.

'You need to answer aloud,' Elma reminded him. 'For the recording.'

'Yes,' Unnar said huskily. 'I knew Lise was pregnant.'

'When did she tell you?'

'On the Friday before the weekend she left.'

'You mean the weekend she died,' Elma said, and Unnar nodded again.

'And what did you do when she broke the news to you?'

'I didn't do anything, I...' Unnar bent forwards, rubbing his forehead with both hands. 'It looks so bad, but I swear I didn't do anything to Lise. Honestly.'

'Did Lise want to keep the child, was that it?' Sævar asked. 'Or was she planning to tell Laufey?'

'Yes, but ... No, she wasn't planning to tell Laufey anything.'

'How did you react?' Elma asked. 'Lise's injuries show that she received a blow to the back of her head. Can you explain that?'

Unnar's silence told them everything they needed to know.

'So when Andri came home on Saturday night and told you Lise had stayed behind at Marinó's house, you decided to go and fetch her. Only, by the time you got there, Lise was dead. Or did she maybe die while you were with her?' Elma studied Unnar, the thin hair on the crown of his head, the eyebrows tufty from where he had rubbed them, the neatly trimmed stubble.

He closed his eyes and suddenly began to shake. For a moment or two, Elma thought he was crying, but then she saw the smile spreading across his face.

'You ... this ... This whole thing's a joke. It's a fucking joke.'

'I just don't understand how Marinó got mixed up in it,' Elma said. 'Why did he agree to help you hide her body? Did you promise him money, or threaten him, maybe? And why did he have to die? Was it to silence him?'

'Seriously?' Unnar said. 'Do you seriously believe that? Marinó was a friend of my son's. I've known Marinó since he was a little boy and I would never have laid a finger on him.'

'Then can you tell us where you were?' Sævar asked and proceeded to read out the dates of the weekends when Lise and then Marinó had died. Like Elma, he had been taken aback by the laughter. There was something unhinged about it.

Unnar filled his lungs again and his smile vanished. 'I was babysitting the girls the first weekend because Laufey was out with her friends. The second weekend I hosted a dinner party, and I can give you the names of my friends who'll confirm it.'

'But that was only during the evening,' Elma said. 'Data from your phone indicates that you were near Marinó's house that night.'

Unnar was visibly shocked. 'That has nothing to do with me.'

'Then answer the question,' Sævar said.

'No,' Unnar replied, lowering his eyes. 'Not without a lawyer.'

Friday

'Are we looking for anything in particular?'

'A down jacket. A black down jacket with a fur trim.' Elma was standing in the kitchen, doing her best not to get in the way of the forensics team. Laufey had gone out with her daughters while the house was being searched. Elma watched as one of the technicians bagged up Unnar's shoes while another removed the home computer. There was no doubt in her mind that Unnar had inflicted the blow that led to Lise's death, but the sequence of events after that remained murky. Elma found it hard to believe that Unnar had murdered Marinó, despite the evidence of his phone. Why would he have gone to the trouble of spiking Marinó's drink with sleeping pills and setting fire to his house, only to leave Lise's body in the shed? There were too many loose ends for Elma's liking and too much that she didn't understand.

'Like this one?'

A female member of the crime-scene team was holding up a bulky black jacket, similar to the one worn by the suspect in the video footage.

'Yes, like that,' Elma said. She didn't let herself get excited, because down jackets were so common in Iceland that you would expect to find them in many homes, or at least in those whose owners had enough money to shell out a fortune on outdoor wear. 'What if he's washed it?'

'There could still be traces,' the woman said. 'A standard washing machine wouldn't be able to entirely remove petrol from clothes.'

Elma went over to the fridge, which was covered in pieces of paper, fixed with magnets. Two timetables, a certificate of progress in gymnastics and a drawing of a windmill with two girls standing on a riverbank, one smaller than the other.

Amsterdam.

Elma was sure the girls in the picture were meant to be Lise and Klara. She had noticed the drawings in Klara's room, which displayed surprising maturity for her age. Muted colours and carefully drawn lines, no scribbling. The figures were out of proportion, but not in the way that children would normally draw them: more as if they were supposed to be like that; as if the effect was deliberate.

Elma went back into Klara's room and examined the drawings on her desk. Her eyes wandered from one to the next, unsure exactly what she was looking for. There was the house, the garden and a boy with a football – obviously Andri: Klara had captured his nose and hair so well that he was unmistakable.

And, there, a picture of the garage and a girl.

Elma bent closer, frowning. It was an unusual drawing. The garage was depicted as if it stood on its own, surrounded by high trees that bowed over it. The proportions gave the impression of a dream rather than reality; the lines were all slanting, the shapes vague, again as if the effect was deliberate. There was a window in the garage wall with a curtain obviously drawn across it, and the door was closed. Outside it stood a girl, viewed from behind. Her face couldn't be seen, only her long, dark hair. It looked as if she was about to knock on the garage door, but her hands were laid flat on the wall either side of it.

'They're asking if there's anything else we need?' It was Sævar. 'Elma?'

Elma was still frowning at the picture, trying to guess who the mysterious girl could be or whether she was just a figment of Klara's imagination.

'Doesn't this strike you as an unusual picture?'

'What? That?' Sævar came to stand beside her and examined the drawing. 'Yes, a bit creepy, like a scene from a horror film.'

'Who do you think the girl is?'

'Lise?'

'Yes, but...' Elma hesitated. It could be Lise. The figure had long, dark hair like her.

'She's bloody good,' Sævar remarked. 'What is she, ten?'

'Yes, Klara's ten.'

'Right, well. Is there anything else we need apart from the shoes, coat and computer?'

'No, that's it, I think.' Elma glanced around. 'Oh, and the luggage, of course. Lise's luggage could be hidden somewhere on the premises.'

'Great, I'll let them know.'

Elma turned to follow him. As she was leaving the room, she cast one more backward glance at the picture, then shook her head. A drawing by a ten-year-old girl was unlikely to tell her anything of significance.

September 2019

Lise didn't return to the house until she was sure Unnar had gone to work. He wouldn't do anything to her while Laufey was home. But, as it turned out, Lise needn't have worried, because Unnar didn't come home for the rest of the day.

The bleeding started on the Saturday morning. At first, it was no more than a small spot on her knickers, but then it got heavier and heavier. Lise stared at the blood, feeling detached from what was happening, as if somehow removed from her own body.

'Are you ready?' Andri asked, sticking his head round Lise's door that evening.

She looked up from where she had been staring blankly at the wall.

'Ready?' she asked.

'Yes, you know. The party at Marinó's.'

'Oh, of course.' Lise looked down at her red-checked pyjama bottoms.

She had been feeling peculiar all day: tired, dazed and lethargic. The back of her head was still aching, and when she stroked the sore area with her fingers she could feel a large bump.

'You've still got time to change,' Andri said awkwardly, after a moment's silence. 'But if you don't want to come, that's fine.'

'No, I'll come,' Lise said hurriedly. The thought of going out wasn't particularly appealing, but the last thing she wanted was to spend all evening in the house.

'Cool,' Andri said. 'Er … just knock on my door when you're ready.'

Lise nodded, forcing her lips into a smile. When he had gone, she closed the door and went to stand in front of the long wall mirror. *This* evening she would go to the party and forget about everything.

Tomorrow she would be gone from here. It didn't matter that she hadn't got round to booking the flight yet. If there were no seats available, she had inherited enough money from her father to stay in a hotel if necessary. And she could ring Anita to let her know her new arrival date. In a few days' time she would be back in Amsterdam, breathing in the familiar smell of the home she had shared with her father, meeting up with Anita, going to a café, and everything that had happened in Iceland would be water under the bridge.

Lise picked up her brush and began dragging it through her hair. She had never developed the knack of putting on make-up like Andri's girlfriends and didn't bother to try now.

After a moment's thought, she pulled her suitcase out from under the bed and wiped the dust off it. How well she remembered her arrival in Akranes, when Unnar had swung the case into the boot of their four-by-four. She had been so excited. Unnar and Laufey had looked like the perfect couple; the kind of couple she wished she'd had as parents. She'd had no idea then about all the little secrets festering under the surface.

Lise opened her case and, rather dazed, began to scoop up as many of her clothes as she could in one go, then dropped them in. Next, she took the drawings Klara had given her, folded them carefully into her diary and laid this on top of the heap of clothes.

It took her only a few short minutes to pack away her life in Iceland, and yet it felt as if a heavy burden had been lifted from her shoulders. She closed the case and sat down on top of it, hiding her face in her hands. In spite of the headache, she couldn't help smiling.

At last she was getting out of here.

Saturday

'Congratulations again,' Elma said, as Hörður entered the meeting room. 'So it was a girl after all.'

'Thanks.' Hörður's face was split by a broad smile. 'That'll teach them not to cheat and try to find out the sex next time.'

He sat down and removed some papers from his briefcase, but he didn't seem able to stop smiling. After a mouthful of coffee, he adopted a more businesslike expression and launched into what he had to say.

'Right, we need to decide our next steps. I've got the report here from forensics. On Unnar's coat they discovered traces of the same kind of petrol as was used to start the fire. On the other hand, nothing was found on any of the shoes confiscated from the house, but we can assume that the pair in question has been thrown away. So, to sum up, we've got the coat and the phone data to locate him in the area at the relevant time. Forensics has also gone through Lise's luggage, which turned up in the garage loft, and discovered a diary she had been keeping. She wrote it in Dutch, so they had to get it translated at short notice, but it states clearly that she and Unnar were involved. However, it seems Unnar was telling the truth when he claimed they only slept together the once and that he avoided her afterwards. In the final entry, Lise describes how he shoved her up against a wall and complains that she's got a headache.'

Elma and Sævar listened in silence until Hörður had finished.

'That should be enough to satisfy the prosecution service, shouldn't it?' Sævar asked.

'Well, we know that Unnar attacked Lise and that his coat connects him to the scene of the fire but...' Hörður paused. 'But we still don't have a motive, do we? We don't know why Unnar would have wanted to murder Marinó.'

'Perhaps Marinó knew what had happened to Lise and was planning to tell people,' Sævar suggested.

'Then why did he stay silent so long?' Hörður asked. 'Personally, I can't see how Unnar could have convinced Marinó to hide Lise's body in his garden shed. And, what's more, we have no evidence of any communication between Marinó and Unnar.'

'But ... the coat,' Sævar protested. 'And the location of his phone. I mean, I admit we don't know exactly how the whole thing played out, but isn't it obvious that Unnar's our man?'

'Another member of the family could have borrowed Unnar's coat,' Elma cautioned.

They all stared in silence at the papers on the table.

'As I said,' Hörður resumed eventually, 'a lot of details remain unclear, and Unnar flat out denies having been involved in Marinó's death. We mustn't forget that the murder was premeditated and carried out by someone the victim almost certainly knew. After all, he let the person into his house and accepted a drink from them. As we know, the drink was spiked with such a large quantity of sleeping pills that Marinó was dead before the fire started.'

'Then why the fire?' Elma asked. 'Why not make do with the sleeping pills? A fire would attract far more attention than an overdose, which could easily be mistaken for suicide.'

'But we've got the phone and the coat,' Sævar said again. 'I don't understand why we should go looking for any other suspects. It seems obvious to me that Unnar acted alone. The fire was probably intended to destroy any evidence that might have been left in Marinó's house.'

'Yes,' Elma said. 'I suppose you're right.'

Sunday

'I'll go.'

'Don't be silly,' Elma said, taking her jacket off its hanger in the cupboard. 'I'm pregnant, not ill. I'm perfectly capable of fetching my own ice-cream.'

'Are you sure?' Sævar asked, without raising his eyes from the television.

'I'm sure.'

Sævar made a face when one of the players fell over and there was a burst of booing from the stands.

'It isn't even your team,' Elma said, shaking her head.

'No, but ... no one went near him.' Sævar looked at Elma indignantly as if expecting her to agree. 'That was a dive!'

'Really, Sævar.' Elma rolled her eyes to show her opinion of this.

On the way to the shop she hummed along to a song on the car radio. The rain was lashing the windscreen so hard that the wipers could scarcely keep up.

Earlier that day she had read the entire translation of Lise's diary. It had felt wrong, unethical, to read someone's private diary, but at least she now knew Lise a little better. The girl had been strikingly intelligent and had written beautifully, almost lyrically in places, though the translation, produced in haste, was unlikely to do it justice. Lise had obviously been very close to her father and her grief was so sincere and crushing that at times Elma had found it painful to keep reading.

Lise's feelings for Unnar seemed to have been complicated. She was obviously ashamed of what had happened between them and blamed herself, though it was clear to an observer how Unnar had flirted with her beforehand. After they slept together, however, he had become distant.

Nowhere was there any mention of Unnar being violent towards her, apart from that one incident at the end. On the contrary, Lise described him as nice and kind. It was only when she told him she was pregnant that he had lost his temper. She herself seemed to have had difficulty believing he could have done something so out of character.

As she read, Elma could see that this was no marriage wrecker but a fragile young girl struggling to cope with grief. Her desire for a family was almost palpable; it dripped from every page, and Elma would have given anything to be able to reach out and hug her.

She could understand why Lise hadn't wanted the abortion Unnar had tried to insist on. The girl had no family left, and the baby might have been her only chance to start one of her own.

The diary ended the day Lise had gone to the party with Andri. In the last entry it also emerged that she had started bleeding, which meant she must have been aware of the miscarriage.

According to Andri's friends, she had drunk a lot that evening. And by Andri's own account, he had come home without Lise and bumped into his father, who had asked where she was then gone out to find her.

After that, the sequence of events became hazy, but over the next few days the police would attempt to construct a sufficiently strong case against Unnar. All the evidence pointed to his involvement, but to bring a prosecution they would still have to tie up the loose ends. Elma just hoped Unnar would give in and confess. That would simplify everything.

After going to the shop, she unwrapped the ice lolly and took the long way home, eating it as she drove. She had started having cravings for lollies and other cold foods: if nothing else was available, she chewed ice cubes in the evenings.

On the coast road above Langisandur beach, she spotted a familiar-looking figure walking along the pavement with a backpack slung over one shoulder and his hand buried deep in his trouser pocket. He seemed indifferent to the rain, perhaps because he was already drenched.

Elma slowed the car and rolled down her window. In the circumstances, he might not feel like accepting a favour from the police, but she called out to him anyway: 'Andri! Would you like a lift?'

Andri hesitated a moment, then came over. His hair was wet, his fringe getting in his eyes as he bent down. A small drip ran off a strand of hair onto his cheek.

'That's OK.'

'Jump in,' Elma insisted.

'Are you sure? I don't mind walking.'

'Sure, it's no problem. I'm not going anywhere in particular.'

Andri got into the passenger seat and smiled at her. He smelt of sweat and rain, and his hands were bright red with the cold.

'Were you at training?' she asked.

'Yes, hopefully for the last time.'

'Oh, yes, of course, you're going abroad soon, aren't you? Assuming that's still the plan?'

The family's situation had undergone a drastic change when his father was taken into custody. Elma still didn't know how Laufey was taking it; whether she would choose to believe her husband and stand by him.

'In two days, yeah.'

'Great. I'm glad you're still intending to go.'

'Yeah,' Andri said. 'My sisters are coming too.'

'Oh, that's nice.' They drove past the nursing home and the new block of flats that had been given the odd name of the Black Diamond. At least it was better than 'Graveside', which was how the townspeople had referred to it while it was under construction, thanks to its proximity to the nursing home.

'What, er … Do you think he'll go to prison?' Andri didn't need to explain who he was referring to.

Elma paused before replying: 'I don't know. I suppose we'll just have to wait and see.'

'Yeah.' Andri leant his head back and sighed. 'I hope he does.'

Elma darted him a questioning look.

'Oh, it's just … Dad's never been particularly … He was never good to Mum.'

'I'm sorry.' They had reached Andri's house, and Elma stopped the car outside.

'Yeah. You know, he never hurt her physically, like he did Lise, but he did a lot of things that were worse. He got Lise pregnant and … and everyone in town knows that he's always with some woman or other. He doesn't give a shit about us.'

Elma didn't know what to say. She felt sorry for Andri. She couldn't imagine what it was like to grow up with all that gossip doing the rounds about your father.

Andri picked up his backpack from the floor and thanked her for the lift. Elma watched him walk towards the garage with his face raised a little to catch the raindrops. He cast a glance back at her before going inside and closing the door.

Elma was about to pull away when she saw Klara and Anna walking along the pavement. She darted a quick glance at the house before getting out of the car. She was well aware that she was in a grey area, talking to minors without the permission of their parents, but it wasn't as if she was planning to interrogate them.

'Hi,' she said, going to meet them. She gave Anna a smile but it was her older sister she addressed: 'Your name's Klara, isn't it?'

'Yes.' Both girls stopped when she was still a few steps away. Klara was wearing a yellow waterproof, but the long, curly hair sticking out from under her hood was dripping wet.

'I hear you're really good at drawing,' Elma said.

Klara didn't answer.

'I, um…' Elma tried again: 'I saw this amazing drawing in your room of a girl who … who was looking in a window.'

Klara still didn't answer. The girls just stared at her, puzzled, and Elma realised this must sound very odd to them. They might not remember her as the detective who had come round to their house, or understand how she'd come to see the picture on the desk in Klara's room.

'Do you know which drawing I'm talking about?' Elma persisted.

Klara nodded.

'I'm so curious about the girl in the picture. Is she someone you know or…?'

To Elma's surprise, Klara seemed to flinch at the question. She stiffened, her eyes opening wide in alarm.

'Klara.' Elma took a step forwards. 'Is everything all right?'

Before Elma could say another word, Klara had darted past her. The slam of the front door echoed over the sound of the rain. Elma sighed and turned to go back to the car but then noticed that Anna was still standing there, looking at her.

'It's Lise,' the little girl said, narrowing her eyes a little. She bent towards Elma and added confidingly: 'We've both seen her in the night.'

'In the night?' A cold gust of wind blew rain into Elma's face and she hugged her coat to her body.

'She's dead but…' Anna lowered her voice '…but she hasn't gone away.'

September 2019

'Come in,' Fríða said, opening the door to Lise and Andri. She was wearing a strappy top and slippers without socks.

Loud music was blaring from the sitting room, but the noise was abruptly cut off when the draught made the hall door slam shut.

'Whoops,' Fríða said, closing the front door. 'We've got the garden door open. Marinó's barbecuing burgers.'

'Cool. I'll go and see if he needs any help.' Andri went past them and out onto the deck to join Marinó.

On the kitchen island there was a crate of beer and a variety of other bottles, along with a bunch of mint and a packet of sugar. A small puddle had formed around a bag of ice that was lying beside the large blender.

'Do you want something to drink?' Fríða asked. 'I'm making mojitos.'

'Yes, please.'

The next track came on: 'I Don't Care' by Justin Bieber – the song Anna had been playing nonstop all summer. The little girl was crazy about the singer and had a poster of him on her wall. Three years ago Anna had gone to a Bieber concert and bought a T-shirt with his face on the front that was way too big for her. She wore it constantly, over tight leggings, which made it look like a dress. Lise smiled at the thought. She would miss the girls. In spite of everything, she regarded them almost like little sisters and had grown so fond of them that she felt choked up at the thought she would probably never see them again.

'Where are the boys?' Sonja had materialised in the kitchen. 'Oh hi, Lise.'

'Hi.'

Lise always felt a little shy in the presence of Sonja, whose life seemed so hectic and beset with problems: Ísak, the baby, the flat, her job, and some man who wouldn't leave her alone. Lise had only met her a few times, but the conversation invariably revolved around Sonja and her problems. In fact, Lise suspected it was Sonja who went looking for problems, rather than the other way round. She was the sort of person who seemed to thrive on drama and friction.

'Could you make mine extra strong?' Sonja asked Fríða.

'Sure,' Fríða said. 'The boys are outside, by the way.'

Sonja took her drink and went out to join them.

'I bet she's going to start having a go at Ísak,' Fríða whispered. 'It probably wasn't a very wise idea to invite them both round at the same time when they're drinking.'

'Why not?'

'Oh.' Fríða hesitated. 'They've been having a lot of problems. They're not a good fit.'

'They're not?'

'No, their relationship's nothing but trouble. Though don't tell Sonja I said that.' Fríða handed Lise a drink and smiled. 'Have you noticed that Andri's always looking at you?'

'What, really?' Lise glanced over at the boys and caught Andri dropping his eyes. 'There's nothing going on between us. We're just friends.'

'If you say so,' Fríða replied.

Lise nodded and sucked on her straw. The sweet, fresh-tasting cocktail slipped easily down her throat. She had taken a painkiller for her headache before coming out and was feeling a little better. She went outside to join the others. The warm sun, the appetising smell of grilling burgers and the alcohol in her veins helped her temporarily forget her troubles, just as she had hoped.

The shopping bags weren't particularly heavy, even though Elma had ended up buying far more than just an ice lolly, yet Sævar rushed over to relieve her of them. Elma thought she would enjoy the rest of her pregnancy if he was going to wait on her hand and foot like this.

'Are you hungry?' Sævar asked, as they were putting the food away in the fridge.

'Starving.'

'Were you seriously planning to eat these?' He was holding up a packet of spring rolls.

'Oh, come on, they're good.'

'Elma,' Sævar said sternly. 'They're not good. But I'll make you something that is.' He took a box of eggs and some other ingredients out of the fridge and ordered Elma to sit down on the sofa. As always, Birta shuffled up to press against her, resting her muzzle on Elma's thigh.

Elma's clothes were still damp from standing out in the rain, talking to Klara and Anna. She thought about what the girls had said: no doubt they were traumatised by the recent events and had started imagining that they could see Lise. Children had difficulty grasping the finality of death, and Elma thought this might be a manifestation of that. Although she was no expert in child psychology, she had completed two years of her degree before dropping out. Perhaps Laufey would agree to her daughters' receiving trauma counselling, in the hope that this would help them sleep at night.

'Did you know that there's a study that shows women are attracted to men who are psychopaths?' Elma remarked, easing Birta's head off her leg and going over to stand beside Sævar, who was frying slices of bread with eggs dropped into holes in the middle.

'Is that why you fancy me so much?' Sævar grinned.

'Ted Bundy was inundated with love letters in prison.'

'You're kidding?'

'I'm not. I think he even had a child.'

'Interesting,' Sævar said, putting a plate on the table and ordering her to sit down.

Later that evening, as Elma was brushing her teeth, she remembered her conversation with Andri. Evidently he didn't have much time for Unnar, and she couldn't blame him. Father and son had probably never been that close. What's more, Andri seemed to feel a protective urge towards his mother and obviously hated seeing how his father treated her.

But there was one thing he'd said that stayed with her, and the more Elma thought about it, the more convinced she became that there was something fishy about it.

Monday

As Laufey shut the last suitcase, she was seized by the urge to pack all their luggage into the boot of the car and set off at once. She had been waiting so long that she couldn't bear it another minute. She wanted to get out of this house, out of Akranes and Iceland. The flat she had rented for them in Sweden was ready, fully furnished with everything they would need. The forecast for Örebro was sunny. It had been more than 20°C yesterday, and the next few days were supposed to be equally fine.

She pictured herself spreading a picnic blanket on the small lawn in front of the house and relaxing while Anna practised her gymnastics and Klara read. They would be happy there.

Laufey wondered when she should tell them that they wouldn't be coming back to Iceland. Should she do it on the plane or wait until they got to Sweden? It would probably be better to delay it a little. Enjoy the first few days in their new surroundings, show them around the town. There was a beach on the lakeshore within walking distance of their house; perhaps she'd break the news to them there. Although she was fully expecting Anna to protest, she wasn't worried about her: Anna found it easy to make friends and would fit in anywhere.

And Klara was unlikely to take it badly. She wasn't happy at school in Akranes. The class she was in was wrong for her; dominated by strong personalities, among whom Klara seemed lost. Although she'd been at the school for five years, she had no real friends.

The girls would get on OK. Andri could play football, and if he didn't want to do that, he could continue with his education.

It didn't matter, she would support him whatever he decided to do.

Laufey also had a back-up plan, in case the children were reluctant to accept the situation: a dog. She was going to buy a large, shaggy animal that she could take for walks by the lake during the day and which would sleep on the floor by her bed at night.

The girls would do anything for a dog.

'Mummy, what are you doing? What's in that suitcase?' Anna jumped onto Laufey and Unnar's bed. She was barefoot, with painted toes, and although she had obviously applied the nail polish herself, she had done a pretty good job for a seven-year-old.

'Our clothes.' Laufey watched as Anna wrinkled her nose.

'Why?'

'I was going to tell you this evening, but…' Laufey leant forwards and whispered: 'We're going to Sweden with Andri.'

'Really?' Anna began to bounce up and down on the bed in her excitement. 'Can I miss school?'

'Yes.' Laufey smiled. 'For now.' This was one of the details she had yet to sort out. She hadn't spoken to the schools, either here or in Örebro. She was too afraid that her secret plan would be exposed if she did. All it would take was one email, one phone call, and Unnar would discover the whole thing. She couldn't take that risk.

'Oh, great! I'm going to ring Ína and tell her.'

'No.' Laufey grabbed Anna's arm. 'You must promise not to tell anyone. It's a secret.'

'Oh, just Ína – nobody else.'

'No, I'm sorry, darling.' Laufey reminded herself to keep an eye on the phone so Anna couldn't sneakily make a call, something she was all too capable of.

'What about Daddy? Is he coming too?'

To Laufey's relief, the doorbell rang, sparing her the need to answer.

Although she could tell she wasn't welcome, Elma didn't mind; she was used to it. In fact, she was always rather surprised when members of the public welcomed the police in and offered them coffee. It was more common for people to want to get rid of them as soon as possible.

'Is Andri in?' Elma asked.

'Yes,' Laufey said. 'He's in the shower.'

'Great. Maybe I could wait for him then?'

'Sure.' Laufey snatched a glance over her shoulder, and Elma realised the girls were home. Two school bags were propped against the wall, and a noisy cartoon was playing in the other room. She hoped the girls wouldn't come out and see her, as it could give rise to awkward questions.

'Can I offer you something?' Laufey asked eventually, as if compelled by her innate sense of hospitality.

'No, thanks,' Elma said, then changed her mind: 'Maybe a glass of water.'

She followed Laufey into the kitchen and stood there while she drank the water.

'How are you all coping?'

'Fine,' Laufey said, smiling dully. 'We'll survive.'

'Of course.' Elma wanted to ask if she had suspected Unnar of having an affair with Lise but felt it would be inappropriate. Laufey had probably had enough of talking about Unnar. 'Andri said you were going abroad soon.'

'Yes, we're going to Sweden with him.'

'The girls too?'

'Yes, I think we could all do with holiday.' Laufey started as a door slammed in the hallway. 'There you go, Andri's finished in the shower.'

Laufey hurried out, and Elma heard them talking in low voices.

Andri came in shortly afterwards, dressed in tracksuit bottoms and a T-shirt. He seemed wary as he greeted her.

'Hello again,' Elma said, giving him a friendly smile. Laufey didn't come back, so it was just the two of them in the kitchen.

'Yeah, hi.' Andri opened one of the cupboards and took out a glass. 'What did you want to see me about?'

'I have a couple more questions, if that's OK?'

Andri didn't say anything, just looked at her with his eyebrows raised. Elma took this as assent.

'I was wondering about your relationship with Lise – were you good friends?' When Elma had put the same question to him before, she had been left with the impression that they were no more than casual acquaintances. Andri had said he'd invited her along to meet his mates sometimes, to please his mother, who was worried about Lise being lonely.

'No, not really.' Andri turned on the tap and filled the glass with water.

'The thing is, we – the police, that is – haven't made all the information about the case public.' Elma rephrased this: 'By which I mean, there are details that only we know.'

Andri waited.

'But yesterday, when I gave you a lift, you said something that … well, that you couldn't have known unless Lise had confided in you.'

'What did I say?'

'You said that Lise was pregnant.' Elma waited for a reaction but there was none. 'How did you know?'

Andri shrugged. 'She told me.'

'I don't understand,' Elma said. 'If you knew your father and Lise were having an affair, why didn't you say anything? Did it never occur to you that it might have played a part in her death? Did it not strike you as important information?'

Andri drained the glass in one go then put it in the sink.

'So you knew all along that your father and Lise were sleeping together. Not only that but you told us your father asked you where she was the evening she vanished; you knew he'd gone after her.'

'I...' Andri's face was twisted with pain when he turned round. 'It wasn't like that.'

'What was it like, then, Andri? Did you or did you not know about their relationship? And why didn't you tell us?'

Andri hesitated, rubbing his forehead with the tips of his fingers. Elma noticed that his hands were shaking.

'Andri,' Elma said, taking a step closer. 'What happened?'

'I thought she fancied me,' Andri said. 'I really believed Lise fancied me. I thought she was different, that I could talk to her, but ... but she turned out to be pregnant by my dad.' He spat out the final words in disgust.

'Andri,' Elma said quietly. 'Did you do something to Lise when she rejected you?'

Before Andri could answer, the silence was broken by a quiet click.

September 2019

The toilet bowl had become all too familiar a sight. Lise could no longer hear anyone knocking on the door; they had finally left her in peace. She sat on the floor, leaning her head against the side of the bath. The sweat on her forehead was cold now, the painkillers had stopped working some time ago, and she felt as if someone was banging a drum inside her head.

What on earth had happened?

She remembered dancing and talking far too much. She had even told them about her father and burst into tears like an idiot. Cried on Fríða's shoulder while the other girl stroked her hair.

Nausea prevented Lise from recalling anything else.

After she had spat a few times into the toilet bowl, she rose groggily to her feet and looked in the mirror. She smoothed down her hair with her fingers, drank some water straight from the tap and rinsed her mouth out.

It was time to go home, she thought. Now she could go home.

When she emerged, the music was still playing but the volume had been turned down. She found Andri in the sitting room, absorbed in his phone.

'Were you waiting for me?' she asked.

'Yeah. Are you OK or…?'

Lise shrugged.

'Do you want to lie down?' a voice behind her asked. Lise looked round and saw Marinó holding a cloth and an empty beer can. 'I'm just tidying up a bit before Mum and Dad get back from their trip,' he explained, smiling. 'But you can lie down if you like. Fríða's staying with Hrafnkell, so her bed's free.'

Lise would have preferred to go home but suddenly she felt an urgent need to lie down. She stood there blinking, the earth moving in waves under her feet.

'I'll show you,' Andri said. He took her by the arm and led her to one of the bedrooms.

Laufey's hands were steady, her stare unwavering. The woman standing in front of Elma, pointing a shotgun at her, appeared perfectly calm and resolute.

Elma felt herself stiffening up with fear. 'Laufey,' she said, trying to fight down a rising sense of panic, 'there's absolutely no need for that. I'm not going to—'

'No,' Laufey said. 'But I can't risk you going back to the police station.'

'Mummy,' one of the girls called, but Laufey didn't let this put her off.

'Andri, go to your sisters. Make sure they don't leave the TV room.'

Out of the corner of her eye, Elma saw Andri wipe a hand over his face. He didn't look at her as he left the kitchen; Laufey, on the other hand, never took her eyes off her.

'It was an accident,' Laufey said. 'Andri never meant to hurt her. Was he supposed to call the police and ruin his life? Who would have believed him?'

'What happened?' Elma asked, doing her best to keep her voice steady, despite her pounding heart. She had no idea if Laufey had ever fired a gun before, but knew that if the woman made even the slightest movement, deliberate or not, the gun could go off.

'He can't even remember himself,' Laufey said. 'He passed out drunk and when he woke up Lise was lying there dead beside him. Why should he go to prison for something he can't even re-member doing? And what about his football? What about everything he's worked for since he was a little boy? He couldn't afford to be mixed up in a case like that, not when he'd finally got the chance to go abroad. If the police had been called, they'd have jumped to the wrong conclusions.'

'Andri didn't kill Lise,' Elma said quickly. The sequence of events was becoming clear now, and she realised that the whole thing had indeed been triggered by one big misunderstanding.

Laufey frowned.

'Lise had a rare condition,' Elma went on, before the other woman could speak. 'She had a blood-clotting defect that meant a blow would have much more serious repercussions for her than for other people. When Unnar pushed her against the wall and she banged her head, it caused a brain haemorrhage that eventually killed her.' Elma could hear the desperation in her voice, as if she thought this information alone might be enough to persuade Laufey to put the gun down.

'But...'

'Andri didn't kill Lise,' Elma repeated urgently. 'He doesn't remember it because it didn't happen. Lise's death had nothing whatsoever to do with Andri.'

Laufey lowered the gun slightly, and Elma saw that she was fighting back tears. 'So Unnar...'

'Yes, it was Unnar's fault that she died,' Elma said. 'But he would never be convicted of premeditated murder. He had no way of knowing that Lise would die as a result of banging her head.'

Laufey tightened her grip on the gun. 'But that makes no difference now, does it? Andri would go to prison anyway for concealing the body, and, even if he didn't go to prison, his life would be ruined. He would always carry the stigma.'

The cartoon abruptly went quiet, and one of the girls called out to Laufey again.

'Mummy's just coming,' Laufey answered in a cheerful voice.

They heard Andri say something, then the door closed and their voices were cut off.

Elma seized the chance while Laufey was distracted to scan

the kitchen. Was there anything on the table she could use to defend herself? There was a chopping board and a salt cellar, but no knives or heavy objects. Outside, a car drove past but didn't stop.

No one knew where Elma was. The evening before she had mentioned her suspicions to Sævar, saying that maybe Andri knew more than he was letting on, but she wasn't sure Sævar had taken it in. When she came into the bedroom he was asleep, and although he had opened his eyes and nodded while she was talking to him, she wasn't sure he'd been fully conscious.

'Come on,' Laufey said, gesturing with the gun towards the hall. She seemed to be having trouble with her eyes all of a sudden; she kept blinking rapidly and taking gasping breaths.

'Why did Marinó have to die?' Elma asked, delaying.

'It was an accident; it wasn't supposed to happen – none of it was supposed to happen.' Laufey suddenly lowered the gun and leant against the wall. She closed her eyes and sank down to the floor. 'I don't feel well, I don't think I can…'

Elma grabbed her chance and took a step towards her. She bent down cautiously and was just reaching for the gun when she felt a sharp pain in her head.

September 2019

Andri led Lise into Fríða's room and helped her lie down. It was comfortable and the bedspread was soft, but her head was agony and the world was spinning. She closed her eyes. Slowly, she became aware of a hand stroking her forehead. Was it Andri? Lise rose up on her elbow and looked around.

'Feeling any better?' *Andri was sitting beside her, watching her.*

'What time is it?'

'Three.'

'Oh. Maybe we should...'

Andri stood up and Lise fell silent. Then he sat down beside her again with his hands in his pockets and, not looking at her, asked: 'Why did you come here?'

'What?'

'I said: why did you decide to come here? Why would anyone choose to come to Akranes of all places?' *He was squinting and seemed to be having trouble keeping his eyes open.*

'Are you drunk?' *Lise had been under the impression that Andri didn't drink.*

'A bit,' *he said, and smiled. He blinked a few times then cleared his throat.* 'I'm not as drunk as I look.'

'No problem.'

'I never usually touch alcohol.'

'No.'

'I have to stay fit.' *His face loomed closer, and Lise withdrew slightly.*

'What are you doing, Andri?'

'You're pretty. Not conventionally pretty, you know. Not like that. More ... more kind of ordinary.'

'Ordinary?' Lise asked.

'Yeah, like natural. All the girls around here are so ... so plastered in make-up, with dyed hair and fake this and fake that. You're just natural. None of that artificial crap.'

'You mean like Júlía?'

'I mean like Júlía,' Andri agreed, and laughed. 'She's not like you.'

'Like me?'

'Yeah, you know. Kind of...' Andri's head sank slowly towards her as if he were falling. Then he twitched and his pupils slid to the front again.

'Kind of ordinary?' Lise asked, and smiled.

'Hey.' Andri sat up. He gazed at her for a while before speaking again. Pulled himself up straighter. 'They're so stupid. So vacant. Sometimes I listen to them yakking on and I want to scream. All they talk about is boys and clothes and ... and what fucking mascara – or whatever you call it – is best. You're not like that.' He stroked a finger over her forehead and down her cheek. Lise felt a ticklish sensation, the touch of his finger burning her face.

'I...' she began, but didn't get any further.

Andri lunged forwards. She gasped but didn't move away. His lips felt like tiny butterflies on her skin. He kissed her lightly, resting his hot, salty lips against hers. She opened her mouth a little. Felt the heat as his wet tongue gently touched hers. Through the smell of alcohol and cigarettes there was a hint of aftershave – the same aftershave Unnar used.

'Stop,' she said suddenly in a low voice, but Andri didn't seem to hear. She pushed him away and studied him. He had such a beautiful face, so innocent. So unlike Unnar's face.

'Don't you want...?' Andri asked in hazy surprise.

Lise swallowed but knew she would have to explain why she couldn't be with him. She just hoped he wouldn't take it too badly. Gazing into his beautiful eyes, she sat up.

'Andri, there's something you should know.'

'You shouldn't have come.'

The voice seemed to be speaking from the other side of the room. Elma blinked and became aware that her mouth was dry. The lights were off but it wasn't completely dark. Although the garage windows were small, they still admitted a dim, grey daylight. She didn't know what time it was; the sun was hidden behind a thick layer of cloud.

When she tried to sit up, she realised why her wrists were hurting so much. They were tightly bound with thin twine that was cutting into her skin. She tried to move her hands but the twine had been wound round them so many times that it was almost impossible.

'We were planning to go away and try to put this behind us,' Andri said. 'Mum had arranged everything.'

'You don't need to do this: you didn't kill Lise,' Elma said desperately. 'There must be another way to solve this. I'm sure you wouldn't get a long sentence; you'd probably avoid prison altogether. It was your father who—'

'Yes, but Dad didn't hide the body and Dad didn't kill Marinó.' Andri's voice was calm and sounded oddly innocent, but there was a new, unsettling expression in his eyes; a brazen quality.

Elma studied him, taking in the way he was standing, hands in his pockets, like when she'd seen him walking home yesterday. Far from being worked up, he appeared to be amused. A small smile twitched his lips, and he seemed quite different from earlier. It was as if he had switched off an act and the show was over. She was frightened by how calm and dispassionate he seemed.

'What happened to Marinó?' she asked quietly.

'He was going to talk,' Andri said. 'He couldn't keep quiet

about what happened to Lise. We hid her body in the shed and were going to get rid of it somewhere the following weekend, but when it came to the point, he chickened out.'

'So you killed him?'

'No, I…' Andri paused, then, instead of finishing what he had been going to say, he turned to leave.

Elma asked quickly: 'Did you start the fire too?'

'No, I didn't start the fire.'

'Then who…?' Elma groaned, and then it came to her in a flash who had helped Andri.

'Mum was only looking out for me,' Andri said, meeting her eye.

'So she went and set fire to Marinó's house? But why?'

'Because if she hadn't, the police would have found out that I'd been there; they'd have discovered my fingerprints or … or something.'

Andri turned away again and took hold of the door handle.

'But Andri,' Elma said. 'You know that—'

'Sorry,' Andri interrupted, not looking at her. 'It's just got to be done.'

❦

Sævar couldn't stop whistling. He knew it was driving his colleagues up the wall but he couldn't help himself. Begga had even put her head round his door to ask if she could close it. The look she directed at him hadn't been particularly friendly.

For the last few days he had been in unusually high spirits. The mundane tasks that generally got on his nerves no longer bothered him. Even all the reports he still had to write didn't seem so bad. Nothing could dent his good mood. The rain outside, the storm that was forecast – they just made him look forward all the more to cuddling up on the sofa with Elma to watch a film together over a nice meal.

So he carried on whistling, and the time flew by. Towards midday he stood up and stretched. As things were quiet in the office, he thought maybe the two of them could pop out for lunch.

Elma's door was ajar. Sævar looked inside, expecting to see her sitting at the desk, but to his surprise her office was empty. At first, he thought she must be in the kitchen or with Begga, as it wasn't unusual for them to lose track of time while they were chatting, but then he noticed that Elma's bag wasn't by her desk and there was no coat hanging on the peg by the door. That was strange; normally she wouldn't go out without telling him.

Sævar went into the kitchen and found Begga there with Kári. 'Have either of you seen Elma?' he asked.

They both said no, so Sævar went back to his own office and tried calling her. When her phone went straight to voicemail, Sævar sat down again, trying to push away an uneasy feeling in the pit of his stomach. He was no longer in the mood to whistle.

'You must see, you must understand…' Laufey said, sounding disturbingly over-friendly. 'It wasn't Andri's fault. I had to do something or he would have been sent to prison.'

It was a while since Andri had left Elma in the garage. In the meantime, she had been struggling in vain to gnaw through the twine binding her hands. Her wrists had begun to bleed under the tight bonds, and it hurt so much when the twine dug into the cuts that it brought tears to her eyes.

The wait had also given her time to piece things together. She understood now how Andri had managed to fool them all. He may not have killed Lise but he had carried her body to the shed with Marinó's help, then murdered Marinó in cold blood. Andri seemed content to let his father take the rap for his crimes, which Elma found pretty ruthless, even allowing for their bad relationship.

'I had no choice,' Laufey continued. 'If I hadn't set fire to the house, Marinó would have been found, and the police would probably have arrested Andri. Have you any idea how serious the consequences would have been for him? Even if he wasn't convicted of murder, his career would have been over. No team would want to be associated with a player who had a history like that.'

There was a level on which Elma could understand that Laufey felt she'd had no choice. Yet it still seemed unbelievable that the woman should have agreed to do this for her son. Elma stared at her, with her head on one side.

Laufey met her eye resolutely, as if she could read her mind. 'I'd do anything for my children.'

'I know.' Elma leant back against the cold concrete wall, grimacing as the twine cut deeper into her wrists. She could tell there was no point trying to talk Laufey round.

'You don't have any children, do you?' Laufey asked.

'No, but…' Elma hesitated, then said: 'I'm pregnant.'

Laufey smiled for a moment as if pleased for her, then her expression grew sad.

'You know, I really don't want to do this.' She looked down at the gun and heaved a breath.

'You don't have to.' Elma closed her eyes, suddenly unable to speak.

She wanted to beg Laufey to let her go. Not for her own sake but out of a desperate desire for her and Sævar's child to be allowed to live.

Yesterday evening, she and Sævar had searched online to see what the foetus would look like at this stage. Incredibly, it had already taken on the appearance of a human being, with tiny hands and feet. The fingers had even started to form. As she looked at the images, Elma had been filled with wonder at the thought that, if all went well, in just a few short months from now she would be holding a fully formed baby in her arms. Their child would be its own person, with its own character and thoughts, and she couldn't wait to meet it.

But that would never happen now; she would never get to hold her baby.

'I'm afraid I have no choice,' Laufey said, smiling sadly at her.

She aimed the gun, and Elma felt her heart pounding frantically. She was filled with a despairing sense of helplessness when she realised that there was nothing she could do. Yet, at the same time, the situation seemed so unreal. This couldn't be happening; not to her.

'How?' she burst out. 'How ... What was Unnar doing there?'

'What?'

'Unnar's phone data,' Elma said in a rush. 'He was at Marinó's house that night. And we found traces of petrol on his coat.'

'Oh, yes.' Laufey smiled faintly. 'That was accidental; I put on Unnar's coat, and he always forgets his phone in the pocket. I'm forever telling him to be more careful, but now ... well, I expect he's finally learnt his lesson.'

'Did you know about him and Lise?'

'I found out later,' Laufey said, adding in a derisive tone: 'In the last week I've found out a number of things about my dear husband. For all I care, he can spend a few more days behind bars.'

'If you were wearing Unnar's coat, where was he?'

'I slipped a sleeping pill into his drink and waited until he was in bed. Then I put on his coat, with his phone in the pocket, and did what had to be done.'

'How did you get into Marinó's house?'

'Andri knew where the spare keys were kept.'

Outside, they heard Andri's voice calling Laufey. She brushed a lock of hair from her face and sighed. 'Anyway...'

'I used to babysit for Andri when he was small,' Elma blurted out, in yet another attempt to delay the inevitable. 'Or rather a friend of mine looked after him, and I often helped her.'

'Wait a minute, what was her name again? Silvía or…?'

'Silja.'

'Oh yes, Silja, that's right.'

'He was such a sweet little kid.'

'Yes,' Laufey said, her eyes suddenly misty. 'He still is. To me he'll always be that beautiful little boy who I'd do anything to protect.'

Laufey's chest expanded as she tightened her grip on the gun. Elma closed her eyes and waited.

✦

'Do you need to come in?'

Elma's neighbour opened the door to the entrance hall. The two little boys with her were in a race to see who could get outside first.

'No, that's OK,' Sævar said. He had already tried Elma's bell three times and was sure she wasn't home.

The woman smiled, then told the boys not to run outside before her. They ignored her.

Sævar returned to the car once the woman had gone. He sat there for a while, thinking back over the day yet again to make sure he hadn't missed anything. They had driven to work at the same time, each in their own cars as usual; had coffee, then gone to their separate offices. He remembered seeing Elma heading in the direction of the ladies at ten, but he hadn't seen her after that. Since midday he'd been trying repeatedly to call her but had got her voicemail every time. It was five o'clock now, and there was still no sign of her.

He decided to drive past her parents' house, though it made him feel like a stalker. He only meant to check if her car was there, then he'd go. Sævar finished the rest of yesterday's luke-warm fizzy drink, then backed out of the parking space.

Elma's parents lived in a cul-de-sac not far from her flat. Sævar had already met them several times and liked them; it would be impossible not to. Aðalheiður, Elma's mother, talked nonstop and was always bustling around the house. Sævar could hardly ever remember seeing her sit still. He'd been won over by the fact she knew almost more about English football than he did. Elma took more after her father, Jón, who was a gentle, placid character. But when he was in the mood, he and Sævar could talk for ages about anything under the sun. Although Jón hid it better, he was just as nosy as his wife. He was also fascinated by the technical side of police work and liked to bombard Sævar with questions.

When Sævar reached Jón and Aðalheiður's house, there were no cars in the drive. Elma clearly wasn't at her parents' place.

Sævar couldn't understand it. Unable to face going home without knowing where Elma was, he started driving aimlessly around town in the hope of coming across her. He drove past the hospital, checking, with his heart in his mouth, to see if her car was there, but fortunately there was no sign of it.

Something must have happened; he simply couldn't work out what.

When Sævar eventually parked outside his own block of flats, instinct told him he shouldn't go in. But there was nothing he could do, and he had no idea of where to look for Elma, so in the end he switched off his engine and went inside.

♦

The girls chattered all the way to the airport. They were so excited that they couldn't shut up for a second. Andri was playing a game on his phone, staring down absorbed, his thumbs moving rapidly over the screen. Laufey tried unsuccessfully to control her shaking.

She had been assailed by a powerful sense of unreality when she lowered the gun, staring at Elma on the garage floor. She had backed out of the door, her legs feeling heavy yet oddly weight-less at the same time. She wanted to run but instead she had closed and locked the garage, although it had taken her shaking fingers forever to insert the key in the lock.

After that, she had booked them onto the next flight out of the country, finished the packing, then hurried the kids out to the car. The whole thing had taken less than an hour, and her body seemed to be functioning on automatic, because her con-scious mind was entirely taken up with what she had done. She had planned everything so well: nothing must be allowed to go wrong now just because one person knew too much. She couldn't let it happen.

Laufey checked the clock on the dashboard. The plane was due to take off in under two hours, and they were almost at the airport. She wondered when she would start feeling like herself again and lose this sense of dislocation.

She glanced sideways at Andri and saw, as always, the little boy he had once been. The dark-blond hair, small hands and solemn face that would light up as soon as he had a ball at his feet.

Andri wasn't the same child anymore, she knew that. He was an adult now, and her little boy would never come back. The thought filled her with a sense of loss, which was foolish because Andri was still there, sitting right beside her. And of course she wanted her children to grow up and become adults.

Her thoughts returned to the night she had started the fire. Andri had come to her in such a state, utterly distraught about what had happened. He had acted without thinking and im-mediately regretted it. He begged her to help him. He was still holding the key to Marinó's house, having for some reason felt he should lock the door behind him when he left.

Laufey had taken the key and told Andri to go to bed. She had crushed a sleeping pill and put it in Unnar's drink, then waited for him to fall asleep. When she entered Finnur and Gerða's house, there had been dead silence. She couldn't remember whether she had found the bedroom immediately or had to search for it. All she remembered was standing there, looking down at the boy lying in bed, while she summoned up her courage. It had only taken her a minute or two to pour the petrol over the floor, then throw a match on it. She'd felt oddly detached, just as she did now, as if she weren't fully awake. As if a switch inside her had been flipped to automatic and she had acted without even thinking.

Of course, it must have helped that she was drunk and the only thought in her head had been to save Andri. The damage had been done, and all she had to do was ensure that no incriminating evidence would lead the police to her son.

Although she knew Marinó was already dead, part of her had been expecting to hear screams of terror behind her, but they hadn't come. The only sound had been the crackling of the flames as they spread so fast that she'd been forced to run out of the house.

'Andri.'

'Mm.' He didn't look up. His thumbs kept moving over the screen. Laufey saw that he was playing a football game. She swallowed. There was so much she wanted to ask but she didn't dare. Was she really that afraid of the answer?

'You know we'll have to go somewhere else,' she said eventually.

'I know.'

'That you won't be able to play for the club.'

'I don't care.' Andri finally looked up from his game. 'I couldn't care less about the club or about football, I just want to get away.'

❧

Elma had always been impulsive. If she got an idea, she generally went ahead and acted on it without stopping to think. This had become abundantly clear to Sævar after knowing her for two years. It wasn't just their spur-of-the-moment Tenerife trip last Christmas, but all kinds of more minor incidents connected to cooking or DIY projects. The window frame she hadn't realised you couldn't drill into, resulting in a cracked pane of glass, or the wall tiles she had painted without any preparation, which had started to peel after only a couple of days.

This tendency towards impetuous behaviour also spilled over into her job, where her curiosity led her astray at times. Instead of letting her colleagues know when she was going to see people, she had a tendency to act spontaneously on her hunches. More than once Sævar had to remind her that she wasn't in a TV programme or crime novel: the guidelines were there to ensure their safety.

Something Elma said yesterday evening had been bothering Sævar all day. It had only been a passing comment: Elma had thought it might be significant that Andri knew about Lise's pregnancy, since this information had not been made public. Nobody knew that Lise had died from a blow inflicted at least thirty-six hours before she died, and no one but Unnar had known she was pregnant.

Yet Andri had been in on the secret, which meant he had been lying to them. He had allowed them to believe that he and Lise were no more than casual acquaintances, and he had kept quiet about the fact she was pregnant by his father. When Elma drew attention to this last night, Sævar hadn't thought it was significant. He just assumed Andri was ashamed or trying to protect his father. Whatever the reason, Sævar reckoned there must be an innocent explanation.

But he wasn't sure that Elma believed this, so, after sitting around at home for an hour, unable to settle to anything, Sævar decided to call round at Laufey and Unnar's house. He knocked on his neighbour's door and asked if he could look after Birta, then headed out.

The first thing he saw when he got there was Elma's car, parked opposite. Sævar's momentary wave of relief gave way to concern.

Laufey and Unnar's house was obviously empty: there were no cars in the drive and all the lights were off. Yet he went up to the front door and knocked, first lightly, then harder, until his knuckles ached.

He could feel sweat breaking out all over his body but tried to think rationally. If Elma's car was here, she must have come round to see Andri. In that case, where was Andri?

Sævar went over to the garage where Andri had his flat. He knocked on the door but didn't wait long for an answer, peering through the window instead. Inside, as far as he could see, the room was a shambles. There was a pile of clothes on the bed, and a mess of plates and mugs on the desk. Sævar tried Elma's phone again but it went straight to voicemail. He walked round into the garden and pressed his face to all the windows. The curtains were drawn in what must be the master bedroom, but he could see into the other rooms. One of them was a typical little girl's room with a dressing table and dolls, the other was more grown-up, with a desk, colouring crayons and books. As he stepped onto the deck, he noticed the next-door neighbour eyeing him suspiciously. He must look like a burglar, prowling around, casing the joint. As a detective, he never wore a uniform, so no wonder the neighbour was concerned.

Ignoring the man, Sævar tried to make sense of what he was seeing. The house looked as if the occupants had just stepped out and were intending to return any minute. There were dishes on the table, and clothes and toys on the floor. Yet it was getting on for seven p.m. and no one was home. Then there was the presence of Elma's car. She had to be here somewhere. It occurred to him that she might know someone else who lived in the street; that the whole thing might be a misunderstanding. But that was impossible. She would never disappear for this long without letting him know. Although they weren't married or co-habiting, it was just so unlike her.

Deciding to ignore common sense, he tried the French windows. They were locked, but he shook them in an attempt to force them open. If the neighbour was concerned before, he was bound to be on the phone to the police by now. Sævar cursed when the doors failed to open. He scratched his head.

It occurred to him to ring the family, so he tried Laufey first but got her voicemail. Next, he tried Andri, whose phone rang twice before the call was cancelled. Sævar rang again, but this time it went straight to voicemail.

Sævar's heart was pounding as he shoved his phone back in his pocket. He gnawed at his lip, racking his brains. He couldn't break in, could he? He took hold of the door handle again, glancing over at the house next door. The neighbour was standing, watching him and talking on the phone.

Sævar put his shoulder to the glass door, stepped back a moment, then rammed it with all his might.

The frame broke and the door flew open. Sævar almost fell through the gap, then, recovering his balance, he scanned his surroundings.

'Elma!' he shouted.

There was no answer.

He knew his colleagues would be here soon, asking questions. How was he going to explain his actions? Sævar started to race around the house, opening all the doors and calling Elma's name. In the master bedroom, clothes had been piled on the bed as they had in Andri's room. All the evidence suggested the family had made a quick getaway.

Sævar ran a hand through his hair, trying to think, and his gaze fell on the window. He realised there was only one place he hadn't properly checked.

The cupboard in the hall turned out to be full of bunches of keys. Sævar grabbed them all and went outside.

He hammered on the garage door, shouting Elma's name. Then he started frantically sorting through the keys for one that might fit the lock.

The first likely looking one didn't work, nor did the second.

But the third slid in and turned without the need for any force. Out of the corner of his eye, he saw a police car pulling up in front of the house but he didn't bother to go over and explain himself, just flipped the light switch by the door.

It was then that he saw Elma.

'Sævar,' shouted a voice outside the garage. 'Sævar, what the hell are you doing?'

Sævar recognised Kári's voice but didn't answer. He couldn't think about anything but Elma.

She was lying against the wall, and Sævar felt as if he had been punched in the guts when he saw her face. She looked so ashen and ill. Her hands were lashed to a wall-mounted metal shelving unit, full of boxes.

'Elma.' He crouched down beside her and stroked her hair. Her wrists were bound with narrow twine and her hands were so white they must be drained of blood.

'What happened, Elma?'

She coughed and grimaced. 'Can you...?'

'Untie you?'

'I can't feel them anymore ... my hands...'

Sævar tried to loosen the twine but it was tied so tightly that he couldn't prise open the knots.

'What happened? Was it Andri?'

'Andri, yes,' Elma croaked. 'And Laufey.'

'Kári,' Sævar said in a louder voice, without turning round. 'Call back-up.'

'It'll be too late,' Elma whispered. She winced as Sævar attacked a knot in the twine, so she must have some feeling left. 'They had a flight booked today. I've been here since this morning. What time is it?'

'Nearly seven.'

'Seven.' Elma closed her eyes and swallowed with difficulty. 'They'll have gone.'

Kári had stepped back outside where they could hear him talking on the phone.

'Where? Where were they going?' Sævar asked, glancing around for a knife or any sharp implement he could use to cut the twine.

'I don't know.' Elma's voice was so hoarse it was almost inaudible. 'Out of the country, anyway.'

Sævar spotted a toolbox and opened it. He found a carpet knife and slid it cautiously under the twine, which snapped instantly. Elma let out a groan of relief. She rubbed her hands painfully, looking utterly exhausted. Suddenly Sævar couldn't give a damn about Laufey and Andri. All he wanted was to get Elma out of here.

'Are you OK?' he asked gently.

'I…' Elma gave a wobbly smile that threatened to tip over into tears. 'She was going to shoot me. She had a gun, she was pointing it at me with her finger on the trigger. I thought I was a goner.'

'What happened?'

'Laufey admitted everything,' Elma whispered. 'Andri thought he'd killed Lise, and Marinó helped him hide her body. But then Marinó wanted to tell the police, so Andri killed him. But it was Laufey who started the fire.'

Kári came back into the garage. 'The ambulance is here.'

'Ambulance ?' Elma began struggling to stand up. 'I don't need an ambulance. I just feel a bit dizzy but apart…'

Sævar grabbed her as she swayed. 'Elma, love.'

'I'm all right,' Elma insisted weakly, trying to recover her balance. 'I'm just so thirsty – and hungry.'

'Then we'll get you a drink and feed you.' Sævar smiled and helped her outside. 'At the hospital.'

October 2019

Laufey went to the window. The street outside was busy, even though this was a quiet suburb of the city. And the people behaved quite differently from those at home in Iceland: there was none of that nosiness and staring; everyone just got on with their own business. But then the sea of humanity was so unimaginably vast and the population so varied. Every time she went out with the girls it was an adventure. All the bustling life in the streets, all the plants and animals, were like a fairy tale to them.

When Laufey said they could choose new names for themselves and that they were going to get a dog, the girls had reacted as if Christmas had come early. They could hardly contain their excitement. It turned out that there were various methods of disappearing and plenty of people willing to help – for the right sum. The first day had been the biggest risk. They had left the country using their own passports, which would make it easy for the Icelandic authorities to discover that they had landed in France. What they had needed was a good head-start and they had got one. It wasn't until hours after they arrived that Laufey had seen their names appear in the Icelandic media. Within minutes she had given her and Andri's phones to a homeless family living in an alleyway.

After that they had boarded a train. Laufey had stayed awake all night as they raced through the darkness. She had watched over her three beautiful children, sending up a fervent prayer that nothing bad would happen to them; that everything would work out. When they disembarked eight hours later, to be greeted by warm sunshine and the smell of the sea, Laufey finally felt safe.

Her thoughts returned to the dinner party she and Unnar had given, and how everything had changed in a single night. When she'd glanced out of the window and seen Unnar and Harpa kissing in the garden, something inside her had broken. For years she had convinced herself that her marriage would improve if only she weren't so stressed all the time. But that night, seeing Unnar with Harpa, she had almost burst out laughing at the absurdity of it all. When the laughter dried up, she'd felt ashamed. Thinking back, she realised how naive and subservient she had been. As she stood there in the dark kitchen, she had felt her cheeks burning with the humiliation. Yet she kept watching them. Saw Unnar squeezing Harpa's breast, then moving his hand lower. Saw his eagerness, how they didn't stop until they were drenched by the rain. She forced herself to watch the whole thing, afraid that if she looked away she would start making excuses for Unnar again, just as she had all these years.

'Mum.'

Laufey turned to look at Andri. 'What is it, love?'

'I'm going out to kick a ball around.'

'Could you take your sisters with you?'

'No problem.' Andri smiled and called the girls, who came running.

Laufey watched them walk off in the direction of the nearby football pitch. Andri was so handsome and, above all, so kind. Ever since they arrived he had made sure his sisters were never bored. He'd taken them out and invented games for them, which gave Laufey time to sort out the flat. To make it homely. She still had no idea what the future would hold, only that sooner or later she would have to decide their next step.

Until then she was content just to be here, safe, with her children.

News Flash 03.11.2019

Last night, police arrested a woman believed to be connected to the house fire in Akranes on 15 September this year. The woman had fled the country with her son and two daughters in September. The daughters are now being cared for by their father.

The woman was arrested on arrival at Keflavík Airport after handing herself in. She is being held in custody while the case is under investigation.

The woman's son, Andri Unnarsson, is still wanted by the police. Anyone who may have information about Andri is requested to contact the police.

November 2019

Her mother wasn't answering the phone. Sonja tried her for what must be the twentieth time without success. She paced restlessly around the flat. Jóel was asleep: he had a bit of a cold, so she had put him down in his cot instead of outside in his pram, Icelandic fashion. She had already cleaned the whole place from top to bottom, simply because she couldn't sit still. Ever since she saw the news about Laufey's return to Iceland, she hadn't been able to think about anything else. Because if Laufey was back, she might know where Andri was hiding, and Sonja wanted to get hold of Andri. She needed to get hold of him urgently.

At that moment the doorbell rang, and Sonja put down her phone. Instantly recognising the policeman's voice over the entry phone, she buzzed him in.

'Hi,' the man said when she opened the door. 'I'm Sævar and this is Elma – we met a while ago.'

'Yes, I remember.' Sonja tried to disguise the tremor in her voice. What were the police doing at her flat?

'Is there somewhere we could sit down?' Elma asked. Her belly had expanded considerably since Sonja last saw her: there was no doubt she was pregnant.

'We can go into the sitting room,' Sonja said.

'Did you see on the news that Andri's mother, Laufey, has turned up?' Sævar asked in a conversational tone.

'Yes,' Sonja replied. 'I saw that.'

'Andri's on his way home too,' Sævar added.

Sonja's heart lurched and she could feel the colour draining from her face. 'Really?'

'Yes,' Sævar said. 'His plane is due to land this evening.'

Sonja was silent, aware that the purpose of their visit was not to tell her about Andri. She had an uneasy premonition about what was coming next.

'We've already talked to Andri,' Sævar continued. 'And he's got quite an interesting story to tell. According to him, you put sleeping pills in Marinó's drink without Andri's knowledge. He says the two of you went round to Marinó's house on the evening of Saturday the fourteenth of September to discuss how to dispose of the body of Lise Ragnarsdóttir Visser, who had died at Marinó's house the previous weekend.'

Sonja tried to send Jóel a telepathic message to wake up. She needed an excuse to step out of the room for a moment; needed to get her thoughts under control so she could come up with a plausible story.

'Marinó wanted to confess, but you two were against it, weren't you?' Sævar said. Without waiting for an answer, he went on: 'According to Andri, you went into the kitchen and mixed cocktails for the three of you, but he didn't know what you put in Marinó's drink until it was too late.'

'No.' Sonja shook her head. 'No, that's a lie. I don't know why Andri would say that. I suppose he's afraid of going to prison.'

'Before coming to see you, we paid your mother a visit,' Elma said, taking over from Sævar. 'She was very surprised when we asked if any medicine had gone missing from her bathroom cabinet in the last few months, as it turns out that her entire stock of sleeping pills had vanished the very weekend that Marinó was murdered.'

'You went to my mother's?' Sonja's voice was barely audible. Why hadn't her mother called to warn her? She was the only person in the world who had always stood by Sonja, but now she had betrayed her too, just like all the rest. Like Ísak, her father and Andri.

'Sonja,' Elma said, her voice so gentle that Sonja suddenly felt her throat closing with tears.

'I did it for Andri,' she sobbed.

'All right, Sonja,' Elma said. 'We need to take you into the police station to give a statement. It's your right to have a lawyer present.'

'But what about Jóel?'

'We'll wait for your mother to get here,' Elma said, her voice still kind.

Feeling a little calmer, Sonja smiled through her tears.

September 2019

When Andri awoke, his tongue was glued to the roof of his mouth, as dry as paper. He still felt drunk. For a moment or two he couldn't work out where he was, then he looked round blearily and made out Lise's shape beside him in the bed. She had obviously fallen asleep too and was lying on her back with her head turned towards him.

He stared at her, trying in vain to remember what had happened. Through the fog of alcohol, snatches of their conversation came back to him. Lise, a girl his age, had slept with his dad. The thought of them together was crazy, absurd, but he wouldn't put it past his dad – Andri had often heard the gossip about him in town. But to sleep with the au pair and get her pregnant as well ... that must set a new record for stupidity.

Andri felt his gorge rising and saliva flooding his mouth. He swallowed hard. After a moment, the nausea passed, and he started to wonder why he and Lise were in bed together.

He tried to picture what had happened last night after her revelation, but he couldn't remember how he had reacted. At some point he had obviously fallen asleep, or crashed out drunk, and presumably she had too. Lise appeared to be sleeping deeply, not making a sound. In fact, now that his eyes had grown accustomed to the darkness, he noticed that she was lying incredibly still.

Andri propped himself up on his elbow, peering at her. Was she unnaturally still? Her ribcage didn't seem to be rising or falling, and he couldn't hear her breathing, despite the quietness in the room.

He touched her arm; she was cold. Not icy cold, but colder

than him. He raised a wary finger to her nose, expecting to feel the warmth of her breath, but there was nothing.

Panic crashed over him. He could hear the rasping sound of his breathing. Feeling the hard shape of his phone in his trouser pocket, he took it out, switched on the torch with a trembling hand and shone it at Lise. Her head was turned towards him, but her eyes weren't shut as he had assumed: they were half open and appeared strangely dull. A moan of horror burst from his lips.

Andri eased himself out of bed and stood there, shaken by his heartbeat, his mind blank. The whole thing seemed so unreal that it occurred to him he might be dreaming. As if to check, he switched on his phone torch again and shone it round the room.

He moved the beam down Lise's body, pausing halfway. There were dark stains – red stains – on her trousers and the white sheet. Andri felt the blood throbbing in his head. He could hear screaming or groaning – it sounded as if it was coming from somebody else, not him.

Almost instantly the door opened, and Sonja appeared.

'What's going on?' she asked, looking from him to the still figure in the bed.

' I… I don't know…' The words stuck in Andri's throat.

'What's happened?'

Andri just stood there, paralysed, trying to piece the sequence of events together. What had he done? He remembered Lise rejecting him and how much it had hurt. Then his pain turning to rage when she told him the reason. After that there was a blank.

'What's up with Lise?' Sonja switched on the overhead light and the scene sprang into sudden, sharp clarity: Lise's dull eyes, the blood on the sheets. Sonja showed no emotion. Her only response was to look back at him, her face unreadable.

'I don't know what happened,' Andri said, when he could finally stammer out the words. 'She was like that when I woke up. I didn't do it. She just … she was just lying there like that.'

'Is she dead?' Sonja moved closer to the bed, studying Lise.

Andri couldn't see her expression. He repeated that he hadn't done it, perhaps to convince himself as much as Sonja. He was almost sure he was incapable of hurting Lise, and yet the reality seemed to make a mockery of this belief. Because there she lay, unquestionably dead.

When Sonja turned back to him, she seemed shockingly calm. 'Did you have sex?' she asked.

'No,' he said quickly, because he was sure of that. He would have remembered. There was no chance he'd have slept with Lise after what she told him.

'Are you sure?' Sonja asked.

'Yes, nothing like that happened.'

Her question struck him as odd. Lise was dead, yet all Sonja wanted to know was if he'd had sex with her. He was well aware that Sonja fancied him, but surely that was irrelevant right now.

Then he realised what must have happened.

'Lise was pregnant,' he said in a rush. 'She must have … she must have lost the baby.' That would explain the blood. Andri felt relief coursing through him. He'd had nothing to do with Lise's death: something must have happened to the baby and she'd died because of that.

'She was pregnant?' Sonja frowned. 'Who was the father?'

'Not me,' Andri said quickly.

'Then who?'

Andri hesitated, then said he didn't know.

Sonja's eyes narrowed. 'She's got a massive bruise on her arm.'

Andri looked past Sonja and in the bright-yellow glow of the ceiling light he saw a dark mark on Lise's arm that he hadn't noticed before. He felt an overwhelming urge to disappear. To walk out and pretend he'd never been here.

Sonja drew a deep breath. 'We'd better call the emergency line.'

'Shouldn't we just leave?'

'Leave?' Sonja echoed. 'Why? You didn't do anything … did you?'

'No,' he said, his voice high with desperation. It sounded un-convincing. Because the truth was he had no idea what had happened. Not that this would matter once other people got in-volved. He had woken up in bed beside a dead girl who'd probably had a miscarriage and who had an ugly bruise on her arm as well. His DNA would be in the bed and on Lise. Maybe inside her too, though he found that impossible to believe. No one would care what he did or didn't remember.

Andri felt sick. He pictured his mother, his little sisters, his friends and teammates. This would be the end of everything: his dreams of a football career, of moving abroad and making some-thing of himself. Making everyone proud. Whatever the final verdict, he knew you only had to be associated with something like this for all the doors to slam shut in your face.

'Sonja,' he groaned. 'This looks bad. Fuck, this looks really bad.'

Sonja waited.

'Can we…?' he began, then stopped.

What was he actually asking? What did he want to do? His strongest desire was to disappear, but that wasn't possible.

But there was another option: they could make Lise disappear.

He thought back over the previous evening. His parents were under the impression that Lise was on her way to Amsterdam. She'd told him she was planning to book a flight. No one would ask any questions if she wasn't seen again in Akranes, and it wasn't as if she had much family left in the Netherlands. No parents or close relatives to notice she was missing and raise the alarm.

'Don't you want me to ring, then?' Sonja asked.

'I don't know,' Andri said. 'You've got to believe me – I didn't lay a finger on Lise. But if the police arrive and see this … It looks bad, Sonja. Really bad. I'll lose everything.'

'What are you saying, Andri?'

He swallowed, rubbing his damp forehead. His hands were

shaking, and he felt faint and dizzy from all the booze he had put away that evening. Could feel it clouding his judgement, making it hard to think.

'I just mean I'm not ready to lose everything.' Moving closer to Sonja, he put a hand on her shoulder.

'Then what do you want to do?' she whispered, sounding suddenly breathless.

'Can't we just move her or something. Is that so crazy? I mean, she's dead anyway and it's not like ringing the police will change that. It'll just mean that we all get into trouble.'

'Oh, Andri, I don't know.' Sonja raised her eyes to his.

'Please, Sonja,' Andri said, stroking her hair. 'If we make the call, there'll be a huge fuss involving the police and our parents, and the whole town talking about us. It'll be all over the news.'

'Yes, but … the police or the doctor who examines her must be able to see what happened and they're hardly going to blame you or us for that.'

Andri grimaced, struggling to think rationally. Maybe he was worrying unnecessarily. Maybe Lise had simply died and he'd had nothing to do with it. Christ, if only he could remember. But everything following the moment when Lise had told him about her and his dad was a big, black hole. He couldn't risk calling the police. He had to convince Sonja.

'In the end, it probably won't matter what actually happened, just what people think happened. Can't you see how it will look for me?' Andri swallowed, his voice threatening to break. 'In football you only have to be mentioned in connection with something like this for your career to be over.'

'Yes, but you didn't do anything,' Sonja protested.

'I know,' Andri replied, a little too roughly. He softened his voice, holding Sonja's eyes with his. 'It makes no difference. We could make this disappear, Sonja. Together.'

Sonja was silent for a moment, but when she raised her eyes to Andri's again, he knew she was on his side.

'OK,' she said, smiling hesitantly. 'If you're serious about us doing it … together.'

Andri grasped instantly what she was implying and knew that he had no choice. So he nodded and didn't move away when she reached up to put her arms round his neck.

A sudden movement in the doorway made them spring apart. Marinó was standing there, staring at them, yet it was as if he wasn't really seeing them. Then he looked over at the bed, where Lise was lying, and staggered, throwing out an arm to support himself against the doorframe.

Andri couldn't ever remember having seen his friend that drunk before.

For a few agonising moments none of them spoke, but when Marinó lost his balance again, Sonja hurried over and caught his arm. She made him sit down. Andri watched as she explained to him what had happened. Marinó just sat there, staring at the floor. He appeared to be struggling to keep his eyes open.

'But we can't take her anywhere now. You understand that, don't you?' Sonja leant closer to Marinó, trying to make eye contact with him. Eventually, he looked up at her and nodded. 'We need to hide her for a couple of days while we work out a good place, just to be on the safe side,' Sonja continued. 'Can you think of somewhere we could put her?'

Marinó's gaze travelled to the window, and Sonja and Andri turned to see where he was looking. Outside, it was beginning to grow light and they could see the garden clearly enough to make out the shape of a small shed that Andri couldn't re-member ever having been inside.

'You think we could hide Lise in there?' he asked.

Marinó's eyes wandered back to Lise's body lying in the bed. 'What happened?' he asked, frowning in an effort to focus, his face so white that for a moment Andri thought he was going to be sick.

Still fighting back his own nausea, Andri was seized by a

frantic need to get this over with – so he could go home to bed and pretend this night had never happened. Kneeling down beside the bed, he grabbed Marinó by the shoulder.

'It was an accident, Marinó, like Sonja told you. But you know what people are like, don't you? They won't understand, and everything will be ruined. Please, I'm begging you. If you'll tell us where the keys to the shed are kept, Sonja and I will take care of it. You just go and lie down, OK?'

Andri wasn't sure if Marinó had followed what he said, but his friend nodded vaguely and rose unsteadily to his feet. Somehow he managed to explain that the keys to the shed were hanging in the key cupboard in the hall. After that, Andri helped him to his room, where Marinó collapsed onto his bed.

Andri stood there for a while, watching him uncertainly, wondering if he should ask again if it was OK; if Marinó understood what they had said to him. But then he heard a jingling from the hall and realised that Sonja had already started going through the keys in the cupboard.

Andri closed his eyes briefly, feeling as if the floor was moving in waves under his feet. When he opened them again, he wasn't sure if he was asleep or awake, and pinched his arm as hard as he could, but didn't feel any pain.

He didn't feel anything at all.

November 2019

Jóel had begun to stir, giving Sonja an excuse to leave the room at last. In the bedroom she picked him up and held him tight, her brain working overtime.

Her thoughts flew back to the moment when Andri had finally kissed her. She had been so upset and angry when he and Lise vanished into the bedroom together that she had lurked outside in a torment, waiting for him to emerge.

But later he had seen how much she was prepared to sacrifice for him. She had been ready to help him hide Lise's body so he wouldn't get into trouble. Sonja had understood how bad it looked for Andri; and it hadn't occurred to her for a second that he had played any role in Lise's death. She'd known him long enough to be sure he wasn't capable of hurting anyone.

After putting Marinó to bed, they had carried Lise out to the shed together and covered her with a blanket and some plastic sheeting they found there.

The trouble had begun when Marinó had surfaced the next day – sober and horrified by what they had done. By the following weekend, he was behaving as if he'd lost his mind. He kept muttering about what he had done – what *they* had done. Sonja, terrified he would blurt it all out, had dragged him into the bedroom with her. There she had done her best to distract him by making up some story about how Ísak had hit her.

She had realised, even as she did so, that Marinó wasn't tough enough to keep quiet about Lise; sooner or later he would talk. So Sonja had gone home and laid her plans.

The following evening she had picked Andri up from Júlía's place, and together they had driven to Marinó's house.

Once they were inside, she'd asked if she could borrow Marinó's laptop. Sonja thought this her stroke of genius – she'd said she was checking her messages, but instead she created a pretty incriminating search history for the police to find later.

After that, she had offered to mix some drinks for the boys, using the same blender as Fríða had used to make their cocktails the night before. First she had made a drink of frozen straw-berries, vodka and lemon for her and Andri, then she had prepared one for Marinó, adding all the sleeping pills she had stolen from her mother's bathroom cabinet.

She had watched as Marinó drained the entire glass, every single drop, without noticing anything amiss. Soon after that he had grown drowsy and complained of feeling weird. He had got into bed and, before long, rattling sounds started emanating from his throat.

Andri had rushed over to try and help him, but Sonja had caught hold of his arm.

At that moment it had dawned on Andri what she'd done. He had stood there for an instant, frozen, watching as Marinó lost consciousness. Then Andri twitched, and was suddenly retching and throwing up all over the floor.

When he recovered, still in a panic, he had grabbed Sonja and they had fled the house.

If Andri hadn't thrown up in his room, Marinó's death would have looked like suicide. But thanks to the vomit on the floor, the police were bound to find out that Andri had been involved – that he had been with Marinó that evening. When Sonja parted from Andri he was in such a state that he was shaking all over.

The following morning she had woken up to news of the fire.

Several days later, Sonja had finally told Andri how she really felt about him. Their relationship hadn't moved on to the next stage following their kiss, and she'd got the distinct impression that Andri was avoiding her. She suspected that he might still be sneakily meeting up with Júlía, despite all she had done for him.

So she had gone round to his garage flat and told him she loved him, that they were in this together and she would never tell anyone – as long as he loved her back.

Andri had looked at her strangely, but in the end he had returned her kiss and promised to dump his girlfriend, though he warned her they would have to wait a bit before getting together or it would look suspicious. Sonja had agreed to this. Yet she didn't entirely trust Andri and had gone round to his house several times, just to make sure Júlía wasn't there.

And now he had betrayed her.

Jóel yawned and snuggled against her neck, snapping her thoughts back to the present and the problem of the police in other room. They didn't have that much evidence against her; only the business of the sleeping pills and Andri's statement. She could say that Andri had told her to steal the pills; that he had threatened her. Yes, she would make up some story, and then it would only be Andri's word against hers. Andri wouldn't get off that lightly; not if she had anything to do with it.

Sonja kissed Jóel on the cheek before putting him down again. Then she bent over him and whispered: 'It's going to be all right, don't worry. We're going to be OK.'

Acknowledgements

This was the book I never thought I'd finish. I started writing it at the beginning of 2020, and we all know how that year went. For some writers it was a quiet time with lots of hours to write at home. For me it was being at home with three young children, and on top of that we were moving. By summer 2020 I had written only half a book that should've been complete by then. So I truly mean it when I say that this book could not have been written without the help of the incredible people around me.

First, thank you to my Icelandic publishers at Bjartur & Veröld, Bjarni and Pétur – for all the talks and encouragement when I've needed it; and yes, I have needed it many times! To be published by such a wonderful and close-knit publishing house is a privilege.

I am fortunate to be published in English by the awesome team at Orenda. Karen, West and all the people that work so hard on each book, I am forever grateful for all your suggestions, dedication and encouragement.

Thank you to my translator, Vicky Cribb, who has such an amazing eye for detail and is just as wonderful person as she is a translator.

Thank you to the greatest literary agent, David Headley, for taking me on, being my friend and teaching me how to drink champagne. Without you I don't think I'd be working now as a full-time writer – which is a dream come true. I feel so lucky to have you!

During the pandemic it was invaluable to have parents and

parents-in-law to babysit when possible. Thanks for this, and thank you for your pride in me and for all your support.

Thank you to my grandparents (I'm lucky enough still to have both pairs) for all the phone calls while I waited nervously for the reaction the first days after the new book had been published. Writing a book is such a weird experience: working on something for so long, sending it out in to the world and then just sitting and waiting and hoping it's OK and that someone will like it. Your phone calls make it all a bit easier.

Last but not least, thank you to my husband, Gunnar, for taking our kids out to play or telling me to lock myself in the bedroom so I could write. Thank you for reading my book a billion times and not complaining once, but being truly excited every time. Thank you for listening to me talk about my books over dinners, during movies and at night when I can't sleep. This isn't my journey, it's ours, and I could not think of anyone else to have by my side.

'Chilling and addictive, with a completely unexpected twist ... I loved it'
Shari Lapena

'Another beautifully written novel from one of the rising stars of Nordic Noir' **Victoria Selman**

'A creepily compelling Icelandic mystery that had me hooked from page one. *Night Shadows* will make you want to sleep with the lights on' **Heidi Amsinck**

The small community of Akranes is devastated when a young man dies in a mysterious house fire, and when Detective Elma and her colleagues from West Iceland CID discover the fire was arson, they become embroiled in an increasingly perplexing case involving multiple suspects. What's more, the dead man's final online search raises fears that they could be investigating not one murder, but two.

A few months before the fire, a young Dutch woman takes a job as an au pair in Iceland, desperate to make a new life for herself after the death of her father. But the seemingly perfect family who employs her turns out to have problems of its own and she soon discovers that she's running out of people to turn to.

As the police begin to home in on the truth, Elma, already struggling to come to terms with a life-changing event, finds herself in mortal danger as it becomes clear that someone has shocking secrets they'll do anything to hide...

'I loved everything about this book: the characters, the setting, the storyline, an intricately woven cast ... this book had me utterly gripped!' **J M Hewitt**

'With the third release in the Forbidden Iceland series, Eva Björg establishes herself as not just one of the brightest names in Icelandic crime fiction, but in crime fiction full stop. *Night Shadows* is an absolute must-read!' **Nordic Watchlist**

'The author writes so beautifully you are immediately immersed in the chilly surrounds ... a genuinely excellent novel' **Liz Loves Books**

'One of the most compelling contemporary writers of crime fiction and psychological suspense' **Duncan Beattie, Fiction from Afar**

Translated by
Victoria Cribb

Cover design by kid-ethic.com
Cover photography © Shutterstock

£9.99
ISBN: 978-1-914585-20-3

9 781914 585203

www.orendabooks.co.uk

@OrendaBooks
@evaaegisdottir
#NightShadows
#ForbiddenIceland